EVEN NOW

KAREN KINGSBURY

WALKER LARGE PRINT

An imprint of Thomson Gale, a part of The Thomson Corporation

THOMSON
™
GALE

————————————————————————————

Detroit • New York • San Francisco • New Haven, Conn. • Waterville, Maine • London

THOMSON

GALE

LIBRARY OF CONGRESS CATALOGING-IN-PUBLICATION DATA

Kingsbury, Karen.
    Even now / by Karen Kingsbury.
      p. cm. — (Thorndike Press large print Christian fiction.)
    Originally published: Minneapolis, Minn. : Bethany House, c2005.
(Dakotah treasures ; 4)
    ISBN 0-7862-8684-9 (lg. print : hc : alk. paper)
    ISBN 1-59415-137-7 (lg. print : sc : alk. paper)
    1. Birthmothers — Fiction. 2. Mothers and daughters — Fiction. 3. Large type books. 4. Domestic fiction. I. Title. II. Thorndike Press large print Christian fiction series.
PS3561.I4873E94 2006
813'.54—dc22
                                             2006008365

ISBN 13: 978-1-59415-137-8 (sc)

Published in 2007 by arrangement with The Zondervan Corporation LLC.

Printed in the United States of America on permanent paper
10 9 8 7 6 5 4 3 2 1

Dedicated to . . .

Donald, my best friend, my prince charming. The years have flown past, and I'm amazed that we're into our eighteenth year of marriage. I remember our honeymoon and how you'd look at me every few hours and say, "It took so long to get here; I can't believe we're finally married!" That'll teach us to hurry time. With you, Donald, the dance is a beautiful one, sometimes slow, sometimes tapped out at a frantic pace. But I wish the music would go on forever, because every day is better than the last. Can you feel it? How we're entering this new phase of life with teenagers? Stay close by and keep praying! I think we're going to need each other more in the coming years than ever. I love being your wife.

Kelsey, my precious daughter. I had a sudden disconnect the other day when I took you to get your driver's permit. I glanced at the little girl beside me, half-expecting to see a ponytailed sixth grader. Because this is supposed to go on forever, right? The part where I drive you places and we hold deep, meaningful conversations about your friendships and your faith? But instead, there you sat, a willowy young woman with the future shining in your eyes. Has anyone ever been more excited to get behind the wheel of a car? Hmmm. Every minute matters, honey. I'm grateful for the relationship we've shared — and the one that will take us into this next stage of your life. Don't ever forget you're a one-in-a-million girl, Kels. I love you. Shine for Jesus!

Tyler, my oldest son. This has been an amazing year for you, my Broadway boy! A lead part in a professional local theater company? I stand back in awe at how God has brought you from that precocious kindergartner walking around the house in an Annie wig singing "Tomorrow" at the top of your lungs, to the self-possessed young man, serious about shaping your voice and your acting skills so that you can be an even brighter light for the Lord. Your song is still the soundtrack of our lives, Ty. I love you. Keep singing for Him!

Sean, my smiley boy. Everyone who sees you or gets to know you says the same thing: "That kid is always so happy!" You've been home more than four years now, but it feels like you've been here since the beginning. I love your smile and your energy, the way you listen at devotions every morning. You've blossomed in so many ways. God has big plans for you, Sean. Keep trying your best and reaching for the stars! I love you, honey.

Josh, my soccer star. When it comes to picking teams, everyone wants you, and you're the first to explain the reason: "God made me an athlete." The same is true for your brothers, but I have a feeling Jesus will use your athleticism in a very special way. I marvel at your confidence, the easy way you have of excelling in everything from art to keeping your room clean. But the reason I'm most glad you're on *our* team is because of your desire to please the Lord. Everyone else might be asleep, but there you are, a flashlight under the covers, reading your Bible. Keep your determination, Josh. I love you. Keep first place for God and all the rest will come.

EJ, my determined chosen child. Long ago, God could've led us to any of a million little boys who needed a family. But He chose you, and we quickly did the same. You are living proof of how love and determination, boundaries and praise can change someone for Jesus. You have no quit in you, EJ, and I stand in awe at that. I love when you think no one's watching and suddenly you launch into a silly song or dance. My heart delights in knowing that your talents are more than running faster than anyone at school. You make us laugh, and one day I pray God uses you to bring a smile to the faces of many people. I love you. Keep smiling when no one's looking.

Austin, my miracle boy. You will always be my little Isaac, the child we were given and then nearly lost. But sweet boy, you are simply growing up too fast, coming to me more often than before with sweatpants that hit above your ankle. I thank God that you're still a towhead, still adorable with that toothless grin of yours. Yesterday I found a dinosaur on my bathroom floor and I realized you'd been in there an hour earlier. I went to move it, but then I stopped myself and let it stay. My days of dinosaurs on the bathroom floor are numbered. I love watching you run and gun on the basketball court, love hearing the other coaches ask, "Hey, that blond kid who's a head taller than the other boys, is he really in first grade?" I'm so proud of your hustle and the way you listen to your daddy. He's the best coach of all, honey. Now and in the years to come — whether the sport is basketball, baseball, or walking with God. I'm so glad you're healthy and strong. I love you.

And to God Almighty, who has — for now — blessed me with these.

Acknowledgments

No book comes together without the help of many people. A thanks to my great friends at Zondervan Publishing, including my greatest supporters: Bruce Ryskamp, Doug Lockhart, Sue Brower, Chris Ornsdorff, Karen Campbell, my friends in England, and everyone who has helped make my place at Zondervan so enjoyable. These books are touching and changing lives, and you play a significant part in that. I'm honored to be working with you. A special thanks to my amazing editor, Karen Ball. You continue to challenge me and help me bring glory to God with the gift He's given me. Don't ever stop!

A big thank you to my agent, Rick Christian, president of Alive Communications. I am more amazed as every day passes at your integrity, your talent, and your commitment to getting my Life-Changing Fiction™ out to people all over the world. You are a strong man of God, Rick. You care for my career as if you are personally responsible for the souls God touches through these books. Thank you for looking out for my spiritual growth, my personal time, and my relationships with my husband and kids. I couldn't do this without you.

As always, my book writing depends on the help of my husband and kids, who are so good about eating tuna sandwiches and quesadillas when I'm on deadline. Thanks for understanding the sometimes-crazy life I lead and for always being my greatest support.

Thanks to my friends and family — especially my once-in-awhile assistants, Susan Kane and Tricia Kingsbury, and all of you who continue to surround me with love and prayers and support. I couldn't write without you lifting me to the Lord and covering my work and my family in prayer.

A very special thanks to my mother and assistant, Anne Kingsbury, for having a great sensitivity and love for my readers. Your personal touch is so precious to me — thank you with all my heart. In the same light, thanks to my father, Ted Kingsbury, who remains my biggest supporter. You believed in me way, way back — proof that parents must always encourage the dreams of their child.

Thanks also to my office assistant, Katie Johnson, who stepped in this year and helped me more than I could've imagined. I pray that you will be a part of this ministry for years to come. Also to Nicole Chapman for filling in on days when the tasks were overwhelming, and Katy Head and Tim Head for your assistance in some of the practical aspects of my working day.

And a thank you to God Almighty, the greatest author of all — the Author of Life. The gift is yours. I pray I might have the incredible opportunity and responsibility to use it for You all the days of my life.

Prologue

Christmas 2006

It was time.

Emily Anderson had waited all her life for this moment.

The box on the floor in front of her held the hope of a lifetime . . . *her* lifetime. Inside could be a window, a glimpse, a pathway to the past, to a time still littered with question marks. But what if it wasn't? What if it was nothing?

For a moment Emily could only sit, stone still, and stare at it. Doubts gathered around her like summer storm clouds. This was her last chance. If the box held only high school mementoes, framed photographs, and old stuffed animals, then she'd know she'd reached her final dead end.

And barring a miracle, her search for her parents would be over.

She laid her hands on the dusty cardboard top and traced her fingers across the words. *Lauren's Things.* The box would be nearly nineteen years old now.

A lump stuck in her throat and she swallowed, forcing it down. "Mom . . ." she stared at her mother's name. "Did you leave me a trail?" She closed her eyes and hugged the box. "Please, God, let there be something here."

Downstairs her grandparents were fixing dinner. They'd given her this time. Her tender old papa had found the worn box in the garage stashed away in a cobwebbed corner with a dozen other forgotten cartons. He had known how much it would mean to her, how long she'd been waiting for a breakthrough like this.

"Emily, honey," he'd told her when she came home from college that day. "This belonged to your mother." He held the box in his hands. As tall as she was, she still felt tiny next to him. He had to look around the brown edges of the box to see her. "I'll take it to your room. You'll need some time."

Indeed.

She opened her eyes and stared at the box, hard and long, drilling imaginary holes through the flimsy cardboard. As if maybe she could see inside before she tore into it and found out for sure. Panic tap-danced around her, and she grabbed two quick breaths. What if she went through the whole thing and found no clues at all? Two more breaths. *Come on, Emily. Exhale.* She tightened her middle, pursed her lips, and blew out. *God, get me through this. There has to be something.*

How many times had she prayed for a clue or a sign? A trail that would lead her to her parents, even for a day? Then she could ask them why they'd left and how come they never cared to find out what happened to their little girl?

Emotion flooded her, tightening her throat, closing her eyes. Memories rushed back like forgotten classmates — hateful ones, who used to laugh when you weren't picked at recess.

Suddenly she was in kindergarten again, at the Mother's Day luncheon. She and the other boys and girls had made place mats with bright green handprints and pretty painted flowers coming from the top of every finger. They sang a song, and Emily could hear their young, off-key voices booming out, "Thanks for all you do . . . Mommy, I love you!"

As with everything around Mother's Day, Emily directed the words to her grandma.

17

Even back then, she'd known. She was the only kindergartner without a mother. The only one whose mommy left when she was just a few weeks old. Now she watched her kindergarten self as the memory of what happened next played back, every painful detail intact . . .

"Grandma," she asked, "where is my mommy? Do you know?"

Her grandmother got sort of nervous. "No, sweetie. Papa and I tried to find her but, well, we haven't had any luck."

Emily had felt suddenly lost. Like the day she was at the park and couldn't find her papa. Then an idea came to her. She smoothed her fancy dress and swung her legs, setting her patent-leather shoes in motion. "Maybe *I* could find her!"

"Honey." Her grandma patted her hair. "I don't think she wants to be found."

And that was that.

Emily drew a shuddering breath, relieved that the memory was over. But on its heels came another. The time she was thirteen and all of eighth grade was getting "the talk."

"I feel funny talking about girl stuff in school," she told one of her friends at lunch that day. "Seems like it should be private."

"So talk to your mom." The friend

smiled. "Moms are great for that."

The emptiness and loss were so terrible, Emily felt like there was an actual hole in her heart, a hole so thorough she bet her friend could see straight through her. That afternoon, Emily went home and made a promise.

Someday, I'm going to find my parents. No matter what.

Emily brushed a hand across her face, as though she could free her mind from the haunting thoughts. She opened her eyes and stared at the box.

Eventually her grandparents got Internet access. After that there were days of typing in her mother's name — L-a-u-r-e-n A-n-d-e-r-s-o-n — and searching through lists of schoolteachers and scientists and track stars, but never — not in all the thousand entries that popped up, making her breathless with possibility — did she find her mother. Same with her dad. She'd spent hopeless afternoons looking for him any way she could imagine.

And now, at eighteen, she was no closer to finding them than when she first started. What she wanted — what she'd *always* wanted — was the truth. Because the sketchy details she knew made up barely a handful of dots. Nowhere near enough to connect.

19

Cobwebs stuck to the top of the box, and Emily brushed them off. She let her hands rest on the old, worn carton, wondering. Could it be? Did this box hold the secrets — secrets that would answer the questions that had haunted Emily all her life?

Why did her mother leave? Where was she? Why hadn't she been in touch since she ran away? Had her parents ever connected again?

She gripped the top of the box. Maybe . . . maybe she was about to discover enough pieces to put together a trail.

And maybe the trail would lead her to the story.

She couldn't wait another minute as she opened the side flaps. It was really happening; she was about to see her mother's things, touch them and read them and breathe them in. Her heart beat so hard and fast she wondered if her grandparents could hear it downstairs.

She peered inside. The first few items were framed photographs of her parents. Emily reached in, lifting them with careful fingers. Beneath them were yearbooks and folded handwritten letters. Emily's heart jumped. Hours of exploration stretched before her. As she pulled out the contents of the box, she lay each item on her bed, staring at it even as she reached for the next item.

Did the letters hold declarations of love from her dad to her mom, maybe words that explained the feelings they had for each other or their plans for after their baby was born? She would read them later. For now she had to keep digging, because she had to make it through the entire box, just in case.

In case the answers lay somewhere near the bottom.

She reached back into the carton and pulled out another layer of pictures and photo albums, and two thirds of the way down, a tattered stuffed bear. Only after the bear was removed did she see something that caused her loud, demanding heart to jerk to a silent halt.

Journals. Eight . . . maybe ten of them. And beneath those, what looked like notebooks, dozens of notebooks.

Emily rifled through the carton, collecting the journals and placing them on the bed next to the photos, yearbooks, and letters. Then she pulled out the first notebook and opened it. The pages were a little warped and yellowed, filled with page after page of narrative and dialogue. Emily scanned the text and caught her breath.

She'd found it. A missing piece.

Her mother was a writer! She set that notebook on the bedspread and reached for another. This one was thicker, and on the front someone — her mother probably — had written, *"Lauren loves Shane."* Emily stared at the words and felt the sting of tears in her eyes. Her hands trembled and she ran her thumb over the words.

She slid further back on the bed, until she was leaning against the wall. She propped a pillow behind her and settled in. The clues she'd been hunting for all her life had to be here, buried somewhere between the paper covers of these spiral-bound notebooks. In the stories her mother had written, the stories she'd left behind.

Tales of her parents' love. Maybe the story of their loss. And perhaps even the reason why they'd gone away and left their baby to live without them.

Biting her lip, Emily turned the page.

And then, carefully so as not to miss a single detail, she began to read.

One

March 12, 1988

The death of a friendship was usually slow and insidious, like the wearing away of a hillside after years of too much rain. A handful of misunderstandings, a season of miscommunication, the passing of time, and where once stood two women with a dozen years of memories and tears and conversation and laughter — where once stood two women closer than sisters — now stood two strangers.

But Angela Anderson had no time to consider those things, no warning that such a death was about to occur. Because her friendship with Sheila Galanter died a sudden death the afternoon of March 12, 1988, in the time it took Angela to say a single sentence:

"Lauren wants to keep the baby."

That was it. The look on Sheila's face said it all.

23

Angela's teenage daughter, Lauren, had been in love with Sheila's son, Shane, since the kids were ten years old. Both families were Chicago upper crust with healthy six-figure incomes, known in all the right circles across the city, prominent members at the most elite clubs. Their husbands owned a bank together, and by all estimates the kids' futures were figured out.

On afternoons when Angela and Sheila bared their hearts, snickering about the pompous women they knew, planning trips to London, and complaining about the five pounds they'd gained over the holidays, they sometimes dreamed about their children's future. The engagement that would likely come after college, the ring, and, of course, the wedding.

Then, to leave room for the kids to make up their own minds, they'd laugh about how silly they were and let the dreams pass. But as the years wore on, Shane grew smitten with Lauren, and there seemed more truth than silliness to the possibility. When the kids started their junior year in high school, Shane had — between baseball games — started referring to the impending wedding.

"After I marry your daughter," he'd tell Angela and her husband, Bill, "the four of us can vacation in Mexico." Or he'd look at his own parents and say, "Where should we have the reception?"

Shane's pretentious statements made Lauren blush and kept the adults amused, but secretly every one of them believed it would happen. That one day, sometime after the kids finished university — probably at Wheaton College — after Shane found his place at the family-owned First Chicago Trust, he and Lauren would marry. And the four of them — Angela and Bill, and Sheila and Samuel — would finish their years not only the best of friends and business partners, but family. Family in every sense of the word.

The bombshell came the day before Christmas.

Lauren and Shane called a meeting after dinner. The talk was held at the Galanter house, and Sheila slipped a frozen pie in the oven for the occasion. Whatever the occasion might be.

Lauren looked thin and pale, her light blonde hair almost white against her black cable-knit sweater. "Shane and I . . ." Her mouth hung open and she stared at her tennis shoes. "We have something to tell you."

Shane sat next to her, holding her hand.

25

Their knuckles were tight, their posture tense. Only then did Angela sense that whatever was coming couldn't possibly be good. Shane slipped his arm around Lauren, shielding her. He was tall and dark and rugged looking, a product of his Greek heritage. Lauren seemed even more fair than usual next to him.

"What Lauren's trying to say is —" Shane ran his tongue along his lower lip; his voice trembled — "she's pregnant. It was an accident, but it . . ." He looked straight at his father. "It was an accident."

Angela would never forget the silence that cloaked the room. She wanted to reach for Bill's hand, but she didn't dare move, couldn't consider drawing a breath or trying to process the news. It was impossible. Shane and Lauren were good kids, kids who spent less time together than they did practicing their sports — Lauren her sprinting and Shane his pitching and throwing and hitting. They were raised in the church! Maybe they weren't regular churchgoers, but the kids went to youth group every Wednesday, right? Wasn't that supposed to count for something?

Across from the adults, Shane pulled Lauren close and whispered something near her ear. Their faces were masked in fear and shame.

As the first bit of air seeped through Angela's teeth, she glanced at her friend. Sheila sat at an unnatural tilt, frozen. Next to her, Samuel dug his elbows into his knees and hung his head. But it was the look on Sheila's face that caused a ripple of offense in Angela's heart. Sheila was staring at Lauren, her eyes angry and intense, like two lasers drilling into Lauren's being.

It wasn't a look of shock or horror or sorrow. Rather it was a look of blame.

Sheila was the first to speak. "Well —" she stood and smoothed the wrinkles in her dress slacks — "when is the . . . baby due?"

Shane blinked. "Uh . . ." He looked at Lauren. "Mid-July, right?"

"Yes." She tried to sit a little straighter, but she looked sick to her stomach. She crossed her arms over her midsection and leaned into Shane once more.

Angela wanted to go to her, take her in her arms, and rock away the hurt, like she used to when Lauren was little and came home sad after a hard day. But this was so much bigger. And with everyone watching, going to Lauren would only look like she

27

approved of the situation somehow. *Honey.* Angela gripped the seat of the chair and stayed put, her eyes on Lauren. *Honey, I'm so sorry.*

Again Sheila took the initiative. "Certainly you're much too young to have a baby." She looked at her husband, Samuel, but his eyes were still aimed at the floor. Sheila turned her attention back to Lauren. "You'll be giving the baby up for adoption, is that right?"

Angela wanted to cut in. Why was Sheila acting so harsh? She didn't need to presume anything at this point. Angela held her breath. Shock must be having its way with her friend. That had to be it. Shock was having its way with all of them. How could anyone discuss adoption when they were still absorbing the idea of a baby?

Bill cleared his throat. "Let's not be hasty, Sheila." His tone was gentle, though Angela heard the weight of disappointment in his words. "This is hard for all of us. We need to hear the kids out."

"Actually —" Shane looked from Bill back to his parents — "Lauren and I . . . well, we want to keep the baby. We'll still finish high school, and I'll go to college the way I'd planned." He licked his lips, but his words sounded like they were stuck to the roof of his mouth. "It won't be easy." He looked at Lauren and smoothed his hand over her hair. "But we know we can make it. We're sure."

The anger that sparked in Sheila's eyes next was something new, something Angela had never seen before. Her friend paced to the window, stopped and spun around, all her focus on Shane. "That's the most insane thing I've ever heard."

Angela's head was spinning. All around her people were making sweeping statements, statements that would change the course of their lives forever. Lauren was pregnant halfway through her junior year in high school? She was about to become a mother at just seventeen? How irresponsible and sneaky the kids had been, and how little Shane had cared for Lauren's virtue. As if that wasn't enough shock, Sheila already had the baby signed off and sent to another family. What about Shane's desire to raise the baby and still attend college in a year?

None of it made sense, and in the end — after very little discussion — they could only agree on one thing: any decision on the matter would have to wait. Finally as the group stood, and an uncomfortable silence fell around them, Angela took Bill's hand and went to Lauren. This was her little girl, her only child.

Angela searched her daughter's face. All her dreams for Lauren were gone now, too far gone to salvage. Angela wanted to shake Lauren, scold her for compromising everything she held to be true, scream at her for being a party to the disaster at hand. The news was the worst Angela had ever dreamed possible.

But as bad as it was, it had to be worse for Lauren.

Surrounded by a silence that had gone from uncomfortable to awkward, Angela finally held out her arms and let Lauren come to her. It was Lauren's life that would change the most now, so what option was there but to embrace her and give her the love and support she needed? After a few seconds, Bill put his arms around both of them and joined their tight circle. Angela wasn't sure how long they stayed close like that, but finally they parted and the three of them left.

It took less than a week for Angela and Bill to reluctantly agree that Sheila — though hasty — was probably right. The best choice was for the kids to give up the baby. That way some of high school could be salvaged, and college would still lie ahead. They pulled Lauren aside on New Year's Eve and shared their thoughts.

"We'd like to help you find an adoption agency." Angela put her hand on her daughter's shoulder. "It'd be the best thing for everyone, especially the baby."

Lauren jerked away. "It isn't up to you." Her wide eyes darted from Angela to Bill. "It's not up to Shane's parents, either." Her hand was on her abdomen, as if she were protecting her unborn baby from a life she had little control over. "Shane has a plan. He'll still go to college."

"It won't work, Lauren." Bill crossed his arms, the lines on his forehead deeper than before. He'd spent a lifetime adoring their daughter. Now his eyes made it clear he was hurting, buried beneath the burden of the trouble she was in. "You're too young to raise a child. Where would you live?"

Angela forced herself to remain calm. "Besides, you're a bright girl. You're cheating yourself and your baby if you decide to raise a child now. You should be thinking of college, not how to change diapers."

"I'm a writer, Mother." She strained with every word, her cheeks red. "I don't need school for that."

"Yes, you do." Angela looked at Bill. "Tell her."

"Your mom's right." He put his arm around Lauren's shoulder. "Honey, the timing is wrong. Think of the baby."

Lauren pulled away from him and ran to her room. Her crying filled the house all that week, bringing a somber end to Christmas break. On Sunday, Lauren called Shane and the two talked for hours. When she came out of her room, her eyes were swollen from crying. Angela and Bill tried to talk to her, but she had only a few words for them. "We won't do it." She sniffed and ran her fingers beneath her eyes. "We won't give up our baby."

The discussion wore on every day for weeks after that, though Angela and Bill avoided telling Sheila and Samuel about the kids' decision. School started again, and Lauren and Shane managed to keep their news a secret from their peers. At least three times a week, Sheila Galanter called and gave what felt like an ultimatum: "Talk some sense into her, Angela. I don't want these kids to lose everything over one mistake."

Angela should've seen the signs those first few months of the new year, should've realized what was coming. Sheila's clipped tone whenever she called, the absence of dinner invitations and shared weekend evenings. Most of all, the way things changed between the men. For a decade, investors had come to Bill and Samuel with offers to buy their bank. Once in a while the men would talk about selling and investing the profits in something new, maybe moving their families to the suburbs. But they never seriously considered the idea.

Not until after Lauren and Shane's announcement.

When an offer on the bank came in late January, the four of them decided to sell and move on. Though they talked about heading to the Chicago suburbs, by March the Galanters had a different plan.

"We're moving to Los Angeles."

Angela stared from her friend to Samuel, speechless. They'd stopped by unexpectedly, saying they had something to tell Angela and Bill. Just Angela and Bill.

Not the kids.

"We have other investments there. I know it's a long ways away, but we'll still see each other." Sheila's smile looked forced. "And this way the kids can have a break from each other."

Angela and Bill agonized long hours about telling Lauren, but in the end they kept the news to themselves. The move was still months off, and there was no

33

point fueling the intensity of the kids' feelings for each other. As the Galanters' secret plans quickly came together, Sheila continued her phone calls to Angela. "She's your daughter. Talk some sense into her. These kids don't need that sort of responsibility. Not yet." On another phone call she pushed it further. "Maybe you should tell Lauren we're thinking of moving. Maybe that would change her mind."

Angela was appalled. "You mean blackmail her? Tell her you'll stay if she gives up the baby?"

"I'm just saying it might make a difference. We need an answer, Angela. Tell us what she's going to do."

The entire situation felt like it was attached to one of those odd-shaped bouncy balls, ricocheting out of control. Twice more Angela talked with Lauren about her intentions, but her daughter never wavered.

She and Shane wanted to keep their baby. As soon as they were out of high school, they would marry and start their lives together.

Finally Angela couldn't put Sheila off another day. On March 12, Angela asked her friend over so she could break the news. She served coffee and cream, and they took their places in the Andersons' familiar sunroom.

Angela wasted no time getting to the point. "Lauren wants to keep the baby." She folded her hands in her lap. They were sitting on white wicker furniture, the sun streaming through the window. Bill was at the new bank in Wheaton, an hour out of Chicago, getting things set up. Lauren was at school.

"That's ridiculous." Sheila brushed her hand through the air, erasing Angela's statement. "She's too young to know what she wants."

"Sheila, listen —" Angela searched her friend's eyes — "I can't change her mind. I won't."

At that, Sheila's expression hardened, and her cheeks grew red. "Of course you can, Angela. You're her mother. She's a minor. She'll do whatever you tell her to do."

"You're serious, aren't you?"

"Dead serious." Sheila's voice raised a notch.

"You think I can force my daughter to give away her baby?" Angela squinted at the woman sitting next to her. When had Sheila become so heartless? "She may be a minor, but the baby is *hers.* I can't make this decision for her."

"Of course you can." Sheila set her coffee cup down and slid to the edge of the sofa. Even as her voice fell, her sharp tone sliced through the growing tension. "*My* son has a future. He isn't going to stay here while his pregnant girlfriend has a baby." A fine layer of perspiration broke out across her brow. "Absolutely not."

"His pregnant girlfriend?" Angela laughed, but without a trace of humor. "Is that all Lauren is now? Shane's pregnant girlfriend? Shane had a little something to do with it too."

"Shane's a teenage boy." Sheila spat the words. "If a girl makes herself available, what teenage boy wouldn't take advantage of her?"

A chill passed over Angela. "Listen to you." She stood and looked down at the woman she'd considered her friend. Had she ever really known her? "This is *Lauren* you're talking about."

"No." Sheila raised her hand. Her fingers were shaking. "This is my son's future we're talking about." She sat back a few inches and the lines in her forehead eased. "Be sensible, Angela. The last thing these kids need is more time together. We're both moving the first week of June. Shane's coming with us. That's final." Her hesitation was cool, indifferent.

Angela felt like she'd been kicked in the gut. How had Angela been so wrong about the woman, trusting her all these years? "We've been friends for a long time, Sheila."

"And my son's future will go on far longer." Sheila's tone lightened some. "I'm sorry, Angela. This isn't your fault, it's just —" she narrowed her eyes, intent — "the kids need to be apart."

Her words put their friendship on the firing line. Angela was angry at Sheila's tone and her accusation that Lauren's pregnancy made Shane a victim and Lauren the villain. But suddenly there was more, and Angela was able to look ahead.

In that moment she could stare hard down the road and see what her daughter's life would be like with Sheila Galanter as a mother-in-law.

It would be a life doomed to guilt and shame and never being good enough. The past would forever be brought out and examined, commented on with a series of tongue clucks and disdainful looks in Lauren's direction. The idea made Angela's heart hurt. She would never wish that for her daughter. How *dare* Sheila take that attitude about Lauren, as if Shane were the only one affected by what had happened?

"Okay." Angela straightened in the chair and leveled her gaze at Sheila. "I agree."

Sheila sat all the way back, the fight suddenly gone. "You do?"

"Yes. Completely."

Sheila's voice was almost a whisper. "What about the baby?"

Angela knew the answer as well as she knew her own name. Lauren was going to keep the child. She and Bill would do whatever they could to help Lauren be successful as a single mom. For however long Lauren needed them.

She cleared her throat. "We'll talk to Lauren again. I think you're right. We can convince her about this. Especially if Shane's gone from her life."

Of course, it was a lie. Lauren wouldn't give up her baby. But saying the false words came easily now that she too was ready to cut ties with the Galanters. Angela didn't blink. "That'll be best for everyone."

Relief flooded Sheila's features. "Yes. I'd hate to have a grandchild on the other side of the country and not know about it."

Angela wanted to stand up and shout at the woman. *You* already *have a grandchild growing inside my daughter! You're so blind and vain and empty you'd do anything to protect your son's reputation. Even this.* Instead she stood and motioned to the door. "She'll give the baby up. Don't worry about it." She crossed her arms and took a step toward the backyard. "Now, if you'll excuse me, I have things to do. As you said, there's no point pretending about our friendship."

Sheila looked almost as if she might apologize for making such a statement, but the look passed. She stood, collected her purse and car keys, and headed for the entryway. When Angela heard the door shut it was like gunfire, and something deep inside her heart took its last breath, shuddered, and died. Angela knew exactly what it was.

Her friendship with Sheila Galanter.

Two

Something was wrong with their parents.

Lauren was sitting in Shane's Camry, just outside her parents' house, and she could feel it. Almost like a force, something bigger than the two of them or their families or anything they'd ever come up against. A steady snow had been falling on the windshield for half an hour and now they couldn't see out. It was a picture of their lives, really. Living life on the inside, with no way to see out, no way for anyone else to see in.

Shane gripped the steering wheel with both hands and looked straight ahead at the white nothingness. They'd known each other as far back as they could remember, and Shane was always the first one in a room to smile or tell a joke. But in the last few months he'd grown quiet and anxious, trapped and searching for a way out. "Maybe —" he looked at her, looked straight to her soul — "we should drive off and never look back."

"Maybe." She turned and leaned against the passenger door.

They were supposed to see a movie that night, but instead they drove around town, scared and silent. No one at school knew she was pregnant, but they would soon. She was four months along now. Already she could barely button her jeans. Reality was closing in on them like a vice grip.

A year ago she'd seen a movie with her dad where the main character was trapped in a hallway with no doors and no windows. Scary music pounded from the big screen as the walls began closing in, closer and closer, leaving the guy no way to escape, no way out. Just when it looked like he'd be crushed, he spotted a trap door and got out with his life.

That's the way it was with her and Shane now. The walls were closing in — but there was no trap door. No way of escape in sight.

They never meant to sleep together, but it happened. Not once, but a few times. Only a few times. Lauren stared at her hands. Her fingers were trembling. Proof that she was falling apart a little more every day. She'd fought so hard to get a little freedom from her parents. To get them to trust her. Getting them to let her go alone with Shane to youth group had been a major deal. But finally they gave in. Let her have some freedom.

Maybe too much.

Over the summer, their parents started letting them hang out together in their bedrooms with the doors closed. At first Lauren was thrilled. But now . . . She shook her head. What did they think was going on in there? Especially in the past year, since Shane had his own car and didn't take her home until hours after his parents were asleep.

"We trust you," her mother said once. "As long as you're with Shane."

Lauren felt a wave of disgust well up inside her. Why would that make things safe between them? Knowing someone as long as she'd known Shane made it *more* dangerous, not less. They were so comfortable together that giving in, going all the way, seemed like nothing more than an extension of kissing. Until it was over.

The first time, when they were finished and they got dressed, they both were scared to death. "God'll punish us for sure," Lauren told him.

Shane hadn't argued. They skipped youth group that week — and the next too.

After that it was easier not to go, not to look in the faces of their leaders and lie about how well they were doing or how they were praying or reading their Bibles.

The punishment came, all right. A positive pregnancy test six weeks later. Since then everything changed between her and Shane.

Everything but this one fact: they loved each other. And it wasn't just a kid thing. They loved with a realness and a longing that consumed them. Yeah, they'd messed up and they were sorry. One of the youth group leaders knew about their situation, and the guy had met with them and their families a few times to pray and ask for God's wisdom.

But the punishment remained. She was seventeen and pregnant, and her parents' friendship with Shane's parents seemed to have all but disappeared. Their fathers were even breaking up their business relationship. Where would they work once they sold the bank?

Lauren had a hard time breathing whenever she thought about it. She studied Shane again.

His jaw was set, his eyes distant. He hit the steering wheel with his right hand. "I *hate* this." He let his head fall back against the seat. "Something's going on, but not one of them is talking."

"Tell me about the bank again." Lauren's stomach hurt. She leaned over and studied his profile.

Shane closed his eyes. "I heard my dad on the phone. He said something about the sale of the bank, how it would close in a few weeks and then he could make the investment. Some new investment."

Panic made her squirm. "If they're selling the bank, why haven't my parents told me? That's the part I don't get."

For a long time he was quiet, then he turned and let his hands fall from the steering wheel. "Lauren . . ." His expression softened. "There's more." He took hold of her fingers, sheltering them with his own. His eyes told her more than his words ever could, that he loved her, that he wanted to make this work but he was just a kid and he didn't know how. He ran his thumbs along the edge of her hands.

"What?" Her word was barely loud enough to hear. The inside of her throat was so dry she couldn't swallow right. It was hard to believe there was more, that something else could be wrong.

He hung his head for a moment and then looked her straight in the eyes. "I think we're moving." Fear took over his expression and he blinked it back.

"Moving?" She shook her head slowly, not wanting the word to sink in, not wanting anything to do with it.

"In that same phone call." He swallowed hard. "My dad said something about going to Los Angeles in June, when school was out."

"*LA?*" She grew still, and from somewhere deep inside her she felt the faintest fluttering. "Why . . . why would they do that?"

His expression was intense, more serious than she'd ever seen it. "I think they're trying to keep us apart." He released her hands and shoved his fingers through his hair. "I don't know what to do, Lauren. I won't let them tear us apart, even if I have to live on the streets, I won't let them."

Her heart raced and her breathing grew shallow. It wasn't real, was it? His family wouldn't move him across the country a little more than a month before their baby was due, would they? "In June?" She gulped, trying to find her voice. "They might move to LA in June?"

He searched her eyes. "I'm sure your parents know. They all know. We're the only ones they aren't telling." His eyes grew watery, and he gritted his teeth. "They can't do this. We need to know their plans so we can fight against them, okay?"

Fight against her parents? When they'd finally accepted the fact that she was keeping her baby? If they didn't have her parents or his parents, who would they have? Who would support them? She wanted to ask Shane, but she bit her lip instead. Her hand came up to his face and she touched his cheek with her fingertips. "I'll find out what I can."

He gave a quick nod and looked at the snow-covered windshield again. His eyes were still serious, as if he were searching through a list of options trying to find one that made sense. Finally he looked at her and gave a sad shake of his head. "I can't believe this."

"Me either." She looked at her watch. It was midnight, time for her to get inside. She leaned close to him and kissed him, slow and tender. They hadn't shared more than an occasional kiss since they found out she was pregnant. Almost as if they'd found a way back to how things had been before Shane had a car, back when holding hands and sharing a once-in-a-while kiss was the extent of their physical relationship.

"Lauren." His eyes had a sweet intensity. "Promise me nothing will change, no matter what they try to do to us."

She needed to get inside, but he still held tight to her hands. Her heart melted and she slid closer, slipping her arms around his neck. "I love you, Shane. I'll never love anyone else."

"I want to be older." He pulled back, his eyes wide and intense. "I wanna wake up tomorrow and be twenty-five, with a college degree and a job and a ring in my hand."

A ring? "A wedding ring?"

"Yes." He framed her face with his hands. "I want to marry you. I always have. This is *our* situation, our problem. But we need to figure it out, even if we *are* young." He was breathing hard, almost frantic with hopelessness. "I'm not letting you go." He kissed her again. "I love you, Lauren. I don't care how old I am; I'll never love anyone like this. Never."

"I love you too, Shane. You won't have to let go. I promise." She spoke the words straight to his heart and when she was sure she'd start crying if she didn't leave, she opened the door and stepped out into the snow. She waved once more as she turned and took light, careful steps up the walkway.

Inside, she leaned against the front door and waited until she heard his car drive away. The worse things got, the more she loved him, the more certain she was that somehow they could handle the days ahead. If only their parents would give them the chance.

Her father's voice came from the den down the hall and she followed the sound. What was he saying? Something about the bank? She slowed her pace. He mustn't have heard her come in. She tiptoed to the edge of the door so she could hear better.

"How far is it from here?" It was her mother's voice. She must've been filing papers, because a rustling sound made it hard to understand her.

"Only about an hour. The town's great, wonderful schools. Lauren can have the baby this summer and start her senior year fresh, no baggage."

"I'm not sure." Her mother sounded skeptical. "If she keeps the baby, we'll have more than prom and college applications to deal with."

"If she does or if she doesn't, I want her to have a fresh start. You know how it'll be around here, Angela. She'll always be the good girl who went and got pregnant with the school's baseball jock."

Anger surged into her veins, but Lauren didn't move. They might have more to say, and she didn't want to miss it.

"Come on, Bill." Kindness filled her mother's tone. "Shane's more than the school's baseball jock."

"I know that." Her father's words were fast and frustrated, like hail in a summer thunderstorm. "But right now the two of them need to be apart. That's what's best for them."

"And Sheila and Samuel found something in LA?"

"Definitely." For the first time in the exchange, her father's voice relaxed some. "They'll be gone by mid-June." He paused. "I never realized how hard it is to work with Samuel Galanter. The man's a control freak, and so's his wife."

"They used to be our friends." Her mother's voice was soft, defeated. "It's like we didn't know them."

"In a few months, we won't." His words sounded pinched. "The nerve of that kid to take advantage of my little girl. We'll see how much time he gets with her once they move to California."

Lauren had heard enough. She burst through the doorway, hands on her hips. "Don't you listen for the door?"

Both her parents opened their mouths, shock written in their expressions. "Lauren!" Her mother was on her feet. She tried a smile, but it died long before it hit her eyes. "No . . . we didn't hear you come in."

"Obviously." She paced in front of them, looking from her mother to her father and back again. "So you're part of this . . . this moving to California thing?" Her face was hot.

"We're not part of it." Her mother was at her side, touching her shoulder. "We wouldn't have anything to do with another family moving away, honey."

"But that's it, isn't it?" Her voice was louder than before. She glared at her father. "You and Mr. Galanter sold your bank, and now you're going your own ways. And if that breaks up me and Shane then so be it, right?"

"The Galanters might be moving, yes." Her mother's voice was calm, and that was bad. The more upset her mom got, the calmer her voice. "That plays a factor in what we're doing, obviously. We're selling the bank, so —"

"Right!" She was shouting now. "That's what I mean. How come Shane had to tell me? Why didn't I hear anything before this?"

"Watch your tone, young lady." Her father stood and walked closer, his finger pointed at her. "We've been conducting business in this family for years without consulting you. You might be seventeen and pregnant, but that doesn't mean you're an adult, and it certainly doesn't mean you'll be privy to everything your mother and I do."

His tone wounded her, hurt her to the depths of her soul. Shane was right. The sale of the bank, the idea of both families moving, all of it was part of a giant plan to tear them apart. She closed the distance between them and took his hand in hers. "Why, Daddy? Why are you doing this to us?"

He pursed his lips and looked away. When his eyes found her again, they were softer. "There is no *us* when it comes to you and Shane. You're kids, nothing more than children. We're going to save you from yourself, Lauren." His voice was thick. "I love you too much to do anything else."

Her world rocked hard to one side, tilted in a way that made her wonder if it would ever be right side up again. She glanced at her mother, her ally, but she received nothing back. Her mom wouldn't even

51

look at her. One small step at a time, Lauren backed up. Her heart was beating so hard she figured they could hear it across the room. "You won't win this!" Her voice was loud again — loud and shrill.

"You will not talk to us that way, Lauren." Her father's gentleness from a moment earlier was gone. "Go to your room and think about your actions. This is no way for a daughter of mine to act."

She shook her head, stunned. Nothing was making sense, not his words or his expression or his tone of voice. It all ran together and she dropped her voice to little more than a whisper. "You won't win." Wetness filled her eyes, blurred her vision. She couldn't make out the details of her father's face through her tears, but she stared at him anyway. "I love him, Daddy. Selling the bank, moving away . . ." Her throat was too swollen to talk.

"Honey." Again his expression eased. "You don't know what love is."

An ache filled her chest and she could no longer draw a breath. Not with the two of them so close, knowing full well that they'd done this, planned against her and Shane this way. Her tone was still quiet, thick with the pain that coursed through her. "No matter what you and his parents do, the two of us will be together. You can't live our lives for us."

She turned and ran to her room. She was about to throw herself onto the bed, when she remembered the baby. The precious little baby. It wasn't his fault or her fault, but here they were. She sat down on the bed and stretched out on her side. With both hands on her middle, she let the tears come.

All she wanted was to love Shane. How had things gotten so crazy, so mixed up? So she and Shane were young. So what? Did that mean they didn't have a right to try to make this work, to figure out a way to raise their child and find a life together? She looked around her room at the pretty furniture and luxury bedspread.

Her parents had more money than they knew what to do with — and so did Shane's — but somehow they'd all missed out on how to *love*. The more she thought about their houses and their cars, the life-styles they lived, the angrier she got. If they were poor or even average, the way most of her friends were, then this problem wouldn't be nearly as big. Her pregnancy would be a disappointment to them, sure, but she'd stay home and raise her baby, and Shane would visit as often as he could.

Then, when they graduated from high school, they'd get married and everything would work out fine.

It was the money — the power and prestige that came with it. *That's* why they were stuck in this situation. Then for the first time an idea came to her, a crazy, wild idea. She had five thousand dollars in a private account, money she could access if she needed it for clothes or a milk shake. What if she and Shane ran away together? What if they took the money and set out on their own? That could work, couldn't it?

But even as the idea took root, it died. She couldn't run away with Shane. Not when she was expecting a baby. She needed medical care *and* her parents' help if she was going to learn how to be a mother. Still, the thought wouldn't quite go away. And as she lay there, as she stared at the ceiling and thought about Shane and their uncertain future, the movie scene came to mind again. The man in the hallway with the walls closing in, the trap door that had allowed him to escape.

That was them, wasn't it? Exactly like their situation. As she fell asleep she thought about the place they were stuck in, and how the walls were closing in on their plans and their time together. There had to be a way out, didn't there? She could wait until her baby was born and take her money then, right? The thought came to life again and the slightest bit of peace filled her heart.

Yes, the walls were closing in. But maybe — just maybe — their prison might have a trap door too.

Three

Shane Galanter felt like he was drowning.

His mind was stuck on something that happened a few summers back, a terrifying memory that actually fit his life now. He'd been sailing with some friends on Lake Michigan, and the guys took turns diving off the sailboat and swimming fifty yards out and back. Someone had a stopwatch, so it became a competition. One swimmer would best another's time by a few seconds, and everyone would try it again.

Shane was on his third swim out from the sailboat when a strong wind came up. It hit him just about the time his energy ran out. And suddenly there he was — a mile from shore, fifty yards out from the sailboat, paddling toward the vessel and not making any headway at all.

"Help!"

But his shout was lost on the wind. His friends had their backs to him, all but the guy holding the stopwatch. And even he wasn't watching.

Shane kicked harder and harder, but didn't get any closer to the boat. About that time, a wave hit him in the face, and he sucked in a mouthful of water. That's when he realized what was happening. He was starting to drown, right in plain sight of his friends. He was taking in water and sinking a little more every few seconds, spending all his energy and not making any progress.

Suddenly one of his friends stood up and pointed at him. "Hey! Galanter's in trouble!"

Another wave hit him and he swallowed a mouthful of water. The guys adjusted the sails and four of them started paddling. In a few minutes they reached him and pulled him into the boat.

He still remembered how he felt. Remembered swallowing the water, feeling his strength leave him, knowing he wasn't going to make it.

Just like now.

He was in over his head, but this time with no boat or shore or help in sight. One thing was sure, though. If he was going to drown, he wanted to know the details. Every single one of them. When he got home from baseball practice, he searched out his father and found him in his home office on the second floor. Shane walked in and closed the door behind him, just as his father looked up from a stack of papers. He had a pencil tucked behind his ear and a smile on his face.

"How was practice?"

Shane stared at him, stunned. "How was practice?" He gave a bitter laugh. "My girl-friend's pregnant and my parents are having some kind of midlife crisis, and you ask me how was *practice?*" He removed his baseball cap and smoothed his hand over his hair. "Distracting, okay, Dad? How's that for an honest answer?"

His father turned his chair in his direction and crossed one leg over the other. "Okay, Shane." He pointed to the leather sofa next to his desk. "Sit down. Looks like you want to talk."

"Not really." The anger was a part of him at this point. It was there when he woke up and when he lay back down. "I *have* to talk. There's a difference."

"Okay." His father gave a thoughtful nod. "Why don't you tell me what's on your mind?"

Shane sat on the edge of the sofa and dug his elbows into his knees. His eyes locked on his father's. "Why don't *you* tell me about California?"

Surprise filled his father's features. No question he'd caught the man off guard. His dad took a moment to recover, then frowned that practiced sort of frown. The one Shane so often saw him use with his mother when things didn't go his way. "We have investments there, son. You know that."

"We've lived here twelve years and never once have you talked seriously about moving to California." Shane kept his voice controlled. It wouldn't get him anywhere to lose his temper, even if his blood was boiling.

"You're a child, son." His dad squinted, stopping just short of being condescending. "We don't talk to you about everything."

Shane's heart slammed against his chest. "So it's true? We're moving to Los Angeles?"

For a moment his father hesitated, as if maybe he might deny it or try to buy a little more time. But finally he exhaled hard and gave a slow nod. "Yes." He brought his lips together and nodded slower this time. "In June."

"We can't!" Shane was on his feet, ready

to kick something. "Dad, that's a month before the baby comes."

"In my day that would've made June the perfect time to move." The moment his dad's harsh words were out, regret shone in his eyes. He opened his mouth and closed it again. Then he pressed his fist to his forehead and looked at Shane. "I'm sorry. That came out wrong."

Shane sat back against the sofa. "It came out just how you meant it to come out. You're moving so I won't stay with Lauren."

"That's not it." His dad sounded tired, discouraged. "We've been talking about selling the bank for awhile, and a good offer came in." He tossed his hands up. "It was time. What else can I say?"

"Why California, Dad?" Shane uttered a sad chuckle. "Why not move to the suburbs, like Lauren's family? You could invest here, couldn't you?"

"We already have investments in California." His father stood and walked to his bookcase. He took a framed photograph from the top shelf and stared at it — Shane's first-grade baseball photo. He turned and met Shane's eyes again. "This is not how your mother and I pictured your life, son. Expecting a baby before your senior year in high school. Can you understand that?" He put the picture back on the shelf. "We only want the best for you. You and Lauren and the baby. All of you."

"Okay." Shane was on his feet again. His blood was hotter than before, and he was breathing harder. "Help me understand how tearing us apart is good for anyone."

When his dad didn't say anything, Shane turned and stormed out of the office. He had to find Lauren, had to reach her and tell her the truth. His parents were moving him to California; they had to find some way to keep him here, close to her. Maybe if he asked her to marry him now, maybe that would do it. Then they could be together through their senior years, he could go to college and one day he could become a pilot, as he'd always dreamed.

He didn't have much. His car, any money he had — it all belonged to his father. Except his birthday money, maybe four hundred dollars saved up in a box under his bed. He jogged to his room, pulled out the box, and grabbed the handful of bills. A quick count told him it wasn't quite that much, but it was enough.

Their parents couldn't separate them if they were engaged, could they? His parents or hers, *some*one would have to come to their senses and let the two of them stay together. That way they could share the early days with the baby, and when they graduated they could have a wedding.

His mother was shopping, so it was just him and his father at home. Shane stuffed the money in his wallet and shoved his wallet in the pocket of his jeans. Then he tore down the stairs, jumped in his car, and drove to the mall. They always had deals on rings at the mall, didn't they? He knew her ring size, because a few months before she got pregnant they were seeing a movie at the mall and before the show started they stopped in at a jewelry store. It was all pretend and silliness, but he remembered her size. Six. The lady had said Lauren had beautiful, slender fingers. He parked and ran inside. The first jewelry store he saw, he walked straight in and up to the sales clerk.

"I need a ring." He was out of breath. The money felt like a million dollars in his pocket.

"Very well." The woman was older, with soft wrinkles across her cheeks and forehead. "Is this a promise ring, young man?"

He was about to tell her no, that this was an engagement ring. But before the words would come, he realized how they would sound. Ridiculous, that's how. He was just seventeen, and most people told him his baby face made him look younger than that. He met the woman's eyes. "Uh, yes. Yeah. A promise ring." He managed a nervous smile. "Anything like that?"

The woman stood and led him to a section in the glass cabinet with smaller rings. Some of them had white little stones on them, and others had pink or blue. A few had what looked like diamonds. He lifted his eyes to the woman. "I want something real."

"Okay." She smiled again. "A diamond, then?"

"Yes." Definitely a diamond. He'd loved Lauren Anderson since he was in fourth grade. She made him feel things he'd never felt before. She was fun and witty and his best friend of all. Nothing less than a diamond.

"Very well, have you thought of what size stone?" She folded her hands and tilted her head to the side. "Diamonds come in many sizes. Full carat, half, quarter, and so on."

Shane's eyes lit up. "Let's try the full carat." His mother had something like that. A full carat would make a nice ring for Lauren.

"All righty then." She opened the case from behind and pulled out a velvet pad with eight rings stuck into separate sections. Each one glistened and shot colors across the glass counter. "They start at fifteen hundred dollars."

He felt suddenly ill. The smell of mall popcorn and cinnamon buns filled the air, making him queasy. He looked at the woman and gave a tight shake of his head. "Not that big." His shoulders fell a little. "I have three hundred and eighty dollars."

"Well." The woman returned the tray of brilliant rings back to the counter. "We have something in that range. It'll be a circle of maybe some crusted diamond chips. Something totaling about a quarter carat."

The rings she brought out this time were much smaller, without the shimmer. He tried not to frown at them, but he couldn't help it. "Hmm." Then he had an idea. Excitement rang out in his voice in a way he couldn't stop. "Can you engrave them?"

"Definitely. It'll be an extra twenty dollars." She looked over her shoulder at an older man sitting behind a glass partition. "You're in luck. My husband does all the engraving. He can get it done in a few minutes, if you have time to wait."

"Perfect." His palms were sweaty. He rubbed them on his jeans. "I'll wait right here."

She helped him pick out a size six ring that would work with his budget, even with the cost of engraving. The ring was small. The diamonds made a crusty little heart at the center and the band was white gold. But it was pretty, and it would serve the purpose.

While he waited he thought of the talks he'd heard at youth group since he and Lauren had slept together. Just the day before there'd been one. Lauren wasn't there — her parents didn't let her go anymore. But the message hit him straight in the heart. One of the youth pastors had taken two sheets of construction paper, one red, one blue.

"These represent you and your girlfriend." He held them up and looked around the room. Then he took a bottle of white glue and drizzled it over the back side of one of the pieces of paper. He pressed the two pieces of paper together, back to back. "This is what happens when you and your girlfriend have sex."

He set the glued-together papers down on his podium and spent twenty minutes talking about the body, how God had asked His people to set aside their bodies as temples for the Holy Spirit, and how sexual immorality was never right for God's people.

"Basically . . ." The guy smiled. Shane really liked him. He was younger than the main ministers and he talked like one of the guys. "Basically sex is a great thing. But it's only great because God thought it up, and it's only great when the people having sex are married. Because that was God's plan from the beginning." He grew more serious. "Any other sex is sin because God says so. And He says so for our own good. Sex outside of marriage hurts us. It always will, whether we think so or not."

He walked back to the podium and picked up the two glued-together pieces of paper. Then he took hold of the corners of each sheet and slowly pulled them apart so that the fronts of the paper faced the kids in the audience. "See?" He kept pulling until they were completely separated again. "Looks okay on the outside. That's why so many of you think, 'No big deal. I have sex with my girlfriend, so what? We aren't hurting anyone.'"

The room was silent, the kids staring at the two pieces of paper. It felt like everyone in the room knew what was coming.

The pastor turned the pieces of paper over. The red piece was gooey and ripped up, with small sections of blue stuck to it. On the blue piece, small bits of red clung in sections. Both pieces were an ugly mess.

"See." He held the sheets of paper up a little higher. "God tells us to wait until marriage because sex outside marriage hurts us. Sometimes it hurts in a way everyone can see. And other times it hurts in ways only God and us ever know about. The bottom line is this: sex outside marriage will scar us, and we will never, ever be the same again."

The man's words faded from Shane's memory. He blinked and spotted a group of kids his age walking past the jewelry store. They were from another high school, the rivals a few miles east. Two of the girls and three of the guys wore letterman jackets. All of them looked happy and carefree.

He wanted to shout at them, "Don't do it! Don't be alone together, don't take chances, don't do things your way! The Bible's right about sex!" But he only watched them walk off, laughing and teasing and enjoying high school life the way it was meant to be enjoyed.

Shane turned and faced the older couple

working over his ring. Why hadn't he listened? What made him and Lauren think they could beat the odds or get away with something that was so wrong? The bench he was sitting on was cold and uncomfortable, the same way he felt inside. He stood and wandered out into the mall. If only there was a way to go back, to tell God they were sorry and they needed a second chance . . .

Not that he didn't want the baby. He did. He wanted the baby and Lauren and the life they'd have together. But he wished like crazy they'd listened to God. He stared up through a glass window in the roof of the mall. *God . . . we need you so bad. Please . . .* He glanced back at the store, at the couple working on his ring. *Please let this work out.*

A verse came to mind, one that the youth group leader wore once in a while on a T-shirt. It was written in big pink letters on a funky pale green background and it said, "I know the plans I have for you."

He hadn't been in church all that much — his parents were never very good at making Sunday service — but he knew the verse anyway. It was a favorite among the kids because it talked about the very thing they all worried about — tomorrow.

" 'For I know the plans I have for you,' declares the Lord, 'plans to prosper you and not to harm you, plans to give you hope and a future.' " It was from Jeremiah 29:11.

He sighed, and it rattled all the way to his knees. Just then, the old woman gave him a little wave and a nod that told him the ring was ready. He went to the counter and studied it. The words he'd asked them to engrave were the words that summed up how he felt about this season in their lives.

Even now.

Even now, when Lauren was seventeen and pregnant, when their future and the future of their baby hung in the balance, he loved her. He loved her the way he always had, with a singleness and a focus. Even now, because no matter when she would see the ring or read the inscription on the inside of the band, it would be true. Even now, when they were struggling; even now, when they were not sure how to get from today to tomorrow. Even now . . . he loved her.

No, they hadn't done things right. But he would stand by her. He would stand by her as long as the sun came up in the morning, as long as spring followed winter. He paid for the ring, and the woman slipped it in a little velvet gray box.

"I think your girlfriend will love it," the woman was saying.

In the background, her husband gave him a wink. "Young love is so precious."

Shane bit his lip. If they only knew. He thanked them, tucked the bag tight into his coat pocket, and left the mall. Since he was in sixth grade he'd wondered what it would be like to ask Lauren Anderson to marry him. He'd planned to take her to a beautiful mountaintop or a sandy beach overlooking the ocean. He'd get down on one knee and tell her how his life wouldn't be complete unless she was his wife.

But there was no time for anything like that now.

It was mid-April, and his parents wanted to move him to Los Angeles in two months. He needed to set his plans in motion now, to find a way to keep them together. He was the man, after all. It was his job to take care of her and the baby, and he certainly couldn't do that from three thousand miles away.

He drove to her house and knocked on her door. That was something new also. He used to give a quick knock and walk straight in. But these days he felt . . . not quite welcome. Lauren's mother looked out a side window and he heard her yell for

Lauren. After a few minutes she came to the door, her eyes wide.

"I didn't know you were coming." Her sweatshirt was oversized, pulled down around her jeans.

The idea of her pregnancy starting to show sent a wave of fear over him. More proof that he really was drowning. He glanced at the window, but her mother was no longer standing there. "Hi."

"Hi." She stepped out onto the porch and crossed her arms. Her eyes were sad — the way they usually were lately — but a smile tugged at the corners of her lips. "I felt the baby move today."

"You did?" A sense of wonder filled his heart, and it bubbled with life and awe and overwhelming love all at once. He wasn't sure what to say. This should've been something they celebrated under the same roof, ten years from now, when they were married and old enough to have children the way they'd planned. Still, the life within her was *their* child. Too young or not, that baby was growing bigger every day. He reached out and touched his fingers to her stomach. It felt hard and just a little rounder than before. His eyes lifted and he looked straight at her. "What did it feel like?"

"Like butterfly wings." She giggled. "I think it's a girl, Shane." She shrugged with one shoulder, and suddenly she looked like the sweet, silly girl he'd fallen for so many years ago. "I can picture her fingers tickling the inside of my stomach. That's what it felt like."

"Wow." He crossed his arms again and shook his head. "I can't imagine."

"You're the first person I've told." She lowered her chin, her eyes big and a little shy. "I wish you could feel it. It's the most amazing thing."

"Me too." He shifted his weight and stuck his hand in the pocket. The one where the ring box lay deep inside. It was too cold to go for a walk, and inside her house had too much tension. They weren't ready to go out on a date, but an urgency pressed in on him. If he didn't ask her now, another day would slip by — another day when they wouldn't have a plan or a way to stay together even if his family moved to Mars.

He coughed once and raised his shoulders up near his neck. "It's cold out here."

"Yeah." She didn't invite him in. Another bad sign. "Wanna talk in your car?"

It was the perfect idea. "Definitely." He grinned at her, but stopped short of kissing her. Her mother might be somewhere, watching.

The sun was fading, and the snow that had melted in the late afternoon had grown icy and slippery. They took careful steps to his car and climbed into the front seat, him behind the wheel and her next to him. When they were inside, her smile faded. "Is it something else? Something about our parents?"

"No, nothing like that." Shane felt a lump in his throat. Until Lauren's pregnancy, he couldn't remember ever crying. But in the past few months he'd felt tears in his eyes several times. This was one of them. "Lauren . . ." How was he supposed to do this? It wasn't anything like he'd always dreamed it would be. Still, he couldn't have meant it any more if he'd flown a banner from the top of the Empire State Building.

She had a funny look on her face, almost a smile but not quite. "What is it, Shane?"

He gulped. Then he pulled the small gray velvet box from his pocket and held it out to her. Her eyebrows lifted, and she looked from the box to him and then back to the box. He opened the lid and showed her the ring inside. His voice cracked as he asked her the question, the emotion leaking in between every word. "Marry me, Lauren. Not today or tomorrow. But as soon as we can, okay? I'll still go to college and I can become a pilot." He released a nervous laugh. "I always wanted to fly, remember?"

"Shane!" She was staring at the ring. She put her fingers over her mouth. Then she reached for it and stopped short. "Do you wanna take it out? So you can put it on my finger?"

He laughed, and it sounded nervous even to him. This wasn't going exactly the way he'd planned. His eyes met hers. "Does that mean you're saying yes?"

"Oh." She gasped and gave a little giggle. "Sorry." Her eyes grew suddenly serious and she sat up straighter, smoothing the wrinkles in her sweatshirt. "Yes, Shane. I'll marry you."

"Good." He smiled, laughing a little now, too. He took the ring from the box and dropped it. "Oops."

The ring bounced on his emergency brake handle and slid down under the seat. "I think I can get it." She eased her hand down the crack next to the seat and felt around for a few seconds. "Hmm. Do you have a flashlight?"

Shane was trying to hold back, but he

couldn't. Not for another minute. The laughter came slowly at first, in quiet bursts. When she saw that he'd given into the humor of the moment, she laughed too. Pretty soon they were both laughing hard, their heads back against the seats. "You know something?" Shanc caught a breath and wiped at his eyes.

"What?" She was still giggling. Her words didn't come easily.

"This is how it'll be if we're married." He laughed again. "Lots of mistakes."

"But we'll —" she drew a long breath and her laughter faded — "we'll learn together. That's what'll make it work."

"That and something we should've had from the beginning." He was calmer now, the laughter gone from his voice. "God in the middle of everything."

"Yes." A shadow fell over her face. "You think He forgives us? I mean, you think He's done punishing us?"

"I don't know if this was a punishment, Lauren." He put his left hand on the steering wheel and cocked his head in her direction. "You getting pregnant, that was a consequence. Okay, maybe it was a punishment too. But it was something that happened because we invited it to happen."

"You mean —" her expression took on a hopeful look — "you think God still cares about us? After what we did?"

"Yes, I think He still cares. Listen to what I heard yesterday."

For the next half hour he told her about it, about the blue paper and the red paper and how they looked after they'd been glued together. Then he told her the rest of the pastor's message. The point was clear. Yes, they might mess up. Some of them in that room had probably already messed up, he told them. The point was to take those mistakes to God, tell Him you were sorry, and then move on in His strength and light, along His path. "See —" he took her hands in his — "we have to find that ring because I want to marry you, Lauren. Then we'll be one again and, well, our backsides won't look so messed up."

"Okay." She giggled again, but she didn't say much about his story. Shane understood. She was bound to feel guilty, and that meant she didn't feel close to God. Not that she ever really had. They were just getting close to Him when this happened. He swallowed back the desire to say anything else. She would feel close to God eventually. If they were married, he was sure about that.

Because with every day he felt surer he couldn't get by without the Lord.

"I'll try once more." She eased her fingers down along the side of the seat and felt around for half a minute. Her eyes lit up then, and she pulled the ring out and held it in the air. "Here you go." She looked at it, then at him. "It's beautiful. Now you can put it on."

"Read it first." He pointed. "There, on the inside."

She held it in the glow of the streetlights. " 'Even now' " She looked at him. Then she held up the ring and read it again. As she did, an understanding came into her eyes. She hesitated some more, and as she looked at him this time, she blinked back tears. "Even now, we have this, right? What we've always had together?"

"Yes. I love you, Lauren Anderson. Even now, when everything in life feels crazy. I love you no matter what."

He took the ring from her, and as he slipped it on her finger, they were both smiling. It was a good sign, a glimpse of hope that maybe they would find their way together and work things out. Maybe one of their sets of parents would let them marry after high school and offer them a room. And yes, their start would be rough.

There would be goofs and laughs and awkward moments, for sure. But they would have each other.

The ring — even with its small bits of crusted diamonds — shimmered in the fading light and Shane took her hand, running his thumb over the white gold. For the briefest moment, it wasn't an engagement ring at all, but the tiniest, most miniature, life preserver. Something to cling to so that just for a moment he could keep his head above water. So the drowning feeling would go away and he could know that God did indeed love them and forgive them. That together they had a future and a hope waiting for them.

Even now.

Four

Angela Anderson was beyond worried.

The kids had talked about wedding plans every day for a month now, and nothing was changing their minds. Clearly they had a plan to convince both sets of parents, and they'd started with her and Bill.

"We want to get married." Shane stood straight and tall, Lauren beside him, when they broke the news. "We're engaged. We need to be together." He hesitated. "If my parents move away, I'd like to ask if I could live here, in the spare bedroom, until I turn eighteen this fall." He swallowed hard. "Then we can get married."

Bill took a deep breath and lit into the kid. "First of all, you're *not* engaged, and you're *not* —"

"Yes, we are, Daddy!" Lauren stepped forward and held up her left hand. It was the first time they'd seen the ring, and both Angela and Bill were silent for a moment. "We're engaged, and we have to be together. Shane's right."

"Do not interrupt me, young lady!" Bill continued his tirade. "You're not engaged because you're too young. You're not going to live together and you're not going to get married the summer before your senior year in high school." He lowered his voice. "None of this is going to work. You need to understand that before another day goes by."

The argument raged, and Angela could feel her heart breaking. Her husband's expression was beyond angry, but she could see his fear. He'd confided to her that he was afraid he was losing Lauren.

"We used to be so . . . so close." He stared out their bedroom window. "Sometimes I wonder if I've lost her for good."

Now his words haunted her, even as he fought with their daughter. And the pain didn't stop there. Shane's face was marked with disappointment, and a gut-wrenching despair filled Lauren's eyes. Their daughter wanted this as badly as Shane did, that much was clear. So what about that? Were she and Bill doing the right thing by forcing their daughter and the boy she loved to part? By giving them no way to make it work?

Finally Shane and Lauren left, but Lauren tried again twice more that week. With each conversation, Angela's doubt grew, and over the next month it caused a quiet crack in her facade of certainty. Shane tried his parents too, and of course they wanted nothing to do with the plan. No way on earth Lauren was moving with *them,* out west. And so, without the help of either set of parents, the kids really didn't have a choice.

Shane didn't have a car of his own or money or a place to stay. For a week or so he talked about quitting school and taking a job at the greasy chicken joint down the street. Then, according to Lauren, his father helped him do the math, showing him that even if he worked sixty hours a week he couldn't afford an apartment, a car, and food. Let alone support a wife and a baby. No, the kids didn't have a chance of staying together without help.

But that wasn't the only issue that kept the weeks through mid-May tense and painful. Sheila called every few days. Whereas in the past they would make small talk and find things to smile and laugh about, now the conversations were about one thing only.

"So —" Sheila's tone seemed harder

with each call — "has she decided to give the baby up for adoption? That's what she needs to do, Angela. You said it was going to happen. You can force her hand in this, you know."

Angela released a heavy breath and explained, yet again, that the decision had to be Lauren's and Shane's. Of course she'd recommended that the kids give the baby up. That would seem the most logical, kindest thing for everyone involved. "But you're missing something here," she finally told Sheila.

"What's that?"

"Our kids love each other. They have for a very long time."

Sheila made a sound that suggested she couldn't have disagreed more. "They don't know what love is."

You don't know what love is. That was the phrase being bandied about among all the adults. Even Angela wanted to go with that. It was neat and tidy and gave them a reason to control the kids, figure things out for them. They didn't know what love was.

But what if they were wrong?

That fear stuck like a thorn in her conscience, and no matter how she tried to work past it or look around it, she couldn't dislodge it. By mid-May, Lauren was seven months pregnant and showing. Angela wanted her daughter to quit school so the kids wouldn't talk. Lauren explained that the kids would talk anyway, and she was right. By then everyone in their circle knew she was pregnant.

What made it more painful for Angela was the loss of Sheila's friendship. The woman had been like a sister, the one she'd shared her deepest insecurities with, her greatest joys and fears. Now Sheila grew less considerate, more accusing of Lauren and even Angela, and finally Angela made a decision. She had to spare her daughter a lifetime of being hated by Shane's family. The two were going to be apart — that much was already decided. The relationship they shared was all but over. Now it was up to Angela to keep Lauren from desiring a place in a family where the parents wanted nothing to do with her. She knew what she had to do next, and it was for Lauren's own good. Because she loved her.

On Saturday afternoon that week, Angela invited Sheila over, and the two of them sat down in the sunroom again. She studied the other woman, choosing her words with care. "Sheila, I know what you're hoping. You're hoping Bill and I were able to talk Lauren into giving the baby up for adoption."

"Yes." Sheila folded her hands in her lap. She was careful not to look too long into Angela's eyes. "It's craziness for a girl her age to keep a baby, Angela. We've been over all this." She paused. "So . . . is that why you called me here?"

"No." Angela took a slow breath and steadied herself. She had thought this through for days and now she believed it was all they had, the only chance of moving forward. "It's about the kids, about our moves coming up next month."

"Our moves?" Sheila looked up and for a fraction of a moment, the old Sheila shone through. The one who was kind and open-minded, the one who would listen and offer support no matter the subject. Every subject except this one.

"Yes." Angela poured them each a cup of coffee. She took a sip of hers and sat it back down again. Bill was out supervising a work crew doing maintenance on some trees near the new bank building in Wheaton. Lauren was up in her room writing, something she did more than ever. Angela closed her eyes and willed herself to move forward with the plan. "I think we should wait at least a month before exchanging phone numbers. After we move, I mean."

Sheila made a face, but gradually the lines in her face eased. "What'll we tell the kids? That we don't want them to talk?"

"No, nothing like that." She lowered her voice. The last thing she wanted was for Lauren to hear her. "We can blame it on the phone company. It can take weeks to set up phone service. That way it'll give Lauren a chance to have the baby and think things through without the pressure of talking to Shane every day, trying to do things as if they were still a couple."

Sheila's arms relaxed to her sides and her face looked almost pleasant. "I like it." She looked at Angela, her eyes imploring her to understand. "I'm glad you're helping me on this. I mean friendship aside, we have to care about our kids. They're too young to be together this way."

"You're right." Angela wasn't so certain, but this was all she and Sheila had left now, a series of actions and reactions, a practice in going through the motions. "Let's see if we can keep them apart for a month, month and a half."

"So when we get to LA — and Shane *is* coming with us to LA, regardless of what he thinks — I give you our new number, but you don't give it to Lauren until forty-five days later. You call me with your new number, but I don't give it to Shane for the same period. Something like that?"

"Exactly."

"I like it a lot. It's a good plan."

"It is. I feel the same as you. They need time apart." The lie made Angela wince. Lauren and Shane would disown them for life if they could hear this conversation. This meeting wasn't about making Sheila happy or believing that the kids were better off staying away from each other. It was about protecting Lauren from the hostility that Shane's family held toward her. For that, she would lie even if it meant hurting Lauren in the short term. She looked at Sheila. "It's only for a month, maybe six weeks. After that they can catch up and we'll see what happens."

Sheila was already on her feet. "Very well." She looked at her watch. "I can't stay. I have a church dinner tonight." Her eyes met Angela's one last time. She stopped short of flashing that phony smile Angela had seen too often in the past months. Instead she let the corners of her mouth raise just a little. "This isn't easy for any of us, Angela." She paused. "Please let us know if you get anywhere with Lauren.

There are so many wonderful families waiting to adopt children. It would be a great sacrifice if Lauren would consider it."

Angela wanted to spit at her. A great sacrifice for Lauren? Yes, and a great victory for Sheila. Angela took a few steps toward the door and held it open wide so Sheila wouldn't stay longer than necessary. Then, since she was on a roll, she told yet another lie. "I was right about adoption, Sheila. Lauren's leaning more toward it every day."

"She is?" Sheila's eyes sparked to life, the same way they did when Bloomingdale's announced a storewide sale.

Angela felt sick to her stomach. She bit her lip and nodded. "Yes. I'm almost positive."

Sheila left, spouting platitudes and half smiles, making comments about things being meant to be and life working out for the best and how every change was like another season meant to be savored and how nothing stays the same anyway.

The silence after Sheila left gave Angela her first peaceful moment all morning. She sat down on the sofa, leaned back, and closed her eyes. She'd done it. She'd convinced Sheila to stay out of her life, out of her daughter's life. At least for a month or more. That meant Lauren could have her baby in peace, without constant phone calls and directives from Sheila about why the baby should be given up and when.

As she sat there, everything about the morning meeting felt right except one thing, the same thing that had troubled Angela for much of the past month: What if the kids' love didn't fade away? What if Sheila and all the adults were wrong? What if age didn't determine whether or not a person could truly understand what love was and whether it was real?

Angela folded her arms and gripped her sides. They were teenagers; of course they would move on. They'd be heartbroken for a season. But they'd get past their grief and given a month or so of separation, they might reevaluate and decide it was better to take time away from each other. In fact, if that happened, Lauren might indeed decide to give her baby up for adoption. And yes, everyone would win in the process.

She blinked her eyes open, stood, and padded her way up to Lauren's bedroom. She did a light knock on the door.

"Come in." Lauren sounded tired and distracted. Shane had baseball all that day, so she'd spent most of the afternoon in her room writing.

"What're you working on?" Angela sat on the edge of her daughter's bed. The memory of her conversation with Sheila burned in her mind. She felt like a traitor.

"A short story." She held up a blue notebook. "I have lots of them."

"What's this one about?"

"A little girl named Emily. She's a princess in a faraway land, where everyone else is a rabbit or a bear or a fox. She goes all her life not knowing where to find her prince until she meets a special woman on the other side of the mountains."

"Hmm." Angela nodded. "I love your imagination."

"Even without a college degree?" She smiled at her mother. The ring Shane gave her was still on her finger, the two of them still believing that somehow one set of parents would give in and let them stay in the same house for the next six months. As Shane had pointed out the week before, they could even get married *now* with their parents' permission. Not that anyone was about to grant that.

Angela stayed silent for awhile and Lauren wrote a few more lines. Then she closed the notebook and looked at her mother. "Why was Mrs. Galanter here?"

Guilt poked pins at Angela and she forced a smile. "We were talking about their move. They haven't decided on a house in California yet."

"Shane's meeting with his dad today. They might let him stay with one of his friends on the baseball team." She smiled, content. No question about it. Lauren really believed it would work out and the two of them wouldn't be separated.

Angela remembered Sheila's tone. *Shane is coming with us, regardless of what he thinks.* She cleared her throat and tried to smile at her daughter. "I'm not sure about that, honey."

"I am." She set her notebook down beside her bed and sat cross-legged near her pillow. "God'll work something out."

"God, huh?" Angela felt a curious twist in her heart. She was the parent, after all. Talk about God at a time like this should've been coming from her and Bill. And it would one day, when they weren't as busy, when they were out in the suburbs in Wheaton and life was simpler. Then they would go to church every weekend and figure out how to get more God into their every day.

Lauren looked out the window, her eyes

gently pensive. "If we'd spent more time talking about God last summer, you know, putting Him first, then maybe we wouldn't have made so many mistakes."

They were quiet for a bit, and outside a light rain started to fall. Finally Angela found the words she was looking for. "Tell me how you feel about Shane." Her voice was soft, not threatening the way so many of their conversations had been since the first of the year. "How do you really feel?"

Lauren wrinkled her nose, and her eyebrows lowered in a soft V. "You already know how I feel, Mom."

"I know what you say. But that's what you're supposed to say. You're pregnant. Of course you're supposed to say you love him. But what does that really mean to you?"

Lauren exhaled slowly and looked out the window again. "It means that no matter what happens, even if they take him from me, a part of me will always stay with him." She looked at her mother. "A part of him will always stay with me." Her hands had been tucked beneath her knees, but now she held out her left hand. "I'll wear his ring forever, Mother." She smiled. "Shane Galanter loves me like no one else ever will. He stands up for me when no one else does, and he believes in me when I don't believe in myself." A laugh sounded low in her throat. "Everyone thinks we're too young to know what love is. But I look at the way you and Daddy and the Galanters are, the way your friendship has died because of this, and you know what I think?"

Angela's throat was thick, her emotions choking her. "What?"

"Being old hasn't helped you know what love is, either."

She didn't want to cry, not with Lauren watching. But the tears came anyway, and since she couldn't speak, she leaned in and hugged her daughter. Hugged her for a long time. As she left her room a few minutes later, the doubt she had about what they were doing to their children was no longer a single small thorn poking at her conscience.

It was a full-size dagger.

Lauren couldn't wait for Shane to show up at her house that night. She hadn't told her parents he was coming, and now it was after eleven o'clock and her mom and dad were in bed. Lauren sat by the window watching the rain. It had been a light sprinkle all day, but now the drops were harder, heavier.

Still, the roads were clear. Shane should be there any time.

In her lap was the story she was working on, the latest one. Ever since she could hold a pencil she'd been writing stories — especially when her heart was full of unresolved emotions. She stared at the notebook in her hands and flipped back to the beginning of the story, reading the first page: *Even Now — the Story of Us* by Lauren Gibbs.

A smile tugged at her lips. *Lauren Gibbs* was the name she always used when she wrote. A long time ago she'd read the name in a book and something about it — the way it fit the character or the strength of it — stayed with her.

The day she'd found it she ran up to her dad, struggling to reign in her enthusiasm. "Dad . . . this is the perfect name."

He was reading the newspaper. The pages crackled in his hands as he bent it in half and lowered it so he could see her. "What's that?"

"The name in this book." She held it up. "It's perfect."

Slowly he began to open the paper again. His eyes darted from the article to her and back again. "Good, honey."

"Dad!" She huffed at him. "You're not listening."

"What?" The paper fell a few inches, and he looked at her. "Of course I am. You like the book you're reading."

"No!" Another huffy breath. "I like the character name in the book."

He blinked. "Character name?"

"Yes. *Lauren Gibbs*." She smiled big again. "Isn't that the greatest name?"

Her dad chuckled a few times. "I think Lauren Anderson is pretty enough."

Lauren stuffed the memory. Her father didn't need to see anything special in the name. She made good on her word. Using it on her short stories was a way to leave herself behind. In her mind, Lauren Gibbs wasn't a seventeen-year-old high school student. She was worldly and wise, with years of education and a fascination with international affairs. She traveled the world and met interesting people from a dozen different cultures.

That was the perspective she wrote from, as if she, like her fictitious alter ego, actually lived such a life.

Her eyes traveled down the page. The first line of the story read: "She watched him from her quiet place at the dinner table. She would remember this day for the rest of time — the day she fell in love with Shane Galanter."

She heard a car in the distance and shut the cover. Once in a while she shared her stories with Shane, but not this time. They had too much else to work through. She set the notebook down and looked out the window again. This was the big chance they'd been waiting for. His father had told him they could talk about the possibility of him living with one of the baseball players for the next year. That would work perfectly. It meant his parents would be out of the picture. The way his mother treated her lately, it would be nice to have some distance between them. Headlights rounded the corner and she squinted into the dark night. It was him. He pulled his Camry up in front of her house and cut the engine. She watched him get out of the car, watched the way his shoulders slumped forward a little, the way his steps were slow.

She sat up a little straighter and a thought hit her, one she had resisted for the past month. What if his dad hadn't given him permission? What if they were insisting Shane move with them? They wouldn't do that, would they? Not when she was wearing his ring. Not when they were engaged to be married.

He was almost to the door, but she reached it first, opening it and motioning for him to be quiet as he stepped inside. Once the door was closed she leaned against it and searched his eyes. "He's going to let you, right?"

"Lauren." He looked down, and in that instant the answer was as clear as the Chicago skyline in August. When he lifted his eyes to hers, they were shiny wet. "He wants me to come to LA for my senior year. Just until I'm finished school. Then he'll do everything he can to help us."

The room felt wobbly, and she wouldn't have been surprised to see the ceiling fall down around their ankles. "You . . . you're leaving? In a month?"

"What else can I do?" A hint of anger colored his tone. "I have nothing, Lauren. No car, no job, no education, not even a lousy twenty dollar bill." He pulled her close. After awhile he leaned back and looked at her again. The sorrow in his eyes was so raw it hurt. "My mom says you're thinking about giving up the baby?"

She shook her head, frustrated. "Never, Shane. Never once." Her hands came in tight around his waist and she held him.

"Why does she keep saying that?"

"It's not just her." His voice was kind, gentle. "Your mom said the same thing."

"What?" She took a step back and shook her head. "Is that what you want?"

"Of course not." He reached for her hands, but she kept her distance. "It's just . . . for the next year, nothing's up to us."

She turned her back to him and stared out the window. A trembling started in her arms and moved to her hands. If Shane was leaving, then maybe she *should* give up the baby. How would she raise it without his support? Her parents had promised their help, but clearly they didn't approve. The trembling moved down her legs to her knees, and suddenly her entire body was shaking.

He came up and slipped his arms around her, resting his hands on her swollen belly. "I want this baby, Lauren. I wish it were coming ten years from now, but I still want it." He eased her around so that she was facing him. "Don't ever think I don't."

"You're really leaving?"

"I won't give up. I'll keep looking for a way, pushing my dad and trying to make this work somehow until the last minute." He took her hands in his. "I promise."

"I know, but —" her teeth were chattering now — "but if it doesn't work out, then we only have a month left together."

"They can take me out of Chicago, but they can't take me out of your life. So we finish up school, Lauren. Then we'll be together. My dad promised."

She wanted to scream or cry or grab him and run as far away as they could get. But they were stuck. The walls closing in a little more every day. She felt the baby move, and it made her eyes fill with tears. "Find a way, Shane." A sob broke free and she buried her face in his shoulder. "Please. I can't do this without you."

He held her, whispering promises that he'd try, that maybe there was something they hadn't thought about. But in the end, as he drove away that night, she was convinced that she wasn't the only one who knew the truth about their situation. He knew it too.

Never mind about love. Good-byes were a month away.

Five

The days passed like so many minutes, each one colored with a different set of new and frightening emotions.

Some afternoons Lauren drove to the lake with Shane, and they'd walk along the shore talking about forever. They barely noticed the strange looks they drew from people who passed by. With her straight blonde hair, she looked younger than her seventeen years. Whispers came with the territory.

Neither of them cared. They were too caught up in their own world to mind what anyone thought. Even their parents.

"I'm talking to one of my teachers about renting a room," Shane told her one sunny afternoon as they sat side by side on the beach. "You know her. Mrs. Tilp."

"Mrs. Tilp, the calculus teacher?" Lauren squinted into the sun. Her abdomen was tight, the baby pressing against her.

"Yeah, she and her husband have an

extra room. I heard her talking about it to another teacher. I asked if I could rent it, you know. Through next year. We could get married in the fall and live there together with the baby."

The possibility sounded doubtful. "Did you tell her it would be you? Or you and me and the baby?"

"Me for now." He adjusted his baseball cap. "I thought I'd ask about the two of you after she says yes."

A day later, Shane had the answer. The teacher didn't want a student boarder. Especially not a minor. Shane's next attempt was a neighbor three doors down, a retired man who lived by himself.

While the possibilities dwindled one at a time, Lauren refused to believe it wouldn't somehow work out. At night, when Shane's school day was over, the two of them were almost always together. They felt uncomfortable in either of their homes, so Shane would pick her up and they'd park someplace to talk.

"What about names?" Shane asked her one night. They'd discussed a few, but hadn't decided anything. "We need a plan, just in case."

"In case?" Lauren searched his eyes, and instantly she understood. "You mean if they take you to California?"

He pressed his lips together and nodded. His eyes fell to her belly and then rose again. "I have one."

This was wonderful, sitting alone with him, pretending they were like any other normal couple about to be parents. She leaned back against the car door and grinned at him. "For a boy or a girl?"

"Girl."

"Okay, what?" The baby moved inside her, and she set her hands over the area. "Here." She took his hand and laid it on her belly. "You haven't felt this yet."

"Really?" His touch was light as they waited. The baby kicked again, and Shane's face lit up. "Wow . . . That was amazing." He put both hands on her now and caressed the place where the baby lay. Then he leaned in and whispered, "Hey, little one, I felt that. You've got a strong kick."

The baby moved again, and the happiness in Lauren was so great she wondered if she was glowing. This was Shane's first contact with their baby. It made everything about her pregnancy feel normal and real and wonderful. The way it was supposed to feel.

Shane ran his hand over her middle once

101

more and then he leaned back against his door and grinned. "Here it is — Emily." His eyes shone. "What do you think?"

"I like it." She pictured her daughter — it was a daughter, she was sure of it — dressed in pink and lace and bearing the sweet, feminine name. Justine or Tabitha had been on her list, something a little modern. But it touched her that Shane had chosen a name. "I didn't know you were thinking about baby names."

"I can't think of anything else." He gave a weak chuckle. "School's barely holding my attention because I'm dreaming about you and the baby, when it'll be born and whether . . ." His smile faded. "Whether we'll be together when it happens."

She ignored that last part. If their parents would let them, she was sure Shane would make the best father ever. Another time when they were together she asked, "What about for a boy?"

"I'm not sure." He made a curious face. "Maybe Josh or Jared. Something like that."

The discussions always felt the same to Lauren. Like they were playing house in the shadow of an impending tidal wave. Still, the normalcy of talking about names made the days bearable. Especially when each one drew them closer to his parents' moving date.

With a week left, the call Lauren had expected all along finally came.

"I have to go." Shane sounded like he'd been crying. "I'll finish school in California and then I'll come find you. Whatever it takes. We'll figure something out from there."

Even then she wasn't ready to give up. All week she tried to talk sense into her parents. "Do something, please!" She took hold of her mother's hand, her father's shoulder. "We love each other; we don't want to be apart. Please, help us."

Her parents listened and once in a while offered some show of sadness on her behalf. But they never once offered a way out. Lauren cornered her mother in the kitchen one day near the end of that week. "Call the Galanters. Have them over. Tell them we can't do this living so far apart. Please, Mother."

"Lauren, things are different. The Galanters have made it clear they want no part of our family."

It was like the shrinking hallway. No doors. No windows. No way out.

Finally it was Sunday night. Shane and his family were leaving the next morning,

103

and he was on his way over to say good-bye. Lauren headed outside to meet him.

"Stay in, honey," her mother called from the kitchen. "We want to say good-bye, too."

"No, you don't. You could care less if he leaves." Lauren's tone was sharp. Things between her and her parents had never been worse. If they didn't want to help keep Shane around, then what good were they? Everyone was against them. She slammed the door behind her, walked to the end of the sidewalk and waited.

She wore a faded oversized yellow T-shirt and her father's navy running shorts. Her middle was gigantic, so big it scared her, and even though the air was heavy and hot, she began to shiver. How had things gotten so crazy? Why hadn't they listened to their youth group pastor before, back when they still had time to finish high school like any other kids?

The moon was full that night, casting light through the trees and spraying shadows around the place where she stood. She heard a car in the distance and she squinted at the headlights coming closer. It was him. She knew the sound of his car. When he stopped and climbed out, she knew for sure. He'd been crying. He still was. He shoved his hands in his pockets, walked around the front of his car, and came to her.

"Lauren . . ." He pulled her into his arms and tried to hug her. But her abdomen was so large that the moment was awkward, and he drew back. "I only have ten minutes. My dad wants the movers to hook the car up to the moving truck."

She searched his face. "What if we give the baby up, would that make them stay?"

"No." He ran his fingers along her brow and into her hairline near her temple. "We've been over this." Question marks danced in his eyes. "Do you want to give the baby up?"

"Of course not." She sniffed and a pounding filled her chest. "But I can't have the baby on my own, without you. My parents aren't on my side, Shane." She took a step back. "I don't know what to do."

He felt her hand, moved his thumb across the surface of her engagement ring. "Remember what it says."

She blinked, trying to see him more clearly. "Yes."

"Even now, Lauren. When everything's falling apart I still love you. I still want to marry you."

The minutes counted down, and finally they were left with only a lingering, desperate hug and a flurry of promises. "I'll call." Shane eased himself from her and started toward his car.

"I'll be waiting." She took a step closer.

"The year'll go fast." He stopped a few feet from his door. "I'll visit, I promise."

"We'll meet you there as soon as you graduate."

"I know." He narrowed his eyes, seeing past her fear and uncertainty. His cheeks were wet. "You gotta keep that promise."

Another step closer. "I'll tell you as soon as I go into labor."

He was about to get into his car, but for a moment he did nothing but keep his eyes on hers. She understood what he was doing. These few seconds would have to last for her too. Then, in a voice quieter than before, he said, "I'll never love anyone like I love you, Lauren. Never."

She massaged her throat and swallowed hard, willing the words to come. "Me neither, not as long as I live."

There was nothing left to say. He climbed into his car and drove away. Only then did she notice the pains in her belly. Not sharp pains, nothing serious. Just an aching sensation.

As if even the baby inside her was grieving.

★ ★ ★

Angela tried not to watch, but she couldn't help it.

She sat in the dark living room, staring out the window as Lauren and Shane said good-bye, as they hugged and wept, and finally as he drove away and Lauren dropped to the grass, her head in her hands. That's when it came over Angela — a suffocating guilt.

"Baby, it'll be okay." She put her fingers against the cool glass, her voice a whisper. "We'll get through this."

She was still sitting there when Bill walked up and put his hand on her shoulder.

"They'll be all right." His voice was low, confident. He hadn't once allowed for any other possibility.

Angela understood. Lauren was so precious to Bill. His protective instinct toward her was intense. This was his way of keeping her from what he believed to be a painful decision. If she and Shane stayed together, she'd keep the baby for sure — even if that wasn't the best decision. If that happened, she'd never get the chance to really grow up, to experience her senior year in high school or her college days after that. Even more, if she married Shane she'd be stuck with in-laws who no longer liked her.

Bill had no doubts at all. Separating Lauren and Shane was the best decision for everyone. Angela wanted to feel the same way, but she was too busy trying to grab a single breath. She put her hand over her husband's. "What if they're not?" She turned and looked at him, and her heart pounded out a strange rhythm. "What if they're not all right? Maybe we're wrong, Bill. This is all our doing, us and the Galanters."

He frowned and looked out the window at their daughter. "They're only kids. They don't know what's right for them." He lifted his chin a little. "I think we all know the best thing for the baby is for Lauren to give it up."

Angela felt the stirrings of anger. "We've been through this. She wants to keep it, you know that."

"But with Shane gone . . ." He shrugged. "With him out of the picture, I think she'll change her mind." He straightened and gave her shoulder a final squeeze. "I hope so."

Then he turned and went back to the living room. She heard the television click on, and after that, the sound of an announcer talking about the Reds and the White Sox and who was in the lineup that night.

Angela watched him go and a soft cry escaped her. She shook her head. No matter how sincere his motives, could he really be a party to breaking the kids up and never have a single doubt? Between them and the Galanters, they had manipulated their kids' futures in every way possible. They had more than a decade of history together, yet the four of them had willingly stood by as their friendship died. Then they'd agreed to keep their new forwarding phone numbers a secret. At least for a month. All so that maybe Lauren would change her mind and give the baby up for adoption. Angela looked out at Lauren and even through the dark night she could see the obvious. Lauren was sobbing, crying alone on the damp early summer grass with no one to comfort her. A chill ran down Angela's spine and she shuddered. The thought wouldn't leave her alone, wouldn't allow her a minute's peace. It was the same thought she'd had all week, all month. Yes, in some twisted way they were all trying to do what was best for the kids.

But what in all of heaven would happen if they were wrong?

Shane couldn't see for the tears.

He was the best player on his baseball team, a kid no one dared cross in the locker room or anywhere else. But in the past month he felt his life falling apart one day at a time. And there was nothing he could do about it. A red light ahead brought him to a stop. He pressed his fists against his eyes and rubbed. They wouldn't have the last word, no, not if he could help it. They could take him away from Chicago, away from Lauren and the baby and all he wanted for their future. But they couldn't change the way he felt about her.

All his life he had pictured himself growing up to be a businessman, an investor like his father; a man who would earn his pilot's license and fly to important meetings. But in the past month that had changed. He had a new outlook on his parents and their world and all they stood for. Somewhere along the way the money had become them, who they were. It was no longer an asset to be used as a tool. The wealth they'd accumulated defined them.

It was their wealth that wouldn't allow for an only son of the Galanter family to be a father the summer before his senior year. That's what the move was about, no matter what they told him. If they could rush him across the country and enroll him in a new school where no one knew him, then life could go on pretty much the way it always had. No worries, no cares, and a future as good as gold.

As if by taking him from Lauren, the truth would somehow disappear.

Instead, the truth had become clearer than ever. The life he would lead one day would never be the life his parents led. He would find meaning and value in something other than money, and he would find it with Lauren and their baby, their children. He remembered the feeling of the baby moving beneath his hands. The child growing inside Lauren was his, and he would spend a lifetime figuring out how to be a daddy.

The light turned green and he pulled into the intersection. His eyes were dry now, the tears gone. In their place was a resolve strong enough to last a lifetime. Because the truth he could see so clearly was this: he really wouldn't love anyone the way he loved Lauren Anderson. One day, as soon as he could make it happen, they would find each other once more. He would add a white gold band to the ring he'd already given her.

And then they'd never be apart again.

Six

Lauren's determination grew with every tear she cried. She and Shane would be together again, sooner than later. The day after Shane left, he called her from a pay phone in Oklahoma somewhere. Static played between his words, but she made out most of what he said.

"My mom told me we won't have a phone at first." He sounded far away, nervous, and rushed for time. "We're at a gas station. They're filling up the car, so I don't have long."

Lauren was confused. "You won't have a phone?" Why was everything starting to feel like a conspiracy against them? "Everyone has a phone, Shane. How come?"

"My parents said it takes time. Something about where our house is. I guess the whole neighborhood's new and phone service could take a few weeks."

Panic welled up in her. "We're moving this Friday." She ran her hand along her forehead and tried to concentrate. "We'll have a new number too. How am I supposed to get it to you if you don't have a phone?"

"My mom's going to talk to your mom. I'm not sure, but maybe through your dad's work or something." His voice was calmer now, but she could hear a car engine in the background. "I called because I want you to remember something, Lauren. If I don't call, I'll be thinking of you. That'll never change. We'll figure out the phone number thing even if it takes a few weeks."

She felt herself relax. "Okay. If our moms have it worked out."

"They do. They have to." He paused. "I gotta go, but how are you feeling?"

"Good. The baby's heartbeat is strong."

"You . . . you haven't changed your mind about anything, have you?"

Why did he keep asking her? She clenched her teeth. "I told you. I've made up my mind, okay?"

"Okay. Hey . . . I have to go. I love you, Lauren. I'll call as soon as I can."

"I love you too."

They hung up and that was the last she heard from him. Now she and her family were completely moved into their new

113

house in the suburbs of Wheaton, a full hour out of the city. They had a new phone number, and once they were unpacked she approached her mother. "How's Shane supposed to get our new number?"

"I'm waiting for his mother to contact us, honey. She'll give it to us when their phone service gets connected."

"Okay, but how will she reach us when our number's new too?" She had two weeks until her due date, and she was uncomfortable most of the time. "I need to talk to him, Mom."

"Oh." Her mother didn't blink. "The phone company has a forwarding service, sweetheart. Anyone can call our old number and get the new one for the next three months."

Light dawned in her heart. A forwarding service? "Really?" She hadn't thought of that. "So he'll call any day."

"Exactly." Her mother smiled.

Three more days passed after that, making it two weeks since she'd heard from Shane. Her back ached and she took a walk down their winding drive to the mailbox. Where was he and what was he doing? Were they unpacked and getting used to their new neighborhood? And what part of Los Angeles had they settled in?

Was it a suburb or near the city, and why hadn't she asked before?

She wandered inside. Her dad was at the new bank, the one near Town Square, and her mother was in the den with an interior decorator, going through a sampling of window coverings. She went to the kitchen, sat at the desk chair, and stared at the telephone. Why wouldn't it ring? No one would go this long without phone service, would they?

But that had to be it, that the phones simply weren't connected. Because Shane would've called the minute he had a chance. She tapped the phone with her finger. As she did, her abdomen tightened, and stayed that way for half a minute. False contractions. She'd been having them for a few days now. She breathed out a few quick times in a row, and tried to remember their last conversation.

What had he said? That he would call as soon as he could, right? She let that play in her mind for a moment. Why hadn't he found another pay phone by now? He could've gone with his parents to the market or the gas station or anyplace in Los Angeles. Pay phones were everywhere. He could call her old number and get the forwarding message, right? But then why hadn't he called yet?

She ran her finger along the receiver. Maybe the information on the forwarding service was wrong, maybe they were a digit or two off, and he couldn't figure out her new number. An idea came upon her slowly, in fits and starts. She could call their old number, couldn't she? Then she could hear the recording for herself, make sure it gave the right new number. Why hadn't she thought of that sooner?

Her mother's lighthearted laughter sounded in the background. Most of her time had been spent with the decorator lately, and her father was practically never home. Board meetings with the new trustees, an intensive program of learning the operations systems, and meeting the employees.

So maybe it was up to her to figure out how to reach Shane.

She picked up the receiver and dialed her old number. A one and the area code, and the seven digits that had been as familiar to her as her first name. As soon as the numbers were all in, she waited for the ringing. But it never came. Instead a strange tone sounded in her ear, and a mechanical voice said, "The number you've reached has been disconnected. No new number is available."

What? No new number is . . . Gradually, like the slow collapse of a line of dominoes, the floor began to fall away beneath her. She gripped the receiver. The recording was still playing. "— you've reached has been disconnected. No new —"

Her mother had lied to her. There was no other explanation. They'd disconnected the old number, the one Shane knew, and they'd intentionally left no new number. The reason was as shocking as it was obvious. Her parents didn't want her talking to him. They'd moved her to the suburbs, and now they were preventing phone contact.

Lauren was on her feet. She slammed the receiver down. "Mother!" Her voice boomed across the house. "I need to talk to you!"

In the other room, her mother's laugh stopped short. "Lauren . . . I'm busy. Can't it wait?"

She stormed through the kitchen, down the hall, and into the den. The decorator was watching, eyes wide. Lauren glared at her mother. "I need to talk to you right now." Her tone was angry and just barely controlled. She stepped back into the hall and headed for the kitchen. Then she spun around and waited.

117

Her mother whispered something to the decorator Lauren couldn't make out, then she slipped into the hallway and locked eyes with Lauren. Her mother should've been angry. After all, Lauren had interrupted her in the middle of a business meeting, with a tone of voice that would never have been acceptable in the past.

But as her mother walked toward her, her eyes didn't hold a bit of anger. They held concern and anxiety and fear. Most of all, fear. Her mom waited until they were inches apart, then she folded her arms. "Are you in labor?"

"Do I *look* like I'm in labor?" She snapped the words. Her voice was still a little too loud, but she didn't care. "This isn't about me, Mother. It's about you." She pointed to the telephone on the desk behind her. "I called our phone number, our old one."

Her mother looked at the phone and then back at her. The fear in her eyes grew. "And?"

"Oh, don't act surprised." She wanted to scream. It was all she could do to keep her tone somewhat controlled. "You know exactly what I'm about to say."

"Lauren, watch how you talk to me."

"You don't sound very convincing." She

studied her mother's eyes. Who was this woman standing in front of her? All her life her mother had been her friend, her ally. The first one to listen and lend a bit of advice when her girlfriends ganged up against her at different times during her school years, or when a certain teacher gave her a hard time. But ever since she got pregnant, her mother had worked against her at every turn. Her mother and father, and Shane's parents, too.

Her mother shifted her weight. "Maybe you could tell me what you're talking about."

Lauren let out a small scream. "Don't *do* this! You know what I'm talking about. Stop lying to me!" She clenched her fists. "You didn't leave a forwarding number on our old phone. If Shane tried to call me since we moved, he would've gotten nothing, no new number, no clue how to reach me."

"What?" Her mother walked around her to the phone. She picked up the receiver, dialed a series of numbers, and held it to her ear. After several beats, she looked at Lauren and set the phone back down. "No forwarding number."

"Yeah, and you knew that." Her anger was growing with every few words. As she spoke, another wave of tightness seized at her middle. She winced and pointed at her mother. "You lied to me."

"I didn't, Lauren. I promise." Shock filled her voice, and she was suddenly indignant as the implication took root. "I told your father to put the new number on when he disconnected the . . ." Her voice trailed off and she turned slowly to the phone. "I told him . . ."

The tightness was worse now, stronger than it had been all day. "You're saying Dad did this, that you had nothing to do with it?" How could she trust her? How could she believe either of them? "What does it matter? The two of you are determined to tear us apart. I should've run off with Shane." She was yelling now, the truth settling in around her heart.

Her mother shook her head, her voice softer than before. "I swear to you, Lauren, I didn't do this." She picked up the receiver again. This time she punched in fewer numbers. After a moment she said, "Yes, this is Mrs. Anderson. I need to talk with my husband, please."

Lauren had heard enough. What did it matter whose fault it was? One of her parents had kept their new number off the recording so they could separate her from Shane. With her head spinning, she ran upstairs to her room.

Only then did the first real pain grab her. It ripped across her middle and dropped her to the edge of her bed. She bent in half, trying to survive it. When it passed, she eased herself onto the mattress and set her head on the pillow. It was too soon for the baby, but the pain that had just hit her sure felt like the real thing.

She stared at the ceiling, red hot anger flooding her veins. How could her parents have done this? They'd betrayed her, and now how would she get hold of Shane? In the distance she could hear some of what her mother was saying.

"But I thought you'd leave the number, Bill. Lauren's very upset about this and now she thinks I did it on purpose and —"

Another cramping pain hit, hard and sure. She rolled onto her side and drew her knees to her middle. Every breath was a struggle until finally the hurt let up. That's when she knew for sure. These were contractions, and if they were coming this close, she might be in labor.

"Mother!" She shouted as loud as she could. Her mom was at her side in a few minutes.

"Lauren, your father meant to leave the message, but —"

"I'm in labor." She panted, trying to catch her breath. "It hurts so bad." Another pain hit, and she yelled out loud. From downstairs she could hear the decorator gathering her things and shouting a good-bye. There was the sound of the front door shutting behind her, just as the contraction let up.

"We need to get you in." Her mother helped her to her feet, made a few phone calls, and in thirty minutes they were at the local hospital. The plan had been to have the baby in Chicago, at the hospital they were familiar with. But they had no time, and the staff at the local Central DuPage worked quickly to get her into a delivery room.

"She's been in labor for quite some time," the doctor told them. "The baby'll be here within the hour."

Lauren was scared and angry and worn out. She could barely breathe as one wave of pain after another rocked her. She tried to concentrate on the doctor's words. What had he said? Within the hour? How was that possible? Her due date wasn't for two weeks, and until she figured out about her parents' lie, she'd felt fine. Now she was breathless, the pain radiating up through her chest and around to her back. She couldn't begin to sort through her emotions. Shane was completely out of touch, and she would be a mother in an hour. All that, and the fact that her parents weren't on her side.

Her mother touched her elbow. "I'll stay here, honey. Your father's on his way."

Lauren moaned. She wanted to tell her mother to leave. If she really cared she'd help her find a way to reach Shane. But the next contraction was already on her, and she couldn't talk. A memory flashed through her mind. She and her mother at a baby shower for a neighbor. Lauren had been maybe thirteen years old.

"What if I don't know how to have a baby, I mean when it's my turn?" She'd turned to her mother, genuinely anxious about the idea.

Her mother had squeezed her hand. "I'll be there for you, Lauren. I'll tell you what to expect, and I'll help you through it. You'll be just fine."

That's how their relationship was before she got pregnant. Now, here she was, going through the very thing that had frightened her. Yes, her mother was with her, but not really. Their relationship was strained and tense, as if the woman beside her wasn't her mom at all, but someone who only looked like her.

"Are you okay?" Her mother pulled a chair up next to her. She crossed her legs and leaned closer, concern written in the lines of her forehead. "Do you need anything?"

"Yes." Lauren was between contractions. She ran her tongue over her lip and locked eyes with her mother. "Shane."

Her mother didn't ask again.

The doctor's prediction proved to be right on. Exactly fifty minutes after arriving at the hospital, with only a mild amount of medication for the pain, Lauren gave birth to a six-pound, three-ounce baby girl. The moment the doctor held the baby up, tears flooded Lauren's eyes. This was her *daughter,* her child. A part of her and of Shane. She covered her mouth and shook her head, amazed. "She's . . . she's perfect."

The doctor smiled, and in the next chair, her mother was crying too. For some reason Lauren was bothered by her mother's tears. Was she crying because this wasn't how things were supposed to go, or because she was too young to be a grandmother? It was an instant that would never come again — the birth of her first child. It was a time when her mother's emotion should've been joy, not pain.

For Lauren, of course, the tears were joyous, but they were also filled with sorrow. This was her daughter, a fair-skinned beauty who would forever be a part of her, a part of her life. But Shane should've been here, beside her, seeing their daughter for the first time. How long would it be before he knew about her, before his parents would let him fly back to Chicago to see their little girl?

That night, her parents took turns holding the baby and spouting the types of things first-time grandparents were supposed to say. "She has Lauren's chin . . . she's perfect." Or, "Look at those blue eyes!" Her mother was no longer crying. Instead, by the time they were ready to head home, her parents were upbeat, promising to return in the morning.

No one said a word about adoption.

When they left, Lauren held her daughter close against her chest. As terrible as it was that her parents had been trying to keep her from Shane, at least they weren't going to force her to give her daughter up. She studied her little girl's face. "Hi, sweetie. Mommy's here."

The baby squirmed a little, her eyes never veering from Lauren's. "You need me, don't you, little one?"

The precious child in her arms trusted her with her entire being. Lauren had no idea what she was doing, no clue where they would go or how they would find Shane again. But they would find him. They would go to him as soon as they could. She owed Shane that much.

By the end of that first night, she'd given the baby a name: Emily.

Now she would press her parents to do everything in their power to help her find Shane. Then they could figure something out so that they could be a family sooner than later. Little Emily needed her daddy too. In the glow and marvel of those early hours of being a mother, Lauren would've walked barefoot to California with Emily in her arms if it meant finding Shane. If her parents weren't going to help, she would find him on her own. She stared at her ring and brought it to her face, brushing it against her cheek.

Whatever it took for the three of them to be together. The way they should've been now.

The way they would be forever.

Seven

Lauren was determined: she was going to find Shane.

Every day that passed, her resolve grew stronger. She would find him, and she would do it soon. The baby was four weeks old by the time she felt strong enough to take the subject to her parents. It was after eight o'clock on a Monday night the first week of August. Lauren had rocked Emily to sleep and tucked her into her crib. Now she padded down the carpeted hallway toward her parents' den. They often spent time there after dinner. The room had a full-size patio door that led to a covered porch. It was one of the nicest spots in the house.

She was almost to the door when she heard her father's voice. He sounded stern, frustrated. Lauren stopped and listened.

"I don't *want* his contact information, don't you see that, Angela?" He uttered a harsh chuckle. "In fact, this is just how I want it. Our daughter doesn't need any ties to that family, that woman."

"It's both of them." Her mother's voice was tired, the way she often sounded since the move. "Sheila doesn't want her son dragged down by Lauren, but Samuel's right there with her. Believe me, the idea of tearing these kids apart comes from both of them."

"Okay, fine. Exactly." His tone was louder than before. "So why should I take calls from the kid? So he called the bank, so what?"

"Bill." Her mother's voice was slower, more calm. "Listen to yourself. This is Shane we're talking about, honey. He was practically part of the family for all those years, remember?" She sighed loud enough that Lauren could hear it in the hallway. "I mean the kid calls the bank looking for you, looking for some way to reach Lauren, and you have your secretary tell him he's got the wrong bank? Is that fair?"

Lauren's knees felt week. She felt the room begin to spin, and she braced herself against the wall. Shane had called the bank, her father's new bank? And he'd been told he had the wrong place? So what would he think next? Did he even know what Chicago suburb they'd settled in or what neighborhood? She squeezed her eyes shut and forced herself to listen.

"Of course it's fair, Angela. The things Sheila and Samuel said about our daughter, the way they treated her . . . Lauren's my child, Angela. I don't want her around people who don't like her. If she's away from Shane, she'll be away from his parents."

Her mother was quiet for a moment, and Lauren wondered if she was crying. Finally she said, "How did it all turn so bad? They were our friends. Our best friends."

"I've learned something." Her father sounded matter-of-fact. "Playing cards together, vacationing together, doesn't always mean you know people." His voice grew wistful. "I thought I knew Sheila and Sam. But you watched how they handled this. The only thing that mattered was Shane. They would've burned down our house if it meant protecting their boy from his responsibility."

There was silence for a moment. Lauren's entire body shook and she felt sick to her stomach. This was the sign she'd been looking for, the proof that her parents really and truly had conspired against her and Shane. Now she would leave this house, walk out of their lives without looking back, and one day, when she and Shane were settled, she would consider being a part of this family again. But not until then. She was about to burst into the room, but she waited in case there was more.

There was.

After another few seconds, her mother said, "So what did he say? I mean, did he leave a message?"

"He told my secretary his name was Shane Galanter, and he was looking for Bill Anderson." A long sigh came from her father. "I'd already told her that if anyone named Galanter called, she was to say they had the wrong bank. No one there by my name."

Her mother groaned. "The kids miss each other, Bill. What if we're wrong?"

"We're protecting Lauren." Her father was curt, adamant. "It's for her own good, because I love her. Besides, she'll never find out."

"Yes, I will." Lauren stepped into the room, still holding onto the door frame to keep her balance. Her head pounded, and she could barely feel her feet. She stared from her mother to her father, her eyes wide, unblinking. "I heard it all, Daddy. Shane called you at work and you had

130

some . . . some woman tell him he had the wrong bank." She wanted to scream at him, shout at both of them that they couldn't do this. But it was already done. All that was left inside her was an eerie sort of iciness, an anxiety that defied expression.

"Lauren —" Her father was on his feet. His mouth hung open for a few seconds. But he rebounded quickly. "The two of you need time away from each other. The Galanters and we agreed. It's important, so the two of you can figure out what you want from here."

"We already *know* what we want." She was imploding, her voice fading with every few words. "You and Mom don't have any idea what I want." She pressed her hand to her chest. "What Shane and I want. We need to be together."

"Okay." Her father looked across the room.

As if on cue, her mother turned to Lauren. "We'll help you find him, honey. It won't be hard. Your father has ways." She paused. "It's like your dad said. We all felt it would be best if we gave the two of you some time apart. If you could've heard the things Mrs. Galanter said about you, honey . . ."

"I don't care about her. I care about Shane." Her voice was getting louder, and she brought it back down again. "All you've done is tear us apart."

"We were trying to help you."

"The phone connection thing, the made-up forwarding information, and now this — Shane calls the bank and gets a lie." She laughed, but it came out low and sad. "Thanks for the help, Mom." She looked at her father. "You too, Dad." She turned to walk out, but her mother was on her feet, crossing the room and coming toward her.

"Where are you going?"

Lauren was done sharing information with her parents. "My room." She looked at her mother over her shoulder. "I have nothing left to say."

Her parents must've felt the same way, because they didn't speak another word as she walked away. Not until she was in the hallway did she hear her mother's voice. "I'm sorry, Lauren. We . . . we never meant to hurt you."

She stopped and closed her eyes for a few seconds, holding back the sudden rush of tears that stung at her eyes. "I know." She blinked and looked back at them one last time. "I know."

As she made her way through the house and up the stairs to her room, she was certain her mother was telling the truth. In some strange, twisted way the things she and her father had done to keep her and Shane apart really were acted out with the thought that it would be best for her.

But some part of their consciences must've known it was wrong. She sat on the edge of her bed and looked across the room at Emily's crib. The baby stirred and gave a small sneeze.

Lauren stood and went to her. "Hey, little one, you okay? Mommy's here." She leaned out and touched her forehead. It was warm, but that might've been from the blankets or the sticky summer night. Lauren frowned and adjusted the layers so the baby had less over her body.

The most amazing thing about being a new mother was the intensity of the love she felt for her daughter. She would've done anything for little Emily, and come tomorrow she would prove it. She soothed her hand over Emily's forehead again. She wasn't that warm, after all. "Everything's going to be okay."

She should've been furious with her parents, devastated by their betrayal, fighting mad about everything that had happened to Shane and her. Instead, as she stared at her daughter, she felt a surging sense of freedom. She and Emily would be fine on their own.

She leaned over the crib and kissed her daughter on the cheek. Then she went to the top drawer in her nightstand and pulled out the envelope just inside. It held five thousand dollars, money she'd taken from her personal account that afternoon. Since her money was still at the bank in the city, she'd found a local branch first. Her mother thought she was running to the grocery store with Emily, but she stopped at the bank on her way home. It was her money, gifts she'd gotten over the years, money she'd earned babysitting. Some of it was from her parents, but only when it was given as a birthday or Christmas present or for getting A's on her report card.

Now it felt like a million dollars in her hands. With that kind of cash she could take Emily to Los Angeles, find someplace to live, and start searching for Shane. She would try the local banks, places where his father might work. Then once school started again, she would try every high school in Los Angeles if she had to. Her parents would get over her decision. She'd done the unforgivable. By getting pregnant she and Shane had cast a shadow of shame on their families too long and dark and wide to ever step out of. The only way she'd live in the light of happiness and freedom again was by finding Shane.

As she fell asleep, she heard Emily sneeze twice more. Nothing to worry about. Just a small case of the sniffles, probably something all little babies dealt with in the first few months of life. And if she came down with a real full-blown cold, they could stop at any supermarket along the way to California and find something to help her.

The next morning Lauren's father left early, without saying good-bye. Her mother checked in and reported that she was spending the day with the interior decorator.

"We're accessorizing today. Looking at a few of the local boutiques." Her mother gave her a tentative smile. "You're not still upset about your father's situation at the bank, are you?" She paused, the corners of her lips locked in an upward lift. "You and Shane will connect one of these days real soon. We'll help you."

"How, Mom?" She had Emily cradled in her arms. Her suitcases were packed and in the closet. "I don't have his phone number, and he doesn't have mine." She narrowed her eyes. "Where exactly does he live? Do you know that?"

Her mother's shoulders lowered a little. "Los Angeles. That's all they told me."

"Okay, what about his dad's business? He had investments in LA, so what are they? *Where* are they?"

"Gas stations, I think. And a small airport, maybe." She bit her lip. "At least I think so."

"You see?" She made a sound that was part laugh, part moan. "Why say we'll connect soon? Shane found Daddy's bank, which is pretty good with nothing to go on, don't you think?"

Her eyes fell to the floor, but she nodded. "Yes. Yes, it was."

"So he found it, and then someone tells him it's not the right bank. No one there by the name of Bill Anderson." She kept her voice calm so it wouldn't wake Emily. "What makes you think I'll be able to find Shane now?"

A pair of robins sang from a tree outside her window. Her mother looked up and gave the slightest shrug. "I've been asking myself the same thing all night." She hugged her arms tight around her waist.

"Honestly, Lauren, I don't know. I have to believe he'll find you, but I don't know how."

"Maybe if our phone number was listed." She hated the sarcasm in her voice. It made her feel ugly and jaded, like a world of distance lay between her and her mom.

"Lauren —" her mother sighed — "you know we can't list our number, not with your dad's involvement at the bank. We've never been listed, and neither have the Galanters."

It was all she needed to hear. She had to go to Shane. Whether he was in California or on the moon, she had to find him. She held Emily closer. "I love you, Mother, and I always will." Her voice cracked. "But I can't believe what you and Daddy have done to me."

Her mom came to her then and placed her arms around Lauren and Emily, holding them tight. When she drew back, she looked deep into her eyes, "I love you too, honey. I'm sorry. Really."

She turned and walked away. When Lauren heard the front door close behind her, she stood and set Emily down in her crib. With her heart in her throat, she added a few more items to each suitcase.

All of Emily's clothes, and more than enough for herself.

As she left the room, a suitcase in each hand, she stopped and looked back. She scanned the room, taking in her box of short stories and photo albums, her year-books and souvenirs from a childhood that ended far too quickly. She could always come back for those things once she found Shane.

The only memento she packed was a framed photograph of her and Shane, something she would set next to her bed so that wherever the next place was she called home, she would be driven every day to find him.

Only then would she send for the rest of her things.

She packed the car with the suitcases, then came back for Emily. She left a note in Emily's crib that said simply, "Gone to meet Shane. I'll call when I find him. Love, Lauren."

By four that afternoon they were three hundred miles out of Wheaton. Everything ahead of her looked bright and promising. The sky was clear, the map on the seat beside her had the route marked out perfectly. A woman at the local auto club had helped her with the best possible freeways and stopping points. She would get to California in six days and after that she'd find Shane and they could be together. Only one thing caused her even an inkling of doubt.

In the backseat, Emily was still sneezing.

Eight

Something tragic had happened.

By six o'clock that night, Angela Anderson was sure of it. She called Bill at the bank and struggled to keep the panic from her voice. "Have you seen Lauren?"

"Lauren?" His tone told her he was busy. "Of course not. She's home with the baby. You know that."

"She's not here, Bill. I think she's gone."

"If she's not there, then of course she's gone." His impatience grated on her. "Honey, I'm in a meeting. She's probably at the store, and she'll be back in a few minutes."

"What if . . . what if she's gone?"

"Gone where?"

"Gone *gone*. I think she left, maybe to find Shane." Angela's voice was controlled, but only barely. "She didn't leave a note, not one that I could find. I looked in her room, everywhere."

He uttered an exaggerated sigh. "She's out shopping."

"I thought of that, but Bill, I've been home for an hour. She wouldn't be gone this long." She hesitated. "I have a bad feeling."

"All right, well listen." There was kindness in his voice now. "Why don't you check her room again and see what you can find. This is Lauren we're talking about, honey. She wouldn't do anything crazy."

A sense of peace washed over her. Bill was right. Lauren was grounded. Before getting pregnant, she'd been a standout student, a kid who always told them where she was; one who preferred staying home and playing Scrabble and Hearts with her parents and Shane rather than hitting a high school party.

Of course she wouldn't just take Emily and leave.

Still, just to be sure, she needed to check her room one more time. She hurried up the stairs, a sick feeling in her heart. She pulled Lauren's door open and scanned the bed. This time she saw something she hadn't before. Lauren's photo of herself and Shane, which always sat on her bedside table, was gone. Angela looked at the crib again. The bedding was gone too. The first time she'd checked Lauren's room she'd assumed the baby's sheets and blankets were being washed. Her heart beat hard in her throat. What if the bedding was missing for another reason? She moved in closer, her steps slow and fearful.

On the mattress lay a piece of paper, something else she hadn't seen her first time up.

Angela's heart screamed at her to leave the room, run back downstairs and convince herself that Lauren and Emily were only at the store, that they hadn't gone farther away than that. But the note demanded her attention. She forced her feet to take her to the edge of the crib, and then without drawing another breath she lifted the note and read it.

Gone to meet Shane. I'll call when I find him. Love, Lauren.

A burning sensation flooded her veins, a mix of adrenaline and fear all wrapped up in a shock that wouldn't let her believe her own eyes. "No . . ." Even as she spoke, she read the words again, then one more time. "No, Lauren. *No!*" Her hand shook so hard she could barely make out the words.

What was Lauren thinking? She and Emily wouldn't last on a trip across the

142

country by themselves. Lauren had never driven more than an hour or two at any one time. She was only seventeen! How would she know which freeways to take or how to make it from Chicago to Los Angeles?

Angela wasn't sure whom to call first. The note clutched in her hand, she raced down the stairs. Bill. He had to know before anyone else. She had to dial his number three times before getting it right. She had him on the line in less than a minute.

"So —" Angela heard the nervous tension in his voice — "is she home?"

Angela dropped to the nearest chair and grabbed a handful of her hair. *Think! Say something.* She squeezed the receiver and found her voice. "She's gone. She and Emily. I found a note."

"A note?" She had his attention now. She heard a door shut in the background. "What did it say?"

"She's gone to California to find Shane. She'll call when she gets hold of him."

He made a disbelieving sound. "That's ridiculous, Angela. She's just a child. She doesn't have any idea how to drive across the country."

"Or how to care for little Emily."

"I'll be right home. You call the police,

143

and tell them what happened." He was in a hurry now, anxious to fix the problem. "And pray, Angela. I can't have anything happen to her." A catch sounded in his voice. "I can't have it."

She told him she'd do her best, then she hung up and called the local police office. "Our daughter ran away. We need your help."

"Okay, hold on." He connected her to another officer.

"I'm Officer Rayson. Your daughter ran away?"

"Yes." Angela put her hand against her chest. Her heart was racing so fast she could barely feel the beat. "Just today."

"Okay, let's start with her age." His voice held compassion, but still she had the sense this was a routine call for him.

"She's seventeen. She . . . she just had a baby."

The officer hesitated. "A baby? Is the baby with her?"

"Yes. She's four weeks old. My daughter packed a few suitcases, best I can tell, and the two of them set off today. Probably this morning."

"Ma'am, you're asking me to make a report on a seventeen-year-old runaway with a newborn baby?"

144

"Yes." Angela clenched her fists. The man wasn't going to help her. She forced her next words. "Is . . . is that a problem?"

"Sort of." The sound of rustling papers came across the phone line. "Ma'am, she's almost an adult, and since she has a four-week-old baby, we can assume she left on her own without any foul play, is that right?"

"Definitely. She left a note." Angela gripped the counter in front of her and stared at the piece of paper. "She said she was going to California to find the baby's father."

"Okay, then." Resignation rang in his tone. "If she doesn't call in a few weeks, let us know. Maybe we can get someone in California on the case."

What?" It was a shriek. "Sir, we need your help! She's only seventeen. She hasn't had a driver's license for a full year yet!"

"I'm afraid we look at things a little differently." He waited a beat. "She may not be an adult, but because of the baby we see her as one. At that age, they have a pretty good idea of what they want. It's a family issue."

"What about —" She gave a series of light taps to her forehead. *Think, Angela. Come on.* "What about a missing person's report. Couldn't I file one of those even if she's almost an adult?"

"You can file one on a person of any age, ma'am. But they need to be missing for twenty-four hours." He sounded doubtful. "I have to be honest with you, though. We can't put manpower behind every missing person's report."

She couldn't make sense of what was happening. The room felt like it was shaking beneath her feet, and all the colors seemed to melt together. The police couldn't help her? What good was a police force, then? Her daughter was gone, headed one of a dozen different ways toward California. Los Angeles. But LA was a huge city, gigantic. How would Lauren find Shane?

More important, how would she and Bill find their daughter?

Bill came home while she was still sitting there, still poring through the yellow pages looking for someone who could help. She contacted three private investigators, but all of them said it was too soon to do anything. Lauren would be driving for the next week. If she wanted to call, she would. If not, there wasn't much any of them could do. She would need to arrive in Los Angeles and set up residency before they

146

could be of much help.

Bill walked in, set his things on the kitchen counter, and put his hand on her shoulder. "Are the police on their way?"

She looked at him, and for just a moment hatred gripped her. He had done this to them. He and the Galanters. She'd gone along with it because they were convincing. They made her believe the kids really would be better off apart. But hadn't she doubted the decision all along? Watching the two of them say good-bye that night in the city, hadn't she known this could happen?

She blinked, letting the rage go. She could hate him later. Right now they had to find Lauren and Emily. "The police aren't going to help." She explained the situation. "I've tried a few private investigators, but they all say it's too soon."

He hesitated, but only for a handful of seconds. "Then we have no choice." He turned and went to the kitchen cupboard. It was his routine when he came home from work, and now he went ahead with it as if this were nothing more serious than a traffic ticket. He took a glass and filled it with ice water. "We'll have to wait till she gets there." He sipped the water. "I'm sure she'll call."

147

"Bill!" She stood, slamming the chair back in against the counter. "Do you *hear* yourself? Your daughter has run away. She's taken her newborn daughter, our grandchild, and you —" she gestured at him — "calmly pour a glass of water and tell me she'll call?" She was trembling, her voice loud and shrill. "I can't believe who you've become. Sometimes I think I hate you for what you've done to her."

The water was still in his hand, but he set it down. His eyes found hers and a layer of remorse colored his expression. "Angela, calm down." He went to her, but as he tried to touch her shoulder, she jerked away.

"Don't *touch* me." She pushed her finger at his chest. "I didn't want this, Bill. We pushed her out, don't you see that?" Tears flooded her eyes and her throat felt scratchy. "All that mattered to any of you, to any of us, was how things looked. The kids needed to be apart, but why? So we could pretend this never happened, so we could pretend Lauren didn't get pregnant and everything was perfectly normal, right?"

"Lower your voice, please." Though his tone was kind, Angela knew he still didn't understand what she was feeling. "Everything will work out. You'll see."

"No, it won't. We let this happen, and now . . . now we might never see her again."

She spun away from him and hurried around the corner to their bedroom. How had life become so crazy? And where were Lauren and Emily? She wasn't sure she could survive without them. Suddenly she realized her daughter held a piece of her heart, the part that understood life and the purpose and meaning of getting up in the morning. And now that Lauren was gone, that part of Angela was dead.

The part capable of loving.

Even loving the man she had married.

Emily was sick. There was no denying that now. They'd been on the road for two full days, and the baby was burning up. Lauren drove aimlessly through the streets of Oklahoma City trying to decide what to do. She'd already stopped at a drugstore and bought pain reliever, something to lower Emily's fever. That was half an hour ago, and it seemed to be working, but her baby still sounded terrible. She was sneezing and coughing and now she was wheezing every time she breathed in.

A rush of fear and desperation worked

its way through Lauren's veins. Where should she take Emily? She had money, enough to see a doctor, but then what? Would they put the baby in the hospital? Would they find out that Lauren was a seventeen-year-old runaway? And what then? Maybe she would lose her daughter forever.

In the backseat, Emily started to cry, and the sound of it made her wheezing worse.

"Okay, honey, it's okay. Mommy's here."

The words hung in the small, stuffy car and mocked her. Mommy was here? So what? She didn't have a clue how to be a mother, otherwise her baby wouldn't be sick. She was about to get back on the freeway, head for the next town, when she spotted a sign that read, Hospital.

She sped up and pulled into the parking lot. The least she could do was get someone to look at Emily. That shouldn't raise too many flags. She parked and lifted the car seat from the back. Once inside the emergency area, she stood there, shaking, mouth dry. Other people were waiting in the lobby, and most of them turned and looked at her. Could they tell she was on the run? Was it obvious? And what about the people who worked there? What would she say? How would she explain her situation, other than by telling the truth?

A blonde woman behind the counter smiled at her. "Can I help you?"

"Yes." She looked at Emily and back at the woman. "My baby's sick."

The woman handed Lauren a clipboard and a pen. "Fill out the information sheet, and we'll get your baby seen as soon as we have an empty room."

"Okay."

The form asked a dozen questions, some of which she couldn't answer. Address, for instance. And phone number. She also left blank the part about emergency contact information and next of kin. But she filled in Emily's birth date and the fact that they didn't have insurance. Then she signed the form and turned it in. They were called back five minutes later. The woman from the front office led her to a room. "Wait here. Dr. West will be in to see you in just a moment."

"Thank you." Lauren sat on a chair in the corner and slid Emily's car seat close to her feet. She felt her daughter's forehead and a shudder passed through her. The baby was hotter than before. There was a knock at the door.

"Yes?" Lauren gulped. What if they called the police or sent her back home?

What if they could tell she was running?

The door opened and a pretty black woman walked in. "I'm Dr. West." She held her hand out to Lauren. "Let's take a look at your baby. Why don't you get her undressed, everything except her diaper."

Lauren lifted Emily from her car seat and laid her on the cold examination table. She started to cry, and as Lauren undressed her, she noticed that her baby's face was red. "I think she has a cold."

When Emily's hot body had nothing on but her diaper, the doctor held a stethoscope to her chest. She moved it three times before looking up, her face knit in concern. "Her lungs sound pretty full. Do you live nearby?"

"Is it a cold?"

"I'm not sure." The woman gave her a slight frown. "Where did you say you lived? We might have to admit her. I'd like to see her get an X-ray."

Panic coursed through Lauren. She put her hand on Emily's head and patted her hair. "I'm not from around here. I'm . . . I'm moving to California." She looked at her daughter. "The two of us are moving there."

The doctor waited until Lauren looked back up at her. Then she made a thoughtful sort of sound. "I tell you what. Wait here for a minute." She gave a last quick look at Emily and then she left the room.

Lauren couldn't draw a deep breath. Where was the woman going? Was she calling the police or maybe a social services department? Maybe she was doing a check on her name, and by now her parents would've called and reported her missing. That would bring the police for sure. Emily was crying, squirming on the table. Lauren studied her, the look in her eyes. She didn't look that sick. And with the pain reliever and maybe a cough syrup, they should be okay until she got help. There was only one place where she could turn now, and it would feel like utter defeat. But her medical insurance, her support system, everything was in Chicago. She had no choice but to go back.

Then, when Emily was well, they could head for California once more.

"It's all right, sweetie." She cooed at Emily as she slipped the baby's tiny arms into her little sleeper. After four weeks it no longer felt awkward dressing her, but here she felt anxious, like she was doing everything wrong. When her baby was dressed, Lauren picked her up and cradled

153

her close, bouncing her slightly so that she would settle down.

After a minute Emily was quieter, her crying only in small bursts. Lauren checked the clock on the wall. No wonder her baby was upset. It had been four hours since she'd eaten; she was probably starving. The idea brought a memory back to her. She'd been maybe eleven years old, home with the flu, but she came downstairs and found her mother in the kitchen.

"I'm hungry, Mama. Can I eat something, please?"

"That's a great sign." Her mother pulled her close and stroked the back of her head. "Little girls get their appetite back when they're feeling better."

Her mother's words faded from her mind. Hunger meant that children weren't that sick, right? That was what her mother had told her that day. She sat down and adjusted her shirt so she could nurse her daughter. Sure enough. Emily was starving. She made precious little sounds as she ate.

Maybe that's all this was. A little cold, a fever, and a lot of hunger. She'd driven a long way that day. They probably should've stopped sooner.

The doctor walked in then. She was

holding the form Lauren had filled out. "Lauren." Her voice was tender. "I see you've listed no emergency contact and no next of kin."

"No." She looked at Emily. The baby was much happier now, content to be eating. Her eyes lifted to the doctor's. "No, we don't have family at this point. We're making a new life for ourselves out in California."

"Okay." She leaned against the examining table and took a slow breath. "But you're a minor, is that right?"

Lauren searched her mind for the right answer. She hadn't written her age on the form, so how did the doctor know? Had the woman contacted the police or found out that she'd been reported missing? Lauren gulped and just as she was about to shake her head and deny anything of the sort, she felt herself nodding. "Yes. I'm . . . seventeen. I'll be eighteen before Christmas."

"You know what I think?"

"What?" Lauren held Emily a little closer.

"I think you need help, Lauren. We have social workers here in Oklahoma City who can help you if we admit Emily. They can find somewhere for you to stay while your

155

daughter's being treated."

Lauren shook her head and looked at her daughter. "Actually, I think she's doing much better. She's eating." She lifted her eyes to the doctor again. "I think maybe she was just hungry."

"I'm worried she could have pneumonia." The doctor winced. "I can't be sure without an X-ray, but I'm concerned."

"What happens if a social worker helps me? I mean, what happens next?" She hated the thought. It meant that there was a possibility someone would take Emily from her. That's what agencies did to mothers like her, right? Mothers too young to know how to care for a baby?

"We'd have to cross those bridges when we reached them." The doctor frowned again, but Lauren didn't sense any anger from her. Just a compassion she hadn't felt from either of her parents. "Everyone would do their best to keep you and Emily together. I'm sure about that. I think we'd want to run a missing persons check. Just to see if you've been reported missing."

A missing persons check? Lauren felt herself closing down. That wasn't going to happen. The police would come and they'd make sure Emily was admitted to the hospital, then they'd take Lauren to the station and call her parents. Social workers would get involved, and when Emily was better they wouldn't consider giving her back to a seventeen-year-old runaway. Then Lauren would be shipped back to her parents. She might never see her daughter again.

She had to buy time. "Okay." Lauren licked her lips. "Well, first I need to get some things from the car. Then we can talk about it, okay?"

"All right." The doctor straightened and felt Emily's head. "She doesn't feel as warm as before."

She wasn't as warm! That was a good sign — a sign that Lauren could take Emily and race back home and still get her the care she needed without risking the possibility that social services or the police would get involved. Lauren slipped her daughter back into her car seat and thanked the doctor. "I'll be right back."

Dr. West turned a different direction as they left the examination room. Lauren wanted to race out the door. She only had a few minutes to get away without being noticed. But she wouldn't leave without paying. She took two twenty-dollar bills from her purse and set them on the counter since no one was behind the desk at that moment. Without looking back, she hurried out the door.

She drove as fast as she could and was on the freeway before she looked over her shoulder. When she did, Emily was sleeping. Then, for the first time since she'd left home, Lauren thought about God. In the days after she got pregnant, Shane had talked all the time about faith and the Lord and His plans for them. Lauren never quite understood how God could want anything to do with them.

Still, she'd told Him she was sorry for messing up, sorry for sleeping with Shane when this whole mess could've been avoided if they'd only done things the right way. She was forgiven, at least that's what the youth group leaders had told her. It was what Shane said too. But still she'd felt like a failure, a disappointment. If God was her heavenly Father, then she would be the last one He'd want to hear from.

But there, with Emily sick and a thousand miles between her and the help she needed, Lauren couldn't do anything but cry out for help.

"Lord, I'm here again," she whispered the words out loud. "Help me, please! I'll drive fast, I won't stop for food, just gas.

But please get me home so Emily can get help. Don't let her die, God." Suddenly she realized there were tears on her cheeks. What was she doing, turning around from Oklahoma City and heading back to Chicago? She should never have left home in the first place. She should've let her mother take care of Emily. That way she could've gone after Shane on her own, without risking any harm to her daughter.

"God, I'm the worst mother of all. But you're our Father. For both of us. Please get us home safely, and please, please let Emily be okay."

She wanted an answer, a loud shout maybe from the dashboard speakers, something that would tell her everything was going to be all right. Instead, she felt only a sense of urgency. As if maybe God Himself was telling her that Emily was sicker than any of them knew. She pressed her foot on the gas pedal and picked up another ten miles per hour.

Then just as quickly she eased up. She couldn't get pulled over for speeding. That wouldn't do either of them any good. "God, help me!"

Daughter, my peace I give you . . . I am with you always.

The answer might not have come across

159

the stereo speakers, but it resonated in her heart. *I am with you always.* What a wonderful thought. Lauren could feel her heart begin to respond to this truth. She wasn't alone, driving into the dusk and facing fifteen hours of freeway time before she could get help for Emily. She was driving with God right next to her. God Himself.

She leaned back in the seat and relaxed her grip on the steering wheel. He would see her home safely, and He'd help Emily get better. It was all going to be okay. The peace that felt nothing short of divine stayed with her for the next twenty-four hours. It was on the last stretch that everything began falling apart again.

Emily cried all the time and nothing made her feel better. She was burning up and with every breath her little chest rose higher than before. Lauren pulled over at a rest stop and slid into the backseat. She leaned up and locked the doors. It was pitch dark, and there was a group of shady-looking people standing near the water fountain. The stop would have to be a short one. She unbuckled Emily from her seat and felt her fear double. Her daughter's body was still burning up. "Are you hungry, little one?"

Emily's wheezing was worse, but it

wasn't until she refused to eat that Lauren felt truly terrified.

Come on, God . . . I need you. Make her eat, please . . .

She held her daughter tight, tried to help her nurse, but nothing worked. Emily was too sick. Lauren gave her a small dose of cough syrup and another spoon of pain reliever. But still she cried for most of the last five hours of the drive. By the end of that time she sounded so sick, Lauren could barely focus on the road.

All along she'd been blaming herself for being a bad mother, for having no experience, for thinking she could take a newborn on a road trip across the country. But in those final hours, her anger shifted toward her parents. This wasn't her fault, it was theirs. They intentionally separated her from Shane. If he hadn't gone away, she would never have packed up a car and taken Emily on the road.

The whole situation was her parents' fault. Theirs and the Galanters. The people who were supposed to love her and Shane the most had almost destroyed them. Her very own parents had betrayed her by allowing the Galanters to leave without any forwarding information. The reason was obvious now. Shane's parents and hers never had any intention of staying in touch. They'd been willing to sacrifice their friendship for the sake of keeping up appearances.

Lauren's stomach hurt as the reality sank in.

Appearances. That's what it came down to. Shane could have his life without the responsibility of being a teenage father. And with Shane gone, then just maybe she would give up the baby and she too could carry on into her senior year without a care in the world. If things had gone according to her parents' plan, Emily would be safe in the arms of some adoptive family by now.

Lauren gritted her teeth and shifted her lower jaw from one side of her mouth to the other. Were they right? Should she have given little Emily up for adoption? Was that the answer in all of this? She shuddered at the thought of saying good-bye. It wasn't possible; she loved Emily with everything in her.

No, she would take her home, get the help she needed from her parents, and then she would leave them and never look back. Because they would never accept her for who she was, never accept Emily. Her life and the life of her daughter would always feel like second-best to her parents. And she couldn't have that attitude coloring Emily's life. No, they wouldn't stay. They would get help, get Emily better again, and then they would leave.

And this time they would never, ever come back.

Nine

Angela was sitting alone in the dark, her head in her hands, when a car pulled into the driveway. Her heart leaped into her throat and she raced for the door in time to see Lauren get out of the car.

"Mother! I need your help!"

Angela wasn't sure what to do first. The reality was just hitting her. There was Lauren standing in the driveway, when only a minute earlier it seemed they might never see her again. But her tone snapped Angela out of her shock. She stepped out onto the walkway, ran to her daughter, and embraced her. When Lauren remained stiff, unresponsive, Angela drew back and took hold of her daughter's forearms. That's when she saw it. Intense anger and fear, all mixed together, burned in her daughter's eyes.

"Lauren . . ." The fear was hers now. She brought her hand to her daughter's face. "What is it?"

"She's sick." Lauren jerked away. She opened the back door and unbuckled Emily from her car seat.

As Lauren lifted the baby, Angela grabbed a sharp breath. The baby was limp, her face red and blotchy. Angela took a step closer. "How long has she been like this?"

Lauren cradled Emily against her chest. "I don't know." Her face was pale and drawn. She looked as if she hadn't slept in days. "We need to get her to the hospital."

The hospital? Angela's head was spinning. It was just after eleven o'clock at night. "Let me go get your father. He's asleep already and he should —"

"No!" Lauren was wide-eyed. She looked crazed, like maybe she was having a nervous breakdown. "I don't want him coming with us." She held Emily out toward Angela. "Take her, tell me how sick she is."

Angela took the baby in her arms and immediately felt the heat. The child was burning up. Worse, her eyes were open but she was indeed unresponsive. "Is she half asleep?"

"No." Lauren was breathing fast, wiping her palms on her shorts and pacing a few steps in either direction. "She's been like this for a few hours. She won't eat."

Angela held her head near the baby's chest. She was having a terrible time trying to breathe. Angela felt the blood drain from her face. Emily wasn't only sick. She was deathly sick. "Okay —" she nodded toward Lauren's car — "let's get her back in her car seat. She needs a doctor. I'll drive."

They made the trip in silence, Lauren in the backseat with Emily. Angela wanted to ask where Lauren had gone and why she hadn't gotten help in one of the cities she'd passed through along the way. But it was too late for any of that. All that mattered now was Emily.

"Sweetie, it's okay," Lauren cooed at her daughter, but Angela could hear the tears in her voice, hear the way her hushed sobs broke her statements into short bursts of words. "Mommy's here, honey."

When they reached the emergency room entrance at the hospital, Angela directed Lauren to take Emily inside. She parked the car and when she ran in to join them a nurse was taking the baby from Lauren and rushing her through a set of double doors.

"Lauren . . ." Angela stopped, not sure what to do.

Lauren looked over her shoulder. "Follow us!"

They gathered in an examination room just inside the double doors. In seconds, a doctor joined them and began undressing the baby. It took him less than a minute to look up from her, his expression grim. "She has pneumonia. We need to start treatment right away. We'll put her on an IV antibiotic and give her immediate breathing treatments."

He rattled off a series of orders to a few attendants and nurses standing by. When everyone was in action — with one nurse putting an IV in Emily's arm, and another preparing a machine with a miniature face mask — the doctor motioned for the two of them to follow him.

In the hallway outside Emily's room, he directed them to a quiet alcove. Then he held his clipboard to his chest and looked first at Angela, then at Lauren. "I have to be honest with you." His expression was deeply troubled. "She should've come in much sooner. I'm afraid her chances aren't good."

Lauren began to fall, slowly at first and then her knees buckled beneath her. Angela hurried to catch her, but she was out cold.

"We need some help!" The doctor

snapped his finger and a pair of nurses jumped into action. "Smelling salts; let's hurry."

Angela was on her knees, her daughter's head in her lap. Everything was falling apart, and there was nothing she could do to stop it. Emily might not make it? Was that the next terrible thing that would happen? And then what? How would they ever have a restored relationship with Lauren after this? She wanted to pray, but she was out of practice. Besides, they hadn't exactly asked God about what to do when it came to Shane and Lauren. Why ask Him now? He had probably washed His hands of them a long time ago.

The nurses were at Lauren's side now, waving smelling salts beneath her nose. In a few seconds she came to, but she looked deathly white. Her eyes were glazed over, and Angela could only imagine all she'd been through. She must've turned back to Chicago when she realized Emily was so sick. She probably drove straight through, terrified that she wouldn't get back home in time.

Lauren was fully awake now. She sat up and rubbed her eyes. A frantic look came across her face and she stared at the doctor. "Where is she?"

"Your daughter's in the room across the hall, Miss Anderson. We're doing everything we can."

"What was that part you said? Before . . . before I fell?" Lauren didn't look even a little familiar. The fear in her eyes made her look like a crazy person. "Something about my little girl and her chances."

The doctor sighed and helped the nurses get Lauren back to her feet. Then he looked straight into Lauren's eyes. "She's getting everything she needs, but I'm not sure it'll be enough."

"Meaning what?" Lauren's words were fast and hard. "Tell me what that means."

The doctor looked to the nurses and then to Lauren. "Your daughter's very, very sick, Miss Anderson." He pursed his lips and gave a slight shake of his head. "She won't make it without a miracle."

"Lauren . . ." Angela moved to take hold of her daughter's arm, but she pulled away.

"Leave me alone." Her anger lasted only a moment. When she turned back toward the doctor there was no trace of it. "Can I sit in the room with her? I . . . I won't be in the way?"

"Yes." He nodded toward the door. "You can be with her the entire time."

Angela looked at the doctor. "Can I stay too?"

"No!" Lauren held out her hand in a stop-sign fashion. Her eyes were ablaze with anger. "I don't want you in there. This is —" She looked at the doctor. "Excuse us, please."

"Certainly." The doctor cast Angela a quick look as if to ask if Lauren was all right. Angela gave him a slight nod. Everything wasn't okay, of course, but the two of them could work through it. "I'll be coming in often to check on her and give you updates." He hesitated. "I'm sorry."

When he was gone, Lauren's eyes blazed. "I don't want you in the room with us." Her words were a hiss, and Angela took a step back. She'd never seen Lauren act like this, never.

"Honey, I think I should stay."

"Mother, listen to me." The confusion and craziness seemed to fade, and she looked more lucid than she had since she'd pulled in the driveway. She pointed at the door of Emily's room. "My baby's dying in there because you lied to me, you lied to me and you pushed me and Shane apart, and you left me no choice but to go after him." Her voice was a study in controlled fury. "So I'm going in there to sit with her,

170

and I don't want you anywhere near me. Or her. Understand?"

A shiver passed down Angela's spine. "I'm sorry, Lauren. I never meant for this to —"

Lauren wasn't listening. She opened the door, stepped inside the room, and shut it behind her. Only then did Angela turn and walk back to the waiting room. She would stay until Lauren was willing to talk to her again. As she sat there, she was too stunned to cry, too shocked to do anything but go over what had just happened. She'd wondered what the repercussions might be if they separated the kids, if it all didn't go the way they'd planned. She'd doubted Lauren and Shane would be okay, as the others asserted. Agonized over what would happen if they all were wrong.

Well, now Angela knew.

And the worst was yet to come.

Lauren didn't move from her chair for the next six hours. She slid it up against Emily's little bed and watched as one person or another came in to work on her. She watched them monitor Emily and place a plastic mask over her face to help her breathe, and she watched the medicine drip into her daughter's veins.

The whole time she begged God for one thing: that He might find it in His heart to let Emily live.

Through two o'clock and three in the morning, things still seemed horribly grim. The doctor checked on her and shook his head. "I'm not sure she'll make it, Miss Anderson. Babies this sick usually don't go home."

In between his visits, she looked at Emily, afraid to touch her. Once in a while she'd put her fingers against her daughter's forehead and run them down her tiny arm. "I'm sorry, Emily. Mommy's sorry."

Most of the night her eyes were dry. She was too scared to cry, too worried that she might lose a minute of praying and willing life back into her little girl.

Then, at four o'clock, the doctor came in with the best news of the night, the best news of the past two days. "Her white count is better. It looks like she's responding to the antibiotics."

"Really?" Lauren didn't usually say much when the doctor came in. She was too afraid of the answers. But this time she felt a surge of hope so great she couldn't keep quiet. "You mean she might pull out of it?"

"I can't say." He studied Emily, placing his stethoscope to her chest and listening.

When he straightened, he looked at Lauren. "I hear an improvement. I'm amazed, really. If things continue in this direction, she might get better quickly. Once babies make a turn for the better they can be eating in twelve hours." He paused and lowered his brow. "But don't get too excited, Miss Anderson. Your baby is still very sick."

When the doctor left, Lauren felt an absolute certainty. Emily was going to pull through! God had heard her cry and He'd reached down from heaven and given them a miracle. She thought about what the doctor said. Emily could be awake and wanting food in twelve hours. If that were true, she'd need to be rested enough to take care of her. Especially because she didn't want to spend any more time than necessary in Chicago.

She considered her options. What she really needed was sleep. She could take the car and go home, get eight hours of sleep, and then come back. If she stayed at the hospital it wouldn't help Emily, and if she didn't get sleep she'd be no use at all to her daughter. But first she needed to talk to her mother. Lauren wasn't any less angry, but she needed to tell her that Emily was doing better. She deserved to know at least that much.

Emily's breathing sounded better, much better. Lauren hesitated. She hated leaving, hated being apart from her daughter for even a few hours. But she had no choice, not if she was going to be well enough to care for Emily when she woke up. Lauren stood and leaned over her baby. "Keep fighting, Emily." She kissed her daughter's feathery soft cheek. "I love you, sweetheart. I'll be here in the morning."

With one last look at Emily, she left the room and went to the waiting area. Her mother was awake, sitting in a chair at the far end of the room. Their eyes met, and Lauren moved toward her, refusing further eye contact until the last moment.

"Emily's doing better. The doctor says he can't believe it." She sat down in a chair opposite her mother. "I want to be strong for her when she wakes up. I thought I'd go home and get some sleep."

Her mother nodded. "I'll stay here."

Lauren hadn't considered that. She figured her mother would go home, since she might need sleep too. "Are you sure?"

"Yes. I'm fine. I'll go in and sit with her while you're gone."

For a moment Lauren considered telling her mother she was sorry about the scene earlier. But things between them were still a twisted ball of knots. It would take months to unravel all the hurt and resentment. For now she stood and her mother did the same. And even though it went against everything she felt, Lauren hugged her.

It was a short hug, but it was a start.

She drove home, slipped in through the front door, and crawled up the stairs. She was asleep before her head hit the pillow. By the time she woke up, it was two in the afternoon, and the house was silent. She sat straight up and looked at the crib.

Where was Emily?

It took her a few minutes to remember that she'd come home not quite halfway to Los Angeles, and that Emily was sick. And then it all rushed back.

She jumped from the bed. She needed to know how Emily was more than she needed her next breath. She called information and got the number for the hospital, and a minute later she was talking to a nurse.

"Hi." Lauren swallowed. The fear from the night before was back. "My little girl is a patient there. I need to check on her."

"What's her name?" The woman seemed kind, not rushed the way nurses sometimes seemed.

"Emily Anderson."

"Okay, let me check. I'll be right back."

Please, God . . . please.

The seconds passed like hours, and finally the woman came back. "I'm sorry, you're the baby's mother?"

Lauren's heart tripped over itself. "Yes, I need to know . . . how is she?"

"Well . . . I don't know how to tell you this, but she's gone. Just a few hours ago. I'm sorry someone didn't call you and —"

The woman's words grew too dim to hear. Gone? Emily, her baby girl, was gone? Lauren dropped her head in her hand, and the phone slid down her cheek. She could hear the woman speaking, but it didn't matter, it didn't make a bit of difference. Her baby was gone. Just a few hours ago . . . a few hours ago.

God . . . God where were You?

She was the worst mother ever.

Her feet and hands and heart felt numb, and she eased off the bed to her knees. *I begged you, God. You let us down. My baby is dead and I wasn't even there to hold her or tell her it would be okay. You knew . . . You had to know it was going to happen and You didn't make me stay there . . .*

She gripped the edge of the bed and

strained for a single breath, but it wouldn't come. The room was spinning, tilting hard to one side. In the distance a tinny voice was saying, "If you'd like to make a call, please hang up and try again . . . If you'd like to make a call . . ."

God, why? Why didn't You let her live? She was everything I had, all that mattered. Her tears came then, delayed only by the shock racking her being. Waves of tears shook her, tearing at her soul. Emily was gone, and Shane never even had a chance to meet her. *Is that fair to him, Lord? He wanted to be a father and now he'll never even know her!* She squeezed her eyes shut and remembered a few months back, when she was pregnant and sitting beside Shane in his car. He'd put his hand on her belly and felt Emily kick. The wonder and awe on his face . . .

He would've made the most wonderful father, but now . . .

Now he would never have the chance.

Everyone had failed her. Her parents and Shane's parents. And now even God. "Will the punishment never end?" She whispered the words, but as she did the anger came back fast and furious and her voice rose. "Will it never end?" She pounded the bed and opened her eyes, staring out the window. "How could You let her die, God? Why did You take her from me? She never . . . never even got to live."

She sobbed out her anger, her grief, letting her forehead fall against the bed. "Emily . . . baby girl . . ." The fight left her, and all she could do was picture her precious daughter, the way she'd looked in the hospital bed. The doctor said she was doing better, right? So what went wrong? The tears came harder now, and Lauren wondered if they'd fill the room and drown her. "Emily . . . baby, Mommy's sorry." Her words were muffled, spoken into a bunched up section of blankets. "I should've stayed with you, sweetheart." She gasped for whatever air she could get. "Emily . . . I love you, baby. I'm sorry."

It took time, but finally her tears slowed. As they did she was left with an emptiness that knew no bounds, a hollow place that was chilling cold and pitch dark. She could still hear chatter coming from the phone, but she blocked it out. There was only one person she wanted now, one who could hold her and make sense of the nightmare that her life had become.

Shane Galanter.

She wanted him now more than ever before. Lauren stood, slowly and carefully, because the room was still spinning. After a minute she found her balance, drew a slow breath, and walked out of her room. No need to stop and look around, to think of the memories she was leaving behind. Memories of her little girl would live forever in her heart, a single bright light in a place that would be dark until she found Shane.

Emily was gone, and with her every hope for the life the two of them could've lived with Shane. But Shane was still out there. Somewhere. As she drove out of the suburbs toward the freeway, she passed the hospital and thought about going inside. She could at least hold her baby one more time. Certainly her body would still be there. Or maybe not. Maybe they'd already taken her to the morgue. Yes, that would be it. There was no way she could go into the hospital now.

She had a handful of photographs and a month full of memories of Emily Sue Anderson. She was too late even to see her daughter's lifeless body, and beyond that, to see her mother. Not when all of this — every bit of it — could've been prevented if only their parents hadn't separated them.

She and Shane should've been together,

at home with Emily in their arms. Gripped with emotion, Lauren pulled off the road and stared at the hospital. She wouldn't forget her last day with Emily. Watching her breathe, and believing with everything in her that God was going to give them a miracle.

Her lips pressed tight together.

But You didn't do that, did You? You summed up my abilities as a mother, and You chose to take Emily home with You. I'll never forgive You for that, God. Not ever.

She cradled her empty arms against her chest and imagined the feel of Emily against her, warm and alive and fully dependent on her. "I let you down, baby . . . Mommy's sorry." The tears in her heart became sobs, and Lauren let her head fall against the steering wheel. "Emily . . . if I could hold you one more time." But she couldn't, because everyone had worked against her and Shane. Even God. What good was it that Emily was in heaven? *Didn't You have enough babies up there? Did You have to take mine?* As angry and scared and empty as she felt, even that one truth — that Emily was in a better place — meant nothing to her.

Not when all she wanted was one more

180

chance to hold her daughter.

She blinked until she could see. Then she pulled the car onto the road and headed toward the first freeway onramp. She was finished with Chicago, with her parents, with their God . . . with every piece of her past. She would find Shane. They'd make a way to be together. Then later, when they were married and more stable, they could return to Chicago and talk to her parents. They could see about mending ties. Nothing would ever be the same again, but she could always go back home. Always pick up her things.

But she could never have her little Emily again.

Grief filled every breath as she pulled out of town and headed for her new life in Los Angeles. The drive would take six full days, and on the third day she sold her sports car to a dealer in Texas. She used that money to pay cash for another car, a sensible four-door sedan with low mileage.

Not only was the new car more economical, but her parents couldn't trace her license plate. They wouldn't expect her to have a new car, and by the time she registered it in California, she'd think of some way to keep her parents from knowing about it.

By her fifth day on the road, she began to worry about money. She had forty-five hundred dollars left, but it was going fast. Before she could look for Shane she had to have a plan, a place to live, a job.

She settled in a town called Northridge, and on her second day there she drove to the California State University, located in the center of the town. On a bulletin board she found three sets of girls looking for a roommate. One sounded more serious than the others, and the rent was only a couple hundred dollars a month. Perfect for her budget.

She made the call, and by that afternoon she had a place to stay and roommates who seemed nice enough. One of them asked about her age, but she brushed off the comment.

"I look young. Everyone always says so." She smiled, though it felt foreign on her lips. A smile hadn't touched her face since she left Chicago, since she drove away from the place where her daughter had died. But she wouldn't share any of that, not with strangers. Not with anyone except Shane.

One of them, a petite Chinese-American girl, raised a curious eyebrow. "Are you a student at Cal State Northridge?"

"Not yet." Lauren swung her purse over her shoulder. "I need to earn money this semester."

"What was your name again?" A tall, thin brunette leaned against the wall. Her eyes sparkled, and Lauren guessed that a lifetime ago if she'd met the girl, the two might've become friends.

"Lauren."

"Got a last name?"

The cool facade cracked down the middle, but just for a minute. She smoothed her hand over her button-down blouse and grinned. "Sorry. Lauren Gibbs."

"Lauren Gibbs?" The Chinese-American girl made a curious face. "I've seen that somewhere before."

Lauren shrugged. "It's a common name." She kept her breathing even, unwilling to give herself away. "What about you?"

Their names were Kathy, Song, and Debbie. They talked about the campus and classes, and then they all fell silent. Kathy, the girl who seemed most in charge, held out her hand. "Welcome. The first rent is due when you move your stuff in."

"Would now work?" Lauren took out her wallet and pulled out two hundred dollars.

They all laughed, and Lauren went back out to the car for her things. She ached inside. So this was her life now. Lies and making do and pretending she was someone she wasn't. The pain she carried buried deep within her. She blinked tears away.

So be it.

All that mattered was surviving long enough to find Shane.

Her room was small and she shared it with Song. It took thirty minutes to un-pack and get her area set up. She placed the photo of Shane and her on the windowsill. The pictures of Emily she would keep in the drawer. She'd buy a photo album, so she could look at them often.

The next day she found a job waiting ta-bles at Marie Callender's, a restaurant across the street from her apartment. On the application, she wrote Lauren Gibbs, and all her contact information came from the new life she'd started the day before.

By then, she had a plan. When she got her first paycheck, she'd get identification and a driver's license with her new name. It was possible. Especially since she didn't have a Social Security card yet. One of the girls at the restaurant had given her some information, a way to start the process. Once she had her new identity firmly in place, she'd register her car and get on with life.

There was a community college not far from Northridge. She would contact the school and take her GED. Then she'd enroll in classes on that campus for the first two years. After that she'd transfer to Cal State Northridge and earn a degree in journalism. Life would be the way it should have been. At least on the surface.

That afternoon Lauren went back to the apartment and found the single phone on a desk in the living room. She grabbed a pad of paper from the counter and a pen from the drawer. August was too soon for school to be in progress, but by now Shane would be enrolled somewhere. Office staff started earlier than teachers, didn't they? She tapped the pad of paper with her pen. A phone book sat not far away, and she reached for it. A section in the front had the names and numbers of all the local high schools. She started at the beginning

Canoga Park High School.

She picked up the phone and dialed the number.

"Canoga Park High School."

"Yes, hello." She did her best to sound old. After all she'd been through it wasn't a stretch. "I need to verify that our son's en-

185

rolled for the coming semester."

"Very well. Is he a new student?"

It was working! Lauren swallowed hard. "Yes. We just moved here from Chicago."

"Okay, let me get the list of incoming students." She hesitated. "What was the name?"

She closed her eyes and pictured him, his dark hair and damp eyes, the way he'd looked that last day when he told her good-bye. The woman was waiting. "Shane Galanter."

"Shane Galanter." The woman repeated his name slowly, and the rustling of papers sounded in the background. "Nope. He's not registered yet. Would you like me to start the paperwork?"

Lauren opened her eyes and wrote a tiny NO next to the name Canoga Park. "That's okay." She uttered a polite laugh. "I'll talk with my husband. We'll come in later this week. Thank you."

Next on the list was Taft High School.

By three o'clock she'd tried every school in the San Fernando Valley. Shane wasn't enrolled at any of them. But that was okay. She had a room and a job and a plan for the future. And she had a new identity. Lauren Anderson was no more. Her death date was the same as her daughter's. She

186

died the moment the nurse told her that Emily was gone. From that moment on, Lauren had no family, no daughter, no desire to do anything but move on and fulfill her single goal in life: to find Shane. She would look as often as she had a chance, every day, every hour.

Even if it took the rest of her life.

Ten

Shane couldn't think of anything but Lauren.

They'd been tricked, that much was obvious. The whole phone number thing didn't make sense unless it was intentional. At least on the part of Lauren's parents. He'd brought it up to his parents a handful of times, and they always seemed surprised. His mother looked confused the first time he told her about the recording on Lauren's old phone number. "We thought they were leaving a forwarding number. Angela told me they were leaving it on the recording."

"So why didn't they?" Shane was ready to get in his car and go back to Chicago. Except the car wasn't his, and his parents wouldn't let him take it farther than the mall. He fought his frustration as he looked at his mother, trying to figure out the situation. "What do you think happened?"

"Truthfully?" Pained sorrow filled his

mother's face. "I think maybe they wanted to be rid of us . . . rid of you, Shane."

"Why?" He was on his feet. "They know how much Lauren and I want to be together. I can't call her without a phone number." He thought for a minute. "Do they know ours?"

His mother frowned. "I don't see how they could. We're in a new development, and getting our phone service in took a while. You know that." She took hold of his hand. "It feels like they wanted to cut ties, son. I'm sorry."

Time wore on and he watched the calendar. When it came time for Lauren's due date, he waited until he had the house to himself, which happened every afternoon. His father was always at his new mortgage office, and his mother spent her afternoons there helping set it up. So every afternoon Shane worked through a list of hospitals within a hundred-mile radius around the city of Chicago.

"My girlfriend's having a baby," he told the receptionist at the first hospital on his list. "I need to know if you've admitted her."

"Sir, I'm afraid we can't give patient information out to anyone except next of kin."

He felt the frustration build. "You mean if I were her husband you'd tell me if she was there?"

"Exactly."

He didn't have to be told twice. He called the next hospital on his list. "My wife's having a baby. I need to know if you've admitted her."

"Her name?"

He felt a surge of hope. "Lauren Anderson."

The sound of typing filled the phone line. "No, sir. No one here by that name."

Then he'd go to the next hospital on the list. When he was finished, he'd hide the list where his parents wouldn't find it. Not that they'd stop him from trying to find her. But they weren't happy about the pregnancy, and he had the sense it would be better to keep his phone calling to himself.

Each day, after his parents were gone, he'd pull the list from his hiding spot under his bed and start again at the beginning. Lauren's due date was mid-July, and he made the phone calls until the end of the month. Then he began to panic. What if something had happened to the baby, or what if Lauren left the area or decided to give the baby up?

There were nights he couldn't sleep because his mind wouldn't stop thinking of ways to find her. She was in the Chicago suburbs somewhere. He tried calling directory assistance, but none of the Bill Andersons listed outside the city were the right one. That's when he hit on the idea of calling the banks. There were dozens in the suburbs around Chicago, but he had plenty of time.

He made another list and started at the beginning.

"Hi, a friend of mine recently bought a bank in your area. I'm trying to find him. Could you tell me if Bill Anderson is the new owner there?"

"Bill Anderson?"

"Yes. It was only a few months ago."

"No, we've had the same owner for ten years."

The answers were mostly the same. Only a few times did people give him a little bit of possibility. Once he called a bank outside Wheaton and started the conversation the same way:

"A friend of mine bought a bank in your area. Could you tell me if Bill Anderson bought your bank recently?"

"Yes. Could I get your name please?"

Yes? Shane was so excited he stood up

and paced across the empty kitchen. "My name's Shane. Shane Galanter."

"Just a minute please." The woman put him on hold and after a short time she came back. "I'm sorry, that's not the name of our owner."

"But you told me yes, you just said that, remember?" Shane pushed his fingers through his hair and rested his forearms on his knees. "Please, check again."

"Sir, I'm very busy. I don't keep track of the bank owners. Can I help you in any other way? Would you like to open an account?"

Shane slammed the phone in the cradle. He tried that bank three more times, but he never again had the strange response he'd gotten that first time.

At the end of another week the bank list turned up nothing, and that made Shane wonder. Maybe Lauren's father had chosen a different investment, the way his father had. A mortgage company or an insurance office, something new. The possibilities were endless, and that meant another dead end.

He tried the few friends Lauren still had, but none of them had her new contact information. Besides, most of them had faded away by the time summer came.

Teenage girls didn't spend time with one of their own who was seven months pregnant.

More time passed, and now it was late August and school was starting in a week. Shane was going crazy trying to find her. She would have the baby now, and that meant she'd made her decision. Either she was learning how to be a mother with their baby at her side, or she had given the baby up.

One night that week he was quiet at dinner, and his father asked him about it. "You okay, Shane?"

"I can't stop thinking about her."

His father took a bite of his chicken. "Who?"

"*Who?*" He looked from his father to his mother. "Are you serious?"

"Honey, he's talking about Lauren, of course." His mother passed a bowl of mashed potatoes across the table. She looked his way. "Have you tried her old number again? Maybe they've left a forwarding number by now."

"I try it every day." He raked his fork through his green beans and pushed his chair back from the table. "I can't find her. I hate this."

"I'll tell you what, son. You get through

this next year of school, and if she hasn't turned up by then, we'll go looking for her."

By the end of the year? Shane stared at him. Did he really think that was a possibility? That the two of them wouldn't find each other for a whole year? What about the baby? He was a father; he certainly had the right to spend time with his child, to meet him or her.

That night he turned in early. Baseball was done for the summer, and he still had a few days before school started. He opened his closet and pulled out a box he kept near the back. Then he shut his bedroom door, carried the box to his bed, and gently lifted the first thing from the top. It was a framed photo that Lauren had given him at the end of their fifth-grade year. The two of them had just finished a track meet, and they had their arms locked around each others' necks. In the background, he could see her parents, talking to some of the other adults. His mother had taken the picture. He could hear her voice still.

"You two are darling together."

"Mom, come on." He hadn't been into girls back then. Lauren was his friend. "Take the picture."

When she finally snapped it, Lauren grabbed her water bottle and sprayed him. The move took him by surprise. He grabbed his and chased her, but she was fast and she had a head start. They ran, and as he caught up to her he tore the lid from his bottle. He doused her before she could get away, and they both wound up lying on the grass, side by side, soaking wet and laughing hard.

He looked at the picture now. It was faded, and their faces looked so young. Like that moment had happened to a different couple of kids altogether. He reached back into the box and the next thing he brought out was a handmade card, something Lauren had made him for his thirteenth birthday.

On the outside she'd drawn stick figures of the two of them on opposite sides of a football stadium. It reminded him of his parents and hers sitting at a high school football game, talking and laughing and watching the action on the field. He and Lauren had walked down behind the bleachers and there — in the shadows of the stadium — they shared their first kiss.

"Don't tell anyone ever, okay?" Lauren's cheeks were red. She could hardly wait to get back up to the bleachers.

"I won't. We can stay on opposite sides of the stadium, okay?" He grinned at her. "That way no one will ever guess."

"Okay. Let's do that."

He looked at the card now. It was lightly yellowed from the years that had passed. The stick figures couldn't have been farther apart. On the inside she'd written, "How's life on your side of the bleachers?"

He ran his fingers over the cover of the card and slipped it back into the box.

How had everything gone so wrong? They were the couple their friends liked to hold up as the perfect pair. Their families were best friends, they both had a determination to stay away from the pitfalls other couples fell to — either by spending too much time together or by getting too physical. It was that last summer, that's what did them in. When he looked back, it made sense that they'd fallen. They were alone so much of the time, and by then they were almost too comfortable with each other.

He looked back into the box. It was half full of cards and letters. He reached in and pulled out one that was folded into a small square. Carefully so he wouldn't rip the paper, he opened it and found the beginning. "Shane, we were studying zoo animals and Miss Erickson assigned me to work on the monkey. Which made me think of you. Remember the monkey? I never laughed so hard in all my life. Love you lots and lots, Lauren."

The monkey. A chuckle sounded low in his throat. He and Lauren had gone to the zoo with their sixth grade science class. He'd been caught talking to her, and the teacher forced him to give a speech on monkeys to the class.

Again the memory dimmed, and he reached for another folded note. This one had a picture Lauren had drawn. It was a fighter jet with a little man sitting in the cockpit. She'd drawn an arrow to the figure and scrawled the words, "You're gonna fly one day! When you go, take me with you."

The evening wore on that way with one special picture or letter after another. In the end, he packed everything back in the box and slipped it back into his closet. Wherever she was, he needed her. And he was certain she needed him. She was his best friend, the girl at the center of all his good memories of growing up.

He stared out the window into the dark. *God, You know where she is and what she's doing. I have to find her. Please, God. I don't know what else to do.*

The answer came clear and quick.

Follow me, son, follow me.

The words took him by surprise. He hadn't been to youth group or read a Bible since he moved to Los Angeles. What he had done, though, was pray. And prayer felt more and more natural. Okay, so he'd follow Jesus. But what did that mean when it came to Lauren? When he told her he wouldn't ever love anyone the way he loved her, he'd been telling the truth. He needed her like water, like air.

He would pray for her and he would look for her until he found her. As long as he lived he would look. And one day — he believed without a single doubt — he'd find her. And then they could go through the box of memories together and laugh at all the funny times they'd shared.

The stick figures and the stadium, and especially the drawing of the fighter jet. All of that and a baby too. He could hardly wait.

Eleven

Bill Anderson was in his office doing something he'd done every waking hour since Lauren left.

Talking to God.

He braced his elbows on his desk and covered his face with his hands. *I'm back, God. I need to talk to you again about Lauren.* His throat grew thick, and he held his breath to ward off the wave of sorrow. All he ever meant to do was love her. She was his precious girl, his only child. His daughter. Of course he wanted a bright future for her. Before Lauren's pregnancy, if that future had included Shane, then wonderful. Everyone would win. But once a baby was involved . . .

Everything changed.

Bill forced himself to exhale. When he first learned about his daughter's pregnancy, he was crushed. How he hated that his little girl would have to grow up too fast. But he didn't embrace the idea of

199

keeping her from Shane until he saw the shallow, biting reaction from the Galanters. Anger stirred in him again at the thought, and he shifted in his chair. How dare Sheila and Samuel make his daughter out to be nothing more than a cheap tramp! And that's exactly how they treated her at the end. The more he thought about Lauren having the Galanters as in-laws, the more he felt angry and sick. She deserved so much more than that. But now, somehow everything had backfired.

God, I'm sorry. I took matters into my own hands, and now, well, I'm desperate. He made his hands into fists and pressed them against his eyes. He hadn't let Angela see him cry much, but the tears were there. Any time he thought about Lauren. Every few minutes he had an overwhelming desire to get in the car and drive after her, search the highways and byways from Chicago to California until he found her, until he could hold her in his arms and tell her how sorry he was.

I only meant to love her, Lord. Forgive me for not listening to her, for thinking I had all the answers. Give me a second chance with her, please. She's all alone out there, and she needs us. She needs us more than she knows. Thank you, God.

He straightened and lowered his hands to his desk. He still had work to do that day, not the kind that used to keep his attention. But phone calls and meetings with a private investigator, someone who might help him find his daughter.

He pulled a list close and noticed that his hands were trembling. He missed her so much it was a physical pain, an ache slicing right through him. It was there when he woke up and when he turned off the lights each night. Where was she and what was she doing? How was she getting by without her their help?

He let out a shaky sigh. His prayer was right on. Wherever she was, his little girl needed him, the way she always had. But now he understood something he hadn't before.

How desperately he needed her too.

The truth was beginning to sink in.

Lauren was gone from their lives and she wasn't coming back. Three months had passed, and none of their efforts had made a bit of difference. Angela finished cleaning the kitchen and put the kettle on. Tea was always good at this time of the morning, something to give her day a sense of normalcy. As if she wasn't dying a little more every day.

Bill was home because it was Monday, the day he'd dedicated to finding Lauren.

"The business can do without me one day a week," he'd told her. "I can't stop looking. Not ever."

The kettle began to rattle, the water inside halfway to boiling. She leaned back and surveyed her kitchen. It was bright and airy, the sort of kitchen in the sort of home she and Bill had always dreamed of having. But the dream never materialized, because always it had included Lauren. She should've been there, enjoying her upstairs bedroom, excited about her senior year in high school.

Her loss was a constant ache for both of them, the way it would be until they found her. She crossed her arms and heard Bill coming in from the other room. "Making tea?"

"Yes." She smiled at him as he walked through the doorway. "Want some?"

"Sure." He took up his position opposite her, the kitchen island between them. "I have an appointment with another investigator. He wants more information, anything we can remember about her past. Things that might be significant."

Angela took another mug from the cupboard and gave him a sad smile. "Shane

Galanter." She shrugged one shoulder. "That's the most significant thing, right?"

He slumped a little. "Right." He blinked and his eyes looked wet. "Pastor Paul's coming over again tonight. There's three more to the Bible study we're doing."

Bible studies and meetings with pastors, all of it was so new to them. Why hadn't they found the richness of faith before, back when they were still living the perfect dream life, before Shane and Lauren fell to temptation and life turned upside down? How different things might've been if she and Bill had made faith more important to their daughter. To themselves.

The kettle began to whistle, low and steady. She flipped the burner off and poured the tea. "I love meeting with him. Everything he's showing us, it's just what we need."

Bill bit his lip. "It's what we needed years ago." He took his tea, moved around the kitchen island and kissed her tenderly. "I'm sorry, Angela. I'll tell you every day until we find her. It's my fault she left." He pulled back a few inches. "You asked me to think it through, and I didn't do it. I thought . . . I thought I was protecting her, loving her."

"I know." She lifted her eyes to her husband. "We have to keep praying."

"And searching." He took the tea and headed back toward the doorway and the den around the corner. "I have a few phone calls to make before I meet with the PI. I'm guessing by now she's enrolled in college somewhere. The PI wanted me to make a list of the schools she might've been interested in."

"Okay." She watched him go. First it had been a search on Lauren's license plate, and then a search of the hotels she might've stayed in along the way. Next it was hotels in California, and now they were moving on to colleges.

It all felt so futile.

The only bit of searching that had turned up anything at all was the license plate check. According to the information found by the first investigator, Lauren had sold her car in New Mexico. Clearly she must've used the money to buy a new car, but that's where the trail died off. Angela picked up her tea and remembered back, the way she always did at this time of the day. There had been no warnings, no sign that her daughter was about to bolt. Lauren had spent the night at Emily's side, and when she left at four-thirty that morning, it was with the promise that she'd come back after she got some sleep.

Angela closed her eyes and drifted back to that day, the way it had played out hour after hour. By midafternoon she was concerned about Lauren and where she might've gone. She called home, but there was no answer. Finally around six o'clock, Bill called her.

"I'm coming down." He hesitated. "How's Lauren doing?"

Alarm rang through her heart and mind. "Lauren's at home." She pressed the receiver to her ear so she could hear above the commotion in the waiting room.

"No, she isn't." His voice held instant alarm. "I thought she was there."

"Have you checked her room?"

"No, I just thought . . . give me a minute, I'll check." He wasn't gone long. When he returned, his voice was more strained than before. "She's not here. It looks like she slept in her bed, but she's gone. Maybe she's on her way there."

Back then, Angela was still furious with her husband, still barely able to talk to him without feeling hateful toward him for what he'd done by breaking up Shane and Lauren. Even if it had been done with love as the motive. When he suggested that Lauren might be on her way to the hospital, Angela didn't push the issue; she only hurried the phone call and agreed that it would be wise for him to come. Maybe he was right, she'd told herself. Lauren was on her way back; that had to be it. She wouldn't simply leave town — and Emily — without some sort of explanation, would she? Not when she hadn't given them any warning. But after another thirty minutes, she had a certainty equaled only by the pain inside her.

Lauren was gone.

Again Angela called the police, and she was given the same answer: wait twenty-four hours and file a missing persons report. She was frantic at the thought of Lauren back on the road, setting out to find Shane, especially when she was so upset. After an hour Angela went to the nurse's station and questioned everyone on staff, trying to figure out if Lauren had called. By all accounts, she hadn't talked to any of them since she left the hospital that morning.

Angela's only clue came when she talked to the woman manning the desk in the pediatric unit.

"Have you asked anyone in labor and delivery? Sometimes our calls get mixed up."

She thanked the woman and hurried to

the other side of the floor where labor and delivery was housed. The woman at the desk was pleasant, but distracted.

"Can I help you?" She had a novel in her hand, and she seemed anxious to get back to her reading.

"Yes." Angela gripped the edge of the counter. "My daughter is supposed to be here. I'm trying to figure out if she called."

"What's her name?"

"Lauren Anderson. She would've called looking for her infant daughter, Emily."

A light dawned in the woman's eyes, and just as quickly a sheepishness. "You know, something that happened earlier this afternoon's starting to make sense." She nodded. "She might've called."

"What . . . what makes you think so?" Angela wanted to run around the counter and shake the woman. The information wasn't coming nearly fast enough.

"Well —" the nurse closed her book and sat up straighter — "I took a call from a woman looking for an Emily Anderson." She cringed. "I thought she must've been one of our new moms. See, we had a newborn named Emma Henderson who had gone home a few hours earlier."

The pieces swirled in Angela's head. She pressed her fingers to her temples and stared at the woman. "I'm not seeing the connection."

"Sorry." A nervous laugh sounded from her throat. "I think she asked about Emily, and I told her she was gone. That she'd been gone for a few hours." The woman sifted through a pile of papers. "After she hung up, I realized we were maybe talking about different babies. Emily Anderson, Emma Henderson. You know, pretty close."

Angela wanted to scream. "That's it? Did she say anything else?"

"Actually . . ." The nurse's smile faded. "She sounded a little distracted. She never actually said good-bye, just sort of hung up on me."

Angela's heart sank to her knees. "Great."

"The woman who called, she's your daughter?" The nurse seemed sorry, but she was already picking up the novel again, positioning herself to dig into the next chapter.

"Yes." She took a few steps backward and shook her head. "Don't worry about it."

"Yeah, I mean it was an honest mistake." She gave her a weak smile. "Sorry if it caused any confusion."

Any confusion? Angela could barely

make her feet move as she left the labor and delivery area and returned to the pediatric wing. She found a seat in a quiet part of the waiting room and covered her face with her hands. The details were shaky, but they were easy to string together. If Lauren had called and asked about Emily, and if she'd been told that the baby was gone, that she'd been gone for a few hours, then Lauren might've figured —

She could never quite finish the thought. Not then and not now.

Her tea wasn't steaming like before, so she picked it up and cradled her hands around the warm mug. In the days since then it was easier to believe that Lauren had run for other reasons. That she had convinced herself she needed to find Shane before she could be a mother, and that she wasn't able to handle the responsibility at this time in her life.

The alternative was terrifying.

A soft little cry drifted down the stairs, and Angela looked at the clock. Almost eleven, right on schedule. Her days were nothing if not directed by a routine since Lauren had left. It was a good thing, really. The busyness of her day kept her sane, and gave her a reason to hang on.

She set down her tea and headed upstairs. With each step the memory of that awful day returned. Bill had arrived at the hospital minutes after her conversation with the labor and delivery nurse, and after he realized that Lauren was gone again, he dropped to one of the waiting room chairs, and for the first time since she'd known him, he wept. The sobs that came from him that day told her that he was not the hard, dominating person she was beginning to think him. He was a father who had sought the best for his only child, his daughter. But everything he'd done in the past six months had backfired, and now he was as overcome by grief as she.

They filed the missing person's report the next day, but it did no good. The first police officer they'd talked to was right. No one on the force was going to spend man-hours searching for a seventeen-year-old runaway, a girl driving a nearly new sports car and headed for California.

But something happened in the days that followed. Though Angela and Bill came no closer to finding Lauren, they did come closer to each other. They dropped to their knees near the side of Lauren's bed and did something they'd never done together before. They prayed. Since then, though they carried the pain of Lauren's loss with them, they had a strength and a hope that was unexplainable, unearthly.

The cry from the upstairs room grew louder.

"Coming, honey." Angela hurried her pace. She rounded the corner into the room that should've belonged to Lauren. The baby had kicked off her light blanket, her arms and legs flailing as her cry turned lusty. "Emily, shh. It's okay."

She swept the baby up in her arms and cuddled her close against her chest. Lauren was missing so much. Her baby was changing with every passing week, losing that newborn look and getting more of her own personality and facial expressions.

"Shh, sweetheart. It's okay." She held her close and carried her downstairs, cooing at her the whole way. "Grandma'll heat up your bottle, okay?"

Emily settled down, her eyes big and blue as they looked straight at her. She made a soft sound, and Angela had the sense — as she'd had before — that this little girl would be a fighter, a child of determination. Already she knew what she wanted and when, and she wasn't about to go unnoticed.

Angela warmed the bottle and took

Emily to a rocking chair in the living room. They were just seated when Bill came up and stood behind them, his hand on Angela's shoulder.

"She's beautiful."

"Yes."

"Can you see it?" He leaned down and brushed his fingers over Emily's forehead, down the side of her cheek. "The way she looks like her parents."

"I can." Tears stung at Angela's eyes, but she blinked them away. She'd already cried enough tears for a lifetime. Emily needed her now, and she needed her happy and full of energy. "I think she's going to have dark hair like Shane."

"And Lauren's blue eyes."

"Mmm-hmm." She smiled at the baby, but inside her heart was breaking. "Sometimes I'm not sure which hurts more. Missing Lauren, or seeing her every day in Emily's eyes."

Bill didn't say anything. After a few minutes he leaned closer and kissed Emily on the head. Then he straightened and gave Angela a side hug. "I'll let you know how it goes with the PI."

"Okay." She put her hand over his and squeezed. "I'll be praying."

He left through the door to the garage,

and she listened as he started his car and pulled away. Private investigators and phone calls and desperate threads of possibility. That's all they had to go on now, all they could draw from if they wanted to find their daughter.

She ran her thumb along Emily's cheek.

The thing was, Lauren had been crazy for her daughter, completely taken with her. Yes, she wanted to find Shane, and no, her trip west with Emily hadn't gone well. But she wouldn't have walked out of the hospital that day without saying good-bye. She would've at least explained that she needed to find Shane, and that she wanted to hand responsibility to Emily over. For a short time, anyway.

Since she hadn't done that, Angela could only imagine the absolute worst.

Lauren believed Emily was dead. From the way she'd acted when Emily was sick, Angela was terrified that Lauren blamed Bill and her for the baby's death. She probably blamed herself, also. And God. With no baby to bid good-bye, and no desire to talk to her parents, she would've been five hundred miles out of town by midnight.

Grief and guilt settled like a cement blanket on her shoulders. Now that she'd allowed herself to admit that scenario, now that she could give herself permission to believe that was why Lauren had left, it made horrible, perfect sense.

When Bill returned a few hours later, she told him her theory so he could share it with the private investigator. The possibility was enough to make her heart race whenever she thought of it. Because nothing was sadder than the thought of Lauren living on her own, believing her daughter was dead, when in reality she was growing up a little more every day. They would spare no expense; stop at nothing to find Lauren. And one day they would get the call or the clue they were looking for, the information that would bring Lauren and Emily back together again. Angela believed that with all her heart.

Even if they had to spend a lifetime searching.

Twelve

Eighteen years later

Wheaton College was everything Emily Anderson hoped it would be.

The only downside was that it kept her in Illinois, when everything in her wanted to be in Los Angeles. There, or anywhere on the coast of Southern California. Especially this time of year. It was Friday afternoon, and Christmas break was looming.

She stretched her elbow out along her desk and rested her face in her hand. Her feature story on the women's soccer coach was due at five o'clock, but she couldn't focus. Three other journalism students were hanging out at the newspaper office that afternoon, but they were working on a project, so they didn't pay her any attention. The outline for her feature was spread out on the desk in front of her. She glanced at it and tried to be interested. Footsteps sounded from behind, and her professor pulled up a chair beside her.

"Hi, Emily." Ms. Parker was young and likeable. Emily hadn't ever heard anyone say anything bad about her. "How's the story coming?"

She sat up and gave her teacher a weak smile. "Not so good." She looked at the clock. "I still have a few hours."

Ms. Parker found the outline on the desk. "You have your points down."

"Yes." Her heart wasn't into it; that was the problem. She met Ms. Parker's eyes. "Did you always love writing?"

"Not always." She laughed. "Most of my students are the other way around, though. For me, when I was in high school I thought I wanted to be a math teacher. It wasn't until college that I knew I wanted to write."

"Hmm." Emily looked at her notes, not really seeing them. Her eyes lifted to the teacher's again. "Did your mom like to write?"

Ms. Parker angled her head. "Yeah, I guess she did. I never really made the connection." She folded her arms and leaned them on the desk. "She kept a journal and wrote poetry, that sort of thing. Maybe that's where I get it."

Emily nodded. "Maybe."

"Did your mother like writing?" The question was an innocent one. Ms. Parker didn't know Emily well enough to understand the territory she was treading.

Emily forced a smile. "I've never met my mother." She made sure she sounded upbeat. She hated people feeling sorry for her. "My grandma told me she spent time in her room, maybe writing, maybe reading. She isn't sure."

"Oh." Ms. Parker was quiet for a moment. "Well, I bet she was a writer."

"Yeah, maybe."

The instructor tapped lightly on the notes. "You're one of the best soccer players this school has ever had, Emily. A feature on the coach should be easy for you."

"I know." She drew in a long breath and grinned at the woman. The message was clear. Whatever was distracting her, the story had to be written. "I'll get on it."

"Okay." Her smile was compassionate. "Maybe you and your grandma can talk about your mom later tonight." She raised an eyebrow. "When the story's written and put to bed."

Emily made a silly face and nodded, then she took her notes to the computer and in half an hour she had the story finished. Ms. Parker was right. The soccer coach was a burly Nigerian man named Wolf, and if anyone understood him, she did. The man was demanding, but he'd improved her game by miles. If she were more committed, she could make a run at the national team. But competing in college was enough, because she wanted to spend at least some of her time thinking about her future. A future writing for a newspaper in Los Angeles. That's all she'd ever wanted. Talent or no, soccer wasn't her passion. Writing held that spot. It always had.

Writing and her faith in Christ.

From the time she was a little girl her grandma had told her simply, "Your mother and father loved you very much, but they weren't ready to be parents."

The answer sounded sad and empty, but Grandma followed it up with this explanation. "God will always be your daddy, Emily. He'll be there for you wherever you are, wherever you go. He'll never leave you."

Her words proved true year after year, and now Emily considered God more than her father. She considered Him her best friend. He was her life giver, her soul maker, her redeemer. He brought her the greatest gifts — joy and love and forgiveness when she messed up. And He brought her peace. But He couldn't quite fill the emptiness in her heart, in the hidden places where she wondered every day *why.* Why did her mom and dad leave? Why didn't they ever come back for her? She'd met kids without parents and often they were rebellious or angry or distant. Not her. She had a wonderful life. Grandparents who loved her, a beautiful home, and a bright future.

But the emptiness was always there.

Sometimes it made her step back and wonder. Especially when the sky was full of snow clouds and California felt a world away and her heart simply wouldn't leave the past alone. What were her parents like? What sort of people had they become? She focused her attention on the computer screen once more and repositioned her hands over the keyboard. The feature was easy, once she gave it some thought. Wolf had escaped captivity from an underground political group in Nigeria and made it to the United States with just the clothes on his back. He earned a soccer tryout at UCLA and two years later he was on the men's national team. Wheaton College was lucky to have him, and she had quotes from the school's athletic director saying as much.

When she finished the story, she sent it to the editor's desk and stretched her feet out. She was going to spend Christmas break at her grandparents' house, but they weren't expecting her until five-thirty. For now she could surf the Internet, look for something to take her mind off the conversation she'd had with Ms. Parker.

And off her mother.

One headline proclaimed an outbreak of violence had flared up in Iraq. Four U.S. soldiers had been killed when their car hit a roadside bomb, and more troops were being sent over. She scanned the details and tried to imagine life in a war-torn country, a place where bombs and death and violence were commonplace. God is a God of peace, so she didn't understand war or whether the United States should be involved. But she knew this: lots of her friends were fighting in Afghanistan and Iraq, and she supported them with everything she was. Still it was easier not to think about it, not to sort through the whys and how comes. *I don't really understand it, God.*

She typed another Web address into the search line, and in a matter of seconds she was looking at the soccer team's standings. Wheaton was at the top. Unless someone got injured or one of the other teams had an unexplainable surge, Emily was pretty sure her team would stay in first. Wolf had done a great job recruiting over the past few years. For the most part the team was older. Emily was the only freshman.

The room was quieter than before. Two of the three students had gone home, and the other was working at one of the computer stations. She clicked her tongue against the roof of her mouth. Then she typed in *writing* and *genetic*. After a brief pause, the computer screen showed a list that was thousands of websites long. The first one asked this question: "How much of who we are is a result of our parents?" She clicked it, and an article appeared.

"Some things are explainable by science, but some things simply can't be figured out. One such phenomenon that defies scientific understanding is the truth that talent and interests are often passed on from one generation to another. For instance, a person with a talent for writing might well have a child with a similar talent . . ."

The article was dry, poorly written, and made up of unbroken small print. She closed it down and stared at the *welcome* screen. She needed to get going. Her grandma hated when she drove home in the snow, and a storm was forecast for that night. She was about to push her chair back, but she couldn't resist. Her hands found the keyboard again. Every few days she checked, the way she had always done. Because mothers didn't just disappear, did they? Her grandmother had told her the story, at least the basics of it. Emily was sick in the hospital and her mother was given bad information — information that might've convinced her Emily was dead. Probably frightened and confused, maybe devastated over the loss of her little girl, her mother had most likely left for California to find Emily's father. Whatever had driven her, she'd left without saying good-bye. To anyone.

In a familiar rush of letters, she typed, *L-a-u-r-e-n A-n-d-e-r-s-o-n,* and hit the search button. Another list of websites appeared, but a quick scan of the first page told her there was nothing new. The number of sites was the same as last time. Every one of them was a site she'd already checked.

Next she tried her dad's name: *S-h-a-n-e G-a-l-e-n-t-e-r.* But the same thing was true; nothing had been added on the Web under his name, either.

"What are you looking for?" Ms. Parker came up behind her.

Emily shut down the list and closed out of the Internet. She turned wide eyes to her teacher. "Something for another feature. I want to do a comparison of culture and expenses between college life in Chicago and Los Angeles."

She gave a nod of her head. "Sounds interesting. You might need more of a local angle, a stronger hook." She looked at her watch. "But for tonight, how about getting home. Snow's coming soon. I want to lock up."

Emily was out of the chair and gathering her things before Ms. Parker walked away. She didn't grab a full breath until she was outside in the car. Why did it matter so much that she found her mom and dad? They had moved on with their lives, and apparently never looked back. She would follow their lead.

Still . . .

Where had this deep longing come from, to leave the Midwest and live in Southern California? She knew the answer, of course. Knew the region held more draw than sunshine and strong newspapers. It was the place her grandparents always talked about, the place where they thought her mom and dad lived.

Snow began falling, and the clouds overhead grew dark and threatening. Emily didn't mind. She was only twenty minutes from home. A storm didn't frighten her. Funny, how peace was so much a part of how she was raised. Her grandparents explained early on that life wouldn't always go the way she wanted it to. But still she could have peace if she understood that God was in control, that He was there for her no matter what was happening around her.

That's why it was strange when — once in a while — she would come home and find her grandparents huddled together at the dining room table, deep in conversation. At times like that, they looked anything but peaceful. It happened again just a week ago, when she came home. As she walked through the door, her grandparents stopped whatever conversation they were having. She still remembered the strange way they'd acted that day.

"Emily." Her grandma stood up, came to her, and hugged her. "We weren't expecting you until later."

"Journalism let out early." She drew

back and set her purse and books on the kitchen table. "Did I interrupt anything?"

"No." Her grandpa was a successful businessman; even now when he was pushing sixty years old, he was a sharp dresser, a man known throughout Wheaton for his power and influence. But with her he'd always had a soft side. He held out his hand to her and she went to him, taking hold of it.

She bent down and kissed him on the cheek. "It's quiet in here." She gave him a hesitant smile. "You sure you weren't talking about something private?"

For the quickest instant, her grandparents looked at each other, as if to question whether they should go into detail about whatever they'd been discussing. But her grandfather only cleared his throat and gave the dining room table a light slap with his open palm. "Dinner. That's what we're talking about. What we can fix for our young college student, home for the weekend."

Their explanations didn't fool her. They never did. She could only guess that they were talking about the one thing they never brought up in her presence: the search for their daughter, Emily's mother. Emily knew they were still looking for her. Every now and then Emily would bring in the mail and see a bill from a private investigator, or a return letter from a congressman's office in California. But their only conversation about Emily's mother was centered on the happier times, the days when she was growing up.

"Your mother colored just like that, with eighteen shades of green in a single tree," her grandma told her when she was little. And as she grew older, "Your mother had a bicycle like that one, shiny red with streamers flying from the handlebars."

From everything she could determine, her grandparents had been on close terms with their daughter. That's why it didn't make sense that her mother would leave in the weeks after she was born. There were so many missing pieces, there always had been. Through the years she had asked her grandparents whenever she felt driven to understand the past better.

Of course, sometimes she dealt with the loneliness all by herself. Too many nights to count she would smile at her grandparents as they kissed her good night and prayed with her. But when they left her room, she would roll onto her side and stare at the open door, wishing just once that her mom would walk through it. She had a picture in her mind of what her mother would look like, the way her eyes would light up when she saw Emily, the tender smile she'd have. Sometimes her imagination would be so vivid she'd actually imagine her mother walking through the door, taking a seat on the edge of her bed, and smoothing her hair.

"I love you, Emily. I always have," she'd say.

But when her imagination let up even for an instant, the image disappeared.

There were other times — times at the park with her grandparents, when she saw a young couple with their children, and for a moment she'd pretend the couple was her parents. She'd think what it would be like to run up to them and take their hands and hug them.

"Emily," her father might say. "We've been looking all our lives for you. Now you're finally where you belong."

The older she got, the less she pretended that way, but still she kept a picture in her mind, the way her parents might look now. Sometimes she encountered something that it seemed only a mom or a dad could help her with. On those days she'd wait until it was time for bed, then hold quiet, one-sided conversations with them.

Usually her hushed whispers turned into prayers, requests spoken to God, begging Him to bring them back, to reconnect them somehow.

"I know my mom was young," Emily once told her grandparents when she was seventeen. "But why didn't she check to see if I was alive? She wanted to find my dad, right?"

"Right." Her grandmother was folding laundry. She set a towel down on the sofa beside her and looked up at Emily. "But honey, don't think she had any doubts. I really think she thought you were dead."

"Yeah." Emily folded her arms across her middle, warding off the hurt inside. "But wouldn't she have stayed just in case? In case I was still alive?"

"I don't know." Her grandma sounded sad and tired. "She was desperate to find your father. She wanted to find him more than she wanted anything."

"Anything?" The answer stabbed through her soul. "Even me?"

Her grandmother reached out and took careful hold of her hand. "Not you, sweetheart. She wanted you. That's why I'm sure she must've had incorrect information about you."

Emily thought for a minute. "Well . . .

maybe we should go to California and find her."

"We've tried." Grandma smiled, but her eyes stayed flat. "Believe me, Emily, we've done everything we know to do. The only way we're going to find your mother again is if God gives us a miracle."

Now Emily stared at the road ahead of her. The snow was heavier than before. Two miles and she'd be home, ready to sleep in her own bed and cuddle up with her grandparents for a couple of movie nights. She didn't have a boyfriend, and most of her friends were spending Christmas break with their families. Emily was glad for the time that lay ahead. With soccer practice every day, her first semester of college was tougher than she'd expected, and she and her grandparents hadn't had much time together.

She took the exit leading to her house and thought again about what her grandmother had said two years ago. It would take a miracle. Fine. She gripped the steering wheel. If it took a miracle, then that's what she'd keep praying for. Because more often lately she couldn't get through a day without thinking of her mom and dad and what had happened to them. Had her mother found him? If so, did they marry and start a new family? Was it possible she had brothers or sisters out west? And if her mom and dad hadn't found each other, were they happy?

And then there was the hardest truth of all. The truth that threatened to tear at the center of everything peaceful about her life and faith and future. The truth that always brought the sting of tears to her eyes. If her grandma was right then there was no point wondering about when she might come back or what type of life she was living.

If her mother thought she was dead, then by now the truth was painfully clear.

She wasn't coming back. Not ever.

Thirteen

Angela had been looking forward to this day since the semester started. She'd decorated the house and opened the seasonal storage boxes so the ornaments were ready to go on the tree. The red felt Advent calendar hung on the wall, all the numbered hand-sewn ornaments ready to be placed on it — even those that should've been up by now.

This would be a very special Christmas. Special and sad, for reasons they didn't want to tell Emily. Not just yet. The news would mar the season, and Angela didn't want that. She wanted one last Christmas celebrated the special way they'd celebrated it every year since Emily was a little girl. Bill had his favorite Mitch Miller CD in the player and a kettle of hot cinnamon apple cider was simmering on the stove. Time enough for sad announcements and changes later.

For now, all they needed was Emily.

She heard the front door open and the cheerful voice of her granddaughter rang through the house. Her delightful, precious granddaughter. "Hi! I'm home."

"Emily!" She gave the garland a last nudge and hurried toward the front door. When she rounded the corner, her granddaughter flew into her arms before she could take another step.

"It's so good to be home!" She circled her arms around Angela and kissed her cheek. "I finished my finals." She pulled back and grinned. "I even finished my feature on the soccer coach."

Angela looped her arm through Emily's and led her into the kitchen. "How do you think you did?"

"Good." She raised her brow a bit. "I guess the first semester is always hard, but I think my grades'll be up there. A's and B's for the most part." She winced. "Maybe a C in biology and Algebra II."

"That's okay." She smiled. "With your sports and your work at the school paper, I think a few C's are to be expected. First semester of high school was hard too, remember?"

"*Do* I." She gave her a dizzying look as she took a seat on one of the bar stools and leaned her elbows on the counter. "In ninth grade I wasn't sure if I'd make it to graduation."

"Your gold tassel took a few of your teachers by surprise." Angela chuckled as she reached into the cupboard and pulled out three mugs. "But not us, honey. We knew you could do it."

She looked around. "Where's Papa?"

"Upstairs." Angela was careful to keep her expression steady. "He's been a little tired lately. He thought he'd get a short nap before dinner." She handed Emily a mug of steaming cider. "Here. Be careful, it's hot."

"Thanks." She held it in both hands and breathed it in. "This is so great." Her eyes took in the adjacent family room, where Angela had most of the decorations up. "All I did was walk through the door and already it feels like Christmas." She took a small sip of her cider. "Is Papa okay?"

"He'll feel better later. That reminds me!" Angela could feel her eyes light up. "He's taken the next two weeks off. He's never done that around the holidays."

"Two weeks?" Emily set her cup down. "That's great!"

"I know." She gave a sideways shake of her head. "The board told him it was time he took a break. He'll be off through New

Year's Day." She didn't add that he might be home even longer. Again, that could come later.

They shared their drinks, humming along to Mitch Miller when the conversation slowed. Angela checked the oven and the meatloaf and baked potatoes she had inside. "Dinner'll be ready in half an hour."

"Perfect." Emily drank the last of her cider. "I'm going to freshen up. I'll be back down in a little bit." She flashed a quick smile and took light running steps around the corner into the entryway. She left behind a trail of her things — her duffel bag and backpack and purse. But that was Emily. Loving and friendly, but not the neatest person. Much the way Lauren had been when she was —

No. Angela promised herself that this Christmas — with the news about Bill — she wouldn't spend countless hours thinking about Lauren. It was simply more than she could bear. Still . . . with Emily back home it was impossible not to think about the daughter she'd lost, the one who was always only a sad thought away. She checked the dishwasher. The dishes were clean. Time to unload. She put away a row of glasses and then her mind started to drift. How different she was with Emily compared to her days of raising Lauren. With Lauren, everything needed to be perfect. An A minus in algebra meant a brief lecture on the importance of pulling grades up and the necessity of going for the best possible mark. A few scattered items on her bedroom floor, and Angela would've cut out her phone privileges for an entire week.

It was petty and ridiculous how she'd treated Lauren, and all for appearances. So they'd look like the perfect family. Nice house, powerful job, an orderly, intelligent, high-achieving daughter. Just the way she and Bill had always known their lives would play out. But of course, all their plans backfired when they lost Lauren.

Things were entirely different with Emily.

She and Bill prayed with their granddaughter and took her to church. They talked and went on walks around their Wheaton neighborhood and laughed at old movies. Back when Lauren expressed an interest in dance, Angela and Bill signed her up for four classes.

"She's good, she has natural rhythm," Bill said after her first lesson. "We need to be serious about this, help her reach the top. She might be a prima ballerina one day."

Lauren was five at the time.

When Emily showed an interest in soccer, Angela and Bill signed her up, bought her a pink soccer bag, and cheered at her games. Win or lose, they took her out for lunch afterward and didn't talk about the sport again until her next practice session. In the process, she developed a love for the game that went beyond anything Lauren had felt for dance or piano or debate team — the things they'd pushed her toward.

Angela finished her drink and set the cup in the dishwasher. Their attitude toward Emily was different in other ways too. They understood now how fragile life could be. Never had they dreamed they'd go nineteen years without seeing Lauren. If Emily had come home with hair dyed green or a piercing through her eyebrow or a desire for drugs, if she'd come home pregnant by a boy she loved more than life itself, Angela and Bill would never have manipulated her life, the way they did with Lauren. They would've held on to her until love brought her back around again.

Angela shook her head. What irony! The mistakes they'd made with Lauren had taught them how to truly parent. And those lessons allowed Emily the best possible life. Lauren's little girl was grounded in her faith, she had a deep love for the Lord and for Bill and her. She'd never done anything more rebellious than stay on the phone too long once in a while on a school night. Angela drew a deep breath. Emily's future seemed good as gold. She would become a writer — one of the best — and she would go into the world bright and beautiful and sure of herself.

Lauren would've been so proud of her.

She heard the sound of Emily bounding down the stairs. "No soccer practice for two weeks! Isn't that great?"

"Longer than that, right? The season's over." The CD had stopped playing, so she drifted into the family room and started Alabama's *Christmas*, another of Bill's favorites.

"College soccer's a little different." Emily made a face. "We'll be conditioning again, doing scrimmages as soon as the field thaws out. Until then we'll be in the weight room."

The music started, filling the air with the gentle sounds of Christmas, Christmas the way they'd lived it and celebrated it since moving to Wheaton. "How's tomorrow sound for getting the tree?"

"At the farm?" Emily's voice held an excitement reserved for the season. But as she made her way back to the kitchen counter and sat back on the bar stool, she looked distracted.

"As always." Angela followed her and took the spot next to her. "Rain, snow, or sun. You know your papa."

"The cutting is the best part." She brought her hands to her face. "My fingers always smell like pinesap for a week."

"You know what I love?"

"What?" Emily gripped the stool's arms and swung her feet.

"Watching you and your grandfather pick a tree. I think we're twelve years running finding the absolute most interesting tree on the lot."

Emily giggled. "Interesting?"

"Definitely." Angela laughed out loud. "Remember last year? You wanted a tree that would reach the ceiling, but the tall ones were scraggly on top."

"Right." She tipped her head back, her eyes dancing. "That's because a Christmas tree doesn't have to be perfect."

"No, it doesn't." Angela smiled. Neither did people. That was something else she'd learned this second time around.

Their laughter died down and Emily drummed her fingers lightly on the counter, a familiar and comfortable action. It was her sign that she had something deep to talk about. Angela waited. Finally Emily drew a long breath and their eyes met. "Grandma, can we talk about my mom? I wanna know more about her."

Angela steadied herself. Emily had asked this sort of question before, and always she'd been content with basic answers. But Angela had known that one day Emily would want more. She put her hand over her granddaughter's. "What would you like to know?"

"Well . . ." Emily squinted, as if trying to sort through which questions were most important. "You've looked for her, right?"

"Yes." Angela felt a heaviness in her heart. How many hours and conversations and phone calls had they made? As technology advanced, they'd used the Internet, sometimes every day. "Yes, we've looked."

"Okay, but how did she just disappear? I mean, she thought I was dead, but then what? She just drove out of town?"

"It seems that way." Angela ordered herself to stay unemotional. Emily needed her to be calm; she couldn't give in to nineteen years of sorrow. "She was exhausted and

239

frantic. The two of you had just driven back from halfway across the country, and you were very, very sick."

Emily looked like she was trying to imagine how her mother must've felt, scared and tired and then convinced that her baby was dead. "But you think she went to California, right?"

"We have our theories." Her hand was still covering Emily's. She gave it a soft squeeze. "She might not have made it to California, for one."

Emily nodded. "I've thought about that. She might be dead."

"Yes. Or maybe she changed her name. If that's what happened we could look forever and not find her. In my heart I believe she's alive and out there somewhere."

"Me too." Emily looked out the kitchen window.

From the side, her profile was so like Shane's, a mirror of his striking Greek features. Between that and the fact that she had Lauren's eyes, Angela had a constant reminder of the kids they'd lost.

"I was thinking today whether she ever found my dad and whether they got together or not."

Angela doubted that. "Anything's possible."

"So the last time you saw her was at the hospital, right? When I was sick?"

"Yes. She was overwhelmed, honey."

"I was wondering today," Emily looked at her again, "whether she was a writer or not."

"We've talked about that."

"But I wish I knew for sure."

"Wait . . ." Angela straightened. "I just remembered something."

A few days earlier Bill had found a box of Lauren's things in the storage section of the garage. Until then, they'd assumed Lauren had taken all her personal belongings with her. But since they'd just moved to Wheaton at the time of Emily's birth, apparently Lauren's box had been shoved with a dozen others into a corner they'd designated for records and tax documents.

Bill was cleaning out there when he found it and called to her. "Angela, come quick."

She hurried to the garage and over to his side. "What is it?"

"Look at this." He was standing next to a big cardboard carton with Lauren's name scribbled on the side. The sight of her daughter's handwriting brought pangs of both joy and sorrow. They lifted the lid, and inside were what looked like old yearbooks, photo albums, and journals. Everything sentimental that had ever mattered to Lauren. She looked at Bill. "I thought . . . I figured she took this stuff with her."

"Imagine what the private investigators could've done with this if they'd had it back when she first left."

They brought the box inside and took it up to what had been Lauren's room. It was a home office now, a sterile room with a sofa sleeper along one wall. The only trace that it once belonged to Lauren was a photo of her that sat on the desk. That afternoon they spread the contents of the box out and looked at it. Halfway through, though, they stopped and packed it back up. "I can't do this without Emily," Bill said. "There's nothing in here that would help us find Lauren now." He dabbed at his eyes. "Emily deserves to see it first."

Angela agreed, though she thought Bill's reluctance to look through the box had at least as much to do with the fact that it was too painful to sort through. But since Emily was coming home for Christmas, they agreed to wait. It was one more reason she'd been looking forward to the holidays. But in the rush of seeing her and sitting with her, she'd forgotten about the oversized box until just now.

"Grandma, what is it?"

Angela slid down from the bar stool and motioned to her. "Follow me."

They went into the hallway and Angela pointed to the carton in the corner. "We found that a few days ago." She walked closer and put her hand on the edge of the box. "Everything in here belonged to your mother. I'm not sure it'd help us find her now. But . . . we thought it would help you know her a little better."

Emily stared at the carton, her eyes wide and unblinking. When she looked up, tears shimmered on her cheeks. "Do you . . . know what's in it?"

"Some." Angela put her arm around Emily's shoulders. "Yearbooks, photo albums, journals. That sort of thing. Everything that was special to your mother."

A framed photo sat near the top of the box, and Emily reached for it. The image was a picture of Lauren and Shane, taken before a formal dance their freshman year of high school. Emily had seen photos of her parents before, but nothing from a professional photographer. She held it up, studying it. "Look at their eyes."

Angela removed her arm from Emily's shoulders and leaned in closer, staring at their faces. That's when she saw it, saw it clearer than she ever had when the kids had been a part of her life. "Yes. I see."

"Grandma, they were so in love." Emily pressed the photo to her chest. Her eyes were damp, but her smile lit up her expression. "It makes me feel so good to know they loved each other."

Regret wrapped itself around her, squeezing her chest and making it hard to draw a breath. Why hadn't she seen the depth of their feelings for each other back when Lauren and Shane wanted so badly to be together? How different would their lives be if she'd recognized it then? She swallowed her sorrow and gave Emily a partial smile. "That's why we wanted you to have these things, to look through them while you were home." Angela sniffed. Watching Emily cradle the framed picture gave her a flashback, and she saw Lauren, cradling Emily as a baby. The memory was gone as quickly as it had come, but the sadness lingered. Angela had a feeling that not everything Emily would find in the box would leave her feeling happy and whole.

Still it was her right to look through it.

In the background, they heard Bill getting out of bed and heading into the bathroom. "Dinner'll be ready in a few minutes." She looked at the box. "Papa will help you get it up to your room. You can look through it later."

Emily bit her lip. "I can't wait." She kept the photo tight against her heart. "Grandma, can I ask you something else?"

"Yes, honey. Whatever you want."

"My parents didn't have God in their lives, did they? Not God and not peace." She held the photo out enough to see it.

Angela felt the regrets again, as heavy as they'd been in the days and weeks after Lauren left. "No, Em. They didn't have either."

"Do you think they have that now?"

Angela had asked herself the question a hundred times every year. Was Lauren happy and at peace, had she found the faith that had been missing in her childhood? A sad sigh eased up from the deepest corners of her soul. She shook her head. "I don't think so, honey."

Emily looked at the picture again. "It was because of me, right? She got pregnant and everything fell apart."

Angela worked the muscles in her jaw. Emily was right, more so than she knew. There was no way around the truth. "It felt like a tragedy at the time. You understand that, right?"

"Yes." Emily looked up, her expression

far wiser than her eighteen years. She pursed her lips and let her eyes find the faces of her parents once more. "But if my birth tore them apart, then maybe I'm the only one who can bring them back together again."

"Hmm." Angela wanted to warn her not to think that way. If two decades of private investigators and elected officials couldn't find her, what could Emily possibly do to find either of them? Instead she gave a slow nod and framed Emily's face with her hand. "I'm praying for a miracle, Emily. You are too. It's certainly worth a try."

Emily set the photo back down, and the two of them greeted Bill in the hallway.

"Papa! It's so good to see you." Emily threw her arms around his neck and held on tight. "I miss you so much!"

A lump formed in Angela's throat because she knew what Bill was feeling, how precious this Christmas would be with Emily. But it wasn't time for sorrow now. Bill tousled Em's hair and looked her up and down. "Looks like that soccer coach has you down to skin and bones."

"Ah, it's not that bad." She linked arms with him, and the three of them went to the kitchen and worked on dinner. When they were seated at the table, Emily said the prayer. "Jesus, you have me home this Christmas for a reason. I sense that so strongly." Emily squeezed her grandparents' hands. "Thank you for letting my papa find the box of my mom's things. I pray that somewhere inside we'll find a miracle." Her voice was clear, as genuine as a summer sunset. "So that I can meet my mom and dad and help them find the peace that might be missing from their lives. In Jesus' name, amen."

As she finished the prayer, the strangest thing happened in Angela's heart. She felt a surge of hope, the kind she hadn't felt since the first year of Lauren's disappearance. As if maybe God was telling her something very important. That they were indeed standing on the brink of a miracle.

And Emily would have everything to do with it.

Fourteen

War didn't take a break for Christmas. This was Lauren Gibbs's third Christmas season on the war-torn fields of Afghanistan and Iraq, and still it amazed her. The opposing sides would set up roadside bombs, aerial attacks, and raids on insurgent headquarters right through December 25. As if the birth of Christ didn't matter at all.

Not that it affected her one way or the other. Christ's birth didn't mean anything to her. It was four days before Christmas, and she didn't feel anything different — no special magic or joy or desire to marvel at a decorated evergreen tree.

She had her memories. That was enough.

As a correspondent for *Time* magazine, her duty was in Afghanistan. Her assignment was complex. First and foremost, she was responsible for reporting the trends of the war before the competition figured them out. In addition, she looked for daily stories, word pictures, snapshots of a war-torn life. She was also responsible for feature stories and predictions on when the white flags would wave and the American troops would head home.

Her job meant everything to her. She was thirty-six, single, and unattached. Her life in the Middle East was comfortable, an apartment in an eight-story building near the border, a place where dozens of journalists stayed. A few of them had spent years there, the way she had. Her days in the States were so few that she'd sold her condo a year ago. For now she needed to be here. It was almost a calling.

"Hey, Gibbs. Wait up."

She turned and walking toward her was Jeff Scanlon, a *Time* photographer. The two had spent more time together in the past three years than most married couples. But they'd only let their friendship cross lines a few times. Scanlon was interested. His rugged good looks had gotten any girl he wanted in his younger years. Now, at forty, he seemed interested only in spending his days with her.

She was fine with that. He was good company, and he shared her views of peace at all cost. But she didn't want a relationship, not when it meant revealing layers she'd spent a lifetime hiding. Layers that felt like they belonged to someone else altogether.

"Hey." She smiled. It was a beautiful day, clear blue skies and eighty degrees. It could be LA but for the broken buildings and starving people lining the narrow streets. "I wanna get out to that orphanage. The one ten miles from here."

They kept walking, heading for the apartment building. Scanlon had a room there too. "Maybe I can get a photo-essay out of it."

"Perfect." Her pace was fast, the way she liked it. "My story'll be a little longer than usual."

"They always are when kids are involved." He heaved his camera bag higher up on his shoulder and gave her a lopsided grin. "Ever notice that?"

She hesitated. "Yeah, I guess so."

They reached the entrance to the building. A frail-looking woman sat huddled near the door. Next to her were three children, their arms and legs bone thin. The woman didn't say a word, but she held out a cracked ceramic bowl.

Lauren stopped and rifled through her pocket. She pulled out a handful of coins and set them in the container. Scanlon stood nearby while she stooped down and gave a gentle touch to each child's forehead. One of them was a little girl, and her eyes made Lauren's breath catch in her throat. Something about them made her look almost like . . .

No, she wouldn't go there. Not now. Not with Scanlon standing next to her. She blinked and looked back at the mother. In a language that was becoming more familiar to her than English, she said, "I want peace as you do. May I buy you food?"

The woman's eyes widened. She was new to the journalists' building. Most of the street people were regulars and knew to expect help from Lauren. The woman put her arms around her children, clearly protective as she locked eyes with Lauren. "Yes." She spoke with a shame and disbelief that was common among the Afghans. Years of repression had caused most women to fear speaking at all, let alone to an American stranger. The woman lifted her chin a little. "That would be more than I could ask."

"Very well." Lauren nodded to Scanlon. "It's early still. Let's meet down here in half an hour."

"Okay." They went through the doors

together. A café on the first floor was operational now that Western journalists were always passing through the lobby. At the entrance, Scanlon waved. "I'll meet you here."

She nodded and turned her attention to a young girl working behind the café counter. Service was slow, but she paid for four rice bowls and four juice drinks. Then she took them outside and handed them to the children's mother. It was important that the woman be the one to give the food to her own children. It was one small way of giving her back some of her dignity.

"Thank you." There were tears in the woman's eyes. "All Americans, I thank you."

Lauren smiled, but gritted her teeth. Not all Americans. Some Americans still believed they were doing everyone a service by fighting in Afghanistan and Iraq. But whatever slim reason the president might've had for starting the war, it was long past. It was time to call the war off and send over humanitarian help. If *she* were the one in charge, peace in this part of the world would be easy. But it was peace in her own life that was impossible to figure out.

She flipped her straight blonde hair over

her shoulder and nodded at the woman. Then she turned back, went through the entrance, and walked past the elevator. Her room was on the seventh floor, and she always took the stairs. She could lie in foxholes next to soldiers, taking notes and working on a story while missiles exploded all around her. But she couldn't ride an elevator to save her life. The idea of stepping inside one was enough to make her heart race. Just the thought of them made her feel trapped, like she was suffocating.

She headed into the stairwell and started up.

The little Afghani girl's face flashed in her mind. What was it about her? Those eyes maybe, dark striking eyes, like Shane's. The sort of eyes Emily might've had. Of course, if she'd lived, she wouldn't be a little girl now. She'd be a young woman. For a moment Lauren stopped and closed her eyes, her hand tight around the railing.

It hurt so much spending time with children, knowing that her daughter would be alive if she'd been a better mother. If she hadn't taken chances with her baby's life. She opened her eyes and kept walking. As much as it hurt, she'd rather spend time with Afghani children than with any of the adults she'd met. Children reminded her that no matter how frozen her heart felt, no matter how driven she was to be the best, most hard-hitting reporter at *Time*, somewhere inside she was still seventeen years old, driving from Chicago to Los Angeles, grieving the loss of her little Emily. How different her life might've been if her daughter had lived.

Stop it! She'd given herself that same order so many times. Not that it made much difference. She breathed in and closed her eyes for a moment. *How come I can still smell her, still feel her in my arms?*

Enough. Lauren opened her eyes and picked up her pace. Scanlon would be down early, the way he always was. After a few minutes she reached her floor. The stairs were good for her. They helped her stay in shape, a crucial factor if she was going to continue reporting from active areas of the war theater. And she *would* continue, as long as she believed her articles might have even the smallest influence on bringing the war to an end.

She reached room 722, slipped her card in the slot above the door handle, and pushed her way inside. She changed from her heavy khaki pants to a pair of shorts.

The day promised to get hotter and spending time at the orphanage would mean she didn't need extra clothing. There would be no slamming herself into the sand or hiding in craggy bluffs while a battle played out before her eyes.

Most Americans figured the war in Afghanistan was over. But there were uprisings of insurgents all the time, and an entire contingency of U.S. troops were still battling them on a daily basis. The problem wasn't the insurgents, of course. Countries like Afghanistan would always have radical insurgents and terrorist groups. The problem was the innocent people harmed along the way. No wonder the country had so many orphans.

She sat on the edge of her bed and caught her breath. Her chest hurt and she leaned back on her elbows. The stairs must've done it, right? That's why she felt so tight. But even as the thought tried to take root, she let it go. It was a lie. The walk up hadn't made her chest ache. It was the little girl. The child's eyes burned in her mind, taking her back the way orphans' faces often took her back. Back to that terrible day, when she left the life she'd known . . .

She'd driven away from the hospital and

headed for California, determined never to come home again. Her plan had been straightforward. She would live in LA until she found Shane. Three or four months, if it took that long. Then the two of them could find a way to stay together and, when things were stable, they'd go back to Chicago and have a proper burial for Emily. Give their baby the funeral service she deserved.

Much had gone just the way she'd planned. With a place to live, a car, and a job, she had no trouble getting her new ID and her residency established. School came easily, also. She passed the GED without studying at all, and the community college was more than happy to have her. Only one thing hadn't gone according to schedule.

She never found Shane.

As the months turned into years, she thought about going home. She could walk up to the front door and tell her parents she needed their help to find him. By then, maybe they would've known a way to reach Shane. She would hug them and hold them and tell them she forgave them for what they'd done. At least she'd have a family again, even if she never found Shane.

But she couldn't do it. She kept telling herself she needed to find him first. That way she could go home and make a clean start, without the need to hold anything against her parents.

The memories stirred dusty emotions in her soul, making her throat thick. She grabbed a water bottle from the half-full case on the nightstand next to her bed. There wasn't one thing she hadn't done to find Shane Galanter. She called high schools and eventually colleges. She searched out his last name, and three times she had help from one of her university professors, a man who specialized in investigative reporting.

"He must be living under his parents' corporation name," the guy finally concluded. "His parents could've called their California business just about anything. All the assets would be listed under that name."

The question she never asked, the thing that didn't make sense, was why Shane would do such a thing? Didn't he realize she couldn't find him if he lived that way? Of course, by changing *her* name she might've kept him away without meaning to. She'd done it to hide from her parents, not from Shane. Regardless, she kept looking. Every week she thought of something else, but each idea fizzled, turning up no sign of him. Sometimes she thought she'd go crazy looking. Back when every tall, dark-haired, Greek-looking man caused her heart to skip a beat. Back when she would race across a street and into a store or office building chasing after someone with Shane's build, his look.

"Excuse me," she'd shout at the man. "Are you —"

He'd turn and she'd be looking at a complete stranger — who clearly thought she was crazy.

"I'm . . . I'm sorry. I thought you were someone else."

It happened again and again. A different street, different store, different tall, dark man. Sometimes she got close enough to touch his arm or his shoulder before realizing it wasn't Shane.

"I'm sorry." She would back away, her face hot. "I thought you were someone else."

She didn't give up until the ten-year anniversary of Emily's death. On that day she took off Shane's ring and put it in a small, square cardboard jewelry box with the pictures she'd kept: one of the two of them, their arms around each other, and the other of Emily. Before she closed the lid she read the words on the ring, words Shane had engraved for her alone.

Even now.

They were still true that dark day. In some ways they always would be. She loved Shane, even now. Even when he was dead to her, when she had moved a million miles beyond the days of loving him.

As time wore on, she no longer lived under a different name. She *became* Lauren Gibbs. A single woman, alone in a world that had turned upside down overnight. If Shane had tried to find her, he wouldn't have had a clue to look for her under that name. No one would've. Even so, she didn't change her name back. She didn't want to be Lauren Anderson again. That Lauren had been trapped by her circumstances and forced into a series of actions that cost her the two people she loved most.

No, Lauren Anderson was as dead as her baby daughter.

Lauren sat up straighter and took a long swig of the water. It was room temperature, as usual. She swallowed some more and then lowered the bottle back to her lap. A wind had picked up outside, kicking dust into the atmosphere and dulling the blue morning sky. What were her parents doing these days? They would be nearing retirement age, probably traveling and talking about the old days. In the beginning they probably looked for her, but after awhile it would've become obvious that she didn't want to be found. Not then, and not now. Except . . .

Except once in a while, when a cool wind kicked up in the middle of December and she could still feel how it was, sitting around a Christmas tree with her parents and Shane's parents and Shane. She stared out the hotel window, but instead of the wind-beaten sky, she saw a scene from two decades ago, heard the laughter, felt the warmth of shared love.

What would happen if she went back now?

She blinked, and the memory swirled into nothingness, like dust in the desert wind. It didn't matter what would happen, because she couldn't go back. She didn't know the way if she wanted to. Her throat still hurt, and her eyes grew moist. She coughed. *Get a grip, Lauren.*

"Come on, Gibbs. You're tougher than this." She pressed her hands to her eyes and inhaled sharply. "A story's waiting."

She grabbed her backpack and double-checked to see that her lip balm was still inside. Then she snatched a bag of American lollipops from one of her dresser drawers. Lollipops were in high demand at orphanages. It gave her a way to connect with the kids. With that she was out the door and headed down the stairs.

Normally with a story pending, she could shake off any memories of the past. But today it wasn't so easy. Was it Christmas making things so difficult? Whatever it was, times like this she had to wonder which battle affected her more. The one that still raged in parts of Afghanistan.

Or the one deep in her heart.

Fifteen

Shane Galanter had been putting off the engagement party for nearly a month. But when Ellen suggested December 23, he knew he'd run out of excuses. Even the Top Gun flight school where he worked as an instructor was closed down that Friday and the following week. Fighter pilots needed a Christmas break, same as anyone.

Maybe even more so.

The engagement party was at the Marriott in Reno. Ellen had worked with his mother to pull it together. Eighty people in one of the hotel's smaller banquet rooms. Shane left his car with a valet and squinted up at the building. It wasn't true that it never rained in the desert states. That afternoon was fifty degrees with drizzle. Another reason he hated spending a Friday night in a room packed with people.

"Here, sir." A blond surfer kid handed him a claim check.

"Thanks." He stuffed it into his pocket

and faced the hotel entrance.

He wanted to marry Ellen. It wasn't that. But throwing a party to announce their engagement seemed a little outdated. He was thirty-six, after all, and Ellen was twenty-seven. People their age were supposed to have a quiet ceremony and get on with their lives.

He sucked in a quick breath and slipped his hands in his pocket. The party was more his mother's idea than anything. His parents loved Ellen, the way they hadn't loved any of his previous girlfriends. He maneuvered himself through the lobby to the bank of elevators. Not that he'd had many girlfriends.

None that ever really mattered until now.

Ellen Randolph, the daughter of Congressman Terry Randolph, was a Christian connected to the most powerful Republican circles in the country. Shane met her two years earlier at a congressional award dinner. He was receiving an honor for being one of the top fighter pilots in Operation Enduring Freedom. She was working for her father, and he noticed her a minute after entering the room.

Halfway through the night, Shane saw one of the veteran flight instructors talking with her and her father. The man was one of Shane's most respected mentors, so he made his way to the small cluster of people and managed to get an introduction.

He and Ellen had been inseparable ever since.

He stopped at the front desk and waited until one of the attendants looked his way. "Yes, I'm trying to find the Galanter banquet room."

The girl blushed as she looked at him. She was a heavy redhead with pale blue eyes. "The engagement party, right?"

Shane smiled. "That's the one."

"Let's see." She checked a list taped to the desk. "You're in the Hillside Room. It's on the tenth floor, right turn off the elevator." She batted her lashes at him. "You by yourself?"

He gave her a half grin. "I'm the guy getting married."

"Oh." Her cheeks darkened. "Lucky girl."

"I guess." He gave her a nod and headed for the elevator. It had taken him longer to get ready than he'd expected. He'd wrapped things up at the air base early that afternoon and made good time getting back to his home in La Costa. But he'd lost time after he got dressed. He was looking for a certain set of cuff links when he spotted the picture. Her picture.

The one Lauren gave him before he moved.

Seeing her face stopped him cold. He took hold of the photo and found his way to the recliner in the corner of his bedroom. For half an hour he held it, looking at her, studying the way her eyes seemed to look straight at him. He'd never really stopped looking for her. But over time it seemed ridiculous to keep trying so hard. He was through officer's training and naval flight school before his father sat him down and put it to him as kindly as he could. "Son, you need to let her go. She doesn't want to be found or you would've come across her by now."

"I'm not looking." His answer was quick, but it wasn't the truth.

"You are. All of life is out there waiting for you." His dad was sitting across from him in the apartment he was renting at the time. He leaned closer, his expression intense. "Somewhere out there is a woman who will love you and make you happy. If that woman was Lauren Anderson, you'd know."

He didn't want to admit it, but his father's argument made sense. He'd done everything but go door-to-door throughout all of Illinois looking for her. Still, he hated the lack of closure. The last thing he'd told Lauren Anderson was that he'd love her forever. No matter what. Nothing had happened to change that, except the obvious. She'd vanished from his life without a trace, without a single trail to follow.

And yet, here he was, on the night of his engagement party, staring at Lauren's picture and wondering what had happened. When his family first made the move, and it seemed only a matter of days before they could talk to each other, he had believed everything would work out after his senior year. But as months wore on without any way to contact her, he began to suspect his parents.

"You must know how to reach them," he'd say every few days. "Just tell me the number. It's my life. I have to live it the way I want to. And I want Lauren."

But his parents always denied having any of her family's information. "A few weeks separation was all we agreed to," his mother would tell him. "When Angela Anderson calls with their phone number, you'll be the first person to have it."

Shane shook off the memories and looked at his watch. The party was starting in five minutes, and Ellen had asked him to be there half an hour early. He stepped into the elevator and pushed the button for the tenth floor. Four floors up, the lift stopped and a family of three stepped inside. They wore bathing suits and had towels draped around their shoulders.

"Headed for the pool." The man raised one eyebrow as if to say it wasn't his idea.

"Sounds like fun."

"What about you?" The guy surveyed him. "Christmas shindig?"

"Engagement party." Shane leaned against the elevator wall. "Mine."

"Hey —" the man reached out and shook his hand — "congratulations."

"Thanks." He smiled at the guy. His wife was busy helping one of the kids with his shoes.

On the eighth floor the family got off. Shane watched them go, and a sudden stab of envy pierced him. He shook it off. What on earth did he have to be envious about? Just as the door was closing, a blonde woman walked past, headed in the same direction as the family. Probably another swimmer . . .

But Shane hesitated, staring. Almost without thinking, he hit the "door open" button. There was something familiar about her. Something he didn't quite understand — not until she looked over her shoulder.

Shane's breath screeched to a halt.

Lauren!

The girl was the mirror image of Lauren! He let go of the button, intending to step out, but the doors started to close. He slid his hand between them, stopping them. But by the time the doors opened again, she was gone. He checked his watch and frowned. This was crazy. He was already late. Still . . . He couldn't leave without knowing.

It was a long shot, but it was possible. Maybe she'd located him through his rank and file, or found him with the help of a private investigator. How many Shane Galanters could possibly live in the Reno, Nevada, area? Maybe she was staying at the hotel. His heart thudded hard against his chest as he darted off the elevator and jogged down the carpeted hallway. A fitness center and a spa were on opposite sides of the corridor. The pool was at the very end, and since she'd been wearing flip-flops he guessed that was the most likely place to find her.

He passed a few kids on his way, and when he reached the pool door, he flung it open. He hurried inside and scanned the deck area. It took seconds to spot her. She was sitting next to a small-framed older man, watching a couple of older teenage boys in the pool. Was one of them his son? The child he'd never met? Shane clearly wasn't dressed for the pool, and because he'd rushed into the deck area, he suddenly had everyone's attention.

Including hers.

Now that she was looking at him square on, he could see the obvious. It wasn't Lauren. He gave a sheepish nod in her direction, then backed away. He was on the elevator again in less than a minute, his heart still racing. What had he been *thinking?* His days of searching for Lauren were over. He had Ellen now. He wasn't supposed to still be seeing his childhood love behind the sunglasses of every blonde in Nevada.

But for a moment, he'd been overwhelmed by the idea that the woman *was* Lauren — and that could mean one of the teenage boys was his. His very own son. He made a fist and banged it twice against the elevator wall. *Insanity, Galanter. Pure insanity.* He gave up on the idea of having kids years ago. Somewhere out there he had a child, one that was probably being raised by a kind adoptive family. Hadn't he decided that was enough?

He caught his breath and let his arms fall back at his sides. Cold feet, that's all this was. He was marrying a lovely, intelligent girl, someone who would make a wonderful wife. She was articulate and excited about the politics he was passionate for. She didn't want children, either.

That suited him fine. Children would only remind him every day of what he could've had — should've had — with Lauren.

He stepped off the elevator, straightened his suit jacket, and followed the signs to the Hillside Room. Half the guests were already there, mingling around the perimeter of the room. Before he had time to look for her, Ellen was at his side. She wore a conservative blue floor-length evening gown, one that subtly emphasized her figure and complimented her eyes.

"Hi." She eased herself into his arms and smiled at him. Her expression was soft and sexy, her attention his completely. She brought her lips to his and kissed him. It was a kiss slow enough to stir him, but brief enough to keep up the polished look of propriety that was important to both of them. She pulled back a few inches and searched his gaze. Her tone was low and teasing. "Glad you could make it."

"Me too." He refused to think about the blonde at the pool. "You look wonderful. Sorry I'm late."

"It's okay." She flashed him a grin, stepped back and fell in beside him, her arm around his waist. "Come see your mother. She's looking for you."

They crossed the room to a bank of windows on the other side. The view from the tenth floor was stunning. Even under gray skies, the mountains that stretched along the horizon looked spectacular. His mother was by herself, leaning on a handrail and staring out at the view. Ellen kissed his cheek this time. "I'm going to greet some of the guests."

"Okay." He smiled at her as he turned toward his mom.

Her dress was simple and elegant. She looked ten years younger than her age as she glanced at him over her shoulder. He would've expected her to be bubbly and ecstatic that night. It was what she'd always wanted, that he'd marry a girl like Ellen. Instead her expression was shadowed with what looked like doubt and fear.

"Mom, you okay?" He hugged her, and then leaned on the railing next to her. He gave a low chuckle. "You're supposed to be

271

right there with Ellen, remember? The belles of the ball."

She set her chin and looked back out the window. "This is Ellen's party, not mine."

He hesitated. "Hey . . ." He slung his arm over her shoulders and gave her a light squeeze. Whatever was eating at her, it wasn't going away. "I was just kidding."

"I know." She sighed and stood a little straighter. "I'm sorry." Her eyes narrowed, but she kept her gaze straight ahead. "I can't get something out of my head."

"What?" Shane had no idea where she was headed with this. He removed his arm from her shoulders and turned just enough to see her face. His tone was still light. "Don't tell me you changed your mind about having an engagement party."

"No, Shane." She looked at him. "It's more serious than that." Lines webbed out from the corners of her eyes. More lines than usual. "I need to know something."

"Okay." He let the humor fade from the moment. "Shoot."

She looked around the room, as if she wanted to make sure only the two of them could hear what she was about to say. Then her eyes locked on his. "Are you *settling* for Ellen, son? I need to know."

A strange sensation worked its way

through his gut, something he couldn't identify. Lauren's face came to mind again, but only for an instant. He made a sound that was more exasperation than shock. "Of course not. What would make you ask that?"

She'd always been good at reading him. Whenever she looked deep into his soul, he knew better than to hide the truth from her. And she was looking at him that way now. "Shane, the last thing I want you to do is marry someone because you think your father and I like her. That's not the case, is it?"

"Mother." He raised a single eyebrow. "No offense, but you're giving yourself a lot of credit here." There was a small wall that went two feet up toward the window. Shane put his foot on the low sill and leaned toward his knee. "Ellen's perfect for me. Of course I'm not settling for her. I could've stayed single forever if I hadn't met her."

"Because of Lauren, you mean." Her eyes softened. "Right?"

Hearing her name brought the familiar ache. "Lauren's out of my life."

She watched him, studying him. "Don't lie to me, Shane. Please."

"Mom, listen to you!" Her words were

like a slap in the face. "I'm not lying."

"Shane, you loved that girl." She looked back at the view of the distant mountains. "I woke up this morning scared to death that you didn't wind up with her because of something we did. Something her parents did. I just don't want you to marry Ellen if you're still in love with Lauren."

He was about to refute her again, but he couldn't. He let the pretense fall from his eyes. "The truth is," his voice was low, "Lauren's gone forever. I've moved on. That's why I was able to fall in love with Ellen."

She frowned. "You're sure? I don't want you doing this if you're not sure."

"Mother." This time he laughed out loud. "This is ridiculous. Really." He reached for her hand. "Come, enjoy my engagement party with me."

They caught up with Ellen, and his mother stayed with his father and a few of their business associates. He and Ellen made the rounds, visiting with one cluster of their friends after another. Shane focused on matters at hand, refusing to give any real thought to his mother's concerns.

An hour into the party, Ellen's father stepped up to a podium at the center of the room. He tapped the microphone, and when he was satisfied with the sound level, he welcomed everyone.

"The occasion is certainly a wonderful one." He flashed a smile at the crowd, the smile that had earned him a large percentage of the votes in the most recent election. "I want to go on record saying I couldn't be happier about my daughter's choice for her future husband."

A polite round of applause followed.

Shane took hold of Ellen's hand and squeezed it.

Her father went on. "I think it's clear to everyone that Shane Galanter has political potential for the GOP." He found Ellen in the crowd and nodded at her. "I know my daughter thinks so."

Laughter bubbled up around the room.

"He might be a Top Gun instructor today, but the Nevada Senate needs someone like Shane, and one day not too far from now I can see him living in the governor's mansion."

This time a few hoots rippled through the crowd. Shane looked at his feet. What was Ellen's father doing? No one had ever said anything about a political rally. He clenched his jaw. The fact that Ellen's father viewed him as a bright spot on the Republican Party's future road map was clear enough. The point didn't need to be made here, as they announced their engagement.

Besides, Shane hadn't decided anything yet.

He was completely supportive of the party's platform, yes. But he enjoyed flying fighter jets, loved getting into the cockpit with a young gun and showing him the ropes. America relied heavily on her fighter pilots. Maybe teaching the next generation was enough of a contribution.

Her father was saying, "Please help me welcome Ellen and Shane." He stepped back and began the loudest applause yet.

Next to Shane, Ellen beamed. She tugged on his hand. "Come on."

"I'm with you." He took the lead, his head high as he nodded at friends along the way. When they reached the podium, he put his arm around Ellen and dismissed his concerns. This wasn't the time for doubts. He smiled big at the group before him. "Ellen and I will be getting married Saturday, May 20." He directed his grin at her, and then back to the audience. "We wanted you to be the first to know."

The group was warmed up now. They whistled and hollered and called for a toast. By then most of the people in attendance had glasses of champagne. Someone ran a few glasses up to Shane and Ellen, and at the same time her father returned to the microphone.

"To Shane and Ellen. May their influence and power grow even stronger because of their relationship, and may this be a season of love and laughter as they plan their wedding day."

Shane had thought driving over to the hotel that a prayer might be a good idea. He and Ellen both had a strong faith, and since they'd talked about getting even more serious about their relationships with God, the engagement party seemed a good place for a group of people to pray for them. But somehow in a room full of people sipping champagne and celebrating the possibility of another Republican hero in their midst, prayer didn't seem appropriate. Maybe later . . . Before everyone left. Maybe he'd close the night that way.

Ellen's father asked the crowd to return to their discussions and make sure they took a plate of food from the table at the back of the room. The next hour passed in a blur of conversations, nearly every one of which had to do with politics.

"Shane, you'd be perfect for the Senate," people told him time and again. "You'd have my vote, that's for sure."

Not until the party was over and he and Ellen were outside waiting for his car, did she turn to him and take playful hold of his jacket lapels. "What'd you think of Daddy's speech?"

Shane studied her. "His talk? The one he gave before he introduced us?"

"Yes." She bounced a few times, her voice giggly. "It was perfect, don't you think?"

He blinked. Was she saying what he thought she was saying? "What? It was set up?"

She squealed. "Of course it was set up, silly. Nothing a politician says is accidental."

For a moment he stared at her. Then he looked out at the lights along the ridge of mountains and uttered a single laugh. "Was *that* the point of the party?" His eyes found hers again. "A chance for your dad to introduce me as the newest political hopeful?"

Her expression fell and she settled back on her heels. "That's what you want, isn't it?"

"Maybe." He stared at her, then he paced a few steps away. When he turned to face her, his smile was a show of disbelief. "I mean, I haven't signed my campaign contract yet, have I?"

"Shane." Her voice held a reprimand. "Come back here. You're making a scene."

He closed the gap between them and spoke a few inches from her face. "We wouldn't want that, would we?" His tone was just short of rude. "What would your *father* think?"

"Listen." She pointed a finger at his chest. "That speech wasn't my father's idea. It was mine."

"Yours?" Shane wanted to laugh out loud. "You asked your dad to say that without talking to me?"

"I *have* talked to you." She lifted her chin, her composure back in place. "For two years I've talked to you. Every time it comes up you tell me it's your dream, running on the Republican ticket."

Anger rippled through his veins. "I'm excited about the party, that's why." He hissed the words. "And yeah, maybe I'd like to run some day." He crossed his arms. "That doesn't mean I need your dad making an announcement at my engagement party."

"He was trying to help." For the first time since the conversation began, she sounded hurt. "We both were."

Guilt washed over him. Why was he fighting with her? The talk was over, done.

279

What had it hurt that her father was proud of him? The man was as honest a politician as he'd ever known, a leader respected around the country for his values and integrity. Most men would've been thrilled with the sort of speech he'd given that night.

He sighed long and hard. "Ellen." He put his hands on her shoulders. "I'm sorry." He pulled her into a hug. "I guess it just took me by surprise."

She responded to his touch and melted against him. "It's okay." Her cheek pressed against his chest, then she lifted her eyes to him. "You do want it, don't you? A chance to run for office one day?"

The right answer was yes. But standing there in the dark, his arms around her, with the damp December air thick around them, he wasn't sure. "It sounds interesting," he whispered against her dark hair. "I'll have to think more seriously about it."

"Okay. That's all I'm asking." She gave him a squeeze and then stepped back. The valet was pulling up with his car. "I guess I always pictured myself married to a politician like my dad."

They fell silent as they climbed inside. It took half an hour to reach her place, and when he dropped her off he smiled. "Tell your dad thanks for tonight. I'm sure someday I'll be begging him to talk to groups on my behalf."

Her smile lit up her eyes. "You will, Shane. And who knows how far God will let you go with it."

They said good-bye, and Shane drove home. He kept the radio off. The quiet suited his mood better, with all the bits of conversations playing in his mind. Most important were the expectations Ellen and her father had for him. He knew all along they were there, but tonight they'd felt like a noose around his neck. As if his thoughts about the future no longer really mattered. He would be a politician because he stood for all the right things, and because his party needed him. After tonight how could he look at it any other way?

But other memories played in his mind as he pulled into his driveway. His mother and her sudden outpouring of guilt and doubt, for one. Most of the past two years she'd done nothing but gush about Ellen Randolph, the same way his father did.

"A girl like that will suit you well for a lifetime," his father had told him. "We couldn't be happier for you, son."

So what had happened that would make his mother doubt his decision to marry her? And how had she known exactly what had been messing with his mind all day long? He rubbed the back of his neck as he climbed out of his car and went inside. Every now and then, Ellen joined him at his house for a movie or a late dinner. They had agreed to save their physical intimacy for after they were married. Because of that, neither of them thought it was smart to spend too much time alone. Tonight he was glad for the privacy. His thoughts left him feeling like he'd been going Mach five for two hours straight. He went to his room, changed into a pair of sweats and a T-shirt, and dropped into his recliner.

Everything in him wanted to go to his dresser drawer and find Lauren's picture again, let her memory keep him company and help him sort through the strange events of the night. He closed his eyes. *Come on, Shane, get a grip. God, keep me focused.* Lauren Anderson was gone. He couldn't make one more decision with her in mind because she didn't exist. Period.

He willed himself to relax, to let his back muscles unwind against the chair. Something had been missing from the night, but he couldn't think of what it was. He tightened his grip on the chair arms, and then it hit him. He'd forgotten to pray. There they were, a couple of supposedly strong faith, and they'd done a toast — but not a prayer. He frowned and pinched the bridge of his nose with his thumb and forefinger. He didn't even like champagne.

Minutes passed and he still couldn't unwind. Maybe his first instinct had been a good one. He should've avoided an engagement party altogether. That way he wouldn't be thinking about giving up the career he maybe still loved and marrying a girl he maybe only liked.

And he certainly wouldn't be spending the day before Christmas Eve thinking about teenage sons and willowy blondes and the life he could've had. Would have had.

If only he'd found Lauren.

Sixteen

The defender saw Emily coming across the field and she raced toward the wall to stop the pass. She reacted with a quickness that surprised even her. Breathing hard, she drew the ball back, dribbled it through another two defenders, then powered it into the net just as the buzzer sounded.

It was her third score of the morning. A hat trick!

She congratulated her former high school teammates. "It might be the day before Christmas, but it's never a bad time for a game," one of them shouted as she waved. "Tell your grandparents thanks for coming out. They've always been our best fans."

Emily saluted the gang, threw a towel around the back of her neck, and grabbed her gear bag. Her grandparents had a full day lined up for them. Last-minute shopping and an early Christmas Eve service. Playing soccer on Christmas Eve morning was a last-minute plan, but it came to-gether just fine.

A group of girls she'd played with through high school were home for Christmas break. Since the current high school soccer team was always looking for a challenge, they put together a scrimmage at the indoor arena. Emily's squad included three college players. They beat the high schoolers, 8–2.

She found her grandparents sitting in the bleachers on the other side of the Plexiglas wall. "Well," she panted, "what did you think?"

Her grandpa was slow getting up. He looked pale and thinner than usual. Emily studied him. Or maybe it was only his new navy Christmas sweater making him look that way. His eyes sparkled in her direction. "I think I love watching you play." He walked toward her and held out his hand. "You're poetry in motion out there, sweetheart."

"Sorry it had to be on Christmas Eve." She fell in beside him, but glanced back at her grandma. "I know you have lots to do today."

"It's okay." Grandma caught up with them. "It makes me miss the days when you were in high school." She smiled at the

285

two of them. "We had four or five games a week."

"Special times, for sure." Her grandpa patted her shoulder. "I'm gonna hate it when you play your last game."

"That won't be for awhile." Her grandparents had been to all her home games that college season and a few on the road. "You still have three more years to put up with my schedule."

They fell into a comfortable quiet as they made their way to the car. Emily needed to shower, so she stayed home while her grandparents shopped. The afternoon flew by and the Christmas Eve service was beautiful. The pastor talked about looking for God's fingerprints.

"Miracles still happen today," he told them. "God in the flesh? The king of Kings lying in a humble manger?" He smiled at them and held his hands out. "What about you? A healed marriage? A healthy family? A job you love?" He paused, his voice expectant. "Every one of us has been witness to a whole host of miracles. But what will it be this Christmas? Lift that thing to God and let the Lord of all creation meet you near the manger. Let Him have a chance to work a miracle in your life once again."

The choir sang a haunting version of "O Holy Night." In the midst of it, Emily bowed her head and closed her eyes. *God, You know what I need, You know the miracle I'm asking for.*

Daughter, I'm with you.

The familiar peace ran through her veins, softening her heart and soul to the presence of the Holy Spirit. Martha, the pianist, was finishing the song and leading into another, the song they always finished with every Christmas Eve service, "Silent Night." Emily opened her eyes as she let the words fill her. Especially the last part. "Sleep in heavenly peace . . . sleep in heavenly peace."

Back at home, Emily and her grandparents sat around the Christmas tree and opened one present — their Christmas Eve tradition. Emily's gift was a new pair of pajamas, same as every Christmas Eve. She giggled and held them up. They were fuzzy and warm, perfect for the coming winter.

Her grandparents opened one gift from each other. Both packages held new pairs of socks. When they'd cleaned up the wrapping paper and exchanged hugs and conversation, Emily bid them good night. "I want lots of energy for tomorrow."

"Emily." Her grandma lifted her brow

and wagged a finger at her. "You won't be sleeping. You want to go through the box, right?"

She winced and gave a little nod. "Is that okay?" Emily couldn't wait to spend time alone with her mother's photos and year-books. She touched her grandma's elbow. "Maybe I'll find something we can look at tomorrow."

Her grandma's smile was genuine. "That'd be fine, honey. Take your time. Christmas morning can start as late as you'd like."

Before she went to bed, they stood near the tree and held hands. Her grandpa led them in prayer.

"This Christmas is a special one, God. We can all feel it. Please help us find the miracle near the manger this year. The one the pastor referred to." He hesitated, his voice thick. "I think we could really use one. We love you, Lord. In Christ's name."

Emily kissed them both and went up to her room. With the door shut behind her, she pulled the box close to her bed again, sat down on the edge, and began taking things from inside. The framed photo — the one she'd already seen — she set gently near the wall to make room for everything else in the box. Next was a photo album.

She picked it up and opened it on her lap. It smelled musty from being in the garage all those years.

"Wow, Mom." She ran her finger under each of the first photos, beneath which her mother had written a caption. "Look how much you cared."

The pictures started when her mom was in middle school. There were several shots of her with her girlfriends, and Emily studied her mother closely. If her mother's eyes were any indication, she was happy, popular with her friends.

Her light blonde hair hung straight and halfway down her back through most of those early years. Toward the center of the album, her hair got a little shorter, and a boy started appearing in the pictures with her. A smile tugged at Emily's lips. The boy was her father – he had to be. He had the same dark hair and eyes she saw every morning in the mirror. But he was skinny and about an inch shorter than her mother.

Even so, there was no denying how they felt about each other. It was palpable throughout the photo album. Even back then nothing could've kept them apart. "Look at you, Dad." She laid her hand on his picture. "The other guys are hanging out together somewhere, but there's you. Right next to Mom."

The captions grew even more precious toward the back of the book. There was a picture with her dad handing her mother a dandelion. Her mom had written, "Shane is the most romantic guy in eighth grade. Even if I am allergic to dandelions."

On the very last page, she found something that made her gasp. The entire sheet was a letter her dad wrote to her mom. Her mother must've hidden the letter there, because the page was stuck at the back, where most people might not look.

Dear Lauren, I don't think people are supposed to feel this way in eighth grade. All our friends are doing stupid stuff, having their friends ask a girl out for them. You know, that kind of thing. But I feel like I could marry you tomorrow. I'm not even kidding.

Emily put her fingers to her lips. "Dad . . . you were so smitten."

I don't know if I wanna graduate because that means going to high school. And high school means more people to deal with. All the senior guys will fall over each other to get to know you. Anyway, that's all right, 'cause I'm never going to leave you. Not ever. Love you, Lauren. Yours, Shane.

Yours, Shane?
Emily cooed. "You guys were so cute." Her parents were adorable as kids. How could this have been in the garage all those years when she would've given anything to know some of these details? She closed the album and set it aside. The next few items in the box were framed photographs. One showed her parents dressed in sports gear, only it looked like her mother was the football player and her father was a cheerleader. She squinted at the picture. Yes, a cheerleader with eye makeup.

Emily giggled, but she kept her voice hushed. The rest of the lights in the house were off now, and she didn't want to wake her grandparents. She looked at the picture again. What were her parents doing? She spotted something in the background. A carved pumpkin sitting on the porch. Of course, the outfits were costumes. Her parents had probably been invited to a Halloween party.

But even more noticeable than the uniforms was the now-familiar look in their

291

eyes. Like they were born to be together. She set the pictures aside and pulled out a journal. Her fingers trembled as she set the photo album down. It was time to read one of her journals. Emily took hold of the nearest one. She'd waited all of her life for whatever lay between the covers — the short stories and journal entries her grandma had mentioned — because then she'd have the answer she'd been looking for. The answer about whether her mother had a passion for writing, the way she did.

She held the journal, fingering the cover. These pages held an inside look at her mother's heart. Something she'd wanted for as far back as she could remember. Emily frowned, wishing she didn't feel so . . . guilty. Journals were private. She'd kept a little pink diary in second grade, then later on, a full-size journal. Page after page of stories and personal reflections and letters to the Lord. No one had ever read any of them.

Until now.

Emily bit her lip and balanced the journal on her lap, then she exhaled and opened the cover. As she did, her guilt faded. Of course she could read her mother's journals. They might well offer the only chance to get to know her.

The first entry was dated spring 1985.

Shane and I talked about love. Real love. We both think it's weird that our parents don't understand how we feel about each other. They act like we're a couple of kids who have no clue what love is. But here's what I've learned when I'm with Shane. Real love waits in the snow on your front porch so you can walk to school together in the fifth grade. It brings you a chocolate bar when you fall and finish last in the seventh grade Olympics.

Real love whispers something in the middle of algebra about your pink fingernail polish so that you don't forget how to smile when you're doing math, and it saves a seat for you in the lunchroom every Friday through high school. Even when the other baseball players think you're stupid. Real love has time to listen to your hopes and dreams when your parents are too busy with the PTA or the auxiliary club or the business they run at the local bank.

Real love stays up late on a Saturday making chocolate chip cookies together, flicking flour at you and getting

293

eggshells in the batter and making sure you'll remember that night the rest of your life. And real love thinks you're pretty even when your hair is pulled back in a ponytail and you don't stand perfectly straight. Real love is what I have with Shane. I just wanted to say so.

Emily blinked, suddenly aware of tears on her cheeks. She was overwhelmed with the enormity of the find. But more than that, she was struck breathless by her parents' feelings for each other. She wanted to read the entry again, but she was driven to turn the page, to capture another glimpse of her mother's life as a teenager.

What she found as she traveled the pages was a love that she hadn't known about before, a love between her parents that was both triumphant and tragic. Triumphant because it was the picture of how love was supposed to be: patient and kind, trusting and hopeful. Never mind their ages, her mom and dad had known about love. But tragic, because it hadn't lasted, because they'd lost each other, and as far as any of them knew, they'd never found each other again.

The last entries in her mother's journal

must've been written after her dad left for California. One in particular caught Emily's attention.

I'm so mad at my parents. I hate them. They told me they'd leave a forwarding message when they disconnected our old phone service. It should've told anyone who called the house what our new number was. That way Shane could reach me and then he could give me his number.

But now they're telling me the recording isn't working yet. The worst part is this feeling I have that my mom and dad lied to me. Maybe, because shouldn't it be working by now?

My baby's due in a few weeks and I'm convinced Shane's parents and my parents don't want us together anymore. The thing that makes me most afraid is that if they really do feel that way, I think they could keep us apart. How would I know where to get his phone number? How would he know where to get mine? I can only pray that somehow, someway he finds me soon. I can't stand being without him.

"Mom." It was as though Emily were sitting across from her mother. She looked out her window at the dark, snowy sky. "Did you ever find him again? Did Dad ever call you?"

She ached for the loss her parents suffered. For the first time she considered the possibility that maybe her grandparents had played some role in separating her parents. The idea seemed crazy, but why else wouldn't they help figure out the phone number situation in the weeks before her birth?

She looked at the clock and she felt a slow smile creep up her cheeks. It was after midnight, which meant it was Christmas. A quiet, silent Christmas morning, and already — even with the sadness of all her parents had lost — she could see one very obvious miracle in her mind, lying near the manger. The miracle of her parents' love, a love that shone as bright as the star of Bethlehem. And in the glow of that light, she begged God for an even bigger miracle.

That she would be used not only to find her parents, but to bring them back together again.

Seventeen

The meeting Angela had been dreading was about to take place.

She and Bill woke earlier than usual and made Emily her favorite breakfast: cinnamon French toast with scrambled eggs. She came down groggy and smiling, her pink padded slippers scuffling along the floor. "Hey." She gave Bill a hug first and then crossed the kitchen to hug Angela. "You guys are so sweet. Christmas never ends around here."

The words pierced Angela's heart. It would end soon enough. In about an hour, she guessed. Emily was chattering on about what a wonderful Christmas day it had been and how much she liked her new sweaters and her cute purse.

Her chatter was like music. If only they could hold on to that innocence, that joy.

"You were up late again." Angela studied Emily. "Are you finding what you wanted to know?"

"I am." She lowered her chin, her look a mix of gratitude and apology. "You can join me any time, Grandma. But thanks for letting me see it all first." Her eyes shone. "I feel like I actually know Mom now." Her smile faded some. "At least the way she was as a teenager."

"Yes." Angela's throat ached. This was too much. All the memories of Lauren, the terrible awareness of what was coming . . . She didn't want to cry, not yet. "Yes, your mother was quite something back then. Never rebellious or sarcastic, the way so many teenagers are today." She leaned over and kissed Emily's cheek. "She was a lot like you in that way."

"Well, I need a little background music." Bill stood and slipped his Mitch Miller CD back into the player. A few seconds passed, and then the sweet refrains of "White Christmas" filled the room. "I always say Christmas songs should play till January 1." He did a little soft-shoe shuffle on the living room carpet. Then he smiled at the two of them. "That's what I'm talking about."

Emily giggled and waltzed her way into the living room, where she took her grandpa's hand and let him twirl her between the sofa and the television. Their

298

voices mingled, a sound that was glorious, and not because either of them could sing on key. Angela watched them, mesmerized, fighting the sorrow struggling to overtake her.

Precious moments like this needed to be savored, because if the doctors were right their time together would end all too soon. But oh, if only they could go on this way another ten years. And how she wished Bill had danced like that with Lauren. What if he'd been more concerned with making memories than protecting her from Shane's parents?

Angela needed to flip the last batch of French toast, but she couldn't draw herself away from the picture they made. Bill and Emily, waltzing around the room, knocking into a bookcase and stepping on each others' toes. Their singing eventually dissolved to giggles, and before the song ended, they were doubled over, laughing hard at themselves.

They each worked their way to a standing position. With their arms around each others' shoulders, they danced back into the kitchen. Angela pointed to the cupboard, ignoring the way her stomach hurt. "We're ready for the plates."

Breakfast was more of the same, smiles

and laughter and shared memories of Christmases long past. All the while, Angela gave Bill anxious glances. If only they could avoid what was coming, if they could just continue to breeze through the day, enjoying the light of Emily's presence. But that just wasn't an option.

When the dishes were cleared, Angela made three cups of coffee, passed them out, and directed her attention to her granddaughter. "We need to talk, Emily." She looked at Bill. "Let's go sit in the living room."

Emily's expression was blank. She looked from Angela to Bill and back again. "Is something wrong?"

"Yes." It was time to get to the heart of the matter. "Something is wrong, honey." She led the way into the living room. "Come sit down."

Bill took his usual seat, the recliner closest to the television. His cheeks were still full of color from the dance and the laughter. Angela felt a surge of hope. He hadn't looked this well in months. Emily moved slowly, probably because she was caught off guard at the possibility that anything could be wrong.

Angela sat on one end of the tweed sofa and Emily took the other, fidgeting, her eyebrows knit together. All that athletic energy made her struggle with sitting still. That was always the case, but it was especially difficult when something serious was at hand.

"Okay." Emily's tone was a mix of hurt and fear. "So what's wrong? And how come you didn't say anything until now?"

"I'm going to let your papa tell you." Angela swallowed the lump in her throat. She folded her hands and bit her lip, unable to say another word without losing control.

Emily slid to the edge of the sofa, her eyes locked on Bill's. "What, Papa? Tell me."

"Well, honey." Bill coughed and his chin quivered. He shaded his eyes with his hands but only for a few seconds. "See . . . I have cancer." His eyes welled up, but he managed a sad, crooked sort of smile. "Doc says I've got about two months."

Emily was on her feet. The color drained from her face and she began to shake. "Two *months?*" She took a few steps in his direction, stopped, and took a step toward the front door. Another stop, and a step toward the sofa again. She looked like she wasn't sure if she should run out the door and scream or run to her grandpa and hold him tight. Finally she looked over her shoulder at Angela. "Two months? How long . . . how long have you known about this?"

"The doctors have been running tests for a few weeks." Angela blinked back the tears, but it didn't help. Her voice cracked all the same. "They told us the Thursday before you came home. It's all through his body, honey. It's very aggressive."

Emily went to Bill and stood near his chair, her hand on his shoulder. "But, Papa, you look so good. You —" she gestured toward the CD player — "you can sing and dance and laugh." Her eyes found Angela again. "Maybe there's been a mistake."

Angela understood the hope in her granddaughter's voice. Hadn't she felt the same way when the doctors told them the results of the tests? But like the doctors, she had to be honest. "There's no mistake. From the first test they told us this was possible."

Emily shook her head. "What about surgery? What about chemo or radiation or something. I mean —" she shot an anxious look at Angela — "we can't just take a death sentence and not fight it, right?"

"Honey, MRIs don't lie. We had the

tests read by three doctors. The reports came in Thursday and Friday, but we wanted to wait until after Christmas to tell you." Her eyes met her husband's. "That was your papa's wish."

He reached for Emily's hand, and she leaned down, hugging him even as the tears broke free. "No, Papa, no. I still need you."

His arms closed around her. "I still need you, too, honey."

That was all Angela could take. She covered her face with her hands and wept. And across the room she could hear Bill and Emily weeping too. From somewhere in the midst of her pain, Angela heard her granddaughter mumble something about God being in control, and miracles, and how quickly everything would have to come together now. And her sweet Bill was saying something about strength and prayer and feeling healthy enough to fight the cancer. Angela wasn't getting all of it, but she understood why. She couldn't hear it over the loudest sound of all.

The sound of her breaking heart.

It was some horrible nightmare. It had to be.

Even after she finished helping her

grandma with the dishes, and after her grandparents had gone to their room for an early nap, Emily still couldn't believe it.

Papa had cancer? Okay, he looked a little pale and maybe thinner than usual. But that could be a good thing, couldn't it? Maybe the doctors were wrong. Everyone's MRI couldn't possibly be the same. Maybe her grandpa had the sort of blood and bones that tricked machinery like the MRI. She went to her room, sat on her bed cross-legged, and tried to concentrate. Suppose the news was true and her grandpa had only a few months to live. If that was the case, she couldn't wait another day. She couldn't take her time sorting through the box her mother left behind.

They were in a race now. And time wasn't going to win.

The miracle she was praying for wasn't just to find her mom and eventually her dad, but to help her mom make peace with her grandparents. Which meant if it didn't happen in the next few months, it might not happen at all.

She pressed her hands against the sides of her head, shutting out everything but the problem at hand. The cardboard box sat near the end of her bed. It held hours and hours of fascinating, heart-wrenching mementos, but did it really hold any clues to finding her mother or father? It was still only the day after Christmas, so nothing official would be open yet, which meant she had no way to make phone calls that might offer a clue to her mother's whereabouts.

So be it. She'd use this day to get through the box. Just in case something vital lay hidden. She'd already gone through a third of the contents. Most of it she'd stacked along the far wall, out of the way so nothing would be bumped or kicked or stepped on. Now she lifted another photo album from the box and scanned it. She could come back and savor it later.

Two more smaller photo albums were next, and then she found another journal. Again she skimmed, though anything her mother had written had far more potential for holding a clue of some sort. Maybe mention of a favorite place where she and Lauren's dad wanted to live when they were older, or something she'd always wanted to do, a place where she wanted to work. Anything that would shine a light on a trail, no matter how narrow that trail might be.

"Come on, Mom, show me something."

More framed photos and a stack of yearbooks were next. It was all Emily could do to pass over them, to place them in another stack by her wall until later. But the minute she removed the last yearbook, she felt her mouth fall open. A slight gasp escaped her as she reached into the bottom of the carton.

Notebooks.

One after another. Emily's heart raced. These had to be the notebooks her grandma had told her about. The journals held no short stories, so maybe they were here in the notebooks. The ones her mother was always writing in.

A chill ran down Emily's back as she lifted the stack of them — maybe twenty in all — and placed them on her bed. They wouldn't be journals. Her mother seemed to like journaling in hardback books with lined paper and pretty covers. These were simple, ordinary spiral notebooks. She opened the first one and scanned the front page. Half of it was taken up by oversized handwritten letters that read:

The Greatest Walk
by Lauren Gibbs

Emily frowned and ran her thumb over

the words. It was indeed a short story, but who was Lauren Gibbs? If her mother wrote these stories, then why had she used a different last name? Whose last name was it, anyway? She let her eyes move down the page to the beginning of the story.

A sidewalk can be many things to many people. But for Rudy Johnson, in the summer of 1985, the sidewalk was his path to freedom . . .

Emily flipped the pages, one at a time. The story went on for half the notebook. She turned back to the beginning and studied the title page again. Lauren Gibbs? Had a cousin or a friend of her mother's written the story? Emily's eyes narrowed. The story was written by hand, so all she had to do was compare handwriting styles.

She jumped to her feet and grabbed one of her mother's journals from the floor. In a rush she opened the journal, laying it side by side with the notebook. She compared the printing styles, then the cursive. Both had *y*'s that dropped low on the line and *i*'s with tiny circles where the dot should be. It didn't take a detective to see that the writing was from the same person.

No question about it. Her mother wrote the short story.

So where did Lauren *Gibbs* come from?

Emily checked the back of the notebook for more stories, details, anything. It was empty, so she set it to the side and opened the second notebook. The title area on the first page read:

A Summer Sunset
by Lauren Gibbs

Emily's heart began to pound. Whatever it was with *Gibbs,* her mother hadn't merely pretended to be someone else for a single story. She sifted through the entire stack, checking the first page of each notebook. When she was finished, there were goose bumps on her arms.

Every single one was written by Lauren Gibbs.

She swallowed hard and straightened the stack. The name was worth asking about, at least. She was about to stand up and go find her grandparents when something else caught her attention. On the front of one of the notebooks, her mom had scribbled this:

Lauren Anderson loves Shane Galanter.

Only something looked different about it. Emily stared at the sentence for nearly three minutes before it finally hit her. She had always spelled her father's name *Galenter*. She'd never asked her grandparents, not when their conversations about the past were almost entirely taken up by questions about her mother. Somewhere along the years she must've seen her dad's name scribbled somewhere and assumed she was reading an *e* where an *a* should've been.

A fountain of possibility welled within her. She raced to her door, flung it open — and hesitated. It was just past three and the house was quiet. She tiptoed down the stairs and peeked into her grandparents' room. They were both on the bed, still sleeping. She could ask them about the spelling later. She zipped back up the stairs and went into the office, the room that used to belong to her mother.

She flicked on the computer, pulled out the chair, and sat down. "Hurry," she ordered it. "Warm up, already." Her eyes stayed glued to the screen while she massaged her calves. They were still sore from the soccer game the other day, a reminder that she needed to get out and jog. But she couldn't think clearly about anything —

not even breathing — until she at least ran a check.

She'd have to ask her grandma about the Lauren Gibbs thing. Maybe there was a family member who had that name, or a friend out in California. It was the best clue in the entire box, and even then it might be nothing. But her father's name? That was huge. Now that she knew the right spelling, she couldn't wait to Google it.

The computer was up and ready. Next she signed onto the Internet and waited. Her grandparents had a blazing fast connection, and she was online in seconds. She found the search line and took a deep breath. "Okay, here goes." Her father's name was familiar to her, because she'd typed it into a search engine hundreds of times, easily, before she finally gave up. But now . . .

Once more she typed in S-h-a-n-e G-a-l-e-n-t-e-r, just in cased she'd missed something all these years.

The results came up instantly and there in the top corner it said . . .

Her mouth hung open. How come she hadn't seen it before? At the top of the page it read, "Did you mean: *Shane Galanter?*"

She exhaled hard and exaggerated. "Yes.

I meant that, okay?" She clicked the link beneath the correct spelling of his name. Another list came up and Emily felt her heart in her throat. Somewhere in this list of possibilities might lie the information that would lead her to her father. She scanned the few lines of details for the first four websites. Shane Galanter wasn't exactly a common name, but still there were a few hundred entries. The first one was for a Shane Galanter, president of a pest control company.

"Pest control?" Emily wrinkled her nose. "You wouldn't be doing pest control, would you, Dad?" She clicked the link and a home page covered with spiders filled the screen. Once every few seconds a cockroach scurried across the page. Emily shuddered. Bugs were the worst. But where was a picture of this Shane Galanter who owned the company?

She scanned the page and near the top she saw a link that said "Contact Me."

"Okay, I will." She clicked the words and another page popped up. This one had the smiling face of a black man. Next to the photo it said, "Shane Galanter has what you need for pest control!"

Emily blew at a piece of her dark hair. "One down."

311

She hit the back button and returned to the list of websites. One was a playwright, with a photo of a white-haired man in his seventies. Emily returned to the list once more. "Two down."

The next Shane Galanter ran track at Azusa Pacific University. Just for fun, she clicked the link and found his picture. "Hmm." She raised an eyebrow at the online photo. "You're cute, but you're not my dad."

The fourth website had the words *Top Gun flight instructor* next to Shane Galanter. Emily angled her head. "Interesting . . ." She clicked the link, but this time there was no photograph. The page was a listing of personnel at a naval air base outside Reno, Nevada. She clicked the link and read a few paragraphs. In the late 1990s, the Top Gun fighter pilot training academy moved to Nevada, but it was still called Top Gun. Like the old 1980s movie.

Was her dad an instructor for fighter pilots? Her grandma had said he came from a wealthy family, a family involved in banking and investments. Papa said Shane's parents had plans for him to be a businessman. Most likely that's what he had become. She grabbed a pad of paper and scribbled down the information.

She went back to the list of search results again and found a few more possibilities. One Shane Galanter managed a grocery store in Utah, and another served as president of the Boys and Girls Club in Portland, Oregon. She wrote down the details for both, and for one more: a Shane Galanter selling insurance in Riverside, California.

"Perfect!" She stared at her list of details. "One in California!"

The hope inside her doubled. It was Sunday, and with so few Shane Galanters, she could start making phone calls in the morning. Her dad was thirty-six, just like her mom. And she could describe him over the phone or fax a photo if she had to. She looked out the window at the setting sun. Morning couldn't come fast enough.

From downstairs, she heard her grandparents up and moving around. She was on her feet instantly, racing out the room and headed for them. "Grandma! Papa!" Her stocking feet slipped and she nearly lost her balance as she rounded the corner into the kitchen. Adrenaline poured through her body, leaving her out of breath by the time she anchored herself at the kitchen counter and looked from one of them to the other. "I found something."

"You did?" Her grandma was putting a tray of leftover turkey into the oven. Even cold, the smell filled the kitchen. "What'd you find?"

Emily ran her tongue over her lips. Her throat was dry. She looked at her grandpa and then shifted her eyes to her grandma again. "What do you know about the name Lauren Gibbs?"

Her grandma frowned, and her grandpa's expression went slack. He spoke first. "Never heard of her."

Emily's hope leaked from her soul like air from a punctured tire. "Never?"

"Me neither." Her grandma pulled a serving fork from the drawer in the island and set it on the counter. "Where'd you see that, sweetheart? Was it something your mother wrote about?"

She pulled out one of the bar stools and sat down. "It was the name she wrote all her short stories under." Emily used her hands to show the size of the stack of note-books she'd looked through. "Mom had tons of short stories, Grandma." She looked at her grandpa. "Every one of them has a title and under that it says, 'By Lauren Gibbs.' "

"Lauren Gibbs?" Her grandma stopped

moving and wrinkled her nose. "Why in the world would she do that?"

"Wait a minute." At the other side of the kitchen, her grandpa leaned against the refrigerator and waved a finger in the air. He looked at the two of them, one at a time. "Angie, you remember that book Lauren read when she was, I don't know, maybe twelve or thirteen?"

Her grandma released a single baffled laugh. "Honey, I didn't keep track of the books Lauren read. Besides —" she took a stack of plates from the cupboard — "that was twenty-three years ago."

"I know, but I remember her telling me about it. At least . . . I think I do." He squeezed his eyes shut, as if he was trying to take himself back to that time, to remember every detail. When he blinked open, his eyes were brighter. "Yes, I remember exactly. It was one of her favorites. Every few nights she'd come find me and read a chapter out loud." He looked at his wife. "Remember? One of the characters in that book was Lauren Gibbs."

"Really?" Emily felt the thrill of discovery course through her again. She crossed the kitchen and pulled a series of salads and side dishes out of the fridge. There were six in all, and she set them on the counter opposite the oven.

"It doesn't sound even a little familiar." Her grandma slid the green bean casserole into the microwave. She wiped her hands on her apron and turned to her husband. "Did Lauren say something about it?"

"Yes." He punctuated the air in front of him. "I remember now. She told me she loved the name Lauren Gibbs. She liked something about the character, I guess. I remember her saying something about being that way when she grew up."

"So what was the book, Papa?" Emily went to him, her eyes wide as she searched his. "Maybe that'd give us another clue."

He squinted at nothing in particular and waited for several seconds. Then he shook his head and looked at her. "I can't remember."

Emily didn't care. At least it was something to go on. Then there was her father's name, the way it was supposed to be spelled. Over dinner she told them about the Shane Galanters detailed on the website.

"A flight instructor?" Her grandma set her fork down. "What was the other one?"

"An insurance guy from California."

"I'd put money on the insurance guy, if it's either of them." Papa looked tired. His words lacked the energy they'd held even half an hour earlier. "Samuel Galanter's son wouldn't have joined the navy. Not with the business plans that man had for his son."

"I'd have to agree." Her grandmother gave Emily a guarded smile. "But sweetheart, you need to be realistic. There's no reason Shane's name has to be on the Internet. You know that, right?"

"Yes." Emily looked at her nearly full plate. She was far too excited to think about eating. Her eyes found her grandma's again. "It's a long shot." She smiled. "But that's what a miracle is, right?"

"Right." Her grandma's expression softened. "I guess maybe it's time I believed in long shots too."

That night, after they'd watched a movie and talked a little bit more about her papa's cancer, Emily turned in early. She lay in her bed staring at the ceiling, willing the clock to speed past the hours so she could start checking out the Shane Galanters on her list. But that wasn't what filled her mind. She couldn't stop thinking about her mother and the book she'd told Papa about, and how she'd been crazy about the name Lauren Gibbs. Crazy enough to use it as her pen name for every one of her short stories.

"God —" she turned onto her side so she could see out the window — "there has to be something in that box besides a bunch of short stories, doesn't there? Can you help me find what I need? Please?" She thought about her grandpa and the battle that had just begun. "I don't have much time, Lord."

Usually when she talked to God, a peace filled her from the inside out. That was true this time, also, but there was something else. An urging grew within her . . . as if she'd stumbled onto something important.

Now all she had to figure out was what, exactly, it was.

Eighteen

The orphanage story turned out to be more than a sentimental feature.

On Lauren's first visit to the badly damaged building, where a hundred children were housed, she assumed the story was obvious. Capture a detailed look at the children orphaned by war, make it heartfelt, and get it in before her Friday deadline. The feature part of the story had gone as anticipated, and the staff at the New York office was thrilled with the piece.

"This story would make a right-winger do an about-face," her editor told her. "It's a five-hanky read for sure."

That would've been enough, especially combined with the amazing photo-essay Scanlon pulled together during their day with the children. But during lunch, one of the workers carrying a water pitcher came up and whispered something in her ear.

"Some of the babies are American."

Then the worker looked around, her eyes

darting about as if she could be in danger for what she'd just said. "They were fathered by American soldiers."

Lauren wanted to react, but she kept cool. She smiled and pointed to her sandwich and nodded, as if the woman's comment had something to do with the food on her plate. Then she whispered, "I'll meet you outside in five minutes."

The woman refilled Lauren's water, nodded, then moved on down the line. At the right time, Lauren excused herself from the table and found Scanlon. "I'll be right back."

"Where're you going?" He looked nervous. For the past eighteen months he'd taken on the unspoken role of bodyguard for her. She was an easy American target because of her pale blonde hair and her involvement in every facet of life in Afghanistan. Her editors had warned her about being alone, since Westerners were still often the focus of kidnappings for ransom or political favors.

"I'll be fine." She nodded to the courtyard outside the orphanage. "One of the workers needs to talk to me."

Scanlon arched a brow, then shifted from one foot to the other and adjusted his camera. "I'll be here if you need me."

"Okay." She squeezed his shoulder and gave him a quick grin. Then she worked her way through the main room, stopping to chat with three children. When she reached the door, she stretched and drew a deep breath. She looked around — no one seemed to be watching her. Once outside, she spotted the worker near a broken brick wall. The wind was howling, and the woman had a veil over her nose and mouth. She still had the water pitcher in her hand, and Lauren realized she was standing near a leaky tap. Lauren went to her, glancing over her shoulder to make sure they were alone.

"This big," the woman said in broken English. "Your people say Americans here help us." She nodded. "Some yes. Some no. Some sleep with our women and make babies." She pointed back to the orphanage. "American babies have no place here. No one wants them."

Lauren was horrified. Why hadn't the idea occurred to her before? There were thousands of U.S. soldiers in Afghanistan, most of them men. Of course some of them must be having their way with the local women. They probably figured it was one way to spend a weekend. No doubt some of the women were willing parties to that sort of carousing. But until now it hadn't occurred to her that those women might've gotten pregnant.

"Why not keep the babies?" She looked again at the doorway. No one was watching them.

The woman's eyes grew horrified and she shook her head. "No babies when no husband. Not okay."

Right. Women in Afghanistan might be out from beneath the veil, but there were still social codes they had to live by. Being single and pregnant was probably akin to leprosy in biblical times. Another gust of silty air blew across the courtyard, and Lauren shielded her face. When it passed she squinted at the woman. "How do they get their babies here? And what happens to the babies next?"

"There is more." The woman looked around and took a step closer. "I meet you here two weeks. Two weeks. Then I tell rest of story."

The two weeks had passed quickly. A flare-up of violence near the hill country took her and Scanlon away from the apartment for three days after Christmas. Twice they were close enough to the action that she wondered about her sanity. Journalists liked to think of themselves as invincible, mere spectators to the sport of war. But that wasn't true. Lauren was well aware that a number of reporters had lost their lives since the war began more than two years ago.

Now it was January 5, and she and Scanlon caught a ride back to the orphanage. So far she hadn't reported on the situation. She wanted all the details before she wrote it for the magazine. If it played out the way she thought it might, the story could wind up on the cover. American soldiers leaving a generation of orphans behind? It'd be the top story for a month.

The road to the orphanage was dotted with potholes, and she and Scanlon bounced along in the backseat. It was another sunny day, dry and windy the way it had been for the past month. The air was cooler than last time she and Scanlon made the trip out, but not by much. The two of them still wore shorts and tank tops. Next to her, Scanlon looked out the window and exhaled hard. "I have a funny feeling about this story."

"Me too." She picked up her worn shoulder bag and sifted through it. For stories like this she needed more than paper. She had a tape recorder and a supply of fresh tapes and batteries. She looked at

Scanlon. "I have the feeling it'll be the biggest story to come out of Afghanistan in a year."

He shook his head and narrowed his eyes, seeing past her into the barren hillsides beyond the narrow roadway. "Not that sort of feeling." His eyes found hers. "Why couldn't she give you the story when you were there the first time?" He nodded toward the road ahead. "We have to get another driver, make the hour-long trip a second time." He paused and looked at the road ahead of them. "Seems weird to me."

"Scanlon, you worry too much." Lauren scrounged in her bag again and pulled out a bottle of sunscreen. A pair of flies was buzzing around the back window and she waved them off. "The woman was scared to death. Another five minutes with me and she would've fainted from fear."

"Okay." He put his arm up along the back of the seat and leaned against the door. "I still feel funny."

"Well you can feel funny all day long." She patted his knee. "Just get pictures of those fair-skinned babies in the back room."

"Did you see them? I mean, do you know where they are?"

"Of course not." She rubbed lotion onto

her right leg and worked it down to her ankle. "That's part of why we're going back. The woman has more information, and then I'm going to convince her to let me have a look."

"Good luck." His eyes danced and he shook his head. "The woman's scared to talk to you and you think she'll give you a tour of the back room?" He nodded. "If we get that far, don't worry. I'll get a hundred pictures." His smile faded. "Just be careful, Lauren."

"Always." They didn't talk for the rest of the ride. Lauren could hardly wait to get inside, not just to talk with the worker, but because she wanted to see the children. She had several favorites already, kids who had bonded with her the last time she was there. Her bag held another supply of lollipops. If Scanlon didn't mind, she'd stay into the afternoon visiting with them.

When they pulled into the long driveway that led to the isolated building, they paid their driver and climbed out. He had nowhere to go, he told them. No other jobs. He pulled his car next to a scraggly tree and rolled down the windows. "I ready when you are."

"Thank you." Lauren smiled at him and tapped her watch. "Could be many hours."

"Okay." He put his hands together and held them along the side of his face. "I sleep here."

"Good." Lauren nodded at him, and she and Scanlon headed inside. The kids were playing in the courtyard and scattered throughout the main room. If today was like the other day, they would have lunch in fifteen minutes or so.

They were inside for less than a minute when a man approached them. He hadn't been around the other day. "Hello, I'm Feni." His accent was slight, his English strong. "You're here to do a story on our orphans, yes?"

"Yes." Lauren stepped forward. She wasn't about to tell him that she had a private meeting with one of the workers. "People want to know about the children, how the war has hurt them."

"Very good." He smiled. "I am the director of the orphanage. You may find me in the office if you have something to know." He turned his hand palm up and spread it out toward the children on the floor. "Our children are very kind, very hopeful. Please . . . let me know if you need anything."

A gust of wind shook the windows. Lauren held her hand out to Feni. "Thank you. I'll come find you if we have questions."

The man nodded at Scanlon, turned, and walked back to the office. As he left, a chill passed over Lauren's arms. "Why wasn't he here last time?"

"I told you." Scanlon moved closer to her so their arms were touching. "I have a funny feeling about this. Remember what the army's media man told us. Never make an appointment with a local, unless it's in plain sight of everyone. Even then we're supposed to watch our backs."

"Right." She wiped her palms on her shorts and ordered herself not to feel frightened. "This is different, though. The woman was a worker, Scanlon." She gave him a confident look. "Really."

At that moment, a little girl came running up. She had hair halfway down her back, and Lauren recognized her from the other day. She'd been something of a shadow around Lauren through most of her last visit. The girl was adorable, not much older than seven, with one of her front teeth missing.

The girl stopped a foot from her and did a little bow. "Hello, Miss."

"Hello." Lauren smiled at her, looking into her eyes. She held out her hand and the girl took it, squeezing her fingers. "Senia, right?"

"Yes." The girl's eyes danced.

"How are you, Senia?" Lauren kept her smile in place, but felt the grief rise again in her heart. She had missed so much by losing Emily. So very much. But the grief was for more than the loss of her daughter. It was also because her job made it impossible to even consider adopting a girl like Senia.

The child was grinning bigger than before. "I fine." She peered into Lauren's bag. Then she lifted her eyebrows halfway up her forehead. "Sweets, Miss? Sweets, please?" She held out her hand. "Please, Miss."

The children knew very little English, but they took pride in using it. They could've spoken their native tongue, and Lauren would've understood it. Especially in the simple words and phrases the children used. But clearly they wanted to impress her, and so for the most part they spoke English.

Lauren smiled at the girl. "Okay." She pointed to the table already set with lunch plates. "After lunch."

The girl looked at the table and immediately she understood. She nodded and her eyes got shy. "Miss, you pretty."

Next to her, Scanlon had his camera out. He was snapping pictures of the girl, her earnest expression, the way she looked up with adoring eyes at the Americans. "You brought your playing cards, right?" He gave her a light nudge with his knee. "Get 'em out and sit on the floor. You'll be surrounded before you can shuffle the deck."

It was a good idea.

Lauren opened her bag and took out her pack of cards. Then she held them up so the little girl could see them, and she dropped slowly to the floor. "See," she told the girl. "We play a game."

Scanlon stepped back and sure enough, a dozen kids were seated around her in no time, all of them with eyebrows raised at the cards in Lauren's hands. She gave the first boy on her right a four of clubs. "Four," she told him. Then she held up four fingers and counted them down. "One, two, three, four."

A light dawned in the boy's eyes. He bounced a little and took the card, rattling off something about numbers and a game to the girl next to him. The other children held out their hands and waited as she gave each of them a card and explained what it meant. They were still holding their cards when the workers filed out of the kitchen and into the dining area.

"Here —" Lauren held out the card box and slipped the rest of the cards inside. The kids followed her example. "Later." She winked at Senia. "When we have sweets."

The kids spotted the lunch servers, and they jumped to their feet, scrambling to their places at the table.

"Where's the informant?" Scanlon kept his voice low so only she could hear it.

Lauren searched the faces of the women. "She's not there."

"See." The workers walked slowly toward the lunch table. "Something funny's going on."

The lunch women spotted Lauren and Scanlon, and they smiled and waved. There were six long tables squeezed into the room, and each seated twenty children. Lauren was amazed at how quickly the workers slapped sandwiches on the table and poured water for the children. She stopped a few feet away, while Scanlon switched discs in his digital camera.

All along Lauren figured this was the time when she'd meet the woman. They'd spoken during lunch before and they'd been uninterrupted because the kids were preoccupied. But where was she? And was it just Scanlon making her nervous, or did she feel the same thing he did? An uneasiness that somehow, something about the meeting wasn't right?

Feni, the man in the office, stepped out during lunch and watched the children for a minute or two. Then he looked in her direction and gave a little wave. She did the same, and he disappeared back into the room. She looked past him and saw a desk and a phone, not much else.

"That Feni guy makes me nervous." Scanlon had his camera open. He was checking one of the settings. "He seems shady."

Lauren bit her lip. "Maybe he doesn't like Americans hanging out at his orphanage."

"Maybe."

The children were just finishing lunch, and Scanlon was saying something about the workers, how they seemed distracted, when Lauren caught the glimpse of a woman walking across the courtyard toward the front door. She held her breath; it was her informant. She stood in the doorway, and their eyes locked.

"Hey." Lauren leaned close to Scanlon, a smile playing on her lips so she wouldn't catch the attention of any of the adults in the room. "She's here. I'll be right back."

"I'll come too." He slipped his camera into his bag and started in beside her.

"No." She gave him a look that left no room for negotiation. "She wanted me by myself."

He pursed his lips and made a frustrated sound. "All right." He looked around her toward the front door. "Don't go far."

"I won't."

This time as she left the building, she could hear the children calling after her. She looked back over her shoulder and saw Scanlon running interference, gathering them and telling them that she would be right back inside. Lauren picked up her pace.

They didn't have much time. She stepped into the courtyard and was met by yet another gust of gritty wind. Shading her eyes, she looked around, but the woman wasn't there. "Hello?" She took another ten steps and scanned the yard. There were several nooks and small areas near half-standing walls, but the woman was nowhere.

Unease slithered up her spine, and she half-expected to see Feni step out from behind one of the broken walls. She owned a gun, but she didn't carry it with her. If Feni had something planned, she couldn't offer much resistance. She was about to turn around and go back inside, when she heard the sound of children's voices behind her.

"Miss!" It was Senia, leading another little girl and two boys out into the courtyard. "Miss, sweets? Please?"

Lauren was about to tell them no, that the sweets had to be eaten inside and that they needed to go back and wait for her, when an explosion of bullets rang out across the patio. In a blur that took a fraction of a second, she turned toward the sound and saw three figures cloaked in black, each with a machine gun aimed in their direction.

"Stop!" She held out her hand toward them, then spun to look at the children. Two of the kids lay spread out on the ground, their white shirts spattered with blood, a dark pool fanning out beneath them. *"No!"* She was about to run toward them when another round of bullets rang through the air.

A burning sensation ripped through her shoulder and knocked her onto the hot cement. She'd been hit, and even though she kicked her legs and tried to find her way to a sitting position, she couldn't do it, couldn't move. All at once a series of voices began shouting at each other, and she looked toward the desert sand at the place where the gunmen were still standing. They waved their guns and started toward her, and she understood. She was the one they wanted. In the blur of pain and confusion she realized what was happening. Scanlon was right. It was a setup. The story probably held no more truth than half the other crazy lures that had been tossed her way.

Usually she was smart enough to avoid meeting with unnamed informants who promised a shocking truth. But this time it had involved kids . . . babies. She felt herself losing consciousness and she fought to keep her eyes open. The men were coming closer, and she wanted to scream. But that would only make them open fire on her. Instead she lay unmoving. Maybe they would think they'd killed her.

And maybe they had. Her shoulder was on fire, and she felt something warm and wet beneath her. Spots danced before her eyes, and she willed herself not to let go, not to give into the darkness that pulled at her. *No,* she ordered herself. *Not yet!* The children needed her. They were hit, two of them, right?

She inched herself backward, toward them. But as she did, Feni ran out from behind a door across the courtyard, and in a rush of bullets, he shot and laid out the first of the three gunmen. At the same time, bullets came from a window in the orphanage and before the gunmen could react, all three were on the ground.

Feni ran closer and sprayed another round of bullets at them. When he seemed sure they weren't going to move again, he raced to her. She heard Scanlon's voice from behind her at the same time.

"Lauren!" He was at her side, turning her over. "We have to get help." He looked at Feni, who was just reaching them. "Call for help, please!"

She moved her good arm and took hold of Scanlon's ankle. "The children . . ."

"The women are helping them." He gulped. His face was pale and lined with worry. "Don't move, Lauren. Help's coming."

"It's . . . just my shoulder." She winced. Her words were sticking together, and she felt faint again. "I'm . . . okay."

A woman ran up to them with a roll of bandaging. She handed it to Scanlon and he worked fast, pressing it hard against her upper arm. The pain was like white-hot lightning hitting her again and again. It roused her up and brought her back to the moment.

"We need to stop the bleeding."

"The children, Scanlon." She waited until he had her shoulder wrapped tight, then she sat up. Nausea built in her, but she shook it off. Scanlon tried to stop her, but she jerked away from him. Crawling on her knees, she covered the three feet that separated her from the cluster of women. "Please! Let me . . . let me see."

"Move, please," Scanlon took the lead and helped clear a path to the kids at the center of the circle.

Lauren pushed her way closer until she could see them clearly. One of them was a little boy, moaning and moving his head from side to side. He lay on the ground and Lauren looked at the place where the women were working. The child's kneecap had been blown off his leg.

She brought the back of her hand to her mouth, but she stopped herself from getting sick. What about the other child? Two women were kneeling beside her and only then did Lauren notice that they were weeping. Weeping and wailing and stroking the child's hair. Lauren still couldn't quite make her out, so she crept a little closer and then . . .

"No! No, not her!" The words that came from her were almost silent, spoken with what remained of her strength. Senia, the little girl with the missing front tooth. "Oh, please!"

Scanlon dropped down beside her. "Lauren, come on. They're taking care of her."

One of the women let her head drop back. She clenched her fists and shook them at the sky. "Why? Why her?"

Lauren reached out, but she had no more strength, no way to reach the little girl. "Scanlon, is she dead? Tell me if she's dead."

"Lauren —" he put his hand on her shoulder — "let's move. They need room to work."

The wailing from the women grew louder, and others joined them. The only woman missing was the informant, the one who must've gotten away once the shooting began. The one who had set her up. She looked up one last time. The little girl's eyes were open and unblinking. One of the weeping women near her shut first one of Senia's lids, then the other.

Scanlon brought his head close to hers.

"She's gone, Lauren. Let it go. Come on."

She wanted to run to the child and hold her in her arms. They hadn't had time for sweets. That's all the girl wanted. A lollipop. A lollipop and a chance to hold her hand the way she'd done the last time Lauren was there. The spots were back, and she let her forehead rest on the ground. It wasn't too late, was it? The sweets were still in her bag. Maybe if she found one she could give it to Senia and everything would be —

The spots connected, and Lauren felt herself falling, as if she were being dropped from a thirty-story building and there was no way to stop. Something warm and salty was coming from her mouth, but she couldn't move her head, couldn't open her eyes. *Help me* . . . But the words died long before they reached her lips.

She felt the heat from the patio radiating through her arms and legs, and then a dizzying sensation. She was dying. She must've been shot in the chest, not the shoulder. Her heart was spilling out everything within it, the ocean of sorrow, the desire to bring peace to these people, and her will to live. All of it was leaving her.

"Lauren, stay with me!" Scanlon sounded a hundred miles away. His voice was tinny and distant, and she couldn't figure out where it was coming from. He was saying something else, but his voice faded more and more.

And then there was nothing.

Nothing but hot, burning pain, utter sorrow, and darkness.

Nineteen

Shane was finishing up a final briefing with a student fighter pilot. The guy was twenty-four, educated, and had a promising future at the Top Gun academy. He'd been through enough training that he knew what he was doing. But this would be his first solo flight, and Shane couldn't leave anything to chance.

Shane held a checklist in his hands. "Bail-out procedure."

"Bail out." The young man's words were clear and clipped. He stood at attention throughout the short examination, his flight suit perfect, his helmet tucked beneath his arm. Then, as Shane took notes, the guy rattled off a perfect description of the circumstances and situations when a bail out was necessary, and followed it up with a detailed account of the procedure.

"Good." Shane placed a check next to the words *bail out* on the form. They went through three more terms, and then Shane looked at the pilot. "You ready?"

"Sir, yes, sir."

"Okay, call sign Doogie." Shane grinned. "Let's see you fly." He shook the pilot's hand, spun around, and headed for the tower. For the next half hour he was in constant communication with the pilot as he practiced routine flight maneuvers. Finally — right on time — he requested permission to land.

"Roger that, Doogie. Bring 'er in." Another instructor was watching from over Shane's shoulder. Shane held up his hand and the two gave each other a high five. He pressed the radio button one more time. "I can see why they recommended you for Top Gun, Doogie. You're gonna be a good one."

"Thank you, sir."

Shane had some more paperwork and another fifteen minutes with the pilot. Then it was time for lunch. He strutted across the flight deck and wiped the sweat off his brow. The cloudiness of a few weeks ago was gone, and the sun was hotter than usual for January.

He went to the cafeteria, bought himself a chicken Caesar salad, and took a table by himself on the outdoor patio, the one that overlooked the runway. It was loud outside, but Shane didn't mind. Every landing and takeoff still shot adrenaline through him, and made him long to be in the cockpit. He bowed his head and thanked the Lord for his food.

Then he adjusted his sunglasses and stared into the vast blue. There was nothing like taking an F–15 out over Nevada and looping up across New Mexico and down along the coast of California all in less than thirty minutes. That kind of power never left a guy. He leaned forward and anchored his elbows on the glass-top table.

What was it about flying lately? His job as flight instructor had always been rewarding, but these days he couldn't wait to come in and work with the young pilots. Part of his job was to stay adept at the cockpit himself, but since his engagement party he'd been putting in twice the required hours in the sky. As if he couldn't get enough sky time.

He was about to take another bite of his salad when he felt his phone vibrating in his pants pocket. With the noise on the flight deck he'd miss every call if he didn't have it set to vibrate. He pulled the phone out and squinted at the small Caller ID window. Ellen. He waited for the surge of excitement to hit him, but it never came.

He tapped the receive button. "Hey, how's my girl?" He set his fork down and pushed his chair back, giving himself room to cross one of his ankles over his knee.

"Hi." She was talking loud, and he heard a chorus of voices in the background. "I'm in D.C., and you won't believe it!"

D.C.? Had he known she was going there? He massaged his brow with his fingertips. "You're in D.C.?"

She did a frustrated breath. "Yes, Shane. I told you Wednesday I was coming to D.C. for the weekend." Her tone lightened some. "Daddy had some friends he wanted me to meet."

"Oh." Shane let his hands drop back to his lap. He had no memory of her telling him about the trip. Not that it mattered. She flew to Washington, D.C., at least once a month. He removed his sunglasses and checked them for scratches. There were none. "Okay, what's up?"

"I took the red-eye, so I got here in time for some meetings." Excitement made her voice shrill. "A lot of the big guys from the party were here, and Daddy put in a plug for you."

"He did?" Shane slipped the glasses on again and watched a pair of F–16s coming in for a landing. He released a single laugh,

343

but it didn't sound amused, even to him. "I thought we talked about this, Ellen. I'm not running for office."

"I know, but that doesn't matter." She was undaunted, her voice louder still. "Sorry about the noise. The meeting just broke up. Daddy explained it to the group. He told them that by the time you were on a ballot, he wanted everyone to know who you were."

A small thrill ran through Shane. "Everyone?"

"Yes." She paused for effect. "Even the president, Shane. The whole party's excited."

"That's amazing." He tried to imagine Ellen's father getting the big hitters in the Republican Party excited about his future son-in-law. It was a heady picture. "Tell him thanks for me."

"He wants you to come with me next month. Everyone wants to get to know you."

"Sounds good." Another plane was taking off from a different runway. Shane imagined himself behind the controls. He blinked and gripped the arms of his chair. "I'll have to see about getting off."

Ellen giggled. "If the president of the United States wants to meet you, I think the navy might be willing to give you a few days."

"True." He squirmed in his seat and uncrossed his legs. "Hey, listen. Lunch is almost over, I better go."

"Okay, me too." She made a squealing sound. "I'm so excited for you, Shane. For both of us."

"Right. Thanks. Tell your dad I said hi."

The conversation was over before Shane realized that he hadn't told her he loved her. Of course, they didn't say it all the time — mostly only when they were alone or kissing good-bye after an evening together. Even then it felt almost businesslike. He slipped his phone back into his uniform pocket.

If he really wanted to be a politician, if he wanted the chance to represent the people on the Republican ticket, he should've felt like flying across the flight deck without any plane at all. This was the chance most aspiring political leaders only dreamed about. Perfect connections, a groundswell of favorable opinion, the support of leaders — all the way to the president.

Shane picked up his fork and took another bite of his salad. He *should* be excited. He and Ellen had talked more about the idea in the days since the engagement party, and he had to admit the possibility was enticing. The country was ready for someone with his moral fiber, she'd told him. Everyone was saying so.

He poked at his salad. The lettuce had wilted during his phone call, but he was too hungry to care. He chewed another bite and thought about the plan he and Ellen had devised. He would work another year as flight instructor, through the days of their May wedding and their honeymoon to Jamaica. Then as the year drew to a close, he would line himself up for position on a ballot. His parents and Ellen's father would bankroll them for the next year while he built a following in Nevada.

"After that," her father told him the last time they were together, "there'll be no stopping you, my boy."

It sounded wonderful. Who wouldn't be excited about that sort of plan? Still . . . Shane stared into the blue. None of it felt like his plan. Before meeting Ellen, he'd been content to be an instructor at Top Gun. No, not content. That wasn't how he felt. He was living his dream. Yes, the idea of running on the Republican ticket sounded good, but not nearly as good as teaching young guys to be hotshot fighter pilots.

A warm breeze blew over him. *God, everything is happening so fast. I feel like I've lost me.*

He waited for some kind of response, a sign of God's guidance. But today there was nothing like that, no sense of understanding, no quiet inner whispers of reassurance. Shane watched yet another jet leave the runway and lift into the sky above Reno.

Okay, God, I know You're there. Even when I don't feel You. Give me wisdom, please. Just a little wisdom to help me know what to do next.

Still no answer resonated within him. He returned to his salad and suddenly, as it had done every day since his engagement party, Lauren Anderson's face came to mind. He had prayed about that too. He was getting married. It was time to let Lauren go forever. He looked at his salad, and her image faded. The chicken was lukewarm, but it tasted all right. As he ate he thought about his prayer. Wisdom was exactly what he needed. Direction about what to do next, something that would help him understand why he was uncertain about a future that only a few months ago had felt bright and exciting. Yes, wisdom was exactly what he needed.

So he didn't make a decision he'd spend a lifetime regretting.

Twenty

Emily was pretty sure her father was an instructor at the navy's Top Gun training facility. The problem was, she couldn't prove it. She had his birth date, his physical description, and his name. But three times she'd contacted the academy, and all three times she'd come away with no information. The last time she'd called was Friday, two days ago, and her conversation was particularly frustrating.

"Hi." She tried to make herself sound older than her eighteen years. "I'm doing a story on your flight instruction program." She held her breath.

"You'll have to talk to the public information office, ma'am." The guy connected her call to the right department.

Emily didn't mind. This had happened each of the other two times she'd called. She waited until someone picked up the call. "Media relations, Private Walton here."

"Yes, hello." She paused, so she wouldn't seem desperate. "I'm a freelance writer working on a feature story about flight instructors."

"How can I help you?" The woman was pleasant, but her tone said she was in a hurry.

"Actually, I'd like to set up an interview with one specific flight instructor. Shane Galanter."

"Officer Galanter's a busy man. Maybe I can fax you over a list of frequently asked questions and their answers."

"I already have that." She gave a polite laugh. "It's important for the story that I have a chance to meet face-to-face with one of the pilots. I've researched the instructors, and I'd really like to interview Officer Galanter."

"Tell you what, why don't you fax me a list of questions, and I'll see if Officer Galanter can get the answers to you sometime next week." She sounded suddenly distracted. "Anything else?"

"You know," Emily could feel the call slipping away, "maybe you could help me figure something out. I've met Officer Galanter one other time, and I want to make sure we're talking about the same man. He has dark hair, dark eyes, and he's tall, right? Thirty-six years old?"

The woman hesitated. "Ma'am, we do not give out that type of information on our flight instructors, or on anyone else. I'm afraid I can't help you with this particular story." She hung up before Emily could say another word.

Now it was Sunday afternoon, and her frustration was growing by the hour. She'd called the insurance company in Riverside, California. It hadn't taken five minutes to figure out that the fifty-eight-year-old redhead who ran the office wasn't the Shane Galanter she was looking for. The others had been easy to rule out also, so that left two choices. Either her father was an instructor at the Top Gun school, or he wasn't listed anywhere on the Internet.

She sat on her bed surrounded by her mother's journals and short-story notebooks. Her grandparents were at the store, but they wouldn't be gone long. Her grandpa had very little energy these days, and he looked far worse than he had at Christmastime.

"I don't understand," she told her grandma one day the week before. "I never knew cancer could be fast like this."

"It is sometimes." Her grandma was teary-eyed again. She dabbed at her cheek.

"He doesn't have long, Emily. We're both so glad you can be home."

Emily shuddered at the memory. Thank heaven she didn't have to be back to school until the sixth of February. Some of the kids took short, one-unit classes in January, but Emily decided to stay home. Her grandparents needed her. Besides, she had to find her parents. Absolutely *had* to find them. Her grandpa's quick deterioration told her that much. First thing Monday she was going to do what she should've done a week ago. She would call the Top Gun academy and leave a straightforward message. *Please have Shane Galanter contact Emily Anderson in Wheaton, Illinois.* Then she would give her phone number and keep praying.

With that decided she stared at her mother's notebooks and journals, scattered on the bed around her, and willed herself to see something she had missed. She opened one of the journals and read several entries. Each one was another window to the girl her mother had been. But none of them had anything she could go on, nothing that would lead her to wherever her mother was living now. She stood and went to the window. A foot of snow covered the ground, and all of life looked the way the search for her mother felt: freezing and dormant. "God . . ." She looked into the thick gray sky and tried to imagine the Lord looking down on her. "You know where she is. So show me how to find her, okay? I'm running out of time, Lord. Please . . ."

She was quiet, her nose against the cold glass window. Then, in the smallest inner voice, a Scripture began to play in her mind.

I am the Alpha and the Omega, the Beginning and the End . . . I am that I am.

The verse was from Revelation, and it righted her world in a heartbeat. God was everything. He was Lord and Savior, Alpha and Omega. What did she have to worry about? A sense of awe came over her. God had more names than she could imagine, more names than —

Like a bolt of lightning, it hit her.

What if her mother had used more than one name too? Everyone assumed she'd changed her name, otherwise the private investigators hired by her grandparents would've found something by now. She darted back to her bed and grabbed the first spiral notebook she could reach. As fast as her fingers could move, she opened the cover and stared at the title page.

A Summer's Day
by Lauren Gibbs

Maybe her mother was using the name Lauren Gibbs! Emily stared at it, then she smacked her knee. Of *course!* Why hadn't she thought of that sooner? Once her grandpa told her the name came from a fictional character, she assumed there was no point searching it on the Internet. The most she would find would be a novel her mom liked to read as a young teenager. But now . . .

She dropped the notebook and sprinted down the hallway to the office. The computer was on and connected to the Internet in no time.

"God —" she whispered His name, her fingers trembling — "You gave me this. I can feel it." She centered her hands over the keyboard, typed in the name, and hit enter. She couldn't breathe while the machine worked, and then in a flash a list of entries appeared.

Emily stared and began reading them out loud. "*Time* magazine correspondent Lauren Gibbs has been stationed in Afghanistan since —"

Emily's heart raced. *Time* magazine correspondent? Her eyes flew to the next entry. " 'Children of War' — a profile on the orphans of Operation Enduring Freedom, by Lauren Gibbs, *Time* magazine correspondent. Photos by . . ."

One after another she read the entries in the list of hits and by the time she reached the end of the page, she was shaking all the way to her toes. Every entry mentioned Lauren Gibbs as a *Time* magazine reporter. Emily pressed her palm against her forehead, pushing her bangs back, the way she did when a soccer game got too intense. "Okay, God, walk me through this."

Just because Lauren Gibbs wrote for *Time* magazine didn't mean Emily had found her mother. She went back to the search line and typed, "Lauren Gibbs *Time* magazine profile."

The results were just as quick as before. The first link said simply "a profile of Lauren Gibbs, *Time* magazine correspondent." Again Lauren held her breath as she clicked the link. And there, instantly, was a photo that took up a fourth of the screen. The woman was blonde and pretty in a plain sort of way. She wore khaki clothing, and in the background were what looked like army tents. More than that, though, was the look on her face. A haunting look that revealed everything and nothing all at the same time. A look Emily had seen more often than she cared to admit.

In photographs of herself.

"Dear God . . ." Tears filled Emily's eyes, and she reached out, brushing the image with the tips of her fingers. It was her mother, she was absolutely sure. After a lifetime of looking, she'd found the woman who had walked out of her life when she was just an infant. She had no doubts, none at all. Because in more ways than one, looking at the woman's image was like looking at her own.

She brought her hands back to the keyboard and scanned the profile, gobbling up every small detail, all the pieces that had been missing for so long. Lauren Gibbs was based in Los Angeles, but she'd lived in the Middle East for most of the past three years. She was thirty-six years old with a master's degree in journalism from University of Southern California. She interned with the *Los Angeles Times*, and took a position at *Time* magazine a few years later, when she was just twenty-six.

Emily read the last part out loud again. "Lauren Gibbs has won numerous awards for her gutsy reporting throughout the war in Afghanistan and Iraq. She is credited with helping bring humanitarian assistance to the

Middle East and with helping to open a number of orphanages throughout the region. She is single and has no children."

What? Emily sat back, hard. The last line screamed at her, hurting her as much as if she'd been slapped. The single part was sad, but not surprising. Her mother went to Los Angeles to find the love of her life, and her search apparently turned up nothing. But . . .

No children?

"Is that what you tell people, Mom?" Fresh tears slid down her cheeks, and she didn't bother to wipe them away. The information was a lie, and it made her mad. Lauren Gibbs — Lauren *Anderson* — did too have a child. She had a daughter. Even if she thought her daughter was dead, she had a child.

Emily stared at her mother's image, trying to see past the hurt in her eyes. Other people might think the look was stone cold, the way people would expect a hardened journalist to look. But Emily recognized the look. It was the way she, herself, looked when she let circumstances get to her. When going through a tough day without a mom and a dad was more than she could handle, when she saw her teammates scan the sideline and wave to parents and the reminder hit her again. Her parents hadn't seen her play a single game.

Again she touched the image, tracing her mother's cheek, her chin. "Was it that easy to let me go? To tell yourself I never existed?" Her tears became sobs, and she drew back from the computer, hanging her head and giving way to a lifetime of sadness and doubt and question marks.

After a few minutes, she heard someone at the door behind her. "Emily?" It was her grandma's voice, and it was filled with alarm. "What on earth —"

Emily sat up and looked over her shoulder. Between sobs she said, "I found her. I found my mom."

Her grandma looked like she might drop from shock. Her face went pale, and she sat on the arm of the sofa, her eyes glued to the computer screen. "How did you — "

Emily dragged her fists over her eyes and found a trace of control. "Her . . . her name's Lauren Gibbs."

"Lauren Gibbs." Her grandma was on her feet, moving trancelike across the office toward the computer screen. The closer she got the more grief-stricken her face became. She reached toward the image on the screen and a cry left her. "Lauren . . . my baby." She brought her hand to her mouth and shook her head. Again she reached out, as tears flooded her eyes. "My girl."

Emily couldn't stop the sobs. All her life living with her grandparents, they talked about her mother only a handful of times. It was as if they wanted to give her the most normal life possible, and that meant they couldn't raise her in an environment of sorrow and regret. But now — watching her grandmother — she knew the truth.

The woman had grieved the loss of her daughter every day of her life. Emily watched her back up a few steps and sit on the other arm of the sofa, the one closest to the screen. Then she dropped her face into her hands and wept, praying out loud as her emotion allowed. "God, You found her for us. Thank you . . . thank you. My baby girl . . . my Lauren."

Emily went to wrap her arms around her. In every way, her grandmother had been a mother to her, but they both paid the price for being without the woman on the computer screen. Now, their tears were for too many reasons to count. They were for every one of Emily's missed birthdays and lost milestones, for all her school years and teenage years and soccer tournaments when she had privately ached for her mother. And they were tears of relief. Because they'd found her. Finally.

Emily sniffed and grabbed three quick breaths. "It's the miracle we prayed for."

Her grandma uncovered her face and looked at the computer screen again. Beneath her eyes, her mascara had left dark smudges, and her cheeks were red and blotchy. But Emily had never seen her look more joyful. Grandma grabbed two tissues from the office desk and handed one of them to her. They both blew their noses and wiped their eyes some more.

"I still can't believe it." Grandma slumped forward and her eyes found Emily's. "I can't believe we didn't think of it a few weeks ago."

"Me neither." Emily sniffed, but she felt a grin tugging at the corners of her mouth. "I was standing at the window in my room and I begged God to show me the next clue. You know what He did?"

"What?" Her grandma reached out and the two of them joined hands.

"He reminded me of His names, all His marvelous names." She made a sound that was more laugh than cry. "All of a sudden, it was so obvious. God has dozens of names, and some people have multiple names too."

Her grandmother looked drained, as if

she wouldn't have had the energy to stand if she needed to. "What do we do next?"

Emily released her grandma's hands and sat in the computer chair again. She slid it forward and looked once more at the profile next to her mother's picture. At the bottom was the thing she was looking for. A link that read, "Contact Lauren Gibbs." Emily's breath caught in her throat, and she shook her head. It was too much, but she wasn't going to stop now.

She clicked the link and an e-mail template opened up. In the top line was her mother's e-mail address: *Lauren.Gibbs@ TimeMagazine.com.* Her hands were still shaky, but she tabbed down to the subject line and typed, "From Emily." Then she moved the cursor to the text area and drew a deep breath. She'd had a lifetime to think about what to say next. Her fingers began to move across the keyboard, and the words came without any effort at all.

Hi, my name is Emily Anderson, and I'm eighteen years old.

She exhaled and looked at her grandmother. "I can't believe I'm doing this."

Her grandmother looked breathless, dazed. "Keep typing."

"Okay." Emily looked back at the screen.

I believe that you might be my
mother. I've looked for you since I
was old enough to know how to do it. I
live with my grandparents — Bill and
Angela Anderson. They've looked for
you too. But just today I thought about
looking under the name Lauren
Gibbs, because that's the name my
mother used when she was young
and wrote short stories. I found that
out a few weeks ago.
I did a search on the Internet, and I
found your profile. Please, could you
write back and let me know if I have
the right person. This is very important to me, obviously. Sincerely, Emily
Anderson.

She lifted her hands from the keyboard
and scanned the note once more. There
were a million more things she wanted to
say, but she had to make contact first.
Once her mother read the e-mail, they
could talk about all the other details. Why
she'd changed her name and what she'd
been doing for the past nineteen years and
whether she'd ever come close to finding
Shane Galanter.

She exhaled hard. "That'll have to do for now."

Her grandmother made an approving sound. "Send it, honey. Please."

Emily moved the cursor over the send button and clicked it. In an instant, the e-mail was gone. Emily stared at the screen and thought for a moment. They still had some logistical problems to work through. If her mother was overseas in Afghanistan, then maybe she wouldn't see the e-mail right away. Soldiers could get e-mail. Emily knew because she kept in touch with a few guys from high school who were serving overseas. Certainly the same would be true for reporters. Unless she had a different business e-mail address, one that her editors could use for her. The one on the website might only be for readers, and because of that maybe she only checked it when she was stateside.

Emily turned to her grandma and pushed her fears back down. "We need to pray."

"Yes." They held hands. "Let's do that."

Emily closed her eyes and for a few seconds she was too overwhelmed to speak. After a few moments she found her voice. "Dearest Lord, thank You." She giggled and it became a sharp breath. "*Thank You* doesn't even come close. The miracle we asked for is at hand, God, so please . . . let my mother read the e-mail soon. And direct her to respond to me so we can arrange a meeting." She paused, her heart full. "I'm doing what You ask, Lord. I'm praying, expecting you to help us. Thanks in advance, God. In Your name, amen."

When she opened her eyes, her grandma pointed at the screen. "Print me a copy, will you, honey?"

Emily grinned and gave her grandma a quick hug. "Definitely." When the picture was finished printing, Emily picked it up and handed it over. Then she printed another copy for herself.

"Your papa's resting downstairs. He's had so much bad news the past few weeks." Grandma looked at the single page. "Let's go give him the best news ever, news he's waited eighteen years to hear."

Angela felt weak as she took the stairs, arm in arm with Emily.

Her heart was exploding with a dozen brilliant colors, because this was the day she never really believed would come. They'd found Lauren! After all the private detectives and investigators and phone calls to elected officials, they'd found her the simplest way of all. With information that had been sitting for nearly twenty years a dozen yards away in the garage. They went into the family room and found Bill in his chair, his eyes closed.

"Bill." She held out the piece of paper. Emily stayed back as Angela approached him.

He opened his eyes and a slow smile filled his face. He held out his hand toward her. "Hi, love." He looked past her. "Emily, how are you?"

"Good, Papa." She managed a teary smile.

Angela moved closer to him. "Sweetheart, I have something to show you." Her voice was shaky. She wouldn't last long before breaking. She held out the piece of paper. "Emily found Lauren."

Bill sat up straighter in his chair, but his smile faded. He took the paper and looked at it, his expression frozen. "What . . . how did you . . . ?" He sat there, still, searching the information on the page, and then his chin began to tremble.

From the corner of her eye, Angela saw Emily move into the room and sit on the edge of the sofa. It was hard to remember to breathe. She wrapped her arms around her husband's neck. "God answered our prayers, Bill. He did."

Her eyes stung again as she watched him close his eyes and pinch the bridge of his nose. He shook his head, as if to say he couldn't accept the idea that they'd actually found her. Angela straightened and let him have this moment. It was impossible for any of them to really believe she'd been found. All the searching had culminated in this amazing moment.

And God had allowed it when Bill had only weeks to live. Angela's heart felt lighter than it had since Lauren left.

Finally Bill lowered his hand and looked at her. "Why didn't we try that sooner?"

She pressed her finger to his lips and gave a soft shake of her head. "That isn't important. She's found, Bill. We can only move forward."

"But all the lost days and years." His voice was gravelly, the tears still stuck in his throat. He turned his eyes back to her picture. "Look at her, Angie. She looks so much like you."

Angela touched the image, willing away the days until they might see her in person, hold her . . . "She's all grown up."

"A reporter for *Time* magazine." His voice held a new level of concern. "Not married, no children."

"No children?" Angela's heart missed a

beat. She hadn't read every word of the profile yet. Now her conscience felt like it was being ripped apart. "It says that?"

"Here." He pointed to that part of the write-up.

She read it, and the suspicions she'd had since the day Lauren left became realities in as much time as it took her to draw breath. If Lauren wasn't married, then she hadn't found Shane. And if she was telling people she had no children, then she had believed that Emily was dead. Wherever she was, she must still believe it.

Angela looked at Emily and her voice seized up again. "Your mother really does think you're dead, honey."

A lifetime of sorrow flooded Emily's eyes. And in that instant, Angela's grief was so great it nearly knocked her to the floor.

Emily listened to her grandmother. The anger was gone. Her mother wouldn't mention a dead daughter in a professional bio. Of course not. Now the freedom in her heart was more than she could take in. Freedom and a deep sadness for her mother, who had gone her entire adult life not knowing that she had a daughter growing up in the suburbs of Chicago. No wonder she'd wound up alone and working in Afghanistan and Iraq. Her mother's passion for writing had taken her to magazine work, but Lauren couldn't help but feel that her loneliness made her look the way she did. Empty, haunted, so very sad . . .

"Grandma . . ." She stood and went to her. They fell together in an embrace that needed no words, and Emily leaned back, searching her grandmother's eyes. "I hurt for her. She's been so lonely all these years."

Lonely the same way *she* was, but Emily didn't say that. She'd always kept her emptiness to herself, and now her tears told the story, that she'd missed her mother every day since she was old enough to understand that she was missing.

"I'm sorry, Emily." Her grandma brushed her hair off her forehead. "The two of you never should've been apart."

From a few feet away, Papa held out his hand. "Come here, Em."

Emily released her grandma and went to him. "Papa . . ."

"If we would've loved our girl better, if we would've handled her situation differently, then maybe —"

"No, Papa." Emily bent down and kissed his cheek. The loss of so many years together was enormous for all of them. "We can't go back." She sucked in a few fast breaths. "Just pray that she'll write back."

The evening was slow and deep, filled with stories from the past and shared memories of Emily's life, moments her mother had missed along the way. Despite her sorrow and loss, by the time they turned in that night, Emily had never felt happier in all her life. Maybe it was because the photo of her mother did something even her faith hadn't done before. It took away the emptiness inside her. The only thing that marred the moment was watching her papa take slow steps to his bedroom. He was getting sicker; the plans would have to come together soon.

When Emily woke the next morning, she was intent on checking her e-mail and then leaving a message for Shane Galanter at the Top Gun naval air training facility. She was about to run to the office when she heard her grandma finishing a phone call.

"Yes, Doctor. Yes, I understand." Silence. "I'll tell him. Yes, we know. Thank you." The phone call must've ended, because Grandma directed her next words to her husband. "They got your latest tests results." She had fear in her voice. "It's worse than they thought."

Emily sat up in bed and blinked the sleep from her eyes. Worse than they thought? She felt a burst of sheer terror, and she headed straight for the office. Her mother's e-mail couldn't come soon enough. Never mind whatever hurt feelings might've stood between her mother and her grandparents before. If her mother was going to have peace, she needed to know the entire story. That her daughter was alive and her parents were sorry — and that her father was dying. Yes, Lauren needed to connect with her mother.

Before they all ran out of time.

Twenty-One

Her recovery was happening faster than the doctor expected. The gritty wind that blew across the Afghanistan desert rattled the windows of Lauren's apartment, and made it impossible to sleep. She sat up in bed and surveyed the bandages on her arm. At least she was out of the hospital. That place was terrible, filled with victims of war and people desperate for healing and hope. She could still hear their wailings, mothers called in to identify young sons, soldiers who might've been on the right or the wrong side. Lauren winced as she felt near her wound. Sides didn't matter to a mother.

Lauren closed her eyes, recalling one grief-stricken woman. Her son had been in the next room, but he hadn't survived the night. The next morning the mother stood at his bedside, screaming his name, shouting at the heavens that she wanted him back, *had* to have him back.

All Lauren could think about was her own family. The way she'd felt when Emily died; the way her parents must feel now. If they were still alive, it would've been nearly twenty years since they'd had any idea even where to find her. How had they handled all that time alone together? Had they, too, shared moments of wailing and ranting at the heavens?

She sighed and opened her eyes. It was the first cloudy day in a month, and it fit her mood. Her mind drifted back to the day at the orphanage. Feni had gotten wind that an ambush might take place against visiting Westerners. That's why he was in the office that morning, armed and ready in case she and Scanlon were the intended targets.

An American army captain filled her in on the other details at the hospital.

The woman wasn't an orphanage worker at all. She'd blended in with the others, pretending to be a volunteer. Orphanages were always shorthanded, so no one would've questioned her motives. The only uncertain thing was how she'd known Lauren and Scanlon were coming in that first day, but the army had its theory on that too.

The driver of the car on that first visit

must've been connected with the group. He could easily have called and tipped them off. Lauren and Scanlon talked openly about their plans for a story and their concerns about the orphanage.

"This is a bad group, Miss Gibbs," the captain told her. "They run a terrorist training camp, an operation we're trying to shut down. We've had some success, but they're spread out. We haven't found them all."

"Why'd they want me?" She was numb to the pain by then, six hours on a medication that barely allowed her to stay awake. A surgeon removed two bullets from beneath her shoulder. The wounds were deep and dangerous, but her joint hadn't been affected. They expected her to heal completely.

The captain thought about her question. "You represent America." He raised an eyebrow, as if he didn't agree with that assessment. "At least, that's the way *they* see it. They probably wanted to wound you. Take you captive. Most journalists and photographers aren't armed, and Feni rarely works out of the orphanage." He shrugged. "They weren't expecting retaliation."

She looked away. "They weren't expecting to kill children, either."

"Maybe, maybe not." He was a big man, his hair cropped short against his square face. "When kids die, Americans always get the blame. They might've shot at the children on purpose."

Lauren blinked away the memory of the conversation and winced as she tried to move her arm. All this time she had sympathized with the insurgents. Yes, they were violent and sometimes behaved in a crazed manner. But this was their homeland. Didn't they have a right to want Americans to stay out? Even if they desired a type of government Americans didn't agree with, should it concern the U.S.? Was democracy the only valid form of leadership?

But now . . .

Now she didn't know what to think. People had a right to form their own government, but if that government was ruthless and brutal, then what? If she had to do it over again, she would've thrown herself in front of the children to keep them from being hit. She would've gladly taken the bullets intended for them if it meant saving their lives. And wasn't that all the U.S. troops were doing, really? Bad people had taken over the Middle East, and innocent people were living in fear, oppressed, and sometimes killed. If Lauren wouldn't stand by and watch that sort of behavior take place, then how could she expect the U.S. to do so?

She shuddered and gave a quick shake of her head. The medicine was making her loopy. There had to be another answer, something better than fighting and bombings and war. Solutions could be worked out at bargaining tables or in courtrooms, couldn't they? The entire mess gave her a headache. The political picture was more complicated than she first thought, that much was certain. But what mattered was this: Because she and Scanlon had gone back to the orphanage, little Senia was dead. A girl whose eyes were bright enough to light up the room. Now she was gone.

Lauren hated crying. She feared that sort of emotion almost as much as she feared elevators. Giving in to sorrow would be like driving a freightliner through the dam in her heart. The emotion of nearly twenty years would become a flood that would drown her. But in the days since she'd been released from the hospital, she could barely last an hour without feeling tears on her cheeks.

She would've adopted little Senia if she'd had the chance.

How could she know that the woman was working for the insurgents, or that the whole story had been concocted? The army captain told her that a thorough check had been done. "We have birth records for every child in that orphanage." His eyes blazed. "Not a child there has a single drop of American blood."

Lauren had hung her head then, not sure what to say.

The captain wasn't finished. "I'm surprised you didn't go with the story before the second meeting." The sarcasm in his laugh cut at her. "Can you imagine the headlines? Orphanages overflowing with the children of American soldiers?"

Her eyes met his. "I didn't have enough information. Of course I wouldn't have written the story before I had the facts."

The captain only raised his eyebrow at her again. "Okay. Whatever." His look was utter disgust. "Maybe we should talk about something else."

"We don't have to talk at all." She'd hated the way he treated her. As though she were the enemy.

"Look, ma'am, I've been assigned to guard you as long as you're in this hospital." He shifted to the front of his chair. "Fine with me if you don't wanna talk."

By the time Scanlon came to take her home, Lauren had no doubt about the army's viewpoint of her reporting. The captain picked apart ten of her top stories from the last two years. She had untrustworthy sources and a strong bias, he told her. She wasn't there to find the truth, but to make the U.S. armed forces the enemy.

The last thing he said before he left would stay with Lauren for the rest of her days: "You think the military's all gung ho for war, that we're a bunch of bullies coming over here and flexing our muscles." He pointed at her, and his voice grew low and intense. "Let me tell you something, lady. We want peace as much as you do. Maybe more." He thumbed himself in the chest. "Because *we're* layin' our lives down for it." He took a few steps back. "Don't forget that."

She turned away, not willing to respond or bid him good-bye. But his speech affected her more than she'd been willing to admit. Now it was Wednesday, and she'd been home for two days. Scanlon was in often, making sure she had water and meals and whatever else she needed.

It was time for more pain medication.

She took the bottle from beside her bed and brought it close. Her fingers on her left arm worked fine, as long as she didn't move her arm. She tapped a single pill into her palm. Then she used the water bottle lying on the pillow next to her to wash it down.

Once the pills were back on the nightstand, she lifted her arm again and let it fall quickly to her side. The pain was still intense. An army nurse was coming by three times a day to change the dressing and administer a shot of antibiotics. But one day soon her arm would heal. Her heart? Well, that was another matter.

She swung her feet over the edge of the bed and stared at the room around her. Life was happening outside her apartment building. Life and conflict and heartache, all translating into stories that needed to be written. That she needed to write. She hoped to be off bed rest by the end of the week.

Her eyes followed a familiar trail around the room, but this time they landed on her computer. She could at least check e-mail. That wasn't much removed from bed rest, was it? She took a deep breath. Why hadn't she thought of that sooner? She could've been researching and checking in with her editors instead of staring at the walls all day from her spot on the lumpy bed.

She stood and steadied herself for a few seconds. Amazing how weak she'd become after just five days of inactivity. She shuffled across the room and fell, exhausted, onto the hard-framed chair in front of her computer. The thud of her heart made her feel light-headed and dizzy. She turned on the computer and waited.

There was a knock on her door. "Lauren, you in there?"

It was Scanlon. She'd given him a key to her apartment a long time ago. She cleared her throat. "Come on in."

He opened the door and gave her a hesitant look. In his arms was a case of water bottles. "Aren't you supposed to be in bed?"

"They told me to rest." She gave him a wry look and faced the computer screen. "How 'bout *you* lie on the bed, and I'll sit here."

He set the case of water on a table in her makeshift kitchen, at the other side of the room. Lauren watched him. His face was tanned, his hair cut short the way he liked it. He was nice looking, in his own way.

She could tell he didn't have the desire

to fight with her. He shrugged. "Okay." He went to her bed and flopped down. "I am kinda tired."

She laughed, but her energy was waning fast. "Don't get too comfortable. I won't be here long."

"Still weak?" He sat up, his legs straight in front of him. "Is that normal?"

"Yeah." She wiped her hand over her damp forehead. "I felt this way once when I had the flu for a week, back when I was a teenager."

"In Chicago?" He put his hand behind his head and leaned against the wall above her tiny headboard. "Remember, Lauren? You already told me about Chicago."

"I was drunk." She signed onto the Internet and waited for the connection. "That doesn't count."

"Okay, but I still know." The tenderness in his voice was evidence that he cared deeply for her. "Everyone has a past. You wouldn't be living here if that wasn't the case."

She let his comment pass. She was connected to her server, and she found the little mailbox icon at the top of her home page. The number on top of the box read 68. Sixty-eight new e-mails. Even looking at them felt overwhelming. Especially now, when she could feel her strength ebbing with every minute.

"Forget the e-mail. Come here." From the corner of her eye she saw Scanlon move to one side of the bed. "There, you have room now. I'll keep my hands to myself. Promise."

"Not yet." She tried to draw a full breath, but she was too shaky. She felt this way one other time since she'd been living in the Middle East, when the area store ran out of food and she drank coffee for three days straight. Still, if she didn't fight it, how was she going to get stronger?

Summoning her energy, she clicked her in-box, and scanned the list of e-mails. Most were from other staff members who'd learned of her injury. The subjects read, "Get better!" and "Close call!" and "Time to come home, friend!" A few were from her editor, with subject lines that said, "Say the word," or "Maybe it's time."

She was halfway down the page when she stopped cold. Her heart thudded faster and harder. The subject line read simply: "From Emily." Lauren blinked and read it a second time. What sort of strange timing was this, anyway? She'd been lying in bed thinking about peace and how she and her family had never found any, and here was a

380

letter from a reader named — of all things — Emily.

A soft laugh left her, and from off to her side she saw Scanlon open his eyes. "What's so funny?"

"Nothing." She gave a shake of her head and brushed off his question. Her eyes were still locked onto the e-mail from Emily. Okay, so what did this Emily want? Lauren hadn't planned to actually open any of the e-mails. Not when her body was wilting badly. But "From Emily"? She could hardly resist. She clicked the link and the letter came up.

Hi, my name is Emily Anderson, and I'm eighteen years old —

Lauren couldn't catch her breath, couldn't force her lungs to draw even half a mouthful of air. She closed her eyes and gripped the desktop in front of her.

"Hey, Lauren." Scanlon's voice was more urgent. "You okay? Maybe you need to lie down."

She waved him off, but she opened her eyes. Again she tried the e-mail, but she couldn't get past that first line. Emily Anderson? Eighteen? Was this some sort of trick? Her Emily would've been eighteen.

Eighteen years, six months, and twenty-one days. She pursed her lips and forced the air from her lungs. The effort gave her just enough room to take in a small breath. Her injured arm felt numb, and her right hand trembled so hard she could barely scroll down and read the rest.

I believe that you might be my mother.

Lauren felt the room collapse around her. Felt everything begin to spin. What *was* this? And who would've written it? Her daughter was dead, so a letter like this had to be a prank. She willed herself to stay steady long enough to finish reading.

I've looked for you since I was old enough to know how to do it. I live with my grandparents — Bill and Angela Anderson. They've looked for you too. But just today I thought about looking under the name Lauren Gibbs, because that's the name my mother used when she was young and wrote short stories. I found that out a few weeks ago.
I did a search on the Internet, and I found your profile. Please, could you

write back and let me know if I have the right person. This is very important to me, obviously. Sincerely, Emily Anderson.

Lauren couldn't exhale. She read the letter again, and a third time, and all she could do was gasp little breaths. Scanlon was up now, hurrying to her side.

"You're blacking out, Lauren, come on." He eased her up and over to the bed. Then he lowered her to the mattress and rushed to the bathroom. When he came back he put a cool cloth on her head. "You're white as a sheet."

She still couldn't breathe right. Scanlon was asking her something, but she couldn't make out his words. All she could think about was the e-mail. It was a hoax, right? It had to be a hoax. But then the past came trampling into the room, screaming at her. Emily was alive? Could it really have been from her? And if so . . . if so . . .

Her heart raced along at triple speed. No way her baby had lived, no way. She hadn't walked away from a living child and left her parents to raise her. It was impossible. What had the nurse said? Her baby was gone, right? Gone for a few hours by the time Lauren had called. Gone meant dead, didn't it? Three more times she tried to breathe, but the air wouldn't come. Not until she exhaled, and she couldn't do that no matter how hard she tried.

She grabbed her friend's arm and gasped. "Scanlon . . . get me . . . a bag." She was hyperventilating. Her head told her she'd be fine, even if she passed out. A person couldn't die from hyperventilation. But right now she didn't want to battle herself, she wanted to battle the past. The giant, monstrous past. And she couldn't face it for a second until she could breathe.

Scanlon tore across the room, rifled through her kitchen drawers, and finally found a brown paper sack, the kind they used when they needed to pack an overnight meal. He raced it to her and held it to her mouth.

"Breathe, Lauren. Come on." He was genuinely worried, and in the rush of all that was dawning on her, she realized one more thing. Scanlon loved her.

She couldn't sort through that thought any more than she could understand the e-mail she'd just read. Instead she focused all her attention on breathing into the bag. Eventually she felt each breath last a little longer, felt her rib cage relax so she could finally exhale. Only then did she dare move the bag and take the smallest drink of fresh air.

She was drenched with sweat, and she felt weaker than she had all day. But still she struggled to sit up, desperate for a glance at the computer screen. When she was fully sitting, she saw it was still there. An e-mail with the shape and form of the one she'd read a few minutes ago.

Next to her, Scanlon wiped the wet cloth tenderly over her forehead. "What in the world was all that about?"

She sat up straighter on the bed. The she brushed away the wet cloth and looked him straight in the eyes. "Can you do me a favor?"

"Anything." He searched her face, ready to jump.

With her elbow she motioned toward the computer screen. "Could you answer that girl's letter?" She hesitated. "Don't read it, just hit reply, okay?"

"Sure." He let his eyes linger on her, doubt flashing in his expression. "For a person who couldn't breathe a minute ago, you're pretty demanding."

Another out breath. "I know." She leaned forward and dug her elbows into her thighs. "Can you do this, Scanlon? Please?"

"Okay, okay." He went to the computer and sat down. "Don't get crazy on me again."

He clicked the reply link and a blank screen appeared. "Shoot."

"Give me a second." She willed herself to think clearly. What if it wasn't a hoax or a mistake? What if her daughter was really alive and living in Wheaton, Illinois? Maybe in the same house her parents had moved to when she was pregnant? She squeezed her eyes shut and refused to think about anything but the e-mail. "Okay, write this." She paused. "Emily, call me as soon as you can. Here's my number with the country code. Dial it just like this." She was winded again, so she stopped and breathed. "Put the number next, okay?"

He was still typing. "I figured." After a few more key strokes his hands fell silent. "Send it?"

"Yes. Thanks, Scanlon." It wasn't the time to write anything flowery at the end. Because whoever she was, she couldn't be her Emily. The daughter she'd brought into the world. Her Emily was dead.

Scanlon was up and moving back to the bed. She shifted so he could sit beside her, but as he did he met her eyes and held them. "Wanna tell me about it?"

"No." She didn't want to, but she had no choice. Suddenly in all the world, Scanlon felt like her only ally, her only friend. And since the past was threatening to swallow her alive, she had no option but to cut it wide open and let it spill out. She put her hand over Scanlon's, her voice softer than before. "I didn't tell you everything about Chicago."

"Why am I not surprised?" He wove his fingers between hers, his expression softer. "I'm listening."

She nodded, and slowly at first, the story came out. How she'd been so in love with Shane Galanter, and her desperate belief that after he left, she had to find him. She told him about leaving for California and being terrified when little Emily got sick, and she explained how she'd taken her daughter to the clinic, but left when she thought for sure the police would come and take Emily away.

"What happened then?" Scanlon still had his fingers laced between hers. "Did you make it back?"

"I did." She told him how she'd rushed home and begged her mother for help, even though the two of them hadn't been speaking before she left. "We raced to the hospital." Her eyes fell and she shook her head. "It took the doctor ten minutes to tell us he didn't think Emily would survive. In fact, he said it would take a miracle."

Scanlon listened, his eyes full of compassion.

She told him how she'd sat by Emily all night, and how around four in the morning her little girl had taken a turn for the better. "An hour after that, I wasn't sure I'd survive without sleep." She shrugged. "I don't know, I was seventeen and scared out of my mind. I hadn't slept in two days. I wasn't thinking straight or I would've found a bed in the hospital somewhere."

"Your mom was still there, right?"

"Right. She offered to stay. So I went home and fell asleep for ten hours — much longer than I planned. When I woke up I called the hospital and someone connected me to a nurse." Her heart pounded at the memory. She let go of Scanlon's hand and pressed her fingers into her temples. "The woman told me Emily was gone. That she'd been gone for a few hours."

"She died?"

Lauren let her hands fall to her sides. "That's what I thought." She nodded toward the computer. "Until just now, that's what I always thought. I had one baby, and I did everything wrong, so she died."

Scanlon groaned. He slipped his arm around her and pulled her to him. She let her head fall against his shoulder. "The e-mail — it was from an Emily Anderson, who says she's eighteen." She sat up and searched her friend's eyes. "She says she's living with Bill and Angela Anderson in Wheaton and that she thinks I'm her —"

Her cell phone sprang to life, ringing and moving about as it vibrated on the table next to the medicine bottle. She felt her lungs seizing up again, but she willed them to stay calm. Scanlon handed her the phone and she flipped it open.

"Hello?"

"Is this . . . is this Lauren Gibbs?" The voice was young and tender, a voice that sounded like her own, like she'd sounded before everything had gone so terribly wrong.

She breathed out. "Yes." Her head was spinning. "Who's this?"

"This is Emily Anderson." The girl waited a moment. "My mother's been missing for . . . for eighteen years, and I thought maybe you might be —"

"Emily." The girl's name felt wonderful on her lips. She tried to remember to be guarded, to doubt whether the caller was really her daughter. A journalist never

389

trusts people without checking facts. "Is . . . this really you?"

"Yes." Emily started to cry. "Are you —"

This wasn't happening; it couldn't be happening. Lauren gripped Scanlon's arm. She felt a searing white-hot pain in her heart, like the pain that pierced her arm a week ago. As if she was being shot square in the middle. She squeezed her eyes shut and pressed the phone to her ear. "They told me you were dead."

"I know." The girl was crying harder now. "Grandma told me. She thought that's what happened."

Lauren leaned on Scanlon, determined to keep breathing, slow and steady. The phone call was too important to lose. "I never would've left, never! Not if I'd known. I —" Emotions choked her words. She swallowed, searching for a way to sum up a lifetime of feelings. "I thought about you every day, Emily. I still do."

"Me too." Tears filled the girl's voice, but her words rang with a joy that seemed boundless. "Mom, did you ever find him?"

Lauren's tears came then.

She called me Mom . . . I have a daughter! Aching sobs welled up in her. *Emily was alive!* She forced herself to think about Emily's question. "Shane?"

"Yes. Did you ever find him?"

The ache in her heart doubled. She had spent a lifetime missing Emily, but she had missed Shane Galanter too. He was the reason she left Chicago, after all. How long had she looked for him and waited for him, when all along her daughter had been growing up without her? If only she hadn't been so stubborn. She could've gone home and made peace with her parents, and she would've found more than a mended relationship.

She would've found her daughter.

"No, Emily." She pressed her finger against her upper lip and fought to keep control. "No, I never found him."

"I'm sorry." Her voice was thick again. "You loved him very much, didn't you?"

"I did." A few rebel sobs escaped, but she swallowed the rest. "I always told myself I'd go home again once I found him."

"But you never found him, so you never came home."

"No."

They fell quiet. Next to her Scanlon rubbed her good arm, lending whatever support he could. She would've given anything to reach through the phone lines and hold her daughter. "I have so many questions."

Emily laughed. "Me too."

"Listen to you." She clung to the sound of her daughter's laughter, a sound that was like water to her barren soul. "I used to laugh like that when . . . before . . ."

"Before you got pregnant." The laughter faded from her voice. "I was talking to God the other day, and I told Him I knew what had happened. You got pregnant and everything went bad from there." There was no self-pity in her voice. "One event tore everyone apart, didn't it?"

Regret came upon her like a monsoon. "It did."

"So I asked God if one event tore everyone apart, maybe He could use me to bring everyone back together."

Usually, when Lauren heard someone talk about God, she was repulsed — probably because she usually heard such talk from politicians. But now . . . Emily's sincerity — her *daughter's* sincerity — rang across the phone lines. When Lauren didn't say anything, her daughter continued.

"The thing is, Mom, you need to come home quick." She sounded serious. Scared and serious.

It was the first time Lauren considered the possibility that her daughter might not be well. She stiffened, gripping the phone tighter than before. "Are you . . . is every- thing okay?"

"No." She sighed, and her voice filled with fresh tears. "Papa's got cancer. He . . . he doesn't have long."

Papa? Who was . . . ? Understanding dawned. Her father. Was that what Emily called him? Papa? She had a flashback, an image of her daddy swinging her in his arms when she was six or seven years old. Senia's age. She swallowed another wave of sorrow. "My father?"

"Yes." She waited a beat. "I don't know what happened between the three of you, but Grandma and Papa, they're wonderful. They have such a strong faith." She took a quick breath. "I need you, Mom. I've waited all my life for this. But now you have to come fast."

Her new reality was taking shape quicker than she could make sense of it. Her par- ents were wonderful? That wasn't such a surprise, was it? They'd been wonderful all her life until they forced her to separate from Shane. And something else con- sumed her. Emily wasn't only alive, but she wanted Shane and her to connect. What had she said? That she'd waited all her life for this? It was more than Lauren could take in. She shielded her eyes and leaned her head against her hand. How much had she missed over the years? She'd never planned to leave her parents forever, had she? Not even after what they'd done to keep her and Shane apart.

It was just that one year blended into the next, and pretty soon the road home was so overgrown with blame and hurt she couldn't find her way back. Wasn't even sure she wanted to. But now her daddy was dying. "Do they want me there? With my dad so sick?"

Emily laughed again, and it sounded like a release. As if she'd been holding her breath waiting for the answer. "*Yes*, they want you to come home. Please, Mom. Come as fast as you can, okay?"

Lauren straightened. She had vacation time, but she needed a medical release before she could fly home. That, and the debriefing day at the magazine office. "I can be there a week from Saturday. Will that work?"

"Yes! Oh yes!" Again her daughter's voice sang with hope and promise. "Here, write this down."

Lauren motioned to Scanlon that she needed him to take a note. He grabbed the pad of paper and pen on the nightstand

and waited, ready. Lauren held the receiver tight. "Okay, go ahead."

Emily rattled off several phone numbers, one for home and one for her cell. Lauren repeated every digit, watching to make sure Scanlon wrote it correctly. She'd lost Emily once; she wouldn't lose her again.

When she'd given all her contact information, Emily giggled. "Mom . . . I might call you between now and then, if that's okay."

"Emily." She felt her heart bursting within her. "Please do."

"I love you, Mom."

There it was again. The name she'd never been called before. *Mom. I love you, Mom.*

It was still impossible to believe any of it was true, but there was no denying that the caller was her daughter. She swallowed hard. "I love you too, sweetheart. I've loved you and missed you every day of your life." She drew her first full breath in an hour. "I still can't believe you found me."

"I didn't." Certainty filled her tone. "God did." She paused. "But we can talk about that later."

When the call ended, Lauren snapped her cell phone shut. She turned to her friend, so full she thought she might burst. "Oh, Scanlon." She searched his eyes. Whatever happened from here, her life would never be the same. "My daughter is alive!"

"I gathered." He smiled at her. "You're going back to the States?"

"Yes." She pulled away and looked around her room. "As soon as they'll let me go. My father's sick. He . . . he doesn't have long."

"Will you get there in time?"

"I don't know. Maybe."

"Amazing, huh? You go eighteen years without seeing him, and your daughter finds you just in time?"

Lauren felt herself being drawn back to the conversation she'd just had with her daughter. Emily said God had found her. She blinked and looked at her friend again. "Definitely amazing."

A hint of sadness flashed in his eyes, but he smiled. "I'm glad for you, Lauren. Really."

Though it meant she was leaving, and though there was now a sudden possibility that she might never come back, she believed Scanlon really was glad. That was the sort of friend he was. Even so, the uppermost thought in her mind right now wasn't leaving him or the Middle East or the job she so loved. Not even close.

All that was on her mind was the miracle. She had a daughter. A living, breathing young woman with a voice like sunshine. And in just over a week, she was going to meet her. See her face. Hold her in her arms.

And her parents. She would see them again. Feel her mother's arms around her, see her father's face glow with love — a love that had been misguided for a season when she was a teenager — but a love fiercely strong all the same. Yes, she had a daughter to meet and parents to reunite with.

And eighteen lonely years to make up for.

Emily hung up the phone. She was shaking, trembling from her fingertips to her feet. Finding her mother's picture, her identity, had been one thing. But actually *talking* with her? It was more than Emily could've dreamed. Her mom sounded shocked and fearful, disbelieving and overjoyed. But there was something else in her voice. A deep, abiding sorrow. For all the years they'd lost.

Emily stood and stared at the picture

next to her bed, the one of her parents when they were teenagers. "God —" she lifted her eyes to the window, the blue sky beyond — "a miracle is underway, and already it's more than I can take in."

She remembered the pain in her mother's voice when she talked about Shane. Emily still needed to find him, find a way to connect him with her mother. She sucked on the inside of her cheek and remembered something else. The hurt in her mom's voice when she realized Papa was sick. They still had so much healing to work through, so much forgiveness to find if they were going to have peace.

A long sigh eased from her lips. She needed to get downstairs and tell her grandparents about her phone call with her mother. But first she needed more time to talk to God. Because yes, the miracle they all needed was finally underway, but it was hardly finished.

Rather, it was only just beginning.

Twenty-Two

Shane wasn't sure how to break it to her.

After a week of praying and searching his Bible and hitting the gym twice as long as usual, he had the answer he'd been looking for. It jumped out at him just that morning, shouted at him from the book of Proverbs, the third chapter. There in verses five and six it said, *Trust in the Lord with all your heart and lean not on your own understanding; in all your ways acknowledge him, and he will make your paths straight.*

He read the words three more times through, and suddenly the answer was clear. His own understanding had led him into a relationship with Ellen Randolph. His own understanding had allowed Ellen to design a plan for his life, a winding path that would take him where she wanted him to go. And yes, he'd gone along with it, because by his own understanding the plan made sense.

But it wasn't God's understanding.

Shane clenched his fists and looked at his watch. He moved onto the patio, restless. Ellen would be there in ten minutes, and the two of them were supposed to go to dinner. He'd thought all day about whether he should cancel and talk to her before the meal, or wait until afterward. He decided to wait. The least he could do was share one last meal with her before telling her it was over.

He sat down on a chaise lounge and stared up into the palm trees that lined his backyard. Long ago he had put his trust in God. Though his parents moved him to California, and he had felt his heart rip out a little more with every mile that came between him and Lauren, he gave everything over in faith. He trusted the Lord to lead him through the rest of his days. Of course, his parents had their own plans. Plans they'd made clear before the first month of his senior year in high school.

His father came into his room before bedtime one school night that year. "About time to apply for colleges, hey, son? I've talked to my friends at Harvard and Yale, even a few at USC." He winked. "Looks like you're a shoo-in for any of the three."

Not until that moment did Shane fully understand what his parents had done.

400

The move wasn't about investments in California. It was about investing in him, about protecting the plans they had for him, the plans to have him finish high school as an all-American football player with a future as golden as the sun.

That night he told his dad news that shocked him. "I don't want to go to business school, Dad. I don't want an MBA or ownership in a bank or the chance to run a mortgage company. I want to fly a fighter jet."

It took most of the next six months for his wishes to sink in. Even then it was clear his parents were frustrated. They moved him away from Lauren, but nothing they could do would move him away from the plans God had for him. That spring, a few months before he graduated, he ran into a navy recruiter with a booth set up in the lunch area. Shane could almost feel God directing him over, making him pick up a brochure and ask questions.

From there, the pieces fell into place. He went to college at UCLA and then enlisted for officer's training school and naval flight training. By the time the Gulf War came around, he was one of the top fighter pilots in the navy.

His parents learned to accept his decision. In time, they were proud of him for flying jets for the U.S. military, bragging to their friends about his awards and medals. Shane was glad, but it wasn't what motivated him. He was born to fly; that's what the Lord had shown him.

Every time he flew he felt God leading him home at the end of a mission. He was serving his country, serving his fellow man, and following the life God had given him all at the same time. His only sorrow was missing Lauren. For more than a decade that void hit him at the end of every day and between shifts and in noncombat situations when he was forty thousand feet up behind the controls of a jet.

He would gaze into the endless blue and remember the note she'd scribbled for him back when they were kids: *You're gonna fly one day. When you go, take me with you.* Only he never found her, so she never knew. Never knew that he'd done what he wanted to do, what God had created him to do. He breathed in the cool Reno air. And now . . . here he was. On the wrong path again.

How did it happen? How did he let Ellen convince him that a position in politics would be better than working at Top Gun, better than driving out to the naval training base every day and living his dream? There was something else too. Since he'd been seeing Ellen, he'd come to believe that he didn't want children, that with all the plans ahead of him, there wasn't time for raising a family. All because for a short while, his own understanding seemed better than God's.

But not anymore.

The doorbell rang, and then he heard the sound of her in the entryway. "Hello?"

"Ellen. I'm back here." He stood and met her. "You look pretty." He kissed her cheek and led her back into the house. "I'll get my keys."

"Shane." Her tone was a mix of no-nonsense strength with a hint of vulnerability.

He turned around. "Yes?"

She exhaled slow and tired. "It's over, isn't it?"

For an instant, he almost denied it. How could she have known? All he'd told her was that he wanted to talk. Nothing more. He slipped his hands in his pockets and took a few steps closer. Her eyes told him that she wasn't guessing. She knew. Somehow she'd figured it out.

He stopped and looked to the deepest places of her heart. "How did you know?"

"This." She pulled something that looked like a small photograph from her purse and handed it to him. "I found this on the front seat of my car this morning. It must've fallen out of your pocket."

Only when it was in his hands did he look at it. As he did, his heart sank. It was his picture of Lauren. She was right. He'd been looking at it the night before, when she pulled up to take him to dinner. In the rush of the moment, he slid it into his pocket and hurried out to meet her.

Ellen lifted her chin, her pride clearly intact. "I thought you'd let her go, Shane."

"I have —" No. He stopped himself. Anything he said about letting go of Lauren Anderson was a lie. He promised Lauren long ago that he would love her until the day he died. Wasn't that what he'd engraved in the ring he bought her? *Even now*. Even now, when it made no sense to hang onto her memory, his promise was good. He put the photo on the closest bookshelf and took Ellen's hands in his. "I'm sorry." He worked the muscles in his jaw. "I thought I had."

She smiled, and the brilliance of it almost hid the pain in her eyes. "I thought so too." She wriggled the ring from her finger. It contained a total of two carats, nothing like the small ring he'd bought Lauren a lifetime ago. "Here." Her eyes glistened. "I can't be second best, Shane."

"I know." He took the ring and tried to see past her pretense. "I think we would've made a good team."

"Me too." She gave his fingers a heartfelt squeeze. "But I don't want a teammate, Shane. I want someone who adores me."

"I understand." He pulled her to himself and folded her in his arms. "I'm the problem, Ellen. Not you. You're perfect."

She nodded, and when she drew back he noticed her makeup was still intact, her eyes dry. "I've spent the day working through this, so, if you don't mind, I think I'll get going."

"Okay." He released her and she took a step.

Holding her purse close to her side, she nodded at him. "Good-bye, Shane."

"Good-bye." He held up his hand and waited as she turned and headed back to the door.

When she reached it, she looked at him once more over her shoulder. "You didn't want to be governor anyway, did you?"

The sadness in his heart was genuine. She had offered him the kind of life most guys in his place would've jumped at. He felt God's words shouting from the foundation of his heart. *Lean not on your own understanding; in all your ways acknowledge him, and he will make your paths straight.*

Ellen was waiting, watching him. He took a few steps closer one last time and shook his head, his eyes never leaving hers. "No, Ellen. God made me to be a pilot. I love politics, and I'd vote for your father and everyone on the party ticket as long as the issues are what they are today." He brushed his knuckles against her cheek. *God, let her move on quickly from here. She deserves so much more.* "But the • truth is, I only thought I'd like politics because I liked you. Your father was a politician, and I thought it made sense if I became one too."

She covered his hand with her own, and after a few seconds she took hold of the door handle and backed up another step. "You know something?"

"What?"

"I'm glad you figured it out." Her smile was more genuine now, as was her sorrow.

"Me too."

She opened the door and stepped out onto the porch. "And I'm flattered that you liked me that much." She nodded at

406

him and held his eyes another few seconds. Then she turned and walked down his sidewalk to her car waiting along the curb. When she was gone, he grabbed his phone and went back outside on his patio. His chest ached, and he knew why. She wasn't right for him, but he cared about her. He was going to miss her, and once again he was going to be alone.

Now it was time to break the news to his parents.

Sheila Galanter hung up the phone and barely made it into the living room where her husband Samuel was reading the newspaper.

"It's over." She leaned against the doorway. Moving any further into the room wasn't an option. All her energy was taken with trying to sort through the news.

Samuel lowered the newspaper to his lap. "What is?"

"Shane and Ellen. They called it off."

"Hmm." He looked up at the ceiling for a few seconds. "Can't say I blame him."

"Samuel! Listen to you." She was catching her breath now. "Ellen was a lovely girl."

"She was that." He looked at her. "But she had Shane's life planned out for him."

407

"We did the same once, remember?" She walked into the room and sat on the edge of the chair opposite him.

He groaned and released the footrest in the recliner. It snapped down into place, and he sat straighter than before. "Sheila, it was only a few weeks ago that you were chock-full of doubts about this impending marriage."

"*I* didn't have doubts." Her tone changed. "I was worried he did."

"Well —" Samuel leaned forward and gave her knee a quick squeeze — "looks like you were right." He studied her. He knew her so well. "Shane's still young, Sheila. He'll find someone else."

It was exactly what she was thinking. But Shane's age wasn't the problem. The awful reality was that their son hadn't truly loved someone since — "What if this is all our fault, Samuel?" Her voice slipped to a whisper. "Have you ever thought of that?"

A shadow fell over her husband's eyes, and he folded his hands on his lap. For more than a minute he said nothing, as if he was being sucked back to that awful time when they'd felt forced to start a new life in order to protect their son.

A long sigh escaped him. "I haven't wanted to."

"But you have, right?" All those years, two decades since they'd left Chicago, and never once had Sheila gotten up the courage to talk to her husband about this. They made their decision and never looked back. But now the past had limped into the room with them, torn up and bleeding, impossible to ignore. Not that they were crushed about the breakup between Shane and Ellen. But the fact that their son had never let go of Lauren Anderson. She watched her own feelings play out across his face, and she already had her answer. "Samuel, talk to me."

He drew in a deep breath. "When we moved that boy here, I knew with everything I was that it was the right decision." He spoke through clenched teeth, allowing a rare show of emotion. "He was seventeen, Sheila. What were we supposed to do?"

"I don't know." A crack formed in her heart and she hung her head. Samuel was right. They'd wanted only the best for him. The move had been Samuel's idea, but she had supported it. To the point of losing her best friend, she'd supported it.

"He wanted to marry her and . . . and be a father all before he finished high school. I couldn't stand by and let that happen." Samuel spread his fingers over his chest.

"Please . . . tell me you don't blame me, Sheila."

"How can I?" She lifted her hands and let them drop in her lap again. "I was the one meeting with Angela, telling her we needed a plan." The crack widened. "I talked about Lauren like she was —" She looked at the floor, the memories so close she could touch them. "I talked about Lauren like she was completely to blame." She twisted her expression and looked at Samuel again. "I lost my friend because I couldn't, not for one minute, think Shane was anything but a victim."

Samuel took her hands in his. For a long time he ran his thumbs along hers. Then he shook his head. "We were wrong. I've known it for a long time."

"He's looked for Lauren all his life." She felt her eyes grow distant. "Sometimes when I'm on the Internet, I type in her name, just to see what comes up."

He studied her, eyes wide. "I've done that, too."

"We should've looked for Angela and Bill. They would know where to find her."

A strange look came over him and he gave a single shake of his head. "No. They have no idea. At least they didn't five years ago."

What was he saying? She held tighter to his hands so she wouldn't fall off her chair. "You called them?"

"I called Bill one day at work. The conversation was short. No apologies, no accusations. We didn't talk about the baby." He shrugged. "I asked him if he could tell me how to get in touch with Lauren."

"You did that?" She'd been married to him for thirty-eight years. How could they not have talked about something this important?

"Shane was gutsy and strong and a military hero, but he was dying inside for missing that girl." His expression grew soft. "I asked myself how I could show Shane I loved him. How much I really love him." He blinked twice, but his eyes remained damp. "Finding Lauren was the best thing I could think of."

"Sam . . ." She slid to the floor and crawled the few steps that separated them. She had never loved him more. "You were exactly right."

"Only Bill told me he didn't know where she was. She ran away after she had the baby. That was the end of the conversation." He eased his fingers along the back of her hand. "I guess we all paid for what we did to those kids."

A small cry came from her. "If I'd known that was going to be my only grand-child . . ." She hugged his legs and rested her head on his knees. "Oh, Sam. We're *still* paying for what we did."

"Yes." Sadness choked his voice. "Some-times I lie awake at night wondering if the baby was a boy or a girl, and where that eighteen-year-old child might be now."

In that moment, Sheila felt the crack give way, felt her heart tear in half. She knew with utter certainty that she would never be the same. Because here was the truth. She wasn't the only one who dreamed about the grandchild they'd walked away from, or who agonized at her son's loneliness. She and Samuel had lived their lives in a sort of quiet denial, never talking about their biggest decision, never facing how it had forever changed them all.

And what about the Andersons? How could Lauren run away and never look back? Where had she gone? A tingling started at Sheila's forehead and worked its way down her face. Lauren would've only run to one place — Southern California. Because she would've been as driven to find Shane as he had been to find her.

This new realization added yet another layer to the hidden tragedy that was their lives. The only thing that could save them was if the broken pieces all found their way together again. Healing *could* happen if Shane found Lauren, if she and Samuel made things right with the Andersons. But how? How was that even possible?

Guilt and regret smothered her, made her wish with all her being that somehow that might really take place. But it was impossible. Miracles like that simply didn't happen.

At least not to horrible people like them.

Twenty-Three

It was the right decision, but that Monday morning Shane could still feel the ache in his heart. He missed Ellen, missed the way she made him laugh and the animated way she entertained him with stories from her father's world. Without her, the weekend had been quiet and uneventful. Shane didn't need anyone to tell him how the next season of his life would go. It would be a lonely one, maybe the loneliest yet.

He pulled into the parking lot at Top Gun, killed the engine, and climbed out. The day was chilly, but the sky was a brilliant blue. He leaned against his car, crossed his ankles, and stared toward heaven.

"Okay, God, I'm trusting you." He smiled, but it didn't erase his sadness. "Show me what's next." He gave a salute toward the sky. "I'll be on standby until then."

He breathed in and headed toward the

back door of the building. He needed speed, needed to buckle into a cockpit and fly like the wind through the forever sky. Maybe that would help him feel better.

It was 8:50 in the morning when he reported at the desk. He picked up a stack of mail and was on his way toward the instructors' lounge when one of the guys behind the counter motioned to him. "Captain Galanter?"

"Yes?" He kept his eyes on the mail. There was a familiar envelope in the bundle, something from the office of Ellen's father. The young man a few feet from him said something, but Shane missed it. He tucked the mail under his arm and frowned. "Sorry. What'd you say?"

"You have a message, sir." He held it out. "She says it's urgent."

Shane walked back to the counter and took a small slip of paper. "Thanks." He nodded at the guy, turned, and headed down the hall. As he did, he looked at the message. It was handwritten, taken early that morning. He read it: "Please call Emily Anderson in Wheaton, Illinois."

Anderson? Shane came to a slow stop. Emily Anderson in Wheaton? He stared at the number and wondered . . . Emily? Emily Anderson? He leaned against the wall, dizzy with the thoughts racing through his head. Was it possible? The wild hope bursting within him wasn't so much because of her last name, or even because she was from Wheaton. But because her name was Emily.

The name that —

He blinked hard and shook his head. Maybe his thoughts were fuzzy because of Ellen, or because it was a beautiful Monday morning and he couldn't wait to get up in the sky. Either way he needed a clear head. Thinking about Lauren or the baby or anything from the past would only hold him back.

Her name had to be some sort of coincidence. Anderson was a common name and so was Emily. Still, he needed to call the woman. Probably a teacher, someone bringing a group of kids to Lake Tahoe and looking for an educational side trip. Happened all the time. He stepped into his small, boxy office and eased himself into his chair, all while reading the message one more time. It had to be about a tour group, he was convinced.

He dialed the number and waited. He would take care of the call, set up a tour date for the lady, and get into his flight suit.

All before nine o'clock.

Emily was typing another e-mail to her mother. The e-mails and phone calls had given them a wonderful chance to connect, even before a face-to-face meeting. This time the topic was journalism, how badly she wanted to write for a newspaper the way her mother did. She was just finishing it when the phone on the desk next to her rang. She answered it, her eyes still on the computer screen. "Hello?"

"Yes, Emily Anderson, please. This is Captain Shane Galanter returning her call."

She gasped, and then covered her mouth so he wouldn't hear her reaction. There was still no way of knowing if she had the right man. Even so, her heart was in her throat, and she was on her feet. She paced out of the room and to the end of the hallway. "This is Emily." A knot tugged at her stomach. "I'm looking for a Mr. Galanter. I'm just not sure I have the right one."

"Okay." The man sounded at a loss. "There's only one of us at Top Gun, if that helps."

"Well . . ." She stifled a nervous bit of

laughter. What if this *was* him? What if she was actually talking to her father — her very own father! — for the first time in her life? "Actually, I'm not sure that the Shane Galanter I'm looking for is an instructor at Top Gun."

He chuckled. "Why don't you tell me about the one you're missing."

"Good idea." She liked him. He had a kind voice and a sense of humor. "My Shane Galanter has dark hair and dark eyes and he's pretty tall. He grew up in Chicago and dated a girl named Lauren Anderson. Then the summer before his senior —"

"Emily." The teasing lightness in his voice was gone. In its place was a sense of quiet shock. "You have the right Shane Galanter. Now it's my turn." He hesitated. "Who are you?"

She stopped pacing and leaned against the wall. It was him! She'd found him! A smile pushed its way up her cheeks, just as the first tears filled her eyes. After all these years had it really been that easy? A matter of spelling his name right and finding him through the Internet? The story began spilling from her at record speed. "I'm your daughter." A sound came from her, part laugh part sob. "I've looked for you all my life, only I was looking on the Internet and I was spelling your name wrong, until last week when I found my mother's journals and I realized your name had two *a*'s and that's how I —"

"Emily?" He sounded breathless, almost doubtful. "Your mother's name is —"

"Lauren. Lauren Anderson." She giggled out loud. "I found *her* five days ago, the same day I called you."

"I just got the message. I . . . I can't believe this." His voice was thick, choked with what must've been almost overwhelming emotions. "So she did it, she gave you up for adoption."

"No, not at all." Emily exhaled hard. There were so many pieces to pull together. "It's a long story. I'm not sure where to start."

"I don't know anything, Emily." He laughed, his tone soaked in disbelief. "Why don't you start at the beginning."

"Okay." She slid down the wall until she was sitting on the floor. "When you and your family left for California, my mom was desperate to find you . . ."

The story poured out in all its detail. All the while Emily was overcome by a joy that made her feel like she was floating. She'd found her dad! They were actually talking on the phone. It was more than she could imagine. She'd found both her parents in the same week. And now it was up to her to get the information to her dad so he could join them. He would come, she had no doubts. She'd asked for a miracle.

And God was making it happen.

Twenty-Four

Lauren felt like she knew her daughter, and it had only been a week.

During that time over the phone, they'd filled each other in on much of what they'd missed, the facts they hadn't known about each other. Lauren told Emily about her first trip out west, and how sick Emily had gotten.

"I thought it was my fault." Lauren willed her voice to convey the depth of her regret. "When they told me you were gone, I knew I only had one hope left — to find Shane."

She told Emily about coming to Los Angeles and finding an apartment and getting a job. How she'd been determined to finish college and start a writing career, and how every day along the way she never stopped looking for Shane.

Other times the conversation would be about Emily. Lauren learned that her daughter had a deep faith, one that colored everything she did, everything she felt. Emily shared the highlights of her childhood, the special moments at home and in school, and her decision to play soccer.

"I still play now, at Wheaton College." There was pride in the girl's voice. "Grandma says my dad was an athlete."

"Yes." Lauren's heart felt scraped bare. Not only because of all she'd missed, but because Shane's memory was alive and standing next to her all the time now. "He was a baseball player."

They talked about Lauren's parents and how anxious they were to see her, and about Emily's place on the school newspaper. But no matter how many times they talked or how often they exchanged e-mails, Lauren couldn't really believe her daughter was alive — not until she saw her in person.

Finally, on a Saturday afternoon, after five hours of air travel, Lauren grabbed her things from the overhead compartment of a 737 and headed through the plane and down the Jetway into Chicago's O'Hare Airport. Even then she couldn't believe she was home again. Back where it all started, all those years ago. Eighteen years. A lifetime.

Emily's lifetime.

She exited out the gate and followed the signs to baggage claim. Emily was going to meet her near the entrance. Lauren wore a conservative skirt and a jacket with low pumps, the sort of outfit she might wear to the *Time* magazine office. Her hair was freshly trimmed, as long and blonde as it was when she left home. As she walked down the concourse, her heart kept time with her heels. All her life she'd cradled other people's children, wondered what Emily might've looked like if she'd lived. Now, in a few minutes, she would know.

The reunion would be beyond anything she could've dreamed, but it would be marked by sorrow. Emily told her the day before that her dad's cancer was much worse. The doctors were giving him a few weeks at best. Lauren picked up her pace, seeing in her mind's eye her father the way he looked when she left home. Her heart hurt because they had so little time now. But it was impossible to feel only sorrow. After all, whatever time they had was a gift she'd never dreamed of having.

The crowds were heavy, and Lauren dodged around a large group of teenagers dressed in basketball uniforms. Emily probably traveled with her soccer team. Maybe the two of them had passed just like this in an airport sometime and had never known it. She darted toward the escalator, steadying her carry-on bag in front of her and gripping the rubber handrail.

Live combat didn't make her feel this nervous.

The escalator carried her down, slowly, slowly. Lauren peered into the clearing and she saw a hallway and a pair of double doors. Just beyond them was a pretty girl with dark hair, pacing a few steps one way and then the other, her eyes never leaving the doorway. Was that her? Lauren had about five seconds to study the girl, but in the end she didn't need even that long to know. The girl had Shane's dark hair, his striking features. And at the same time she was a brunette replica of herself at that age. Lauren stepped off the escalator and rushed through the doors, out of the way of the flood of people behind her. She stood there, staring at the girl, her heart in her throat.

The reality hit her just as their eyes met, as they held, and as they spoke volumes without saying a word. This was her daughter, her Emily! Her baby girl really was *alive!*

Emily spoke first. "Mom?" She came to her. "It's you, right?"

"Yes, Emily." Lauren dropped her bag and held out her arms. Her daughter came to her then, rushed into her embrace, and stayed there. Lauren rocked her back and forth as tears streamed down her cheeks. Their hug was warm and sure, and it took Lauren back to the last time she'd held Emily. She'd missed a lifetime of rocking her, but she wouldn't miss one second more. "You're so beautiful." She breathed the words into her daughter's hair. "I can't believe you're really here."

"Me neither." Emily drew back. Her eyes were bright as the sun, even though her cheeks were tearstained. "I looked for you all my life."

"I missed you every day." She pressed the side of her face against her daughter's. "If I'd only known."

Emily sniffed, and a bit of laughter came from her. "But you're here! You're really here. Now we'll never be apart again, okay?"

"Okay." She studied her daughter, reveled in the sight of her. They'd missed so much together, that maybe Emily was right. Maybe they would find their way to the same city and never be apart again. It was a piece of the story that hadn't yet been written. Lauren's life had been in the

Middle East, but that was before finding Emily. Now the future held more questions than answers.

"Hey." Emily stepped back and picked up Lauren's bag. "Can we get something to eat? I brought a photo album we can look at."

It was past one o'clock, but until then she hadn't realized how hungry she was. "Here? At the airport?"

"Why not?" Emily linked arms with her. "We're here, right?"

"Right." Lauren couldn't remember feeling this happy, not since her daughter's birth. They collected her two checked bags and headed back through the double doors up the escalator to a small Mexican restaurant.

Emily kept checking her watch and finally Lauren gave her a curious look. "Are we late?"

"No." She laughed, but it sounded nervous. "I told Grandma and Papa we'd take our time."

"Okay, then." They ordered, and Lauren found a table. When they were seated she leaned closer. She couldn't get enough of Emily, the way she looked so much like Shane and so much like herself all at the same time. She covered her daughter's

426

hand with her own. "Why don't you show me your photo album?"

"All right." Emily grinned. "Let's start at the beginning."

The first photos showed her as a toddler, taking her first steps, and sitting in front of a white-and-pink frosted birthday cake with one lit candle in the middle. Each picture was like a precious, painful window to all Lauren missed, all she'd lost out on. Why hadn't she gone back? Even one phone call and all the lonely years could've been avoided. By the second page she felt overcome with sorrow.

"Wait, Emily." She leaned her elbow on the table and shaded her eyes with the back of her hands. "I'm sorry."

"Mom." Emily took tender hold of her wrist and peered in at her. "Hey, don't be sad."

"I am." She sniffed. "I should've been there, and now . . ." A sob slipped free, and she willed herself to find control. "There's no way to get that time back."

"Yes, there is." Emily leaned in and kissed her cheek. "That's what pictures are for. They give you a way back."

"But it hurts so much." She wanted to be strong. This was her first chance in nearly two decades to actually be a mother to her daughter. She shouldn't be the one leaning on Emily. "I'd give anything to go back and do it all over again."

"I know."

"Really?" She lowered her hand and looked into her daughter's eyes. "Really, do you know how much I wish I'd been there?"

"Yes, Mom. I know. I could tell from the first time we talked." She closed the photo album. "We can look at this later."

Lauren sat up a little and stared at the blue leather cover on the book of photos. She could do this, especially with Emily at her side. She could go back to a missed lifetime and watch her little girl grow up in pictures, and somehow she would get through it. Without question she would be stronger for having done so. "No, I want to see them now." She put her arm around her daughter and smiled. "Just don't be embarrassed if I cry, okay?"

"Okay." Emily's eyes shone with compassion.

The next photos showed a preschool Emily riding a shiny red tricycle, then Emily dressed as a fairy princess for Halloween. Before they could turn the page, two of Lauren's teardrops hit the plastic covering. Lauren grinned at Emily. "See? Told you."

They both began to giggle, and then —
for the first time in their lives — Lauren
and Emily fell into a side-splitting round of
laughter, the cleansing, complete sort of
laughter only a mother and daughter can
share.

Emily couldn't get over it.

She and her mother had been together
less than an hour, and already she felt a
bond that would last a lifetime. Neither of
them liked refried beans, but they were
both crazy for spicy guacamole and black
olives. They both broke their chips in half
before dipping them into the salsa. When
they noticed, they laughed again.

The photos and the food, the little habits
they had in common, all of it was a wonderful distraction. And it helped Emily
keep from telling her mother what was
coming next: that she was about to see
Shane Galanter.

Because she couldn't tell her. Not yet.

The phone call with her father had been
amazing, and they too had talked a few
times since.

He had the same strong faith as Emily,
which was not the case with her mother.
And only a week before Emily found him,
he had broken off an engagement. Emily

couldn't help but believe that was somehow part of the miracle God was pulling together.

"So, Mom . . ." They were done eating. Emily planted her elbows on the table and rested her chin in her hands. "Tell me about Dad."

Her mother's eyes grew dreamy and faraway, but defeated at the same time. "He was amazing." She crooked her finger and pressed it first beneath one eye, then the other. "He wanted so much to be your daddy." She hesitated, directing her gaze across the concourse and out the full-length glass windows toward the runway. "He asked me to marry him." Her eyes found Emily again. "Did you know that?"

Joy filled Emily's soul. "No. I didn't." Her grandparents hadn't said anything about an engagement. She felt angry for the briefest instant, but then she let it pass. She could talk to them later about why they hadn't shared that information. The important thing was that long ago her parents had wanted to be married. It was all she could do to stay seated when she wanted to dance around the table and shout out the news. She settled herself down. "Tell me."

"It was before his family moved away." She narrowed her eyes and looked off to the distance again. "He gave me a ring engraved with the words *Even now*. He told me he would always love me, even now when things seemed so impossible." Her eyes glistened. "I wrote a story back then about the two of us in one of my notebooks and that's what I called it. *Even Now*." She took a slow breath, the memories clouding her eyes.

"I found it." She took a quick breath, not wanting to break up the memory. "I haven't read the whole thing. But the message on your ring . . . that's so romantic."

"Yes." A resignation filled her tone. "Shane was always that way."

"So what happened?"

"Nothing, really. Shane thought if we were engaged that our parents would work with us. He tried everything to find a place where he could live while we finished our last year of high school."

"Nothing worked out?" It was all so sad, so tragic. And though she knew what was coming in a half hour, Emily found herself getting teary eyed.

"Our parents just wanted us apart." There was no condemnation in her mother's eyes, no animosity. Just resignation. "Shane's parents owned his car and everything else. After he bought me the ring, he didn't have ten dollars left." She gave a sad laugh. "So they took him to California, promising that he'd have a way back to Chicago as soon as he graduated."

"They lied." The possibility hadn't occurred to Emily before. She might've grown up with her mother and father if these grandparents she didn't know had done something to help their son stay in Illinois. "That's so sad."

"It is." Her nod was firm. "But I forgave them. I had to." She smiled. "Otherwise I would've shriveled up and died from hating them."

Emily watched her mother. Being with her was like opening a chest with layers of treasure that would take a lifetime to experience. She leaned back and squeezed her mother's hand. "You know what I hope?"

"What?"

"I hope I'm loved that way someday."

A bittersweet longing knit her mother's brow together. "Me too, Emily. Me too."

The conversation shifted then. They talked about life in the Middle East and her mother's friend, Scanlon.

It was the first time her mother mentioned him, and Emily felt a ripple of alarm. "Are you two . . . you know, are you dating?"

Her mother gave her a pensive smile. "No —" she raised an eyebrow — "though Scanlon might think we are." She grew more serious. "He's a wonderful man. I think he'd like a future with me, but . . ." She lifted her shoulder. "I know what love is, Emily. I might not have had it for very long, but I had it. Unless I feel that way again, I don't see myself getting too serious with anyone."

They talked more about Scanlon and the recent tragedy at the orphanage. Her mother got tears in her eyes again when she talked about a little girl she'd met there — Senia, a seven-year-old with a missing front tooth.

"I'm sorry." Emily kept her tone low. "How's your arm?"

"It's healing. It still hurts, but even that's fading."

Emily didn't want to think about how different the attack might've played out. How awful it would've been to find her mother and learn that she'd been killed all within a few days. Her mother changed the subject again, telling Emily about the stories she'd covered while in Iraq and Afghanistan. They realized that one of

433

them — a cover story about the veil being removed from the women in the Middle East — was a story Emily had written a report about for her English class.

"Wow." Emily took a sip of her pop. The moment was approaching, and she was getting more excited by the minute. "Who'd have thought my mother would be famous?"

Again they laughed, and her mom went into another tale of danger and a story she'd written early in the Iraqi war. This time Emily was only catching half the details. She was about to burst from keeping the truth in.

Her dad's plane was landing in fifteen minutes!

"Emily?" Her mother angled her head. "Are you okay?"

She jumped to attention. "Of course. I was just thinking how much I'd like writing for a magazine someday." Silently she congratulated herself on the good cover. "Want more chips?"

Her mother looked puzzled. "We stopped eating chips awhile ago, honey." She laughed and gave Emily a silly look. "Let's get home." A ribbon of pain flashed in her eyes. "I want to see Mom and Dad."

"Now?" Emily's toes tapped out a panicky rhythm beneath the table. "I was

434

going to tell you about the soccer season. We almost went to the playoffs, did I mention that?"

"You drove here, right?" Her mother was already pushing back from the table, wiping her mouth and gathering her dishes on the tray.

"Right." Emily grabbed her fork and stuck it into the lukewarm mix of chicken and lettuce that covered her plate. "But I'm still working on my burrito."

She made a pleading look. "Could you maybe bring it with you? I really want to get home."

"Okay. When you put it like that." She grinned and went back to the counter for a carryout box. She took her time scraping the contents of her plate into the container, and then clearing her dishes from the table. She could feel her mother getting antsy, but she had to get the timing perfect.

They'd arranged it all. Her dad would walk off the plane and head down the concourse to the baggage area. When he reached the bottom of the escalator, he would call her cell phone, letting it ring once. She had her phone in her jeans pocket, set on vibrate. His call would cue her to take her mother and meet him.

Without drawing attention, she checked

435

her watch. Five more minutes. Suddenly she had an idea. She swiped her hand over the table, making it look like she was trying to clean off the crumbs. But as she did, she knocked over her pop, splashing it onto the floor and under the table. "Oh!" She jumped back. "I'm so clumsy."

Her mother darted across the café and grabbed a stack of napkins. "Here." She gasped. "Yikes. Emily, look out. It's coming off the table onto your shoe."

"Oops." She sidestepped the stream of pop. "I think I need more napkins."

They worked together to clean the mess, and then Emily stood and tossed the wet garbage into the trash can. "The trouble is, I'm more thirsty than ever."

"Well —" her mother pointed to the pop dispenser — "your cup's okay. Why don't you fill it before we go?" Her eyes danced in a way that was only half teasing. "Maybe you'd better get a lid too."

Emily pointed her finger in the air as if her mother's suggestion was a good one. She was filling her cup with Dr Pepper when the phone in her back pocket vibrated. She gasped and nearly spilled her drink again. But instead she slipped a lid on it and hurried back to her mother. "Okay. I'm ready."

"You sure?" She grabbed her carry-on bag and headed toward the café entrance. They were halfway out the door when her mother pointed back at the table. "Your leftover burrito!"

Emily turned and brushed her hand at it. "I'm not that hungry after all."

Her mother shrugged and gave her a crooked grin. "It's hard to keep up with you, Emily."

"I know it." She looped her arm through her mother's and held her chin high. "Everyone on the soccer team always tells me that."

Her mother hesitated, looking at the signs over the concourse. "Which way do we go?"

"This way." Emily's heart pounded hard within her. She hoped she wouldn't drop from anticipation before they reached him. "We have to go back through the baggage area."

"Isn't there a quicker way to —"

Emily dragged her toward the escalator. "Nope, this is the best way." She cast her mother a quick grin. "Trust me."

Shane Galanter had lived a lifetime for this moment.

He was standing next to his suitcases, at

437

the center of the baggage area, just off the main path leading to the escalator. Even now it felt like he might be dreaming. How many times had he seen a blonde with her build, her graceful mannerisms, and followed her only to realize he'd been wrong again? That initial conversation with Emily was still fresh in his mind. From the first few lines it was clear that he was the man she was looking for and that she wasn't part of any school tour group. But when she explained that she was his daughter . . . It had been more than he could take.

All along he'd wondered about what had happened to his child. Sometimes — as with the woman at the hotel the night of his engagement party — he would see a blonde with older kids and wonder for a minute if maybe one of them was his. But there were so many missing pieces. He wasn't sure if Lauren had kept the baby or not, and if she had, he didn't even know if his baby was a boy or a girl.

When he realized who Emily was, he couldn't make plans fast enough to come out to see her. That was when she told him that Lauren was coming too.

Lauren . . .

How long had he looked for her, wondering if he'd ever find her again? The photo he had of her was getting worn around the edges. He looked at it all the time, dreaming of this day, praying it might happen. What would it be like, seeing her after so many years? His heart pounded and he tried to dismiss his fears. What if she'd changed and her feelings for him were long dead? It would almost be easier never to see her again than to look in her eyes and know she'd left her love for him somewhere in the past.

No. As hard as it might be, he wouldn't trade what was coming. He loved Lauren still, there was no way around the fact. Whatever the coming hour held, he would let his heart ride it out.

He wore jeans and a white button-down shirt. Civilian clothes. Emily hadn't told him much, but she'd mentioned that Lauren was a reporter for *Time* magazine, a correspondent in the Middle East. That meant that they might have far less in common now than they once had. It was something he didn't want to think about, not yet. A wave of people filed off the escalator and out the double doors, but none of them was Lauren. Three more people, an older couple carrying a boxed up poodle, and then . . .

They were walking arm in arm, two

women with the same look, one blonde, one brunette. He straightened, willing himself to hold up. He wasn't sure about the girl, but the woman was Lauren. He'd seen her in his dreams every night since he moved to California. She was older, but the years had only made her more beautiful.

The younger of the two — Emily, it had to be — stopped and looked first one way, then the other, and then straight at him. Her eyes lit up, and he could hear her gasp from twenty feet away. For a second she turned to Lauren, but then she looked back at him again, as if she didn't know what to do first.

She tugged Lauren a few feet in his direction, and then she let go and ran the rest of the way. "Dad!" Her arms were around him, and she was crying.

"Emily . . ."

Here she was, the child he'd longed for, the one he'd never forgotten. His daughter, his very own! This was the girl who kicked at his hand as an unborn baby. That was their last contact until now.

They hugged arms tight around each other, before his daughter leaned back and looked him up and down. "Look at you! No wonder Mom was crazy about you."

He laughed and framed her face with his hands. The face that was so like his own. "I never thought I'd see this day, Emily." He wanted to look at Lauren, see if she'd followed their daughter closer. But he needed to have this moment first. "I promise you I'll spend the rest of my life making up for the years we've lost."

Emily gave him a quick hug, then — as if she suddenly remembered — she jumped back and both of them looked at Lauren. Her bags had fallen over, and she stood there, frozen in place, her mouth open.

The minute their eyes met he felt it, the connection. How had he thought for a minute that what they shared might've changed over the years? He had always known nothing could change it, and he was right. For a long moment they stood there, trying to believe what they were seeing. Tears ran down Lauren's cheeks, and finally he couldn't wait another second. He went to her at the moment she started toward him, and they met in the middle. If it were a movie scene, he would've swept her up, twirled her around in a circle, and kissed her the way a soldier kisses his girl after a long tour of duty.

But this moment held as much sorrow as it did triumph. As wonderful as it was to

441

see each other, Shane couldn't help feeling desperately sad. They'd lost two decades. And the privilege of raising their child together. That loss would always be with them. They stopped in front of each other, and slowly, with all the tenderness he had to give, he drew her into his arms. The lost years slipped away like so many seconds, and he soaked in the feel of her. They fit perfectly together, the way they always had.

"Lauren . . . I can't believe it's you." He could feel her heart pounding against his chest.

She held him tighter. "I looked for you . . . for so long . . ." She drew back and searched his eyes. "Where've you been, Shane?" Her crying grew harder, her voice the barest whisper. "I couldn't find you."

People were milling past, casting curious glances at them. Not far away Emily had righted her mother's luggage and now she was watching them, her face taken by a smile that stretched from ear to ear. Shane tucked Lauren's head in close to his chest and swayed with her, feeling himself responding to her presence. "I thought I'd lost you forever." He kissed the top of her head.

"Me too." Her voice was a mumble

against his shirt. After a few seconds she took a step back and studied him. "In my dreams you looked just like this, Shane."

"You too." They had so much to catch up on. He wanted to ask her why she changed her name, and what life had done to her way of thinking now that she was a *Time* magazine correspondent. He needed to tell her that he was in the navy, a fighter pilot, but all that could wait. He smiled at her. "Emily found me a few days ago." He leaned sideways and flashed their daughter a grin.

She gave him a cute little wave, and he did the same.

"I asked her not to tell you." He put his hands on her shoulders and searched her eyes. Looking into them was like getting his first drink after years in the desert. "I wanted you to be surprised."

"Surprised?" She took a few steps back and bent at the waist, bracing herself on her knees. When she looked up her expression was still filled with disbelief. "I'm surprised my heart's still beating."

He laughed and took her hands. They stood there, not quite able to get enough of each other. Finally he felt his smile fade. "You know about your parents?"

She nodded. "Daddy's sick. He might

only have a few weeks to live."

"Emily told me." He motioned for their daughter to join them. When she did, he put one arm around her and one arm around Lauren. He felt a rush of joy at the way they felt against him. Lauren and Emily, both of them. The feeling was amazing, like he'd found a missing part of himself and now — finally — he was whole again. He blinked back the wetness in his eyes and gave them each a light squeeze. "Let's get back to the house."

Emily nodded. Fresh tears filled her eyes, but she smiled at both of them. They were halfway to the parking lot when Emily said, "This is it, exactly."

"This moment, you mean?" Lauren looked around him and smiled at their daughter. Shane's throat tightened. Their daughter. Their little girl. A part of each of them . . .

"Yes. When I asked God for a miracle, a picture came to my mind." Emily skipped a few steps in front of them and turned around, her arms spread wide. "This picture. Exactly this."

Twenty-Five

It was the first day Bill hadn't felt like getting out of bed.

Angela asked him a few times, suggesting that he join her at the kitchen table for hot oatmeal or later that he sit on the sofa with her and watch a movie. The kids would be there by four o'clock. It was important that he stay awake and alert.

But he had only taken her hand and looked straight to the part of her that belonged to him alone. "Everything hurts, Angie. I'm sorry."

His answer dropped her to the edge of the bed. She sat there shaking. It took awhile until she said anything. "You never told me."

"I didn't want to." He smiled and laced his fingers between hers. "I have pills if I need them. It's just that I want to be alert when the kids come." His shoulders slid up and down against the pillow. "I figured if I rested all day I could fake it a little tonight."

That was at noon. He slept most of the day and now he was up and sitting in his recliner in the family room. She studied him from the kitchen and wondered how he would look to Lauren and Shane. Older, of course. But he was thin now, much thinner than before. His face was gaunt and the cancer had left his complexion ashy gray. He was cold too. No matter how high she kept the thermostat, he needed a blanket across his legs. Tonight he was using two — both of them extra thick.

Still, with all the changes and the pain he was in, his eyes glowed as he looked at her. "Any minute!"

"Yes." All their searching and praying and wanting their daughter had come to this. Lauren and Shane together again in the same room. With their daughter. And with them.

Part of her was so excited she could barely put the apple pie in the oven. But another part of her was terrified because she and Bill were at least partly responsible for separating them. If only Bill had asked the phone company to leave forwarding information on the recording connected to their old number. It was something he regretted every day. She wasn't about to bring it up now.

Once the pie was set, she poured the two of them coffee and joined him in the family room. She took the chair she liked best — the one closest to him. Just as she sat down, she heard a car, and after a few minutes, the sound of Emily's voice. Angela closed her eyes and reached for her husband's foot. "Father God, be here tonight."

She expected them to ring the doorbell, then realized Emily would never do such a thing. So she wasn't surprised when she heard the group come into the entryway, and after a bit of hushed conversation, she heard Emily's voice heading up the stairs with what must've been Shane. Angela stood and waited, her heart barely beating. Were Emily and Shane giving them this time alone with Lauren? It was something she had wanted, but never voiced. There was silence in the entryway for a few seconds, and then the sound of heels on the tile floor.

And suddenly — there she was. Standing before them, like something from a dream.

"Lauren . . ." Tears blurred Angela's vision and a sob caught in her throat. She was afraid to move or cry or say the wrong thing.

Lauren blinked and tears slid down her cheeks. Their eyes locked and she massaged her throat. "Mom . . ." Her eyes shifted to Bill. "Dad . . ."

Angela couldn't wait. She crossed the room, and carefully, as if her daughter might break, she took Lauren into her arms. With one hand on the back of Lauren's head and the other pressed to the small of her daughter's waist, Angela cradled her the way she'd done when Lauren was little, when she'd come home from kindergarten with a skinned knee.

Only this time she and Bill had caused her daughter's pain. And it went far deeper than any childhood scrape. "I'm so sorry, honey." She muttered the words against the side of Lauren's face. "I've spent my life being sorry."

Lauren felt stiff at first, as if the awkwardness of the moment kept her from giving in to her emotions. But as they embraced, Angela felt her daughter letting go, felt the sobs shaking her slight frame. "I'm . . . I'm sorry too."

When their tears slowed some, Lauren took a step back and turned toward Bill. Angela watched them. *God . . . You did this. You brought her home while we still had a chance to be together. All of us, the way we should've been from the beginning.*

"Daddy, how are you?" She reached the edge of his chair and he held his hand out to her. She took it and leaned closer, hugging him for what seemed like a minute. She eased onto her knees, bringing them face-to-face. "Does it hurt?"

He shook his head and brought his hand up along her face. "Not anymore." With his other hand, he brought her fingers to his lips and kissed them. "We were wrong, Lauren. I'm so, so sorry, baby."

Angela felt her composure slipping. He was a strong man, Bill Anderson. Strong and intelligent and not given easily to shows of emotion. At least, not before Lauren left. When she didn't come back and they couldn't find her, she'd watched him change. What he'd done by leaving their forwarding information off the recording, he'd done in love. He loved Lauren and would've gone to any lengths to protect her. It was that protective instinct of his that longed for Lauren with every passing hour. She was his little girl, and in some ways he hadn't been complete until just this minute. With her safely in his arms again.

Lauren looked weak as she struggled to her feet. The day had been an emotional one for all of them. She wiped her cheeks with her knuckles and looked at Angela and then Bill. Her eyes settled on Bill. "I'm the one who left." She lifted her chin a few inches. "I thought Emily was dead and I panicked. I never . . ." Her voice cracked and she held on to the back of Bill's chair for support. "I never should've gone without saying good-bye." Her expression was a twisted mass of sorrow and regret. "Forgive me . . . please?"

She dropped to the arm of Bill's chair and put her arm around him, leaning close and letting her head rest against his. "I missed you, Daddy." She looked up and turned the other way. "You too, Mom. How did so many years get away from us?"

Angela came to them, and the three formed a hug full of hope and promise and second chances. There was no talk about Shane, but Angela knew that would come. They couldn't move too far ahead without first letting go of the past.

Lauren lifted her head and looked at Bill again. "I'm sorry . . . about the cancer."

"I didn't ask God to make me better." His voice was hoarse, barely understandable. He framed her face with his fingers again. "I only asked him to bring you home."

★ ★ ★

The three of them talked in whispered tones before Angela found a box of tissues and passed them out. Lauren took one and stood. "Can Shane come in now? He wants to see you."

Angela felt like the worst person in the world. He was really there, the charming young man who had loved her daughter with such devotion, the kid who had purchased a wedding ring and asked Lauren to marry him so they wouldn't be torn apart. He had come, even though she and Bill had acted to keep them separate from each other.

"Yes, Lauren. Bring him in."

She left the room, and Angela turned to Bill. "Can you believe it? She's really home."

"She's beautiful." He sat up a little and pulled the blankets higher on his lap. "But her eyes aren't what they were. Do you see it?"

Angela hadn't wanted to admit that. To do so meant taking blame for even more damage. But Bill was right. "I see it. I think it has to do with her faith."

"Does she . . . have faith?" He winced, as if the pain of thinking such a thing was worse than anything the cancer was doing to him.

451

"I don't know." She took hold of his shoulder. "I can only believe that with the miracles God has brought about in the last few weeks, He won't stop short of that one."

Bill nodded, and as he did, they heard footsteps in the entry again. This time all three of them filed into the family room, with Shane leading the way.

He smiled and came to them, giving Bill a firm handshake. "Mr. Anderson, it's good to see you." Then he turned to her. "Mrs. Anderson." He released Bill's hand and hugged her. It wasn't the hug they'd received from Lauren, but it was one that spoke forgiveness. Whatever Shane Galanter had once held against them, those feelings were no longer a part of him.

"Shane." Bill coughed and held his hand out to Shane once more.

"Yes, sir?" The handshake held.

"My wife and I owe you an apology." Bill's eyes had been dry until now. But here, with Lauren and Emily standing a few feet away arm in arm, and all of them gathered together for the first time, tears welled up and trickled down his leathery cheeks.

"It's over with, sir." Shane kept hold of Bill's hand. "God made it clear to me a long time ago that we can't go back." He looked over his shoulder at Lauren and Emily, and then at Bill once more. "We can only be glad for today."

"Something else." He rubbed at his throat, his voice raspy. "I understand you're a captain in the navy, a fighter pilot, is that right?"

Angela watched Lauren's expression change. She looked down at the floor, but only for a minute.

"Yes, sir. I train fighter pilots at the Top Gun facility in Reno, Nevada."

"Well, then, I have to tell you —" Bill gripped Shane's hand harder than before — "I couldn't be prouder of you if you were my own son."

Again a shadow passed over Lauren's eyes, and Angela felt a strong prompting to pray. *What is it, God? Does she disapprove of Shane's job?* With Shane and Bill discussing the navy, and Emily grinning, talking about how her dad was going to take her up in an F-16, it hit Angela. Of course Lauren had a problem with Shane's job.

She'd been covering the war for *Time* magazine for the past two years. Her political views and Shane's would be at polar ends of the spectrum by now. What if Lauren found all of them too conservative, their faith too upfront? What if she stayed for only a few days and then ran away again, certain she could never belong? Fear wanted a place in the midst of their group, but Angela wouldn't allow it.

God, this is Your territory. The years might've changed Lauren, but that's okay. She's entitled to her opinion — whatever that opinion is. She settled her gaze on Lauren, aching to go to her and hold her again, her only daughter. Instead she finished her prayer. *Father, let her feel Your love this week. I know I'm asking for a lot, God, but please use this time to stir in her the faith we share with Emily and Shane. Please . . .*

Even as her prayer ended, she felt a deep uneasiness, a sorrow that their decisions twenty years ago had pushed Lauren far away, not only from them, but from God. The Lord had been so good to them in the years since Lauren left. The tragedy of losing her, of raising Emily without her parents had turned them to a deep, life-sustaining faith. From what Emily told them, in his pain and loneliness, Shane had found a relationship with Christ also.

Now she would pray with every breath that one day soon the same would be true for Lauren.

Twenty-Six

Lauren had been waiting for this moment all day. Waiting for it and dreading it all at the same time. She and Shane were about to be alone for the first time in two decades. The night had been amazing. All five of them had talked and cried and told funny stories about the years they'd missed until finally her dad was too tired to last another minute. Her mother walked him to their room, and Emily stayed up talking with Lauren and Shane until just a few minutes ago. After so many years, none of them could get enough of each other.

Now it was after midnight, and she and Shane and Emily were heading upstairs to tell Emily good night.

"Can I ask you something?" A smile played on Emily's lips, as they reached the top of the stairs and she looked at the two of them standing together. "I always used to wonder what it would be like to have my parents tuck me in. You know, like other kids." Her eyes were dry, but her tone rang with sincerity. "Would you do that? Please?"

Lauren's heart sang. She felt honored her daughter would even ask. Emily was no longer a child, after all. How wonderful that she didn't feel too old to still be a kid around them. She tugged on Emily's sweater sleeve. "You lead the way."

And so the three of them trucked down the hall to Emily's room, Lauren and Shane a few steps behind. Shane held her hand, and the sensation stirred countless emotions in her. How often had she dreamed of this, the normalcy of such a moment? That she and Shane might be heading upstairs to bid their daughter good night, the way real families did.

Emily slipped into her bathroom to put on her pajamas, leaving Lauren and Shane standing near the doorway. He slid his arms around her waist, and she let him draw her close. No matter how long she looked at him, she couldn't get enough. It was as though they'd never been apart. All evening they'd sat close together, and she could hardly think for the way Shane's fingers felt linked with hers.

It was the same way now, in his arms. She came to him willingly. Time had done nothing to dim the desire between them, that much was certain. "Can you believe we're here?" His voice was low, his breath soft against her cheek. He nuzzled his face against hers. "You feel so good, Lauren."

"I used to fall asleep each night wishing . . ." She traced her finger along his collarbone. "Wishing I'd wake up in the morning and you'd be there beside me. That we were married and together." She dragged her hand through the air beside them. "Like all this would just be a terrible nightmare."

"Mmm." He breathed in near the nape of her neck and then drew back enough to meet her eyes again. "We should've had a lifetime of that by now." He lifted his hands to her face and worked his fingers into her hairline. A low groan came from him. "It kills me to think of all we missed."

The bathroom door opened, and Shane pulled back. He took hold of Lauren's hand, but he hit the light switch and Lauren could see him grinning at both of them in the dark. "Okay, young lady, time for bed."

Emily giggled and padded past them in her socks. Then she climbed in between the covers and pulled them up near her chin. "Can you pray with me? That's part of tucking in."

Lauren shifted, but tried not to show her discomfort. She'd considered God an enemy since she got the news that Emily was dead, since she'd driven away from Chicago that terrible day. Faith belonged to the rest of them, not her. It wasn't something she wanted, either. If there *was* a God, He had let them lose a lifetime together. Why Emily and Shane cared for such a God, she didn't understand.

Still she wasn't about to resist. This wasn't a debate on theology. She let Shane lead her to the side of Emily's bed. Suddenly the full extent of what was happening hit her square in the heart. She was saying good night to her daughter — the baby girl she'd thought was dead! She was sitting next to her in a dark room, getting one of her first chances to be Emily's mom. She sat on the edge of the mattress and ran her fingers through Emily's bangs. Next to her Shane's quiet voice rang out clear and confident, full of a faith Lauren had stopped believing in years ago.

"Dear God, we're here tonight because You allowed it." He drew a deep breath. "I thought I'd live my life never finding either of these two, but You — You brought us together. We pray Emily will sleep well, and that tomorrow we'll all wake up and find that it's really happening, that it's not just a wonderful dream." He hesitated, and his tone grew heavier. "Help us not to be angry or sad over all we've lost. But help us celebrate what You've given us today. In Jesus' name, amen."

Shane leaned down and kissed Emily on the cheek. "Good night, Emily." He tapped the tip of her nose. "Thank you."

She smiled, and the little girl she must've been shone in her eyes. "For what?"

"For letting God use you." He stood and headed for the doorway.

It was Lauren's turn. She looked down at Emily and once more brushed her thumb across her daughter's forehead. "I remember the last time I did this."

"At the hospital?" Emily rolled onto her side so they could see each other better.

"Mmm-hmm. You were so sick, so hot. I sat there next to your bed and I did this. I touched your forehead, begging God to let you live, to bring you back to me."

Emily searched her eyes. "Don't you see, Mom?"

"See what?"

"He answered your prayers." She gave a little shrug. "Here we are, just like you asked."

A lump lodged in her throat, but her

words found their way around it. "I like your attitude, Miss Emily. I'm proud to be your mother." She leaned in and kissed her on the forehead. Then she whispered, "Good night, sweet daughter. I love you." The words felt wonderful on her lips. "I can't say it enough."

"Love you too."

Shane was waiting for her out in the hallway. Without saying a word he eased his fingers between hers again and led her back down the stairs to the living room. Gentle flames danced in the fireplace, and through the oversized picture window it was snowing.

He turned out the lights, and when they reached a spot near the fireplace, he stopped and tugged her into his arms again. "Hi." He brushed his cheek against hers, holding her with a gentle firmness.

"Hi." Panic tried to interrupt the moment. Were they going to talk or was it just assumed that they would start up again where they'd left off?

"Here we are." He searched her eyes . . . Was he going to kiss her? Did she want him to? She swallowed. Her knees were weak and her heart was racing hard. Of course she wanted him to kiss her. But was it right, when they hadn't talked yet?

Before she could answer her own questions, he began humming a James Taylor song, one that had been their favorite the year she got pregnant. Slowly, and with his eyes still locked on hers, he swayed her in a dance that made her head spin. She felt herself being sucked in, pulled to a place where she wouldn't ever want anything but the feeling of his arms around her.

What little resistance she'd brought with her to Chicago melted like the snowflakes hitting the window outside. Maybe they didn't have to talk, not yet. This was what she'd wanted all those years, wasn't it? A chance to be in Shane Galanter's arms again, alone in a dark room with just the sound of a fire crackling in the background.

Their swaying slowed and he brought his hands to her face. In an unhurried, barely controlled way, he worked his fingers into her hair again and brushed his lips against her cheek. "I never stopped loving you."

"Me neither." She breathed in the scent of him — his warm breath, his fresh shampoo and cologne. He smelled wonderful. The day had already been so emotional, and now this. Their eyes held, and she knew. It was going to happen.

His lips found hers first, and he left the

lightest kiss there. "Lauren . . . don't ever let go."

"I won't." Her heart was talking now. This time she found his lips and kissed him the way she was dying to. Full and slow and with a lifetime of bottled-up passion. His arms tightened around her, and they swayed every now and then, and after a few minutes they made their way up against the wall closest to the window.

The air between them changed, and she felt the same trembling in his body that was moving over her. Shane pulled back first, pursing his lips and exhaling hard. His eyes blazed with desire, mirroring the feelings that had to show in her face as well.

"Okay." He chuckled and rubbed the back of his neck. He let her go and crossed the living room where he sat at one end of the sofa. "Looks like some things haven't changed."

She let her arms hang at her sides and she shook them. No one made her feel the way Shane did. She grinned at him through the dim light of the fire. "No, some things definitely haven't changed." He was waiting for her, so she crossed the room and sat a foot away from him. A little space would be good right now.

Something he'd said made her wonder. Maybe she wasn't the only one afraid of sorting through the years and taking a harder look at who they'd become. She ran her finger down his forearm. "Did you mean —" her voice was kind — "that some things *have* changed?"

His expression gave him away. He looked down but only for an instant. When his eyes found hers again, he gave her a sad smile. "I know who you are, Lauren Gibbs."

"Lauren Gibbs?" She lowered her chin. How much did he know? She kept her tone light, not wanting to lose what they'd found in the past hour. "Does my fighter pilot read *Time* magazine?"

The sorrow in his face deepened. "He does."

An awful feeling crept into the moment. A year ago she'd written an article stating that Iraqi residents had no respect for American fighter pilots. She'd quoted one man saying, "They are the epitome of the ugly American. Cowards afraid to face their enemies. Flying overhead and destroying our towns and villages, our homes and neighborhoods with the push of a button."

The article included a brief paragraph

detailing a response from the air force and another from the navy, rhetoric about how air strikes were actually more humane because the targets could be pinpointed within a few feet. Had he seen that story? She had the awful feeling that he had. She sighed. "You saw my piece on fighter pilots?"

He brushed his knuckles against her cheek, the love in his eyes still strong. "It was posted at the base for six months." He chuckled. "Just about every fighter pilot wrote a rebuttal. Last time I checked, your story was pretty well surrounded."

She groaned and let her head fall back against the sofa. "Shane . . ." She sat straight again searching his eyes. "How did you wind up on the wrong side of this war?"

He took her hand and in the smoothest sensation he brought it to his lips and kissed it. "The question is —" his voice held no accusation; only the same love from earlier that night — "how did you?"

His words placed a thin line between them. "Shane, just for a minute forget all your naval air training." She was careful not to sound hard or sarcastic. "You're a Christian."

"I am." His kindness didn't waver.

"So Jesus taught about peace, right? He came to bring us peace."

"Actually, He came to bring us life." Shane's words were slow, easy. His eyes still held hers and his tone was relaxed. "Life to the fullest measure."

"Okay, good." She bit her lip. "If He came to bring us *life,* then how can you be part of a war that kills people?"

"Lauren." He ran his fingers along her forearm. "Conflict has been around since Cain and Abel. For most of time people have fought wars, lots of them with God's approval."

She could feel her blood pressure rising. "Okay." She breathed out, "How can you support a God who would want war? Innocent people killed?" She sat straighter, putting another few inches between her and Shane. "Isn't the goal supposed to be peace?"

"Yes." His voice was a little more intense. "Do you think I don't want peace in Iraq? Peace in Afghanistan?" He pulled one knee up on the sofa and turned to face her. "Because I fly fighter jets?"

The question threw her. She'd had these talks with conservatives before. Even military conservatives. They always trotted out the causes for war: weapons of mass destruction, vicious dictators, torture among civilians. But no matter how long and fast they talked, she felt the same. How did two wrongs make a right? How could the U.S. take a stand against dangerous weapons in Iraq, and then drop dangerous weapons to make its point?

But never, in all her days of reporting in the Middle East, had she heard a military captain say that he wanted peace. She searched his eyes. "Peace, Shane?" Her voice held question marks, nothing more. "You spend your days training fighter pilots how to find and destroy enemy targets, and you want peace?"

He was quiet for a minute. The slight rise in his intensity faded. "Where were you on September 11, 2001?"

She didn't want to talk about the terrorist attacks. It was the same story with half the war supporters she'd interviewed. It made the U.S. military sound like a bunch of whiny kids. *They hit us first . . .* Still, this was Shane. Regardless of their differences this side of yesterday, she owed him a thoughtful answer. She crossed her arms and pressed her good shoulder into the back of the sofa. "I was in Los Angeles at the office." The memory came sidling up like a smelly drunk at a bar. "I watched it, horrified like everyone else."

"Did you know anyone in those buildings?"

"I didn't." She drew her feet up in front of her and hugged her knees. "But I was one of the reporters on it. I interviewed people in Los Angeles who'd lost friends or family." The sick feeling she'd known all that week came back. "It was awful." She studied his face. Maybe he had other reasons for asking about it. She reached out and touched his hand. "What about you?"

He stared at the fire, his eyes full of something she couldn't make out. "I was in Reno, at the Top Gun facility. Got a call the night before from a buddy of mine, went through navy fighter pilot training with him. Only Benny didn't want to be a career fighter pilot. He wanted to be a firefighter. FDNY." Shane squinted at what must've been the garish glare of the past. "We talked about his wife and kids, the great weather they were having." Shane smiled at Lauren. "I told him he should come out to Top Gun and take a ride in an F–16 with me."

Lauren knew what was coming. She looped her fingers around his. "He was on duty the next morning?"

"He was." Shane looked at the fire again.

"His wife told me he made it to the sixty-first floor before the South Tower fell." He met her eyes again. "They never found his body."

She waited a minute, giving the story time to fill her heart. "I'm sorry."

"Thanks." He gave her fingers a light squeeze. "I've thought a lot about peace. I studied it in school, believe it or not."

"Really?" Her tone told him she was teasing in a gentle sort of way. She tried to picture him hanging out with the people she knew in college, the journalism students. "You wore tie-dye and sandals in college, did you?"

"Close." He chuckled. "The sandals, anyway." He rested his arm along the sofa back and ran his fingers over her shoulder. "I didn't want what my parents had. Materialism and business investments and a life of plastic facades. I knew that much." He gave her a serious frown. "College was interesting for me. I asked a lot of questions, studied the history of civilizations and what exactly constituted peace."

She was impressed. A large number of her liberal friends hadn't done that. Yes, she agreed with them, but that didn't mean their opinions were based on fact. Hers were. She interviewed people all day long.

If anyone should have the facts on why war wasn't worth fighting, she should.

He must have seen she was interested, because he continued. "Time and again I saw the same thing, Lauren." His eyes implored her to hear him. Really hear him. "I saw that we could have peace only through strength."

Another military motto, one she'd heard bantered about far too often. Still, she stopped herself from reacting. "What does that *mean,* Shane? Peace through strength?"

He gave her question some thought. "I guess it's like this. We've lost an awful lot of men in this war, and that's a tragedy. One life lost is a tragedy. But when we look at the plans the terrorists had for this country, I see the benefit of strength. The peaceful benefit." He ran his thumb over the top of her hand. "They had very detailed plans, Lauren. I saw them. They thought they'd make September 11 look like a minor incident."

Even after a lifetime of standing on the other side of this fence, she wanted to understand him. If things had been different, they wouldn't be having this talk. No doubt she would've been on his side, searching for a way to justify the things she inherently believed. "So . . ."

He held his hands out to the sides, face up. "They haven't struck again, Lauren. Their plans fell to rubble. Their rubble."

"They messed with the wrong people, right?" Again she was careful to sound open, interested. Not condemning. "That's what you're saying?"

"Sort of. I mean you're over there, Lauren. You walk down the streets and shop in the villages and see the people." He paused. "When's the last time you saw an air raid, an air attack by a U.S. fighter pilot?" A partial smile played on his lips. "The only reason we're still there is to help the new government get set up. And that's peaceful, right? We pull out and, well, you know what'll break loose over there."

She thought about the attack on the orphanage. "It's already loose. I didn't make the article up, Shane." She sighed. "The people I talk to live in fear and stay indoors most of the time."

"Yes." A hint of frustration crept into his tone. "Because those are the people your magazine *wants* you to talk to."

"Okay." She eased her feet back to the floor, her eyes never leaving his. "You think we have peace through strength because we flexed our muscle, right? We showed them. If they thought they could mess with

470

us, they had another think coming. Something like that?" Her opinions were coming
through a little too loudly. She drew a slow
breath to bring down her tone. "But
maybe that only makes us bullies."

"Lauren." He took hold of both her
hands. "Do you really want to talk about
this tonight?"

"Do you really want to avoid it?" Her
answer was quick, and regret filled her. She
ached to go to him, lose herself in his
arms, and kiss him all night long. "I'm
sorry."

He reached for her and she slid closer to
him. "You see things your way, and I see
them mine. Can't we be okay with that for
now?"

"Yes." She looked at him. Their faces
were close again. "For now."

"Meaning what?" He angled his body toward her, tracing her jaw with his finger.

"Meaning we don't have to talk about it
this week, Shane. We can figure it out later,
when it's time to go home."

He kissed her then, and in the time it
took her to respond, all the passion from
earlier was back. He eased himself from
her and took a breath. That's when she noticed his eyes — they were eyes that belonged to a seventeen-year-old boy she'd

promised to love forever.

"You're forgetting one thing."

"What?" She didn't want to talk. She wanted to be lost in his arms, searching desperately for a way back to what they'd shared before.

"You forgot that this *is* home. Here." He kissed her again and another time. "Right here, with me."

She wanted to believe him. Oh, how she wanted to. But she couldn't. He was wrong. Home was her apartment in Afghanistan, where she wrote stories that shed light on the reasons war could never bring about peace. Home was hitting the dusty roads with Scanlon beside her, his big canvas camera bag sitting on the seat between them. But she couldn't say so.

Not when she planned to spend the next week pretending he was right.

Twenty-Seven

Emily woke to the clipped sound of a single siren.

She sat straight up and looked at her dresser alarm clock. Six a.m. Lights were flashing outside the window and suddenly she was awake enough to understand what was going on. Her heart felt like it was turning somersaults inside her chest. Something must've happened with Papa.

Her mom was sleeping in the office; her dad on the living room sofa. Now she and her mother met in the hallway and hurried down the stairs. They were halfway down when they saw her grandpa on a stretcher, being taken out through the front door. Her grandma was saying, "I'll be right out. I want to ride with him." She shot them a quick glance. "He had a seizure. They want to admit him, just in case there's something they can do."

Near the side entrance to the living room, Emily's dad walked up and gave his

473

head a quick shake. "Mrs. Anderson, can I do anything?"

"Bring the others." Her grandma ran into the entryway with Papa's two blankets. Then she took quick hold of Shane's wrist and looked at the rest of them. "He's stable. He'll be okay for now. Come later this morning, okay?"

Emily padded down the stairs the rest of the way and darted over to her grand-mother, giving her a fast hug. She had never been more afraid in all her life. "Tell him we're praying for him."

"I will." She paused, and Emily thought she looked about to collapse. "The doctor told me seizures would mean he was close to the end." She took another step toward the door. "I thought you should know." She bid them good-bye and then she left.

The three of them stood in the entryway, listening to the ambulance pull away. Every few seconds the sirens gave a short blast — probably so they wouldn't disturb the neighborhood any more than neces-sary.

Emily's throat was tight. "I can't go back to sleep."

"No." Her mother took slow steps the rest of the way down. She wore a white T-shirt and what looked like black running pants. "Let's go sit on the couch."

Emily couldn't help but notice the way her mom went to her dad and slid one arm under his and up along his back. Emily had wondered what their time alone would bring about, and now she had her answer. They were happy and in love and probably making plans to get married. Just like she'd always dreamed. But there was one problem. In her dream, Papa wasn't on the verge of dying just when everything was coming together.

They sat on the sofa, her dad in the middle, and for the next two hours they took turns talking and dozing off, leaning their heads on each others' shoulders. At eight o'clock her dad stood and stretched. "I'm going to take a shower." He looked at the clock near the front door. "Let's try to leave in an hour."

When he was gone, Emily slid closer to her mother. She was terrified about her grandpa, but she couldn't let that stop her from enjoying this time with her mom. For a few moments she leaned into her, resting her head on her mother's good shoulder. Then she sat up and gave her mom a hopeful look. "So, is he just like you remembered?"

"Shane?"

Her mother's reaction wasn't quite right. She smiled, but she didn't light up like she should've.

"He's very handsome, if that's what you mean."

"He is." Emily giggled. "But I meant the other stuff." She scrunched her shoulders up a few inches. "Do you think you'll be back together after this?"

Her mom looked at her, and then let out a sad, frustrated sigh. "Honey, seeing him again . . . this time together is wonderful." Her tone softened. "But don't get your hopes up." She sighed and took hold of Emily's hand. "We've grown up a lot in eighteen years."

Emily tried not to gulp. She'd wondered but been afraid to ask. With their opposing occupations, her mom and dad had to be in opposite corners, for sure. "It's about the war, right?"

"That's one area." Her answer was quick and it shook Emily's confidence. "We've become very different people."

"It doesn't seem that way. Not when I look at you."

She smiled. "I like being with him. That part's easy."

"Well . . . then maybe it'll work out after all."

"Emily." Her mom lowered her chin, and in a nice way her look said the conversation was over. "Let's just enjoy this week." Her smile faded. "We have Papa to think about. That's most important right now, okay?"

Her answer didn't come easily. "Okay."

She wanted to scream or run or keep them together in this same house until the end of time. But none of that would bring her parents together the way they'd been before, in a way where their politics and differences wouldn't matter.

Only God could do that.

Emily's questions had Lauren off balance all day. But she couldn't spend much time thinking about Shane or how they'd changed or whether they could find something again when this week was over. Her father was far too sick to think of anything but him and her mother and how quickly the end was coming.

She and Shane and Emily arrived at the hospital just after nine. Her mother met them in the hall outside his room. Lauren took the lead, meeting her mom halfway and taking her hands. "How is he?"

"It's moving so fast. It could be anytime." She looked down and their foreheads came together.

Lauren gripped her mother's arm at the news. "No . . ."

It was too soon. She hadn't had time to talk to him or find out what she'd missed for all those years. On the hardest days in the Middle East, she always believed she could go back home if she wanted to. Her daddy would always take her back. But now he would be gone, and a place in her heart would never be the same again.

Her mother was trembling, probably tired and scared and trying not to break down. A moment later Emily and Shane came up and circled their arms around the two of them.

"Is he awake?" Shane's voice rang with compassion. "I'd like to see him. Maybe pray with him."

"He is." Her mom sniffed and straightened a little. "We should all go in. He's been asking for you."

Why did she run when she did? Why didn't she at least call? Just one call and she would've found Emily and her parents. Together they might even have found Shane. Maybe she'd be writing for the *Tribune* and covering features or entertainment — something less life shattering than war.

She trailed the others into the room. Her

heart felt like it was being dragged behind her on a chain. Had she done this to her father? Had his grief and longing and missing her all those years given him a deadly disease?

No. She couldn't think that way, not now when he needed her smiling face at his bedside. He was greeting Emily, and she watched her daughter lay her head on her grandpa's chest. "Papa, we're gonna stay here all day, okay?"

"I'm . . . sorry I'm sick." He gave her a weak smile and then looked around the room at the rest of them. "Not much of a party, huh?"

Emily nuzzled her face against his. "We don't need a party, Papa. We just need you."

Shane looked back at Lauren and motioned for her to come closer. She did so without hesitation, but her attention was still on her father and Emily, the relationship they had. Emily had told her that her dad had changed, that he wasn't the way he'd been, wasn't the man who'd hurt her so. Watching the two of them, the way her dad held Emily's hand and spoke softly to her, she knew the truth. Her daughter was right.

In some ways, it was another loss. Had

479

she come home sooner, she would've had time to share that same sort of tender relationship with him. Emily gave him one more hug and then she stepped back. Next, Shane put his hand on Lauren's father's shoulder. "God has a plan in all this." Shane's voice was strong and compassionate, a tone that showed how much he cared and that he held no hard feelings toward the man. "Don't forget that, okay?"

Her dad looked intently at Shane. "My girls are going to need you."

"Yes." His chin trembled, but he clenched his jaw and nodded. "I know."

"Don't leave them, okay?" He glanced at the others. His eyes settled on Lauren, and she wasn't sure who his next words were directed at. "They need you . . . even if they don't think they do."

Shane reached back and took Lauren's hand. "I know, sir. I'm not going anywhere." He eased back against the wall and gave Lauren a look that melted her.

It was her turn. She came to her father's side. "Hi, Daddy."

"Hi, little girl."

Her eyes were dry, but a sob caught in her throat. She remembered a thousand times when she'd greeted him that way, back before she'd taken up with Shane, when he thought of her as the girl who couldn't do anything wrong. In some ways this was better. Because he certainly knew the truth. She was miles from perfect, yet his eyes told her he loved her no less. In fact he cared for her more than ever. His hand was rough against hers. Rough and dry and cold, as if death was already staking its claim on him. She leaned close and kissed his fingers. "We need more time."

"Yes." His voice was gravelly, so low it was impossible to hear him without leaning closer. "You know . . . what I'm going to tell you."

She wrinkled her nose, confused. "No, Dad." Her heart skipped a beat. Was this when he'd remind her that the whole tragedy of their lives was her fault, that she never should've slept with Shane in the first place? He wouldn't do that now, would he? She swallowed her fears. "What do you want to tell me?"

"About Shane." The words were an effort for him. "That young man has loved you forever." He took a rest and for a moment he did nothing but breathe. "He still loves you." His look grew more intense. "And you love him too, I . . . know you do."

She felt the sting of tears. She'd spent all these years forcing herself not to cry. But now, crying was as familiar as breathing. "Yes." She didn't turn around or look at Shane. She wasn't even sure he could hear them. "Shane loves me."

"Don't . . . don't let him go again. Love doesn't mean . . . seeing eye to eye on everything."

Was her father that aware of what was happening around him? Had he really known that who they'd become as adults could make her and Shane walk away from this week and close the door on their past for good? Even thinking about it hurt her, but what choice did they have? She drew a steadying breath. "Dad, I —"

"Shh." He held her hand to his cheek and winked at her. His eyes danced as they hadn't since the group of them walked into his hospital room. "Don't analyze. I'm right about this." His lungs sounded raspier than before. "You've lost so much, Lauren. Don't lose what God wants to give you now."

Lauren felt her own wisdom dissolving. He was right, wasn't he? She had lost so very much. They all had. Losing Shane now would be tragic, even if she still couldn't see a way for it to work between them. She leaned over and put her cheek against his. "Daddy!" She hugged him, wishing she still had a thousand more times to do this. "How do you still know me so well?"

"Because —" he brushed his scruffy unshaven face against hers, the way he'd done when she was little — "daddies never forget their little girls." He looked at her, leaving just enough space between them so he could search her eyes. "When I get to heaven . . . I won't forget you even then. I'll be waiting . . . for you there, believing you'll be along one day. Just like I . . . believed you'd be along one day . . . for the last eighteen years."

She couldn't talk, couldn't squeeze a single word past the emotions stuck in her throat. Instead she held him and willed life into him. He was kind and wise and gentle, and he loved her — he always had. Even when he hadn't used the best judgment in showing her, still he loved her. Now she wanted another thirty years with him. At least.

Please . . . please . . .

She didn't know who she was pleading with, but it didn't matter. She had to try. Snuggling against him, her knees ached from the awkward position, but she didn't move until there was a sound at the door. Only then did she straighten and look past the years to his tender soul. "I love you, Daddy."

He gave her hand another squeeze. "I love you, sweetheart."

At that moment, a familiar-looking couple in their late fifties or early sixties walked through the door. Lauren looked at them and frowned. She knew them from somewhere. Their eyes held the haunting look of guilt and trepidation, as if maybe they were entering a place where they weren't welcome. In a rush, Shane went to them — and in a sudden flash she understood.

Sheila and Samuel Galanter. Shane's parents. The people who had once been her parents' closest friends. The people who took Shane from her. Lauren felt her knees start to shake and she braced herself against the hospital bed. Why had they come, and what could they possibly say now? For a moment she couldn't decide whether to excuse herself from the room or stay and hear what they had to say. She looked at the floor, her heart racing, and she made up her mind. She would stay.

Whatever was about to take place, she wanted a front-row seat to see it.

Angela was trying to keep from falling to the floor.

She was standing on the other side of Bill, opposite Lauren, when first Samuel, then Sheila walked through the door. At first Angela couldn't make herself believe what she was seeing. The stress of Bill's illness, the wonder at having Shane and Lauren back, all of it was maybe making her a little loopy.

But then Shane went to them. "Mom, Dad." He hugged them one at a time and then stepped back.

Angela couldn't see Shane's face, but she had the sense he wasn't surprised. Had he called them, asked them to come? Across the room, Emily moved close to Lauren and whispered something. Lauren nodded, her face pale.

Next to Angela, Bill slid a little higher on his pillow. "I can't believe it." He looked up at her, his voice hushed. The Galanters were still talking to Shane near the door, so they couldn't hear him. Bill covered her hand with his. "Did you know about this?"

Angela shook her head. Fear and trepidation filled her. What would the four of them say after so many years, so many hurts? She kept her eyes on Bill, her whispered words shaky. "I thought I was seeing things."

The Galanters made the first move. Sheila took a few steps into the room, her eyes vulnerable and heavy with . . . could it be? Was it remorse? The beginnings of hope stirred in Angela's soul. Ten feet away now, Sheila looked at Bill, and then, after a long beat, she shifted her gaze. Angela swallowed hard as her eyes met that of her long-ago friend.

Sheila's voice broke as the first words left her lips. "I'm sorry, Angela. I was . . . so wrong."

Angela couldn't speak or move. She didn't dare draw a breath or blink until the words found her heart. Sheila was here and she was sorry? Was it really true?

"Bill, Sheila's right." Samuel took a step closer and put his hand on the foot of Bill's bed. "We —" His eyes fell, and Sheila reached for his hand. When he looked up, his eyes shone with emotion. "We were wrong. We owe you an apology."

The entire scene played out in a handful of seconds, but still, so far she and Bill hadn't said a word. Angela's eyes were full, blurring her vision. What could she say after such a long time? Shane backed up and stood next to Emily and Lauren, the three of them doing their best to blend into the background.

Samuel cleared his throat and continued. "We were wrong, how we handled the situation with our kids." He narrowed his eyes and worked the muscles in his jaw. Then he gave a solid shake of his head. "We were wrong in too many ways to count."

"We knew Shane was here." Sheila took another step toward them. She looked at Bill. "We knew you were sick. And we had to come. We've let so much time pass."

Angela hung her head for a moment. Her knees were steady, but her whole body shook. There had been years and years when she believed she'd see Lauren again, and maybe even Shane. But she never once thought she'd see this — these old friends finding a way back to the same place. She looked up and her eyes met Sheila's. "I . . . can't believe you came."

"We're so sorry." Samuel put his arm around Sheila's waist. He had been an intimidating businessman in his day, a man who neither smiled nor laughed easily. But now — if the sincerity in his eyes was any indication — he was a changed man.

Sheila held her hand out. "Forgive me, Angela . . . please."

Angela felt herself break, felt Sheila's

words finally connect in her heart. Her tears fell hot and quick onto her cheeks as she held her hands out to her lost friend. "Sheila . . . of course. It wasn't just you. We were all . . . all of us were at fault." She embraced Sheila, overcome. There was no going back, no way to regain the years they'd lost, no way to undo the damage they'd done to their kids. But here now, forgiveness was happening, and it was the most wonderful feeling in the world.

She drew back and made a sad sound. "Why were we so stubborn?"

"I don't know." Sheila sniffed and smiled through her tears. A smile that showed how deeply she meant the apology, how sorry she was for everything that had happened between them.

Angela's heart soared as the moment played out. The four of them had made a plan that separated their friendship, yes. But it had done more than that. Their actions had cost Lauren and Shane every hope of a future, of being a family with Emily. The cost was too high to measure.

Samuel worked his way toward Bill's bed. With both hands he clasped his outstretched fingers. "It's been too long, Bill."

"Yes." Bill kept his hands locked with Samuel's for a long time. Long enough to erase the differences that had brought them to this point. Bill's chin quivered as he looked up. "All that matters is you're here now. And that you understand something."

"What?" Samuel's voice was thick with feeling.

"We're every bit as sorry as you. What we did . . ." he looked the other direction at Lauren and Shane and Emily. Then he turned back to Samuel. "What we did to those kids was wrong."

"It was." Samuel looked at Lauren. "Forgive me. We . . . we didn't know what we were doing."

Angela studied Lauren, saw the doubt in her eyes and the small hesitancy in her expression. Apologies were well and good, but the things done to Lauren and Shane had changed their lives. Forgiveness would take time.

Lauren gave Samuel a stiff nod. "I know." She gave Emily a slight hug and reached out to rest her hand on Shane's shoulder. "We all would do things differently if we had another chance."

Lauren couldn't believe her eyes. She was still processing the scene playing out in the hospital room, and now Shane's father had apologized. Next to her, Emily leaned closer. "Another miracle," she whispered. "I prayed for this too."

But Lauren wasn't sure. How was it a miracle that the people who had separated her and Shane were here now? This was a private moment, her last few hours with her dad. She wanted to tell the Galanters to leave and come back in a year or so. When she'd had time to process everything that was happening.

All around her the apologies continued, and after a few minutes the two older couples found their way again, the way long lost friends do. Even when their differences had cost them half a lifetime, even when Lauren wasn't sure she liked the idea.

Throughout the day she and Emily and Shane stayed close, walking down to the cafeteria together at lunchtime and giving the friends time to catch up. For two days they stayed almost constantly around her father's bed, the sweet, tender moments with him marred only by the occasional update from the doctors that there was nothing they could do. He didn't have long. There was talk about him going home, but the decision was made that it would be too painful to move him.

He was comfortable in the hospital, the

pain medication flowing through his IV at just the right rate to allow him conversations with her and Shane and Emily, with the Galanters, and especially with her mother. Once, sometime Monday afternoon, Lauren and Shane spent an hour in the cafeteria alone. Their conversations had been so consumed with her father that they hadn't talked much about each other.

"So . . ." Shane sat across from her and covered her hands with his.

She knew what he meant, the way she'd always known. Their flights were scheduled to leave later that week, and they still hadn't found any answers. None that made sense, anyway. Her eyes held his. "Us, you mean?"

He wrapped his fingers around her hands. "I heard what your dad told you yesterday morning."

"I wondered." Her heart ached just looking at him. His eyes held a depth that took her breath away. He was conservative, a military guy with a fierce support for the war, but he didn't seem like any warmonger she'd ever written about. And how was that? Navy captains weren't supposed to have feelings like this, were they? Still, what was she supposed to say? That she'd move to Reno, Nevada, of all places? Settle

491

down somewhere outside Fallon Naval Base and get excited about the fact that he was training the next generation of fighter pilots? She looked down at the place where their fingers came together. Maybe if she said nothing, they could sit like this forever, holding hands and pretending things were exactly the way they'd been when they were kids.

He tried again. "Can I go on record saying I agree with him?" His voice was light, but his eyes gave him away.

She didn't know what to say, so she fell back on her most familiar ally: teasing. "About what? About heaven?"

"Okay." He gave a thoughtful nod. "That too." His gaze held hers and wouldn't let go. "But mostly that love doesn't mean seeing eye to eye on everything."

She tilted her head, willing him to comprehend what they were up against. "Shane, I'm a senior reporter at one of the top magazines in the country, and I'm in that position because of my stories on the war in the Middle East." Sadness crept between every word. Sadness and longing and resignation. "There isn't a reader in the nation who doesn't know where I stand." She lowered her chin and kept her tone light. "And then there's you, over on the other side of the table."

"Navy captain, supporter of the Republican Party, fan of the president." His eyes melted into hers. He brushed his thumb along the top of her hand.

The move kicked out the foundation of her resolve. "Right."

"So . . ." The people at other tables in the dining room seemed to fade from view, the conversation too deep for any distractions. "We'd have interesting dinner conversations, right?" He gave her the boyish grin that had haunted her dreams for a decade after he left. "Is that so bad?"

"Shane." She felt herself melting. "Really, I mean, think about it. What do we do? Get married and live at the Top Gun facility? So I can write articles condemning the war straight from command central?"

He shrugged. "You'd get quicker feedback."

"Anyway." She couldn't resist him another minute. Her salad was gone, so she pushed her tray back and slipped around the table to his side. "How was your lunch?"

"You changing subjects?" He crooked his finger beneath her chin and eased closer to her.

"You're quick, Shane." She breathed the

words against his chin, moving her lips closer to his. "I always liked that about you."

"Really." His mouth found hers, and he slid his fingers up along her cheekbone. The kiss didn't last long, but it made her dizzy all the same. He drew back. "I thought you liked this." He kissed her again, his eyes full of light and love and humor. The way she remembered them being. "Besides, we wouldn't be the first couple separated by our politics. You've got Schwarzenegger and Shriver . . . Mary Matalin and James Carville."

"I know." She exhaled hard. He wasn't making this easy. If she sat here much longer he might even start making sense. A slight thrill swirled in her heart at the thought, but she looked past it. "Those couples didn't live in different countries, though."

He looked like he wanted to volley back, but he didn't. Instead he brought his lips together and looked deeper into her heart, to the long ago places where memories of him once ruled. "There's always a way, Lauren."

Thoughts of her father drifted through her mind, followed by the fact that in a week or so this time together with Shane

494

would probably be nothing more than a wonderful coda on a lifetime of wondering. Even though they hadn't solved anything, she was grateful to him, glad that he'd kept the discussion silly and lighthearted, and even hopeful. Now, when time was so desperately short, that's what they needed most.

On their way back up to her father's room, Shane eased her into a doorway. "Hi." The word was a breathy whisper as he brushed his face against hers. He kissed her once more and when he pulled away he said, "Just working on military public relations."

She had a serious answer, something about sensibilities and their obvious differences. But it wouldn't come to the surface. Without the words, she returned his kiss, breathless with the way he made her feel. When she took a breath she could do nothing but grin at him. "You know what?"

He brought his lips to hers once more and then found her eyes, his voice full of desire. "What?"

"You're good at it."

Her daddy was going downhill fast.

By the next day he was too weak to do

anything more than look at them through tired eyes. Close friends from her parents' church came by the hospital twice that morning to circle his bed, hold hands, and pray. The first few times Lauren didn't join in.

"I'll wait in the hall." She gave a polite smile, using the moment to visit the restroom or grab a water from the vending machine. But as she left that first time, the pastor's voice stopped her. She hesitated, standing in the hall, listening . . . amazed. She'd prayed that way once, hadn't she? Back when she and Shane were so sorry for sleeping together?

In the course of the day, a dozen different prayers came back to her. She'd begged God to let Emily live and she'd begged him to help her find Shane. It was noon when it hit her. Emily was right.

God had done both. Maybe not in her timing, but then hadn't they always been taught that God had His ways, that His ways were better than their ways, even when it didn't feel like it? Another prayer was happening inside her father's room, so she leaned against the wall outside and tried to remember . . .

How had it happened? How had she and God moved so far away from each other?

The answer was easy. She pictured herself standing over the small hospital bed, Emily lying there gasping for breath, burning up. The doctor told her Emily had almost no chance of living, and so God was the only answer left. Lauren had begged Him to let her live.

She remembered what it felt like hours later to have the nurse tell her Emily was gone, the shakiness in her chest, the terror streaming through her veins. Okay, yes, God had let her daughter live. But hadn't He robbed her of the chance to see Emily grow up, to be a part of her life?

And what about Shane? God knew how badly she wanted to find him. If she'd come across him, then she would've felt compelled to go home again, and there she would've found Emily. A decade sooner or even more. Wasn't that God's fault too?

After starting her new life in Los Angeles, God became just one more part of her past, one more person she'd walked away from. Then, as she got into political reporting and moved her way up on the *Time* magazine staff, she began believing the same thing so many of her peers believed. That Christians were hypocrites.

She had only to check her e-mail to see that much. The meanest, most negative letters often came from readers who called themselves believers. But it wasn't just that. Lauren couldn't understand how a person with faith in Christ could also support the war. She hung her head and listened to the prayer taking place in her dad's room. Prayer wouldn't resolve anything. It wouldn't save her dad. And it wouldn't answer the questions building inside her.

Right on the heels of that thought, a voice raised, the words coming to Lauren as clearly as if she were inside the room rather than in the hallway.

"Lord, we know that all things happen for a reason, but that doesn't mean we understand this. We pray You'll be with our friend, Bill, and that You'll lead him gently from this world to the next. I know You'll be waiting for Him in that beautiful place, the place You've prepared for him. And so we thank You for Bill's life, for every day he's had with us and with his family. Please give them the . . ."

Lauren hugged herself. It took all her strength to stand there and not go into the room, to not join that circle of people. But why? She shook her head. Guilt. Of course. What must her dad think, looking around and seeing her mom and Shane and Emily, special church friends, and even Shane's parents.

But not her.

Dad had been so certain in their talk the day before. When she got to heaven, he'd be waiting for her, just the way he'd waited for her all these years since she'd gone away. And if he was right, if there was a heaven, then her mother would be there, and Shane and Emily. All of them, everyone she loved. But what about her?

What about me, God? She pressed her lips together. Did God strike people dead for being sarcastic? But then, why should He? He hadn't exactly delivered answers to her prayers. The same integrity that drove her to verify sources for her work hit her now like a sledgehammer.

God had *delivered the answers. Just not the way I wanted. So I walked away.* Something she was good at.

Drawing in a steady breath she peeked into the room. They were still praying, and with their eyes closed, heads bowed. Everyone except Shane. He must've heard her, and now he had one eye open and he gave a short nod for her to join him. She skirted silently around the outside of the circle, then slipped in between him and Emily.

Someone was saying, "We thank You most of all for the peace You've given this family. Your peace goes beyond our understanding because it happens on the inside of us, where our hearts are. Not on the outside where life can be so difficult. It's that internal peace You've given them. Restoration and healing, divine redemption, all of it has come to the Andersons in recent days, and we thank You. Your peace should be the goal of every believer, and today, well, we could take a lesson from Bill and Angela and their family."

Lauren felt her sinuses swelling again. Who *were* these people? They sounded so different. They certainly weren't like the Christians she'd known. But that didn't matter. Because something from the man's prayer caught at her. He mentioned peace, but not the peace she spent her days thinking about — not the kind that would bring an end to the war in Iraq and Afghanistan. What had he said? God's peace happens on the inside, where the heart is, right? Not on the outside where life was hard.

She pressed her hands more tightly into Emily's and Shane's. This was the peace she'd searched for all her life, wasn't it? And though she still wasn't sure how to find it or make it happen on the inside, suddenly, in that moment, standing there beside those she loved most in the world, it seemed possible. As she stayed in the circle of prayer she felt love and acceptance raining down on her, showering her with a feeling she hadn't ever known before. It was a feeling that lasted even after the moment ended and the church friends left.

And it had everything to do with prayer.

The hours passed slowly, with little response from her father, and late that night he slipped into a coma. The loss was enormous. Even with Shane and Emily and her mother huddled close around her, Lauren felt like she was falling from an airplane without a chute. All these years, she'd convinced herself her parents had been wrong, that their actions had cost her a lifetime with Shane and Emily. But she'd forgotten the people they really were. The father who had run along beside her when she learned to ride a bike, the one who went running with her on weekend mornings when she was in junior high, and who once in a while stopped to pick her a bouquet of wildflowers on the way home. He loved her as sure as summer followed spring. Love had indeed driven him to do the things he'd done when she was pregnant with Emily.

A pure, misguided sort of love.

Now that she was home, the good times were clear again. Her dad was a kind-hearted, gentle man whose humor and compassion was like balm to a gaping wound that had never come close to healing. This time when the four of them gathered around to pray, Lauren did something she hadn't done since she left home — she silently joined her voice with theirs.

"It won't be long," the doctor told them. "He won't last through the night."

The man was right.

By one o'clock in the morning, her father's breathing slowed. Lauren watched the monitors, counting down as the numbers showing how much oxygen her father was getting fell. 80 . . . 70 . . . 55 . . . 40 . . .

Half an hour later, it was over. Her father's breathing stopped. Lauren stared, disbelieving, at the still form on the bed, then turned to cling to Shane and Emily. She clutched them close, burying her face against them, not sure if the sobs echoing around were hers or theirs. She let them go and turned to her mother, opening her arms and folding them around her as they grieved his loss.

The Galanters were there too, holding onto each other and quietly crying.

How could this be real? How could he be gone? Mere days ago he'd been well enough to sit with them, to visit and hold hands. It had been terrifyingly fast, not at all the way Lauren had thought cancer progressed. But at the same time it was merciful, because there had been little pain, no surgery, no horrendous chemotherapy or radiation. If only she could find some comfort in that. But there was none. Because all she knew was that her daddy was gone, and she'd missed way too many years with him.

Before they left the hospital, her mother looked at each of them, tears still on her cheeks. "For weeks I've been praying for your father to be healed." She folded her arms, hugging herself tightly. "I couldn't understand why God didn't answer me, why the cancer wasn't taken from him. God is the Healer, and we needed His help." She looked intently at Lauren and Shane and Emily, one at a time. "Today while we were praying, God made it clear that my prayers had been heard. Your father, your papa, was healed of something far worse than cancer." She smiled through her tears. "When we found you, Lauren, and you, Shane . . . watching the two of you discover Emily . . . well, Bill was healed of a broken heart."

Sorrow and peace wrapped around her grief, and Lauren held tight to Shane's arm. If only she could have another few weeks with him, another day. Maybe they could've talked about this healing her mother was talking about. She squeezed her eyes shut and leaned her head on Shane's shoulder. *Daddy . . . I can't believe you're gone . . . just when we found each other again.* The pain was so consuming it threatened to bring her to her knees. But if her mother was right, then it wasn't all sad. It couldn't be.

Daddy had been healed in a way that still seemed unbelievable. And that brought about a sort of hope that held her up, kept her from falling. Next to her, Emily had her arm around both of them. Her daughter's tears came harder now, but something was different. Now her sobs were almost joyful. She looked up at her mother and the connection Lauren felt between the two of them was stronger than ever. And suddenly Lauren understood the joy in Emily's tears. She smiled at her daughter and felt the mix of sorrow and triumph in her own expression. Because her father wasn't the only one healed of a broken heart that week.

They all were.

Twenty-Eight

For all they'd lost and all they'd found, in the end they came full circle.

Shane couldn't get past that fact, not through Bill Anderson's touching funeral or in the days that followed. Now it was Saturday, and as he stood near the ticket counter at Chicago O'Hare, Emily and Lauren at his side, Lauren's mother and his parents next to them, the sad truth was glaring. They were right back where they'd left off nearly nineteen years ago — standing on the brink of good-bye.

Shane's parents' plane would be the first one out. Lauren's was next, and his was a few hours later. They walked as far as they could toward the security line, and then his mother turned to Angela. The two hugged and held on for a long while. When they pulled apart, his mother said, "Think about it, will you, Angela? I can't believe God would give us another chance to be neighbors."

"Definitely." Lauren's mother had dark circles under her swollen eyes, and she looked gaunt from the grief. But for all of that, her expression held a supernatural peace. "We'll have to get things in order and sell the house." She looked at Emily, and the two shared a sad smile. "We're ready to move. Emily wants to finish college on the West Coast, anyway. We don't have anything keeping us in Illinois now."

Emily looked at Lauren, and Shane's heart broke for her. His daughter looked like a lost little girl, caught up in more emotions and changes than anyone should have to go through in a week's time. Emily gave Lauren a sad smile. "You can put in a good word for me at USC, right?"

"Of course." So far Lauren had made no promises to any of them, other than the obvious: she would keep in regular contact with Emily. Now she looked weary, buried beneath the weight of the good-byes that lay ahead. She put her arm around Emily and pulled her close. "They'll be lucky to have you."

Shane stood on Emily's other side, and he smiled at her. "Once you move out west, we'll see each other all the time. LA is a day's drive from Reno, and only an hour in the air." He stroked the back of her head, her silky dark hair. Losing Bill had been terribly hard on her. Shane could feel how much she needed her dad now that the most important man in her life was gone.

His parents added their approval. "We've missed so many years with you." His dad held out his arms, and Emily went to him. "All we can do now is catch up."

"Yep." Emily put her arms around Shane's mother too, and a sad sort of quiet fell over them. His dad looked at his watch. "We better get going."

Shane stepped up and gave them each a hug. Though the mistakes his parents made hadn't severed his relationship with them, as it had Lauren and her parents, there still was a sense of loss there, beneath the surface. It was something they never talked about. But that was going to change. Shane knew it. He could feel a new depth to their relationship. One more bit of proof that healing had, indeed, come to all of them. He stepped back beside Emily and held up his hand. "See you next week sometime."

Another round of good-byes was spoken and the four of them watched his parents head through a door and file into the security line. When they were out of sight, an ache settled in Shane's gut. The hardest part lay just ahead.

Emily was still clinging to Lauren, but she was looking down, as if she couldn't face the moment just yet. Lauren held out her hand to her mother. Angela didn't hesitate. She came and the three generations of Anderson women formed a tight knot of tears. Shane wanted to join them, but they needed this time — just the three of them, a picture of what a mother-daughter bond should be. He could hear their voices, and he let their words soak into his soul.

"Do you forgive me?" Angela rested her head on Lauren's. "I'm so sorry, honey. You'll never know —"

"Of course I forgive you, but it was me too." Lauren's voice was raspy. Her shoulders trembled as she spoke. "I only wish I'd come home sooner."

"I'll always see us the way we were in the family room that night." Emily smiled through her tears. "Papa sitting there with his big smile, and all of us together for the first time." She made a sound that was mostly laugh. "I have parents and grandparents, and a legacy of love someone should write a book about! I even have my special papa in heaven waiting for me. What could be better than that?"

Only one thing, of course, but Emily seemed determined not to bring that up. Last night she had found Shane and Lauren seated on the living room sofa, talking. She plopped down between them and announced, "I think you two should get married."

"Is that right?" Lauren looked surprised, but she kept her deeper feelings to herself.

"Yeah, I mean —" she looked at him — "you already asked her."

Shane's eyes widened. "I did?"

Emily poked him with her elbow. "Eighteen years ago, silly."

"Oh." Shane gave Lauren a quick grin. "She has a point."

Emily's eyes found Lauren next. "And you already said yes."

Shane had barely restrained a grin as he held up his finger. "Another point."

But Lauren only gave them both a wistful look. "If only it were that easy."

Emily hadn't pushed the issue, but before she turned in for bed she pulled Shane aside. "I'll never stop praying about it."

He winked at her. "Me neither."

So it was no wonder Emily was being quiet on the matter here, in the midst of good-byes. She'd done what she could.

Now it was up to Lauren and God. Most of all, God.

The group hug among the three women ended, and they pulled apart. Lauren looked over her shoulder at him and held out her hand. Shane took it, savoring the feel of her skin against his.

Angela was asking, "Will you stay in Afghanistan?"

"For now." Lauren's answer was quick, but it cut Shane deep. He tried to catch Lauren's eye, but she kept from looking at either him or Emily. "I love what I do there." She finally looked at Emily, her expression tender. "I can come back often."

Shane wanted to shout, "What about me? What about *us?*" But that would wait until they were alone. Instead he took a deep breath and looked at the faces around him. "I need to get going."

"Me too." Lauren picked up her bag and swung it over her shoulder.

"All right, then," Angela held out her arms and hugged first Shane, then Lauren. She let herself linger with her daughter. "Be careful, Lauren. Please."

"I will." Lauren rubbed her left shoulder, the one that was still healing. "Especially now."

It was Shane's turn. He hugged Lauren's

mother, and then Emily. For a moment, he kept his hand along the side of his daughter's face. He looked down into those dark eyes, marveling.

"I'm so proud of the young woman you are." Time would never come between them again, not the way it had before. The moment he'd seen her, held her in his arms, she'd become part of him. So much so that it was tearing at his composure to leave her. "I'm sorry I wasn't there for you when you were growing up."

She covered his hand with hers and clung tight. "You didn't know."

"But I do now." He kissed her cheek and let his hand slip to her shoulder. "We've got a lot of good times ahead, sweetheart."

"Yep." She hugged him again and their eyes held as he stepped back. She looked at Lauren next. "Mom . . ."

They came together in a last embrace that made Shane's throat thick. There would be phone calls and e-mail and visits, God willing. But with Lauren in the Middle East, any good-bye could be their last.

He watched the two of them, knowing they were too torn up to say anything more. Finally Angela put her arm around Emily, and the two of them waved. Then they turned and headed for the exit. Shane and Lauren watched them until they were gone. Then, without saying a word, Lauren fell into his arms.

"I didn't want the week to end." She mumbled the words against his chest.

"It doesn't have to." He kissed the top of her head.

She said nothing, and after a few seconds he picked up his bag and the two of them walked through the door and got into the security line. They held hands as they walked to her gate. Lauren's plane was already boarding.

He faced her and lifted her chin with his fingers. "Did you hear what I said earlier? What I've been saying all week?"

Her eyes held a sort of torment he hadn't seen before, as if the battle inside her was far more frightening than the one she was going back to write about. She took a step closer, so their legs were touching. "Yes." The word sounded strained. "Yes. I heard."

"So then . . ." He kept his tone easy, his words slow. Even if it killed him to tell her good-bye after finding her again, there would be no last-minute sales pitch to convince her to stay with him. His heart hurt and he wanted to weep, but now wasn't the time. Instead, he dug deep down and found a trace of humor. "Does this mean you're breaking our engagement?"

A single laugh burst from her throat, and she let her forehead fall against his chest. "Shane." She lifted her eyes to his again. "Be serious."

He hesitated. "Why, Lauren?" He felt the smile fade from his face. With his eyes holding hers, he traced her jaw, her neck. "Would that convince you to stay with me?"

She brought her hands up along the sides of his face, and with fresh tears brimming in her eyes, she kissed him. It was a kiss filled with finality, and when she drew back she was breathless, her emotions giving way. "I'll think about it, Shane." She shook her head. "I just don't see how it can work."

He understood. As he searched her eyes, he prayed the way he'd been praying since their first conversation that week. *Please God . . . show us how to make this come together.* And in that instant he realized something. It wasn't only their politics that were different. It was their faith. Without that in common, Lauren might be right. *God we need You . . . she needs You.*

"What are you thinking?" Her voice was

low, her eyes locked on his.

He worked his fingers through her hair and kissed her once more. "I'm trying not to."

"Attention passengers —" a tinny voice came over the loud speaker system — "this is the final boarding call for Flight 92 to Los Angeles. All ticketed passengers please proceed directly to Gate C20 for immediate boarding."

He took a step back and pain cut through him, as though his heart were being ripped in half. He caught his breath, forced himself to smile, to speak. "You better go."

She nodded, too choked up to talk. She mouthed the words, "Bye, Shane." And then, with a last look at him, she turned and headed for the Jetway.

There were no desperate statements, no promises that she'd call or write or stay in touch. She just turned . . . and was gone. Swallowing hard, he stared at the terminal around him without seeing anything. Hoards of people pushed past, but he barely noticed. He just stood there, unable to take a step away from the gate, to be the one to put more space between them.

Finally, his feet took over. He drifted toward the window and watched the plane back away, shift gears, and begin positioning on the runway. He could still see her face, her blonde hair and blue eyes. Could she see him too? Did she feel what he felt? That even though she was leaving, their hearts were still connected? Would always be connected?

Father God . . . help.

Things had worked out for everyone that week. Emily had her parents, and Bill had a place in heaven. His parents and Lauren's had found friendship and healing, and none of them would ever be the same again because of it. Yes, things had worked out for everyone.

Everyone except Lauren and him.

He kept his eyes on the aircraft, watching the same window, the one where he was sure he could see her, no matter now far away the plane was. Finally the craft circled into place, and after a brief pause, barreled down the runway, lifting up through a hole in the sky.

Taking Lauren with it.

Only then, did Shane drop to the nearest chair, cover his face with his hands and let the tears come.

Twenty-Nine

Lauren was one of the first to exit the plane. She collected her things and headed out onto the concourse, not really aware of anything around her. Her mind was consumed with Shane, with their time together, with all she'd turned her back on. How had she let things go so terribly wrong?

For the past six hours she'd done nothing but relive every wonderful moment with him, weighing it against the reality of the life she had in Afghanistan. From Chicago to New York where she had to change planes, she'd asked herself the same question over and over again: it couldn't work, could it?

No. How could it? How could she believe the way she believed or cover the war the way she had always covered it, and spend her nonworking hours sharing a life with a navy flight instructor at the Top Gun facility. And what about their beliefs?

He spoke about God at every turn, and she . . . well, she was still trying to forgive Him.

She and Shane together? The idea was ludicrous. But by the time she reached New York she could no longer deny one very obvious truth. Letting Shane go now was even more so.

When the plane taxied to the gate, she hurried off and talked with the woman at the counter. Yes, the woman told her. She could do this, and yes, they could see that her bags followed her. But she had just thirty minutes if she wanted to make the flight.

Lauren paid the price, then pulled her cell phone from her pocket and dialed the Los Angeles office of *Time* magazine. When she had her editor on the line she had to stifle a bout of giggles. "Listen, I have a favor to ask."

"Whatever you want, Gibbs." She'd worked with this editor for three years. "We just hope you're ready to get back to work. The magazine needs you."

"I'm ready." She swallowed, not quite believing that she was doing this. "But I need time away from Afghanistan. I want a temporary new assignment, if that's all right."

"Sure." Her editor didn't hesitate. "You've earned that much." He hesitated. "Where do you want to go?"

She closed her eyes and lifted her face. "Reno, Nevada."

"Reno?" A pause. "Are you crazy?"

She smiled. "Yes." Another giggle. "You know what? It's wonderful!"

With her editor's promise to make the arrangements, Lauren ran from one concourse to the next, barely making her flight. Now, if the schedules had held up, her plane would land fifteen minutes before his.

Her flight was quick, and before she knew it, she was walking out the door, into the Reno Airport. With each step, she picked up her pace, and with five minutes to spare she found a seat at the gate, his gate. One with a direct view of the Jetway. When she was sure she had enough time, she dug through her bag until she found it. The small cardboard box that was never more than a few yards from her.

The whole week, every time she and Shane were together, she'd wanted to pull it from her bag and share it with him. Because the moment she did so, he'd know. She'd never forgotten, not through the years of college, no matter where her reporting took her. But the moment had never seemed right.

Now she looked at the faded, creased photographs and — careful not to damage the pictures in any way, she took out the ring. It still stirred emotions in her, memories of a love that nothing in all her life had equaled. With deliberate care, she slipped the ring on her baby finger, closed the small box, and placed the box back into her bag. No, she couldn't have brought out these things earlier. This way she'd had time to think it through. It was true, they wouldn't have everything in common. But they shared what mattered most for now, and in time they would figure out if the rest would work or not.

Emily's face danced in her mind, and tears stung Lauren's eyes. They had a daughter — their precious baby girl, all grown up and longing to be loved — and they shared a past and a romance that knew nothing of struggles with faith or political differences. She was pretty sure she believed in God, after all. And if He was real, well then, she and God had some mountains to scale. But mountains were meant to be climbed, right? And the politics thing, well, Shane had been right. If others could pull off a bipartisan marriage, maybe they could do the same thing.

There was a rustling of activity behind the gate counter, and an aircraft pulled into view. Lauren's heart beat so hard she thought it might burst through her chest. But at least it wasn't broken anymore.

She stood, her bag high on her shoulder, and watched the people file through the door. A mother with two babies; a group of businessmen; two couples, tanned and laughing, moving slowly and talking with their hands . . .

And then he was there. At the doorway.

Lauren started to shake. Emotion flooded her, coursing through her veins and making her hands and feet tingle. She felt hot and cold at the same time. Would she fall to her knees, faint from all she was feeling? *Lord, if You're real . . . I can't believe this. What is this feeling?* She wasn't sure what startled her more: her reaction to seeing Shane, or that she'd spoken to God about it.

Sucking in air, she took a step closer, and then another. Shane followed those in front of him through the door, staring at the ground as he walked. He looked so . . . grief stricken. Defeated.

Oh, God, I did that to him. I'm so

sorry . . . I love him so much!

As though he heard her broken inner cry, Shane hesitated — and looked up. Their gazes locked, and she saw the reality hit him like a physical force, saw the emotions flash in his eyes. Disbelief and shock and amazement. And then, shining out with such intensity that it engulfed her, love. A love that made Lauren feel like she could fly.

He moved, slowly at first and then in a rush that closed the distance between them. Before she had time to take a breath, his arms were around her, clutching her, and they were rocking, holding on to each other the way she'd ached to hold him every hour that they'd been apart. Lauren wasn't sure how long they stood there, but finally they shuffled to the side, out of the way of the other passengers. Shane searched her eyes. "What . . . how . . . ?"

She grinned. "I called my editor." Her eyes danced, and the feel of his joy flowed down to her soul. "I told him maybe I better be stationed at Reno for awhile."

"You did?" He clasped his hands at the small of her back, holding tight to her. The familiar teasing filled his voice. "How come?"

She lifted one shoulder. "I figured you

had a point." A giggle slipped from her overjoyed heart.

"A point?"

"Yes." She leaned up and kissed him, kissed him in a way that left no doubts about her feelings. "Magazine reporters are supposed to be unbiased, right?"

"Right." He brought his lips to hers again, cradling her face in his hands. "So?"

"So, maybe it's time I spend a little time on military public relations."

He chuckled, and it became a full-blown bout of laughter. The whole time he held on to her, his head tipped back, delighting in the moment.

When his laughter died down, she pulled the ring from her little finger. "Here." She handed it to him, waiting as he recognized what it was. "Do you still mean it?"

He looked at her, lost in her eyes. Then he took her left hand and with heart-breaking tenderness placed it on her ring finger. "I love you, Lauren Anderson."

"I love you too." She held her breath. He'd stopped short of asking her to marry him, but that was okay. Maybe, if the next season in their lives went the way she wanted it to go, the question would come. For now, though, they could at least give it a try because they had time. Sweet precious time.

He still had her hand in his. "God brought us together, and now nothing can ever take us apart. I'll never love anyone like I love you, the way I love you. Even now."

She hugged him, and suddenly he lifted her off her feet and swung her around in a circle. When he set her down, he raised his fist in the air and shouted out loud. "Thank You, God!"

People passing by looked at them, and a few smiled. In that moment Lauren recognized the feeling inside her, the one that was still flooding her with warmth. Peace. Again not the peace she'd spent so much time thinking about all these years, but a peace that was deeper, more lasting. A peace she wanted to feel all the rest of her days.

Shane was pulling his cell phone from his pocket, opening it and grinning at her.

"What are you doing?" She held onto his elbow, watching him, smiling so big it hurt.

"The thing I've been dying to do since I saw you standing here." He tapped a series of numbers into the phone. "I'm calling our daughter."

Emily hung up the phone with her dad and darted through the house to tell her grandma the news. Her mother and father were together again! Yes, they had a lot to work through, her dad had told her, but they were together. That was all that mattered.

Her mom was as thrilled as she was, but Emily couldn't talk about it for long. She had something important to do first. She went back to the kitchen, grabbed the phone book, and looked up the number for Wheaton College. It was time to make good on a very special promise.

God gave her the miracle she'd prayed for — every last detail of it. They would always miss Papa, but suddenly the future looked like it might be everything she'd ever dreamed of. She'd asked God to make her an instrument of peace. Her birth had torn everyone apart, but in the past few weeks God had used her to bring her family together again. No, the final chapter hadn't been written. But she believed it would be, that the God who had seen to every last detail of this miracle would see her parents through the next season of their lives, as well.

Now she would follow through on what she'd promised Him.

She found the phone number to the university, dialed it, and asked for the journalism instructor. The receptionist put her on hold for a moment, but then a familiar voice picked up the line.

"Hello?"

Emily's heart soared. "Ms. Parker?"

"Yes?"

"This is Emily Anderson. I've, well, I've had some personal issues to deal with at home, but I wanted you to know I'll be back when school starts."

"I heard that your grandpa died." Her voice was warm, sympathetic. "Your grandma called and left a message." She hesitated. "I'm very sorry, Emily."

"Yes." She swallowed. "Me too." A robin landed on a patch of grass where the snow had melted. It hopped around, found a worm, and flew off again. New life was like that, always just beneath the icy surface. Emily blinked and held the phone tighter. "Can I ask you a favor?"

"Of course. Anything."

"Could you save me a spot for a short story in the creative magazine? I know you're assigning articles this week, and I have a special one. It's a story I want the whole world to know."

"Really?" She sounded interested. "What's it about?"

"It's about life and love. And miracles." She grinned and the joy inside her felt absolutely wonderful. "I'm calling it *Even Now*."

From the Author

Dear Reader Friends,

Some time ago I felt the Lord bringing together in my heart a story about peace. Obviously, at this time in our nation's history, peace is a volatile topic, something bantered about in casual conversations and debated by pundits across the country. Where the line between parties once was a picket fence, in many cases now it's solid brick and razor wire.

The war in the Middle East has contributed to this, and so has the strength of both support and animosity toward our current leader, President George Bush. In the news not so long ago, a woman was chased and threatened with her life for having a bumper sticker supporting the president.

The issues surrounding Operation Enduring Freedom are complex. One of the benefits of writing about a character like Lauren Anderson was that I felt sympathy for people on her side of the fence. Lauren had nothing against American soldiers. She simply believed that peace would only be found with peaceful behavior. Shane also was sympathetic. He wasn't a person crazy for war, and he certainly had no blood thirst. Rather he believed peace came through strength. He didn't want to see children orphaned or soldiers killed. He only wanted to help protect and defend.

Because of these two characters, I learned something while writing *Even Now*. I learned that once in a while the two sides are closer than they think. Especially when faith is a common factor. The issues are complex, and so I think sometimes the best way to work things out is, well, not to work them out. If you and someone you love have a difference of opinion on something, maybe it's best to let it stay that way. Respect each other's right to believe what you believe. Respect each other. Agree to disagree, my dad used to say.

When people do that, I've seen the most amazing result: love happens. People start finding the things they do have in common and they start loving the person for simply being a brother or a father or an aunt or a cousin. Obviously there are some differences of opinion that happen because one person is standing by Scripture and another person isn't. In this case, please go ahead and take a stand for the truth. That's what Jesus wants us to do. But at the same time, take your stand in love.

Sometimes we need to say, "I don't agree with that and here are the reasons why. But I love you so much. Let's go to lunch."

Conversations like that will build bridges between you and the people with whom you're at odds. And often, when we love people despite our disagreements with them, we give them a chance to cross that very same bridge. In the process, we may find more common ground than ever before.

Ultimately, I loved writing about Lauren and Shane, because real peace isn't found by either of their methods. It's not found at antiwar protests, and it's not found by dropping bombs — although there are times when both events might be appropriate, so long as our troops are always supported. Here's the point that Emily understood so well: real, lasting peace is only found through a lifesaving relationship with Jesus Christ.

Period.

Knowing Christ means that all the world might be falling apart just outside your front door — maybe just inside it — yet that inner peace, that inner knowing, remains unshaken. A quick formula for all of us would be this: Does your world feel out of control? Are you lacking peace in your marriage, your finances, your health, or your relationships?

Add Christ.

Add prayer and Bible study and conversations with other people who share your faith.

Your mind is only so big. To the degree that it is occupied with Christ, you simply won't have anything left for unrest and worry, frustration or hopelessness.

If you're reading about Jesus for the first time, then please take a few minutes and quietly — in your own words — ask Him to come into your life and clean house. Ask Him to be in charge of you from now on, and let Him be not only your Savior, but your Lord, your Master.

If you make that decision for the first time, here and now, contact a Bible-believing church in your area. Talk to a pastor, get involved in a newcomers' group, and start the greatest journey of your life. If you aren't able to do that, then send me an e-mail and write, "NEW LIFE" in the subject line. My e-mail address is *rtnbykk@aol.com*.

I love receiving letters from so many of you, and recently I received a very sad letter. A woman was alone after her husband had left her, and now she wanted to kill herself. She envied people who had died, because at least they had peace. I was grateful for the chance to tell her that life is always worth living. No matter what your situation, God has a plan in it, a purpose, a reason why your life can make a difference. Many times people who feel this way need professional help and medical advice. But many other people who struggle with such thoughts need to add a whole lot more God to their schedules. Volunteer time, Sunday school, various church ministries. Most churches are crying out for God in prayer, God in Bible study, and God in service. Remember, more God equals more peace. Or as many people say: No God, no peace. Know God, know peace.

Things are going very well — if very busy — in our happy household. My husband is considering staying home from his teaching job next year and homeschooling our boys. It's a funny situation, because we love our local public schools. They're truly wonderful, with many of the old-fashioned benefits that too many schools have let slip away. But we are excited to see what "A Year with Dad" will bring about. Also, it will give us much more time together as a family — since I can write the books God gives me while they're having lessons.

Please continue to pray for us. We greatly appreciate your love and concern, and we feel your prayers time and time again. If you're already receiving my e-mail newsletter, look for the next one soon! If you'd like to receive it, stop by my website at *www.KarenKingsbury.com* and fill in your e-mail address.

As always, I love hearing from you. I pray that you are enjoying the Christmas season, and remembering through it all the call to love one another — even the people sitting opposite the fence from you.

Until next time . . . in His light and love, Karen Kingsbury.

Book Club Questions

Explain how Shane's parents reacted to the news that their son's girlfriend was pregnant. Why do you think they reacted that way?

How about Lauren's parents? How did they react to the news, and why?

"What would Jesus do?" is a common question these days. Analyze both of the above situations and discuss them in light of that question: What *would* Jesus have done in the situation with Shane's parents? What about Lauren's parents?

What were the first signs that the friendship between the two couples was in trouble? Why did the friendship between the two couples fall apart so quickly?

Tell about a time when you were tempted to manipulate a situation to your advantage.

How did the two couples manipulate their children, and what danger signs did they ignore along the way?

Explain how deception played a role in the falling-out that happened between Lauren and her parents.

Tell about a situation where you or a person in your life has come out well-adjusted after a difficult start or a difficult set of circumstances.

What were the signs that Shane wasn't ready to marry the politician's daughter?

Lauren liked to think of herself as a gutsy reporter. What were the signs that she also had a tender heart?

What do you think is important for a marriage to work? Is it important to share political beliefs?

Emily prayed for a miracle and God granted it. How have you seen Him work miracles in your life?

For many years Emily longed for her parents. How is God the parent to those without parents?

God always answers prayers, but not always in our timing or the way we had hoped. Explain how this truth played out in the book, and how has it played out in your life?

Discuss God's provision in the lives of Emily and her family members. How has God provided for you in difficult times?

About the Author

Karen Kingsbury is the author of over thirty titles, including *One Tuesday Morning*, *Beyond Tuesday Morning*, and several other bestsellers, one of which was the basis for a CBS *Movie-of-the-Week*. With more than two million copies of her books in print, she is one of America's favorite inspirational authors. Kingsbury lives in Washington state with her husband, Don, and their six children, three of whom are adopted from Haiti.